THEIR BABY
SURPRISE

BY
JENNIFER TAYLOR

MILLS & BOON

First published in Great Britain 2009
Paperback edition 2010
Harlequin Mills & Boon Limited,
Eton House, 18-24 Paradise Road, Richmond, Surrey TW9 1SR

© Jennifer Taylor 2009

ISBN: 978 0 263 86986 6

Harlequin Mills & Boon policy is to use papers that are natural, renewable and recyclable products and made from wood grown in sustainable forests. The logging and manufacturing process conform to the legal environmental regulations of the country of origin.

Printed and bound in Spain
by Litografia Rosés, S.A., Barcelona

Dear Reader

This is the fourth and final story in my *Dalverston Weddings* series, and I have to admit to feeling a little sad now that I have reached the end. However, helping my hero and heroine discover how much they love one another was a real joy for me—even though it did come as a shock to them!

Rachel Mackenzie and Matthew Thompson have worked together for a number of years, and they have an excellent working relationship based on mutual respect and liking. However, when the wedding of their respective offspring is suddenly cancelled, they find themselves taking a long, hard look at their own feelings and are stunned when they realise that they are attracted to one another. Both are wary of rushing headlong into a situation they might come to regret, and agree that an affair seems like the ideal solution—but will it be enough for either of them?

I hope you enjoy reading this book as much as I enjoyed writing it. I particularly loved planning the last scene, as it reminded me of my daughter's wedding day. I spent many happy hours looking through all the photographs in the name of research!

Best wishes to you all

Jennifer

Jennifer Taylor lives in the north-west of England, in a small village surrounded by some really beautiful countryside. She has written for several different Mills & Boon® series in the past, but it wasn't until she read her first Medical™ Romance that she truly found her niche. She was so captivated by these heart-warming stories that she set out to write them herself!

When she's not writing, or doing research for her latest book, Jennifer's hobbies include reading, gardening, travel, and chatting to friends both on and off-line. She is always delighted to hear from readers, so do visit her website at www.jennifer-taylor.com

Recent titles by the same author:

THE DOCTOR'S BABY BOMBSHELL*
THE GP'S MEANT-TO-BE BRIDE*
MARRYING THE RUNAWAY BRIDE*
THE SURGEON'S FATHERHOOD SURPRISE**

*Dalverston Weddings
**Brides of Penhally Bay

CHAPTER ONE

HE MAY have been putting on a brave face all day but Rachel Mackenzie wasn't deceived. It was no secret to those who knew him that Matthew Thompson adored his only daughter, Heather, so the fact that Heather had decided to cancel her own wedding and leave Dalverston was bound to have caused him a great deal of pain.

Rachel sighed as she followed Matt into his house because it was painful for her too. It had been her son, Ross, who had been due to marry Matt's daughter that day and she couldn't begin to imagine how devastated Ross must be feeling.

'I don't know about you but I could do with a drink.' Matt led the way into the sitting room and went straight to the table under the window that held an array of bottles. Picking up a bottle of whisky, he glanced at her. 'Will you join me, Rachel?'

'All right, but just a small one.' Rachel grimaced as she sank down onto the sofa. 'I'm so exhausted that even a sip of alcohol will probably send me off to sleep.'

'It's been one heck of a day,' Matt concurred, pouring

two small measures of whisky into a pair of cut-glass tumblers. He handed one of the glasses to her then sat down with a sigh that spoke volumes about how he was feeling. Rachel studied him while she sipped her drink.

Normally, Matt was so full of energy that he appeared far younger than his actual age. He ran the busy general practice that served the people of Dalverston with a verve that few could emulate. However, today every one of his forty-eight years showed in the deep lines that were etched onto his handsome face.

At a little under six feet tall, with a powerful physique and thick black hair that was only just starting to turn silver at the temples, Matthew Thompson was a very attractive man. Rachel knew she wasn't alone in thinking that either. Several of her friends, the married ones as well as the single, had remarked on it. In fact, she'd had a job to convince them that she wasn't interested in Matt *that* way and saw him simply as a colleague and a friend.

It was a good job, too, she thought suddenly. Quite apart from the fact that she wasn't interested in having a relationship with anyone at the moment, there was definitely no chance of it happening with Matt. The thought touched a nerve oddly enough and she cleared her throat, unsure why it should trouble her in any way.

'I couldn't believe it when you phoned and told me we had a major incident on our hands. I mean for it to happen today of all days…' She tailed off, not needing to explain why today had been the worst day possible. Instead of celebrating their children's marriage, they had spent a large part of the day dealing with the aftermath of a serious accident on the banks of the canal. Talk about bad timing wasn't in it.

'At least it provided a distraction.' Matt grimaced when he realised how uncaring that must have sounded. 'Sorry. I didn't mean that the way it came out. A number of people were badly injured when that crane collapsed and I certainly wouldn't have wished that on them.'

'I know you wouldn't, but you're right, Matt. At least while we were treating them, it took our minds off this other problem,' Rachel said quickly, not wanting him to feel bad about what he had said.

'Exactly.'

He gave her a tight smile as he raised the glass to his lips. Rachel knew that he rarely drank alcohol, and never during the day, and it just seemed to prove how low he must be feeling. The thought caused her such intense pain that it surprised her. It was only natural that she should feel upset for Ross, but that didn't explain why it was so painful to see the way Matt was suffering, did it?

Rachel wasn't sure what to make of it all. In the end, she decided not to worry about it. Ross had attended the incident along with the rest of the staff from the surgery and she wanted to make sure that he had got home safely. She hunted her mobile phone out of her pocket and stood up. Matt looked up and she felt an odd little frisson run through her when their eyes met.

'I just want to phone Ross and check he's all right,' she explained, trying to stem the shiver that was trickling so disturbingly down her spine. What bothered her most was that she couldn't remember the last time something like this had happened. She kept too tight a rein on her emotions to let them misbehave this way, but obviously recent events had taken their toll.

She had been looking forward to this wedding so much, looking forward to the fact that from here on her son would have the woman he loved by his side to support him. Although she had never met anyone she had wanted to spend the rest of her life with, she believed in marriage, firmly believed that a happy marriage was a wonderful thing.

Was it disappointment that all her hopes for her son's future had amounted to nothing that was making her feel so mixed up? she wondered suddenly. She certainly couldn't remember feeling so emotionally raw before and that could explain the odd way she seemed to be behaving that day.

'You do that while I make us some coffee.' Matt put his glass on the table and stood up. He shrugged as he took Rachel's glass from her and placed it next to his. 'I don't think alcohol is the answer somehow, do you?'

'Probably not.' Rachel summoned a smile as he passed her on his way to the kitchen, but she was aware that it was an effort to behave naturally. Knowing that she wasn't in control of herself as she usually was worried her, too. She certainly didn't want to make a fool of herself in front of Matt.

She sighed softly as she dialled Ross's number. She and Matt had a very good relationship, she'd always thought. They trusted each other in work and enjoyed an easy camaraderie outside the surgery. Recently they had been spending a lot more time together as they had helped their respective offspring finalise the plans for their wedding and she had found herself enjoying his company too. Was that when she had become more aware of Matt as a man and not solely as a colleague? Had those hours they had spent together altered her perception of him?

The thought troubled her. She wasn't sure if she wanted to make any adjustments to how she saw Matt. It seemed rather dangerous to alter the status quo, unpredictable, and if there was one thing Rachel didn't handle well it was the unpredictable. She liked her life to have structure, lots of nice tidy compartments to file away both people and events so she knew how to deal with them.

She frowned. It didn't sound a very appealing way of living, did it? Nevertheless, it had worked all these years for her and worked well too. Maybe this wedding had thrown her off course but she mustn't allow it to affect her too much. Once she got over the shock of it being cancelled, hopefully her life would return to normal.

Matt plugged in the kettle then took a tin of ground coffee out of the freezer. He spooned some into the cafetière then stood staring into space while he waited for the water to heat. It was almost four in the afternoon and if the day had gone as planned, he should have been enjoying the reception now. He would have been gearing himself up for his speech, not that it would have been difficult as wishing Heather and Ross every happiness for their future together was something he had been looking forward to doing. He had been so sure that Heather had found her ideal partner but had it been wishful thinking on his part? Although Heather hadn't said so, was he guilty of pushing her and Ross into this marriage?

Matt had a horrible feeling it might be true. He had been so pleased that Heather had found someone as reliable as Ross that he had overlooked the signs that the relationship maybe wasn't what it should have been. He had put his desire for Heather to have security above everything else and he regretted it now. Deeply.

Maybe he had sworn that he would make sure their daughter was safe after Claire, his wife, had died, but Heather needed more than security. She needed love, laughter, *fun*, and he wasn't sure if Ross could have provided her with all of those things.

The truth was there had always been that vital spark missing, now that he thought about it. That extra dimension needed to take a relationship up a level. He and Claire had had it and it was one of the reasons why he had never been able to imagine falling in love with anyone else. He didn't think any other woman could light that spark inside him again.

'Ross is back at home. He says he's fine, but I'm sure he's only saying that to stop me worrying.'

Rachel came into the kitchen. She gave a gusty sigh as she stared at her phone as though it should be able to tell her if her son was telling the truth, and Matt felt himself grow tense. He couldn't see her face clearly with her head lowered like that so maybe that was why she appeared different all of a sudden, almost like a stranger.

She looked up and his heart gave the oddest little jolt as he found himself taking stock of the familiar yet strangely unfamiliar features—the elegant little nose, the softly rounded cheeks, the lusciously full lips now gnawed clean of any trace of lipstick. She'd had her hair done for the wedding and the soft chestnut curls looked so invitingly silky as they tumbled around her face that he longed to touch them, feel their softness against the palms of his hands, the tips of his fingers, so tempting and alluring…

He took a deep breath and stamped down hard on that thought. There would be no stroking of hair going on here!

'Did Ross say if he'd heard from Heather?' he asked instead, picking up the kettle. He poured the hot water into the pot and pressed down the plunger, quite forgetting to let the coffee brew first.

'No. I didn't ask him, to be honest. Sorry.'

Rachel's pretty face filled with remorse and that odd feeling he'd had about her being a stranger immediately receded. Once again she was Rachel Mackenzie, a woman he liked and respected, and he breathed a little easier at finding himself back on familiar territory. It had been just a blip, he told himself as he took a couple of mugs out of the cupboard, a tiny aberration caused by the stresses of the day and definitely nothing to worry about.

'It doesn't matter. I'm sure Ross would have said if Heather had phoned him,' he said soothingly, filling the mugs with coffee and frowning when he saw how insipid it looked. 'This doesn't look too good. I'll make another pot.'

'It's fine. Don't worry about it.'

Rachel picked up one of the mugs and carried it over to the table. Matt's heart ached when he saw how upset she looked as she sat down. What had happened today had had a big effect on Rachel too and for some reason the thought upset him even more. It wasn't fair that someone as kind and as gentle as Rachel was should have to suffer this way.

He went to join her, trying to find the right words that, hopefully, would make the situation easier for her. 'I know how hard this must be for Ross but he'll get through it, Rachel, you'll see.'

'Do you think so?' She looked up and he could see tears brimming in her huge brown eyes. 'I feel so helpless, Matt. Oh, I know Ross is a grown man and more than capable of running his own life, but he's still my son and I love him dearly.' The tears spilled over and trickled down her cheeks. 'I just can't bear to think of him hurting this way.'

'I know. And I understand how you feel, really I do.'

Matt reached across the table and squeezed her hand. Her hand was so small that his seemed to engulf it and it surprised him how it made him feel—overwhelmed with tenderness and a need to protect her. He cleared his throat but he could hear the roughness in his voice even if Rachel couldn't.

'It's a difficult time for both Heather and Ross but I'm sure they will work things out in the end.'

He withdrew his hand, unsure what was happening and why he felt this way. This was Rachel, he reminded himself, someone he had worked with for a number of years, a trusted colleague as well as a friend. However, the description no longer seemed to fit as accurately as it had done in the past; there seemed to be an extra dimension to Rachel he had never noticed before.

He frowned because that wasn't quite true. If he was honest, his view of her had been changing for a while now. They had spent a lot of time together in recent months planning for the wedding and he had found himself looking forward to it too. She wasn't just a colleague and a friend any longer. He was very much aware that she was a woman as well and a very attractive woman too.

The thought stunned him. For the first time since his wife had died Matt realised that he was aware of another woman's femininity and he couldn't believe that the feelings he had believed long dead were very much alive. His whole body suffused with heat all of a sudden because he was powerless to stop what was happening. When he looked at Rachel, sitting here at his table, what he saw, first and foremost, was a woman he wanted to put his arms around. A woman he wanted to make love to.

CHAPTER TWO

'SORRY. I know this is just as difficult for you as it is for me, Matt.'

Rachel plucked a tissue out of her pocket and wiped her eyes. The last thing she wanted to do was to make the situation even more stressful for Matt.

'There's nothing to apologise for,' Matt said swiftly, and she looked at him in dismay when she realised how strange he sounded. It wasn't that he sounded angry or even upset, just…*odd*.

'Are you all right?' she asked anxiously, leaning forward so she could get a better look at his face. It was early December and the nights soon drew in at this time of the year. They hadn't switched on any lights and Matt's face was in shadow, making it difficult for her to see his expression clearly.

'Yes. Just a bit shaken by what's happened, I suppose,' he replied, and she was relieved to hear him sounding more like he usually did this time.

'You and me both. I was stunned when Ross told me this morning the wedding had been called off.' She gave a little sigh. 'I still find it hard to understand why it's happened, if I'm honest. I always thought he and Heather were a perfect match, didn't you?'

'Ye-es.'

Rachel frowned when Matt seemed to hesitate. 'That sounded almost as though you had your doubts. Did you?'

'Not before this happened, no. However, now I'm not so sure.'

He stood up and switched on the light then sat down again. Rachel could see a glimmer of some emotion in his green eyes that she found it difficult to interpret.

'You don't think their marriage would have worked?' she said slowly, struggling to digest the idea.

'The honest answer is that I don't know any more. I thought they were ideally suited too, but I was thinking about it while I was making the coffee and I realised there was always something missing, that spark which makes a relationship truly special.'

'Do you really think so?' she said in surprise.

'Yes, I do. I only wish I'd realised it sooner. I wouldn't have pushed them into getting married then.'

'You didn't push them, Matt!' she exclaimed. 'It was their decision and it had nothing to do with you or anyone else for that matter.'

'I wish I could believe that but I have a horrible feeling that I'm more than partly responsible for this mess.'

'Rubbish!' She glared at him when he looked at her in surprise. 'I'm sorry but that's exactly what it is— complete and utter rubbish. They're both old enough to know their own minds. It wouldn't have mattered a jot what you thought.'

'Let's hope you're right.' He gave her a quick smile although Rachel could tell that he wasn't convinced. Matt obviously blamed himself for what had happened and that must make the situation even more difficult for him.

There was little she could say to persuade him otherwise, however, so she let the matter drop, talking about what had happened down by the canal instead. They had treated at least a dozen people who had been injured in the accident and it was always useful to compare notes after the event. It was only when Rachel heard the hall clock strike the hour that she realised it was time she left.

'I'd better be off,' she announced, standing up.

'I'll run you home,' Matt offered straight away, following her into the hall. He had collected her in his car along with the rest of the team from the surgery and ferried them to the site of the accident, which was why Rachel didn't have her own car with her. However, as she lived only a ten-minute walk away she immediately protested.

'There's no need, Matt. I can easily walk home from here. There's no point dragging you out of the house.'

'No, it's dark outside and I don't want you walking down that lane on your own.' He took his coat off the hall-stand before she could protest any further and she gave in. There was no point making an issue out of it, was there?

It took them a bare five minutes to drive to her home. She had bought the cottage when she had moved to Dalverston and had spent a lot of time and effort restoring it over the last few years. She had always loved the cottage's quirkiness and its sense of history, not to mention its location, backing onto the river. However, she had to admit that the sight of the darkened windows made her heart sink a little as they drew up outside.

Normally it didn't bother her that she lived on her own. She'd had Ross while she was still in her teens, getting pregnant the first time she had slept with her boyfriend. Ross's father had been just a year older than her, far too young to want to accept responsibility for the child he had fathered.

With her parents' help, Rachel had brought Ross up, working hard to give them both a good life. Getting through medical school had taken a huge amount of determination with a young child to care for but she had succeeded and it had got easier as Ross had grown older. However, one thing she had never factored into her busy life was time for a proper relationship.

She'd had a couple of affairs over the years, and still dated occasionally, but that was all. Although the few men she had been involved with had appeared perfect on paper, she had never been tempted to commit to a long-term relationship with any of them. Quite frankly, she hadn't had any inclination to fall in love with all its attendant pitfalls, especially not after her first disastrous experience. She had been perfectly happy with her life the way it was…

Or so she had thought.

Rachel's breath caught as the doubts slid into her mind. She had everything she had ever dreamed of having, a job she loved, a son she adored, a comfortable home, so what on earth could be missing? Surely she didn't wish that she had someone to come home to, someone who would be waiting for her with a smile and a hug?

'Here we are, then. Want me to come in with you and check everything's all right?'

Matt's voice mingled with her thoughts and Rachel had the craziest urge to shout, Yes, please! Please come in with me. Please stay and talk to me, share this evening and maybe share other evenings with me too, but she managed to stop herself in time. If she took the first step down that route, who knew where she would end up? The thought scared her.

'No, it's fine,' she said, hoping he couldn't hear the panic in her voice.

'Sure?' He stared at the darkened windows and frowned. 'I don't like to think of you going into an empty house on your own.'

'I'll be fine,' Rachel said firmly, as much for her own benefit as his. She grasped the doorhandle, ready to get out of the car, then stopped when he suddenly leant across the seat and kissed her gently on the cheek. His lips were cool from the night air and she shivered when she felt them brush her skin, hastily blanking out the thought of how good it would feel if he kissed her properly on the mouth.

'Take care, Rachel. It's been a tough day for all of us. If you need someone to talk to, you know where I am.'

'I…um…thank you.'

Rachel scrambled out of the car and almost ran up the path to the front door. Her hands were shaking so hard that it took her a moment to fit the key into the lock. Stepping into the tiny vestibule, she switched on the porch light then turned and waved. Matt gave a toot

on his horn and drove away, his taillights rapidly disappearing into the darkness, but it was several minutes
before she closed the door and went inside.

She stood there in the hall, deliberately drinking in
the peace and quiet of her home in the hope that it
would calm her, but for some reason the magic didn't
work that night. Instead of peace all she felt was loneliness, instead of soothing quiet, emptiness, and she bit
her lip. She had thought she was happy with her lot but
all of a sudden she was aware of all that she lacked. She
may have a fulfilling job, good friends, a son she
adored, but she needed more.

She needed someone to love her and hold her in the
night. Someone she could love and hold onto too, but
was it too late for that? She was forty-six years old and
it seemed crazy to be wishing for more than she had,
more than might be good for her. Did she really want
to risk falling in love at this point in her life, always supposing she met someone to fall in love with. Suitable
men weren't exactly thick on the ground.

A picture of Matt suddenly appeared in her mind's
eye and she frowned. If she did fall in love, it would
have to be with someone like Matt, someone she trusted
and respected, someone she found attractive too. But
where could she hope to find anyone like Matt? He was
a one-off. Special. There wasn't another man like Matt
in the whole wide world.

A tiny sigh escaped her as she went into the sitting
room and turned on the lamps, filling the house with
light. There was no point even *thinking* about falling in
love with Matt when there was little likelihood of him

reciprocating her feelings. The only woman Matt had ever loved was his late wife and she certainly couldn't compete with her.

'I'm sorry, Matt, but I've had to add a couple of extra patients onto your list. Rachel asked me if I'd try to make some cuts to Ross's list and it was the only way I could fit everyone in.'

'That's fine, Carol, don't worry about it. We'll just have to pull together until everything settles down.'

Matt smiled at the practice manager, hoping he hadn't visibly reacted at the mention of Rachel's name. It was Monday morning and he had just arrived at the surgery. He had planned on getting there early that day but as luck would have it, he'd had a phone call from the Ambulance Control centre as he'd been about to leave home. By the time he had dealt with that, the traffic had built up in the town centre and he'd had the devil of a job getting through it. Now he had barely five minutes to spare before his first appointment.

'Oh, good, there you are, Matt. What happened? Did you oversleep?'

Matt turned when he heard Rachel's voice, trying to quell the tremor that ran through him when he saw her standing behind him. She was wearing what she normally wore for work—a tailored suit with a white blouse and low-heeled shoes. Today her suit was cherry-red, a colour that shouldn't have worked with her glorious chestnut hair, yet it did. The richness of the hue highlighted her porcelain-fine complexion and made her large brown eyes look darker than ever. She had chosen a slightly deeper shade of lipstick to complement it and the colour emphasised the fullness of her mouth.

Matt felt his stomach lurch as his gaze lingered on her luscious lips. He still didn't understand what was going on. For almost six years, six extremely *comfortable* years too, he had viewed Rachel as a colleague and a friend, but he could no longer think of her solely that way. Far too many times over the weekend he had found his thoughts returning to her and they had been thoughts he had never entertained before. The memory of them made him inwardly squirm and he hurried to reply. Rachel would run a mile if she discovered that he had been fantasising about her sharing his bed!

'Sorry I'm so late. Someone from Ambulance Control phoned as I was about to leave home.' He picked up the bundle of notes Carol had prepared for him and headed to his consulting room, talking to Rachel over his shoulder because it seemed wiser than doing so face to face. At least this way he wouldn't start fantasising about her gorgeous mouth again. 'That's what delayed me.'

'Did they want to know about what happened on Saturday?'

Rachel followed him along the corridor, quickening her pace to keep up with him. At a smidgen over five feet three, she was a lot shorter than he was even in heels. Matt's first instinct was to slow down but the need to curtail all this craziness was just too strong. He had to stop thinking of Rachel as a woman and remember that she was a colleague.

'Uh-huh. That's right.' He stopped when he reached

his room, inwardly groaning when he realised that he couldn't keep avoiding looking at her. Rachel would think it very strange if she had to carry on talking to the back of his head.

He forced himself to smile as he turned to face her. This close he could smell her perfume and his nostrils twitched appreciatively as he inhaled the scent of jasmine mingled with something even more exotic, a fragrance that stirred his blood in a way it hadn't been stirred for years. As the father of a grown-up daughter, Matt was accustomed to the smells of the lotions and potions that women applied to themselves; however, he had to admit that he hadn't smelled anything as delicious as the perfume Rachel was wearing that morning. It was an effort to concentrate when his mind was intent on racing off down a completely different path.

'Ambulance Control want us to send them a detailed report of what we did once we arrived on scene,' he explained, taking a step back in the hope it would make life easier. It did, a bit, but he could still smell jasmine as well as that other fragrance, something exotic and spicy and wickedly sexy…

'It will need to be a joint effort, then, won't it?' Rachel stated, and Matt dragged his wayward thoughts back into line again. At least one of them was functioning with a clear head and he should be grateful for that.

'It will. Everyone did something different, plus we arrived separately too. Ross and Gemma were first on scene and they had already prioritised the casualties by the time we turned up.'

'How long was it before the rapid response unit got there—do you remember?'

Rachel frowned as she tried to recall the exact order of events and Matt sucked in his breath as he watched her brow pucker. When had a frown become so beguiling? he wondered in astonishment, then hastily blanked out the thought because he really and truly didn't want to know the answer.

'About fifteen minutes after us, although I think there was a paramedic car there before then. I'll have to check with Ross about that. He'll have a better idea than me.'

'I hope this isn't going to turn into a major investigation,' Rachel said anxiously. 'There's bound to be a bit of a hullabaloo because most of the rapid-response vehicles were off the road thanks to that problem they had with their fuel supply. That's probably why Ambulance Control want us to write a report. They will need to have a full picture of what went on. I don't want Ross dragged in if there's an inquiry, though. He's got quite enough on his plate at the present time.'

'I can't see why any of us should be involved to that extent,' Matt assured her, hating to hear her sounding so worried. He patted her arm then wished he hadn't done so when he felt his blood pressure soar. 'We'll keep our report as general as possible. There's no reason why individual members of our staff should have to account for their actions at this stage.'

'Good. I don't want to add to the pressure Ross is under at the moment. To be honest, I don't think he should be at work today. It's madness to try and carry on as though nothing has happened.'

'We'll do our best to lighten his load as much as we can,' Matt said soothingly. 'Carol said that you'd asked her to re-jig his lists so that should help. And if it gets too much for him then he must go home.'

'You wouldn't mind?' Rachel smiled in relief when he shook his head. 'Thanks, Matt. I know Ross thinks I'm fussing but I can't help worrying about him.'

'Of course you can't,' Matt replied, his innards doing cartwheels as he basked in the glow of her smile. He cleared his throat and forced himself to focus. 'Right, I'd better get ready before my first patient arrives and catches me on the hop.'

'Me too. There's nothing more offputting for a patient than watching their doctor scrabbling about, trying to find the right case notes. It doesn't exactly inspire confidence, does it?'

Rachel laughed as she hurried away, causing his insides to perform yet another tricky manoeuvre. Matt thankfully went into his room and closed the door, hoping it would provide some protection from what ailed him.

He sighed as he sat down behind his desk. What did ail him, though? Was it the shock of Heather cancelling her wedding and leaving Dalverston that was making him feel as though he was on some sort of emotional roller-coaster ride?

For eight long years, ever since Claire had died so tragically of a stroke, he had felt very little. Every thought, every fibre of his being, had been poured into looking after Heather. Caring for Heather had filled the void left by his wife's death, but now that Heather no longer needed him he had nothing to fill it with. Did that explain why he was suddenly experiencing all these desires and urges he had believed long dead?

Matt tried to tell himself it was that simple but in his heart he knew it wasn't true. He was merely papering over the cracks because he was afraid of what he would find if he delved too deeply. He had loved once and it had been the most wonderful experience of his life. He was too scared to try and repeat it, terrified that it could only end in disappointment. How could he ever hope to find another woman to replace Claire?

He couldn't because Claire had been unique, special. However, it didn't mean that there wasn't someone else equally special in her own unique way. Once again his thoughts returned to Rachel and a little tingle ran through him, like a frisson of static electricity passing over his skin. He could deny it till the moon turned blue but the truth was that Rachel definitely had an effect on him.

CHAPTER THREE

RACHEL heaved a sigh of relief as she sat down at her desk and switched on the computer. She had been dreading seeing Matt after what had happened over the weekend. Time and again she had found herself returning to the thought that he would never love anyone the way he had loved his late wife and it was so stupid to have let the idea upset her. She really couldn't understand why it had become such a big deal when she had always known how he felt.

In the whole time she had worked at Dalverston Surgery, Matt had never shown any interest in another woman. He never dated, never flirted, never even hinted that he was interested in the opposite sex. He had poured all his energy into his job and caring for Heather, and she had admired him for it too, so why had that admiration suddenly changed to concern? Was she reflecting her own emotional turmoil onto him?

Rachel wasn't sure if that was the real answer and it was unsettling to find herself dealing with uncertainties when she preferred absolutes. It was a relief when her first patient arrived and she could concentrate on her instead. Miss Bessie Parish was eighty years old, a spinster who had lived in Dalverston all her life. She was one of Ross's patients normally but she had agreed to see Rachel instead that day. Rachel invited her to sit down and asked her what she could do for her.

'I've not felt at all well lately, Dr Mackenzie,' Miss Parish replied in her forthright way. 'I had a nasty cold a couple of weeks ago and it's left me feeling very wheezy and breathless.'

'I see. Have you had a cough as well?' Rachel asked, picking up her stethoscope.

'Yes, and I've been bringing up phlegm too.'

Miss Parish's mouth pursed with distaste and Rachel nodded sympathetically.

'Horrible for you, I'm sure. Now, I'd just like to listen to your chest, if you wouldn't mind.' She waited while Miss Parish unbuttoned her coat then listened to her chest. 'And I'll take your temperature too,' she told her once she had finished doing that.

Miss Parish sat perfectly still while Rachel checked her temperature. The reading was higher than it should have been and Rachel nodded because it confirmed her suspicions. Sitting down at her desk again, she smiled at the old lady.

'It looks as though you have bronchitis, Miss Parish. The symptoms you described certainly point towards it—wheezing, shortness of breath, a persistent cough that produces considerable quantities of phlegm. Your temperature is higher than it should be, too, which is another indication.'

'Bronchitis? Well, I never!' Miss Parish looked shocked.

'It's an acute form and we can treat it quite easily with a course of antibiotics,' Rachel said soothingly. She wrote out a script and handed it over along with detailed instructions aimed at making the old lady more comfortable in the interim.

Miss Parish listened attentively to what she said then nodded. 'I shall follow your advice, Dr Mackenzie. Thank you. I must say that I was very sorry to hear what had happened to your son. It can't be easy for him, having his wedding cancelled like that.'

'I'm sure Ross will deal with it,' Rachel replied evenly, hoping to avoid any further well-meaning comments.

'Oh, I'm sure he will. Once he gets over the shock, I expect he'll realise that it's better it happened now rather than later.' Miss Parish stood up. 'So many young couples end up getting divorced these days and that must be just as distressing for them, I imagine.'

Rachel frowned as the old lady bade her goodbye and left. Would the marriage have ended in divorce if it had gone ahead? she wondered. A couple of days ago she would have pooh-poohed the idea but she was no longer so sure. Heather obviously had had her doubts and that was why she had called the wedding off.

She sighed because it just proved how difficult relationships really were. Even those that seemed guaranteed to succeed could and did fail. It took both love and an awful lot of commitment to build a lasting relationship, not to mention that vital spark Matt had mentioned. That was essential too. Thinking about Matt immediately reminded her of what had troubled her all weekend and she groaned. She didn't want to go down that road again!

She buzzed in her next patient, a young woman with a screaming toddler suffering from a nasty ear infection. It was hard to make herself heard over the din the poor little mite was making but Rachel was glad because it blotted out any other thoughts. She didn't want to dwell on what a special relationship Matt must have had with his late wife when it was so painful, didn't want to sit here daydreaming about him when she had work to do. It wasn't the best way to get things back onto a normal footing, which was what she desperately needed to do.

Lunchtime arrived and Rachel hurried to Ross's room to see how he had fared. She caught him as he was about to leave and her heart ached with motherly concern when she saw how drawn he looked. Having his wedding cancelled at the eleventh hour must have been a terrible experience for him despite the brave front he was putting up. She wasn't sure that he should be at work, but he was adamant that he wanted to be there when she broached the subject.

They chatted for a couple of minutes, but her heart was heavy as she watched him leave. No matter what Ross claimed, she knew he must be devastated by what had happened. A tear trickled down her cheek and before she could wipe it away, Matt appeared. He took one look at her and gently steered her along the corridor into his room.

'Is it Ross?' he asked as he sat her down in a chair and offered her the box of tissues off his desk.

'How did you guess?' Rachel blew her nose and tried to get a grip on herself. The situation was difficult for Matt too and she didn't want to upset him as well.

'Simple deduction, Watson. If you eliminate everything else, whatever you're left with, no matter how improbable it seems, must be the solution.'

Despite herself Rachel laughed. 'Is that a fact, Sherlock?'

'It certainly is, Doctor.' Matt smiled back her at her and her heart immediately lifted. She couldn't deny that she was touched that he should try to cheer her up when he must be feeling extremely low himself.

'So how is Ross holding up?' he asked, placing the box of tissues back on the desk.

'Fine, according to him.' She shrugged when he looked quizzically at her. 'You know Ross. He isn't one to wear his heart on his sleeve. He was the same when he was a child, very self-contained and serious...a little too serious, in fact.'

'Did he have much contact with his father while he was growing up?' Matt asked quietly, and Rachel tried to hide her surprise. It was the first time he had ever asked her a personal question like that in all the time they had worked together and she couldn't help wondering what had prompted it that day.

'None at all,' she replied, determined that she wasn't going to make too much of his sudden interest. Maybe he wanted to find out more about the past in the hope it would provide a clue as to how to bring Ross and Heather back together? If that was the case then she was all for it. She would do anything at all to see Ross happy again.

'Ross's father made it clear from the outset that he wasn't interested in him,' she explained truthfully. 'I don't blame him in a way because he was only eighteen when Ross was born. Not many boys of that age are ready to become fathers.'

'You were very young to be a mother but you coped,' Matt pointed out, and she sighed.

'Yes, I know, although I wouldn't have managed nearly as well if my parents hadn't supported me. They were marvellous.'

'It must have been hard, though, even with their help.' Matt's tone was gruff and she frowned when she heard it. She couldn't help wondering why he sounded so uptight all of a sudden, apart from the obvious reason, of course. He must miss Heather dreadfully and the thought made her heart ache for him.

'It wasn't easy. Finding the time to study and look after Ross was a real juggle. Looking back, I don't know how I fitted everything in.' She gave a little laugh, hoping it would lighten the sombre mood. 'If I had to do it now, I'd need a few more hours tagged onto the end of each day!'

'I imagine you fitted it all in by dint of sheer hard work. You should be proud of yourself for what you've achieved, Rachel.'

'I am extremely proud of Ross, although I can't claim any credit for how he's turned out,' she said firmly. 'Ross put in the effort himself.'

'I don't just mean raising Ross but what you've

achieved.' Matt leant forward and she could see the light in his eyes, a hint of fire she hadn't noticed before and certainly hadn't expected. Her heart gave a little bounce then started to race as he continued.

'You must have worked incredibly hard to get through medical school. I remember how difficult it was to keep up with all the work and when you factor in a child as well…' He shrugged. 'Not many people could have done what you've done, Rachel.'

'I always dreamed of being a doctor,' she said quietly, deeply moved by the compliment. To know that Matt admired her made all the years of hard work and struggle seem even more worthwhile.

'And you achieved your dream. You're a damned fine doctor. Your patients couldn't speak more highly of you.'

'Thank you. It means a lot to hear you say that,' she murmured, feeling a little choked with emotion.

'It's nothing more than the truth. You should be proud of yourself. You've achieved everything you set out to do.'

Had she? she wondered. Had she really achieved every single dream she'd ever had? Just days ago Rachel would have agreed with him but she was no longer sure if it was true. Once upon a time she'd had other dreams for the future. She had buried them as deeply as she could over the years because there'd been no time to worry about them, but they were still there, maybe not as bright and as shiny as they had been, but still there.

Her heart caught as she looked at Matt and remembered all the hopes she'd had at one time for a happy marriage like her parents', a loving relationship that would sustain her throughout the years. She had abandoned those dreams because she'd been afraid of what would happen if she allowed herself to fall in love again. She had done it once, fallen in love with Ross's father, and it had been a disaster… Hadn't it?

The thought pulled her up short. Having Ross hadn't been a disaster, far from it. It had been a turning point. Knowing she'd had a child to provide for had given her the impetus she had needed, pushed her to make a good life for herself and her son. Without Ross, she might not have studied as hard, but made another mistake and fallen in love with someone else who might have held her back.

Rachel took a deep breath as she faced the facts, head on. Her life could have turned out very differently if she hadn't had her son. For one thing, she might never have met Matt.

Matt decided to stay on after evening surgery ended. He wanted to make a start on that report Ambulance Control had requested while the facts were fresh in his mind. After all, it wasn't as though there was anything to rush home for, was there?

His heart sank at the thought of returning to an empty house, although he knew that he would have to get used to it. With Heather gone he would be spending a lot of time on his own. He had just drafted out a rough timetable of events when there was a tap on his door and Rachel came into the room.

'I spotted your light was still on as I was passing,' she explained, coming over to the desk. She frowned when she saw the timetable he had made. 'Is that about the accident?'

'Yes. I thought I'd better make a start on that report.'

Matt glanced at the notes he had written, trying not to think about the fact that Rachel lived on her own as well. It had no relevance to his situation, especially as it was obviously her choice to do so. By no stretch of the imagination could he believe that she hadn't had lots of offers to change her single status.

'Do you need any help?'

Matt barely heard what she said. Not once in the all the time they had worked together had he wondered why Rachel was single, but now the question clamoured for his attention. She was a beautiful and highly intelligent woman and there must be lots of men keen to share their lives with her, so why had she resisted? Was it because she had never met anyone she had cared enough about to spend her life with?

Thoughts whizzed around inside his head. It was only when he realised that Rachel was waiting for him to answer that he pulled himself together. 'It's kind of you to offer, but I don't expect you to give up your evening as well, Rachel.'

'It's not a big deal, Matt.' She gave a little shrug. 'And it isn't as though I've anything better to do. In fact, I'd be glad to help, if I'm honest. It will stop me worrying about Ross if I have something else to think about.'

'In that case, I'd be glad of your help. Thank you.'

Matt smiled up at her, feeling warmth ripple along his veins when she smiled back. She pulled up a chair and sat down beside him, leaning over so she could read what he had written. Matt felt his whole body grow tense when he inhaled her perfume but he was wise to the effect it could have after that morning and quickly brought himself under control. So long as he focussed on what he was doing, there shouldn't be a problem.

With Rachel's help they soon compiled a list of events and the times they had occurred. Anything hazy—such as what Ross and Gemma, their practice nurse, had been doing before they had arrived—they marked with an asterisk so they could check it later. By eight o'clock they had the bare bones of the report prepared and Matt was delighted they had accomplished so much.

'Excellent!' he said, leaning back in his chair and easing the crick out of his neck. 'I thought it would take a lot longer than that.'

'Two heads, et cetera,' Rachel replied with a grin, and he laughed.

'Too right, especially when the two heads are in tune with one another.' Matt smiled back, feeling more relaxed than he had felt in days. Ever since Heather had told him that she was leaving Dalverston, it had felt as though his nerves had been strung out on a rack. However, after just an hour of working with Rachel he felt much better, so much better, in fact, that he was reluctant to let the evening end there.

'How do you fancy going out for dinner?' he suggested impulsively. 'I don't know about you but all this extra work has given me an appetite. I could eat a horse!'

'I'm not sure if you'll find horse on the menu anywhere in Dalverston,' she replied lightly, although he saw a hint of colour run up her cheeks.

Did she think he was being presumptuous by asking her out? he wondered, then immediately dismissed the idea. Of course Rachel didn't think that. They were colleagues and having dinner together wasn't anything to get worked up about.

'Hmm, good point. I'll have to settle for a steak instead.' He pushed back his chair, not wanting it to appear as though he was pressurising her to go out with him. It was her decision and he would abide by whatever she decided to do, although he really hoped she would say yes.

It was unsettling to realise just how much he wanted her to agree and he hurried on. 'So long as it comes with all the trimmings, I'll be more than happy.'

'I have to confess that I'm hungry too,' she admitted, standing up. 'I can't remember when I last had a decent meal—it must have been last week. I definitely didn't cook anything for myself over the weekend.'

'Me neither,' Matt agreed, sliding the notes they had made into a folder. 'The most I've managed is tea and toast for the past couple of days. My poor stomach must think my throat's been cut.'

She laughed as she headed for the door. 'It sounds as though we're both in desperate need of some proper sustenance. How about that new place on the bypass? I believe they do excellent steaks there.'

'Sounds good to me.'

Matt managed to hide his delight as he switched off the light and followed her along the corridor. It was just dinner with a colleague, he reminded himself, although he had to admit that it felt somewhat different to the usual staff outings he had attended in the past. For one thing, he and Rachel would be by themselves tonight and that was something that didn't usually happen. Even when they had spent all that time planning the wedding, they hadn't been on their own—Ross and Heather had been with them. This would be a whole new experience for them.

He took a steadying breath as he stopped beside the reception desk, determined that he wasn't going to let himself get carried away by the thought. 'I'll set the alarm and follow you out. We can go in my car, if you like. That way you can have a glass of wine with your meal without worrying about driving home.'

'Thanks, but it's easier if we take both our cars. It will save all the hassle in the morning of getting here.'

It was on the tip of Matt's tongue to tell her that he would give her a lift, but he sensed that would be over-stepping the mark. 'Fine. I'll see you there, then.'

He waited until she had left then switched the phone through to their on-call service and set the alarm. There was only his car left in the car park when he went outside and he hurried over to it, shivering as a blast of icy wind blew down from the hills. The temperature had dropped over the weekend and it looked as though they were in for a really cold spell. Still, it wouldn't be long before he got to the restaurant and warmed up, he consoled himself.

He started the engine, smiling at the thought of meeting Rachel there. Maybe it was only dinner with a colleague but it was good to know that he wouldn't be spending the rest of the evening on his own. Was that her main attraction? he wondered suddenly. Was he so eager for her company because he was lonely?

He tested out the theory and discovered that it did fit. However, deep down he knew it was more than that. Loneliness didn't explain the way he had responded to her recently, did it?

CHAPTER FOUR

RACHEL could feel butterflies flitting around her stomach as she entered the restaurant. It wasn't very busy with it being a Monday evening and she had no trouble getting a table. She told the waiter that she was expecting someone to join her and sat down to wait, trying to control the frantic fluttering inside her. It was just dinner with Matt, nothing more, nothing less, and definitely nothing to get worked up about.

Matt arrived a few minutes later, looking big and imposing as he stopped to speak to the waiter. Rachel noticed several women glance his way and look a second time too as he made his way over to her. No wonder, she thought as he took off his coat and draped it over the back of a chair. He was an extremely handsome man and she wouldn't blame any woman for finding him attractive.

'This is nice.' He looked around the restaurant with obvious pleasure. 'It all looks very sleek and modern without being too stark and bare. Call me old-fashioned but I like a bit of clutter around the place.'

'Me too, probably too much clutter,' she agreed ruefully.

'So you don't go in for the minimalist look that Ross favours?' Matt queried, loosening his tie. He undid the top button of his shirt as well and Rachel hurriedly averted her eyes when she felt those pesky butterflies start flapping even more wildly. She had seen Matt wearing a variety of outfits over the years they'd worked together, from the jeans he had worn on staff outings to the suits he preferred for work, so why was she reacting this way to a glimpse of bare tanned flesh?

'No, it's not my taste at all. As for Ross, well, he probably favours that style because it's the complete opposite from what he grew up with.'

Rachel hurriedly dismissed the question. They were there to have dinner, not so she could analyse how she felt about Matt. He was a colleague and a friend, and that was all she needed to know.

'Really?' Matt sat back in his chair, obviously keen to hear more, and she continued, finding it easier to talk about such a safe topic.

'We lived with my parents for a long time, you see, so Ross grew up in a house decorated according to his grandparents' tastes. Mum is very much into chintz and frills and I think that's why Ross rebelled and opted for something very different when he bought his own home.'

'It must have been a help to have your parents on hand,' Matt said quietly, and she nodded.

'Oh, it was. Mum not only looked after Ross while I was studying but while I was doing my rotations as well. I don't know how I'd have managed otherwise. The hours a newly qualified doctor has to work are horrendous.'

'I remember how exhausting it was working such long shifts. My first post was as a junior house officer in A and E at a hospital in London—I don't think I went to bed for three days solid at one point because I was on call.'

'Thank heavens they've put a stop to young doctors working such terrible hours, although it's no picnic for them even now,' she agreed. 'It's madness to expect someone to function properly when they're exhausted.'

'It is. I certainly couldn't have coped with looking after Heather on top of the hours I worked. Thankfully, I didn't need to because Claire took care of all that. She gave up work when Heather was born so she could be a full-time mum.' Matt sighed. 'You've not had an easy time, Rachel, have you? You didn't have that option.'

'It wasn't that bad,' she protested, touched by the concern in his voice. 'As I said, Mum and Dad were marvellous and once I'd completed my GP training, life became much easier. It was still hard work, of course, but at least I didn't need to work such gruellingly long hours.'

'When did you move out of your parents' house?' Matt asked curiously.

'When Ross was about twelve. I was earning a decent salary by then and I was able to afford a mortgage. Mum still helped out if I needed a hand, but it was good to be independent at last.'

'You value your independence, then?' he said quietly, and she frowned when she caught a hint of something she couldn't identify in his tone.

'Yes, I suppose I do. It was a long time before I was able to strike out on my own and it's important to me to know that I'm not beholden to anyone.'

'Is that why you've never married?' He shrugged when she looked at him in surprise. 'It just seems strange that you're still single. It certainly can't be for lack of offers.'

Rachel felt the colour rush to her cheeks and stared down at the table. Had she imagined that sensuous note in Matt's voice, that hint of sexual attraction? She must have done because there was no sign of it on his face when she looked up.

'I guess I've never met anyone I wanted to spend my life with,' she said lightly, opting for a partial truth.

The waiter arrived just then to take their order and by the time they decided what they wanted, the moment had passed. However, several times during the evening Rachel found herself wondering if she should have been more up front with Matt and explained that she had been wary of falling in love in case she had committed another error of judgement. For some reason she couldn't explain it seemed important that he should know the truth. How odd.

They left the restaurant shortly after ten p.m. Matt would have happily stayed there longer but it was obvious the staff were waiting to close for the night. If anything the temperature had dropped even further and he saw Rachel shiver as they walked towards their cars.

'Brr, it's freezing,' she declared, huddling into the collar of her coat. 'Do you think it will snow tonight?'

'It could do, although it's probably a bit too cold at the moment.' Matt carried on past his car and saw her look at him in surprise. 'I'll just make sure you get off safely,' he explained, and she laughed.

'Ever the gentleman even in the freezing cold!' She quickly zapped the locks open and turned to him. 'I enjoyed tonight, Matt. Thank you. Next time, it's my treat.'

'I'll hold you to that,' he said, aiming for lightness and hoping he had succeeded. The thought of them spending another evening together was so enticing that he had a sudden urge to grin but managed to restrain himself. There was no point scaring her into thinking she'd had dinner with a lunatic!

'You do that.'

Before he could say anything else she reached up on tiptoe and kissed him on the cheek. Her lips were cold from the wind and Matt sucked in his breath when he felt them touch his skin. It was just one of those kisses that people exchanged all the time, he told himself firmly, a social nicety, nothing to get steamed up about, but he wasn't convinced. He could call it whatever he liked, but it was still a kiss and his body appreciated that fact even if his brain insisted on trying to rationalise it.

Desire flooded through him, bringing about a very predictable response, or at least one that would have been predictable several years ago. The fact that it hadn't happened in so long he could barely remember the last time made his heart almost stutter to a stop.

Rachel gave him a quick smile as she stepped back.

'I'll see you tomorrow, then. Take care going home. There could be ice on the roads.'

'I…um…you too,' Matt said numbly as she got into her car and closed the door. He waited while she backed out of the parking space, even managed to wave as she drove away, but every action was an effort when his body was clamouring for something it hadn't experienced since Claire had died.

He walked back to his car and got in then sat there, letting the feelings pour through him. This had gone beyond what he had felt at the weekend, way beyond that first tentative awakening of desire. What he was feeling now was something more earthy, more powerful, more urgent. He wanted to make love to Rachel and enjoy every inch of her delectable body, and then enjoy *her* enjoying *him*. Maybe it was the passage of time but he couldn't remember feeling this need so intensely before, not even for Claire.

The thought shook him to the core. His love for Claire had been the mainstay of his life, the one thing that had never been in doubt. Surely he wasn't doubting it now just because he wanted to have sex with another woman?

Matt knew he needed to work out what was going on and that he couldn't do it there. He needed to go home and think about it, calmly, rationally. He drove himself home, keeping his speed well below the limit because he was aware that his reactions weren't as sharp as they should have been. As soon as he got in, he made himself a cup of coffee and took it into the sitting room. There in the room he and Claire had spent so many happy evenings, he let himself remember their life together, all the good times they'd had, the fun, the laughter, the love.

Tears welled to his eyes but he didn't try to stop them falling. He had spent years being strong for his daughter's sake and it was time he allowed himself an outlet for his emotions. He had loved Claire so much, would have loved her for ever more, but she had died and left him on his own. He needed to cry for the woman he had lost and he also needed to cry for himself too.

Rachel drove home carefully, heeding her own advice. Although the main roads had been gritted, she could see a shimmer of frost on the tarmac when she turned into the lane leading to her cottage. She negotiated the bends with extra care and drew up with a sigh of relief. Thank heavens that was over.

Stepping out of the car, she went to hurry up the path and shrieked in alarm when her feet suddenly skidded from under her. She landed with an almighty thud, wincing as her right knee took the brunt of her fall. Getting to her feet again wasn't easy when her knee felt as though it was on fire but she needed to get inside. She certainly couldn't spend the night outdoors in weather as cold as this.

She hobbled up the path and let herself in. It seemed an awful long way to the kitchen but a cold compress should help to prevent her knee swelling up. By leaning against the wall and hopping, she finally made it to the kitchen and dug a bag of frozen peas out of the freezer, wrapping it in a tea-towel before applying it to her knee.

There was already a huge bruise forming and she guessed that the whole knee would be black and blue by the morning.

She sighed as she held the makeshift compress against her swollen joint. What a miserable end to a lovely evening. Maybe it was payback for that kiss? She hadn't planned on it happening—it had been purely an impulse. She wouldn't have given it a second thought normally either. However, the moment her lips had connected with Matt's cheek, she had realised her mistake. Social kissing may be all well and good, but not when the person she was kissing was Matt, apparently.

Her breath caught as she remembered the warmth of his skin against her lips. She touched a finger to her mouth and shuddered when she felt an echo of that heat still lingering there. It was hard to believe the brief contact could have left such a lasting impression. Had it made the same impression on Matt, though?

Common sense insisted that the answer to that question should be a resounding no but she found it difficult to accept it. There had been several occasions recently when he had looked at her with an awareness in his eyes that she hadn't seen there before. Even the interest he had shown tonight when he'd asked her why she had chosen to remain single was a new departure for him and she couldn't help wondering what had changed. Was it possible that Matt no longer saw her simply as a colleague?

The thought made her heart race even though she had no proof that it was true. Rachel sighed as she put the now-soggy bag of peas back into the freezer and lifted out a bag of sprouts. All she knew for certain was that *her* feelings towards Matt had altered recently and altered dramatically too. She would have to be extra careful around him and make sure that she didn't let him know how confused she felt. And that meant no more kissing for *any* reason!

Matt was getting showered the following morning when the telephone rang. Snatching a towel off the rack, he hurried into his bedroom and picked up the receiver. Surprisingly, after all the emotional upheaval of the previous evening, he had slept soundly. It was as though a weight had been lifted from his shoulders, making him see that he had needed an outlet for his feelings for a very long time.

'Matthew Thompson.'

'Matt, it's me, Rachel. I'm sorry to phone you so early but I need a favour.'

Matt felt a rush of heat invade him and sank down onto the bed. Hearing Rachel's voice reminded him vividly of the dreams he'd had during the night, dreams of such an explicit nature that his body immediately quickened as he recalled them. It was an effort to respond calmly when every cell was suddenly on the alert.

'Of course. What can I do for you, Rachel?'

'Can you give me a lift into work? I very stupidly slipped on some ice last night as I got out of my car and hurt my knee. It's not serious,' she added hurriedly, 'but I don't think I can actually drive myself there today.'

'Do you want me to run you to hospital so you can have it X-rayed?' Matt suggested in concern.

'Thanks, but there's no need. I'm sure there's no

serious damage—it's just badly swollen. It should be back to normal in a couple of days' time.'

'Are you sure you should be going into work?' he protested. 'The best thing for it is rest and you won't be able to do that if you're having to jump up and down, attending to patients.'

'I'll manage,' she assured him. 'I've spent the night with a bag of frozen peas strapped to it and that's helped.'

Matt chuckled. 'It's good to know the professionals opt for the same remedies as their patients. Frozen peas indeed!'

Rachel laughed. 'It was either peas or sprouts, and the sprouts were far too lumpy, I discovered. They kept rolling about!'

Her laughter rippled down the line and Matt felt his senses spin all over again. Why had he never realised before what a gorgeously sexy laugh she had? It was an effort to concentrate as she continued.

'I'll be ready any time you say, so when should I expect you?'

He glanced at the bedside clock. 'Will half an hour suit you?'

'Fine. I'll be able to hobble around and make myself some breakfast before you get here. Everything seems to take twice as long as normal when you have a gammy leg.'

She said goodbye and Matt went back to the bathroom. However, the thought of her struggling as she tried to make herself something to eat didn't sit well with him. His conscience simply wouldn't allow him to let her soldier on on her own.

It took him a scant ten minutes to get himself dressed and drive the short distance to Rachel's house, and instead of ringing the front doorbell he went straight round to the back. It would save her having to trek down the hall if he used the rear entrance, he reasoned. He tapped on the door, feeling his heart lurch when she opened it. Rachel in the flesh was every bit as beautiful and as sexy as she had appeared in his dreams.

'You're early!' she exclaimed.

'I thought you could use some help.' He smiled at her, determined to get a grip on such wayward thoughts. 'I'm a dab hand at making tea and toast for the injured.'

'Oh, that's really kind of you, Matt. Thank you.' She hobbled over to a chair and sank gratefully down onto it. 'I hadn't realised how difficult it is to do even simplest tasks like filling the kettle when you need to hang onto something to stay upright.'

'Well, I'm here now so you just sit there and rest that leg.' He glanced at her bruised knee and grimaced. 'That's a real beauty. You really need to raise it to reduce the swelling—here, use this chair.'

He pulled over a chair and gently manoeuvred her leg until it was resting comfortably on the cushion. Rachel groaned, the lines of strain easing from her beautiful face.

'That feels *so* much better.'

'Good.'

He turned away, although he could have happily stood there all day and simply enjoyed looking at her. He set to work instead, scrambling some eggs and making a stack of toast as well as a pot of tea to go with them. Rachel nodded approvingly as he placed everything on the table and sat down.

'This looks delicious. Scrambled eggs are my absolute favourite.'

'We aim to please.' Matt helped himself to a slice of toast, thoroughly enjoying the experience of sharing breakfast with her. He could get used to seeing Rachel across the breakfast table each morning, he decided, very used to it indeed. The thought was so highly inappropriate when he was trying to be sensible that he immediately chased it from his mind and applied himself to his meal.

Rachel scraped the last morsel of eggs off her plate and sighed in contentment. 'My compliments to the chef. That tasted every bit as good as it looked.'

'Thank you kindly.' Matt smiled at her, loving the way her eyes sparkled with golden glints when she was feeling happy. It was something else he hadn't noticed before and he added it to the ever-expanding list. 'Although I have to warn you that my repertoire isn't exactly extensive. I can roast a chicken, grill chops, scramble eggs and that's about it.'

'Better than a lot of men, I imagine,' she said cheerfully, attempting to stand up.

'Whoa!' Matt put out a restraining hand and eased her back down onto the chair. 'Where do you think you're going?'

'I was only going to stack the dishes in the machine,' she protested.

'I'll do that.' He picked up their plates and took them over to the dishwasher, adding the rest of the crockery as well as the pan he had used for the eggs.

'Thank you.' Rachel glared at her knee in frustration. 'It's a real nuisance not being able to do things for myself. I only hope the swelling goes down soon.'

'It will probably take a couple of days before you get your full mobility back and even then you'll need to be careful,' he warned her. 'If you try doing too much too soon, you'll only make matters worse.'

'In other words, I need to be patient.' She grimaced. 'The worst part was last night. The stairs here are really steep and I had a devil of a job getting up them to go to bed. And I had to come down on my bottom this morning—not a pretty sight, believe me!'

Matt laughed at the wry note in her voice although he couldn't help feeling concerned. If there was an emergency, Rachel would have great difficulty getting out of the cottage. 'Maybe you should sleep downstairs until your knee is better.'

'I would do but the bathroom's upstairs, so I have to go up to get to it.' She gave a little shrug as she lifted her leg off the cushion and cautiously stood up. 'Not to worry. I'll soon be back to normal.'

Matt doubted it but he decided not to say so. He waited while she found her coat and bag then offered her his arm so she could lean on him while they went out to his car. It was obvious from the strain on her face that it was an effort for her to walk even that short distance but he knew it was pointless advising her to stay at home and rest. She was far too dedicated to go off sick unless she really couldn't avoid it, and in all truth they would find it very difficult to manage without her when they were trying to lighten Ross's workload.

It was frustrating not to be able to do more to help her, though. Matt resolved to keep an eye on her and make sure she didn't push herself too hard until her knee was better. What Rachel needed at the moment was someone to take care of her and he was more than happy to take on that role. The fact that he wouldn't mind it being a long-term project flashed through his mind but he didn't dwell on it. It was too soon for ideas like that, way too soon.

CHAPTER FIVE

MORNING surgery was exceptionally busy that day. There was a nasty tummy bug doing the rounds and a lot of people wanted to see the doctor. Rachel dispensed sympathy and advice in almost equal measures. Although this type of winter vomiting bug was very upsetting for the victims, so long as they behaved sensibly by restricting their food intake and maintaining their fluid levels, it was rarely life-threatening. The only exceptions were the elderly and the infirm, and young babies and infants. They needed extra care so she was particularly concerned when one young teen-age mum brought in her three-month-old son.

'How long has Charlie been like this, Melanie?' she asked, studying the poor little mite. Little Charlie's lips looked extremely dry and when she gently opened his mouth and checked, his tongue was dry to the touch too, worrying signs in a child this young.

'Since yesterday lunchtime. He was sick after he'd had his bottle and kept being sick all afternoon long. He also had the most horrible nappies,' Melanie added, her nose wrinkling in disgust.

Rachel stifled a sigh. It wasn't the girl's fault that she lacked experience and hadn't realised just how urgent the situation was. 'Has Charlie had anything to drink since then, cool boiled water, for instance?'

'No. The health visitor told me to give him some the other week, but he doesn't like it,' Melanie explained. 'He prefers his milk.'

'I see.' Rachel gently pressed her index finger against the baby's arm and was unsurprised to find that his skin was lacking in elasticity. Charlie was exhibiting all the classic signs of being severely dehydrated and he needed urgent treatment. Picking up the phone, she dialled the emergency services and requested an ambulance, briefly outlining the problem to the operator when she was connected. Melanie looked at her in dismay after Rachel hung up.

'An ambulance! But surely Charlie isn't so ill that he needs to go to the hospital?'

'I'm afraid he is, Melanie,' Rachel replied quietly. 'He's extremely dehydrated and it's very dangerous in a baby this young. He needs to be rehydrated as quickly as possible so he'll be put on an intravenous drip when you reach the hospital.'

'But I thought you'd just give me some medicine to stop him being sick,' Melanie wailed, tears pouring down her face.

'I wish it was that simple.' Rachel struggled to her feet and hobbled around the desk. She placed a comforting arm around the young mother's shoulders. 'The doctor at the hospital will also do a blood test to check Charlie's fluid and salt levels. Once an infant becomes severely dehydrated, it's essential to ensure that the right balance is maintained.'

'I wish I'd known all this before,' Melanie sniffed. 'I'd have brought Charlie in to see you last night if I'd thought he was in any danger.'

'Do you have anyone to help you with him?' Rachel asked and Melanie shook her head.

'No. I was brought up in care. I don't know where my parents are—they never came to visit me while I was in the children's home. And as for Charlie's dad, well, he didn't want to know when I told him I was pregnant.'

'I see.' It was an all too familiar tale and Rachel's heart went out to her. She had been so fortunate to have her parents there to help her through the first difficult years following Ross's birth, she thought.

There wasn't time to dwell on it then, however. The ambulance had arrived so she saw Melanie and baby Charlie out to Reception then went back to her room. However, as she worked through her list, Rachel decided that something needed to be done to help other young mums like Melanie. If they had somewhere they could go for advice it could prevent another situation like this from occurring.

She decided to mention it to Matt and see what he thought about the idea. If they put their heads together, she was confident that they could come up with some sort of a plan. A smile curved her mouth. It may mean extra work for her but working with Matt was always a pleasure and never a chore.

Matt went straight to Rachel's room after his last patient left. He had found himself clock-watching, willing the time to pass so he could check up on her. She was sitting at her desk, her head bowed as she jotted down some notes on a pad.

Matt felt a rush of heat erupt in the centre of his chest. She had no idea he was there so he could study her at his leisure and he made the most of the opportunity. Her hair was a riot of rich chestnut curls as it tumbled around her face. It looked so silky and so soft that once again he was struck by the urge to touch it. Then there was her skin, so smooth and satiny that he ached to touch that too. Everything about her was appealing, seductive, and he couldn't understand why he had never realised it before. Had he been walking around with his eyes closed for the past few years? Or had he been afraid to notice how beautiful she was because of what it could mean? By admitting that he was attracted to her, it meant that he was getting over Claire.

The thought shook him. He had never considered the idea that he had been deliberately clinging on to the past but it was true. He had been afraid to let it go when he had been scared of what the future held. Until Claire had died his life had been mapped out and mapped out in a way he had wanted it to be. He'd had a job he loved, a child he adored and a happy marriage. However, Claire's untimely death had changed everything. He had been cast adrift, his future sent spinning out of his control, and the only way he had been able to cope had been through clinging onto what he'd had—especially his love for Claire.

Deep down he knew it wasn't enough any longer. He

needed more than just his memories. But having more meant taking risks and he couldn't imagine placing himself in the position of getting hurt. Even supposing he found someone else to love, did he have the courage to risk his heart again?

Thoughts tumbled around his head and Matt realised that he needed time to deal with his inner turmoil. He quietly backed out of the room but just as that moment Rachel looked up and saw him. Her face broke into a smile and his heart clenched in fear. Even now it might be too late. He already felt far more for Rachel than he should have done.

'Ah, just the person I wanted to see.' Rachel smiled at Matt across the desk, her mind still busy with the plans she had made for the new teenage pregnancy advisory service she was hoping to set up. She glanced at her notes again and nodded. Yes, it was do-able. Just.

She looked up, eager to share her ideas with him, and frowned when she realised that he hadn't moved an inch. He was still standing in the doorway, looking to all intents and purposes as though he wished he was anywhere but there. What on earth was wrong with him?

'Are you all right, Matt?' she began, but he didn't let her finish.

'I'm sorry, Rachel, but I can't stop right now. I've an urgent call to go to. I'll catch up with you later. OK?'

'I…um…yes, of course,' she murmured, although he couldn't possibly have heard her seeing as he had already left.

Rachel grimaced as she struggled to her feet. It must

be something really important if Matt couldn't spare
even a couple of minutes to talk to her. She gathered up
her case notes and made her way to the office. Carol
leapt up from her desk when she saw Rachel coming in
and rushed over to the door.

'You should have buzzed me,' the receptionist ad-
monished her. 'I'd have come and got those notes off
you. Here, sit yourself down and take the weight off that
knee.'

'Thanks.' Rachel gratefully subsided onto a chair. 'I
never realised before just how long that corridor is,' she
joked, easing her leg onto a handy cardboard box full
of stationery.

'And it'll feel even longer by the end of the day,'
Carol retorted, taking the cushion off her chair and
placing it under Rachel's swollen knee. 'You should be
at home, resting, instead of galloping around this place.'

'I'm not sure galloping is the right way to describe it.
More like a hop, skip and hobble. All I need is a parrot
on my shoulder and I could double for Long John
Silver!'

Carol laughed. 'At least you can see the funny side,
that's something.'

'That's probably all,' Rachel replied pithily. She
looked round when Ross poked his head round the door,
putting up her hand when she saw his expression change
as he spotted her injured leg. She had managed to avoid
telling him what had happened by going straight to her
room when she had arrived that morning. However,
there was no way she could avoid it any longer. 'There's
no need to panic, darling. I just slipped and bumped my

knee getting out of the car last night. It looks far worse than it is.'

'Why on earth didn't you phone me, Mum?' He came into the room and crouched down in front of her, shaking his head when he saw the bruising. 'I'd have come straight round.'

'I know you would but I didn't want to bother you. Anyway, there was no need for you to come haring round,' she added, deliberately distorting the truth a little. The last thing Ross needed at the moment was to have to worry about her. 'Matt sorted me out. He even came round to make breakfast for me this morning *and* drove me to work.'

'Oh, right. I see. Well, that was good of him but you still should have phoned me and let me know.'

Rachel breathed a sigh of relief when Ross accepted her explanation at face value. He wasn't to know that she had struggled on by herself the previous night, neither did she intend him to know. She smiled at him, her heart aching when she saw the shadows in his eyes. There was no doubt at all that recent events had taken their toll on him, despite his attempts to carry on as normal. 'I feel suitably rebuked. I'm sorry, darling.'

'I'll let you off this time so long as it doesn't happen again,' he told her with mock severity, and she laughed. He gave her a peck on the cheek and straightened up. 'Have you got that list of calls ready, Carol?' he asked, turning to the receptionist.

'Here it is. There's nothing urgent. Most folk seem to be suffering from that wretched tummy bug.'

Carol handed over the list of house calls that needed

doing along with a printout of the relevant case notes, and Rachel frowned. Nothing urgent? But what about the call that Matt had gone rushing off to? She waited until Ross had left before broaching the subject.

'Matt mentioned something about an urgent call. Who's he gone to see?'

'Matt?' Carol looked blankly at her. 'Sorry, I don't know what you mean. Ross is on call today, not Matt, and there's been nothing urgent, as I said.'

'My mistake. I must have got the wrong end of the stick. Blame it on the painkillers.'

Rachel passed it off although she couldn't help feeling puzzled. Matt had been very clear about being called out, so what on earth was going on? If he needed to go somewhere then why not say so…? Unless it had had something to do with Heather and he hadn't wanted her to know.

Rachel sighed sadly. She had never known Matt to prevaricate before and it was upsetting to know that he felt he needed to do so now. She must make it clear to him that she had no intention of taking sides when it came to their respective children. She certainly didn't want it to have a detrimental effect on their relationship—whatever that relationship was nowadays.

Once again the uncertainty caused a rush of panic. Mere days ago she had been happy to call Matt her friend but friend wasn't enough any longer, neither was colleague. Matt seemed to have assumed a new role in her life, one that demanded a great deal of her attention, too.

How did he view her? she wondered, harking back to the question that had troubled her the previous night.

Was she still just the same person he had worked with all these years or did he now see her differently too?

One part of her preferred the security of thinking that nothing had changed so far as Matt was concerned while another part knew that it had. The trouble was that she had no idea if it made the situation easier or more complicated. It all depended on *how* Matt felt about her and only time would tell her that.

Matt drove round for almost an hour before he went back to the surgery. By then his initial panic had subsided and had been replaced by a definite feeling of embarrassment. What on earth had he been thinking, rushing off like that after only the flimsiest excuse? he thought grimly as he parked his car. Rachel only needed to check with Carol and she would soon discover that there'd been no emergency and then he would have some explaining to do.

His mouth compressed as he pushed open the surgery door and went inside. He wasn't used to making a fool of himself and he didn't enjoy the experience. From now on he had to stop acting like an idiot and behave like the rational and responsible person he was.

'Matt, hi!'

Rachel's voice brought him to an abrupt halt. He turned slowly around, steeling himself for the questions and the answers as well. How the hell was he going to explain his abrupt departure if she asked him outright where he had been? He may have resorted to a small white lie before but he couldn't lie to her again. He would have to tell her the truth, yet the truth was so terrifying that he didn't dare to imagine her reaction. Could he really see himself confessing that he was attracted to her and that was why he had made such a rapid exit?

'If you have a few minutes to spare any time this afternoon, can we get together? There's something I want to discuss with you.'

She hobbled unsteadily over to the desk and Matt immediately forgot about himself as he grasped hold of her arm. 'You need to sit down and rest that leg. Come on, let's get you back to your room before you do yourself any further damage.'

He held onto her arm as they made their way along the corridor. Rachel sank down onto her chair with a groan of relief that spoke volumes and he shook his head. 'You need to slow down, Rachel, instead of rushing about the place.'

'If only I could rush.'

She smiled up at him, her eyes filled with amusement and just the tiniest smidgen of concern. Matt knew without a word being exchanged that she had found out that he hadn't been to see a patient, only she was too polite to say so. The thought made him feel guiltier than ever as he sat down on the edge of the desk.

'Well, whatever speed you're moving at it's too fast for you. If you need someone to fetch and carry for you then ask, Rachel. That's all it takes.'

'I know, and thank you.' She looked up at him so trustingly that he knew he had to confess, although how he should go about it was another matter entirely.

'About before, when I went rushing off,' he began, but she held up her hand.

'You don't have to explain, Matt. I understand.'

'You do?' He could barely hide his dismay and she sighed softly.

'Yes. You didn't want to upset me, but it's all right. Really it is. I'm not going to take sides. They have to work this out themselves.'

'They do?' Matt murmured, because he had no idea what she was talking about.

'Yes.' She leant forward and he could see the sympathy in her eyes. 'If Heather has contacted you then it's only natural that you should want to see her. I promise I won't say a word to Ross. For one thing I don't intend to interfere and for another I don't want to raise his hopes unnecessarily.'

'Oh. Right. I see.' Matt didn't know what to do. He knew that he should explain that Heather hadn't contacted him but that meant opening up a whole new can of worms. He mentally argued with himself about the rights and wrongs of keeping quiet but still hadn't decided when Rachel changed the subject.

'If you've got a few minutes to spare now, can we talk about this idea I've had?'

She launched into her proposal for a teenage pregnancy advisory service and he didn't interrupt her. Maybe it was cowardly to take the easy way out but it was a lot less stressful for both of them. Admitting that he was attracted to her would alter the dynamics of their relationship and he wasn't sure if it was a good idea. What it all boiled down to was one simple question: was he willing to risk losing Rachel as a friend when he wasn't sure if he was ready for any other kind of a relationship?

CHAPTER SIX

'I KNOW it will mean extra work for us all, but after what happened today with Melanie and baby Charlie, I honestly feel that it would be worth it. If we can prevent another near-tragedy from happening, it has to be a good thing, don't you agree?'

Rachel waited for Matt to answer, hoping that he would see the benefits of her proposal. She hadn't realised how passionately she felt about the idea until she had explained it to him. Now she could only hope that he would share her enthusiasm.

'I think it makes an awful lot of sense,' he said slowly. 'Yes, it will entail extra work, especially while we set everything up, but the flip side is that we may not get so many callouts or visits to the surgery. Once the younger mums gain more confidence, they will be less likely to call us in unnecessarily.'

'Exactly!' Rachel beamed at him, delighted that he had taken her ideas on board. Not that Matt had a closed mind when it came to any new ventures; he was always open to fresh ideas that would benefit their patients. It was one of the things she had always admired about him, his willingness to listen and learn, but there again there were so many other things to admire that it was hard to select just one from the whole delicious package.

She cleared her throat, aware how easily her mind could run off at a tangent if she let it. 'There may be funding available too. I'll need to check on that. But if we could get some sort of a grant, we could buy in extra help as and when it's needed—a midwife to speak to the mums before they give birth, maybe a health visitor or even one of the more experienced mothers to offer practical day-to-day advice—that type of thing. I know some of those services are available already but I get the impression that the younger mums in particular don't feel there is enough help on offer to them.'

'I get the same impression. In fact, one of my patients mentioned only the other day that all the new mums get nowadays by way of guidance are three one-hour sessions before their babies are born. They're supposed to cover everything during that time from the birth right through to the end of the baby's first year.'

'Is that all?' Rachel exclaimed. 'It definitely isn't enough, especially not for the very young mums like Melanie. They need a lot more support than that to prepare them for motherhood.'

'They do. I imagine you're particularly keen to help them because of your own experiences,' Matt suggested quietly.

'You're right, I am. I know what it's like to feel out of your depth, even though I was one of the lucky ones and had my parents to help me.'

'Then if you feel so strongly about it, Rachel, we'll see about setting it up as soon as possible.' He glanced at his watch and grimaced. 'Now I'm afraid I'll have to cut and run. It's my turn for the antenatal clinic so maybe we can continue this discussion later. There's still a lot of ground we need to cover.'

Rachel checked her desk diary and shook her head. 'I won't be able to fit it in today, I'm afraid. I've got the anti-smoking clinic this afternoon so I'll be tied up until evening surgery begins. That clinic always seems to run over time for some reason.'

'How about tonight, then?' Matt stood up to leave. 'If we hope to secure sufficient funding for this scheme to go ahead, we need to work the costs into next year's budget. The figures are due in at the end of January so we'll have to get a move on.'

'If you're sure you don't mind,' she began hesitantly, not wanting him to suspect how much the idea appealed to her. Spending another evening with him was something she hadn't anticipated and her heart was kicking up a storm at the prospect.

'Of course I don't mind.' He gave her a quick grin. 'Let's do it the civilised way and talk it all through over dinner.'

'That would be lovely,' she agreed, and he nodded.

'Good. It's a date.'

He straight left after that but it was a couple of minutes before Rachel followed him from the room. It had been a turn of phrase, that was all, she told herself firmly as she made her way to the meeting room where the anti-smoking clinic was being held. It certainly wasn't a date and she had to get that idea right out of her head. They were just two colleagues who planned on having dinner together while they discussed work-related issues. Yet even though she understood that she couldn't help wishing that he had invited her out for a very different reason. To know that Matt wanted to spend some time with *her* would have meant a great deal.

The afternoon flew past and before Matt knew it, it was time for evening surgery. He saw his first half dozen patients without encountering any major problems. Most people had come with the usual complaints that were the mainstay of any busy general practice— coughs and colds, ear infections and aching joints. He treated everyone the same, taking the time to listen to them and affording them the courtesy they deserved. He liked people and wouldn't have chosen to do this job if he didn't care.

His next patient was a teenage boy called Adam Shaw. He came shuffling into the room, looking very ill at ease. Matt asked him to sit down and smiled encouragingly at him. 'So what can I do for you today, Adam?'

'I…well…um…' Adam turned bright red with embarrassment. It was obviously an ordeal for him to explain the reason why he had come.

'There's no need to be embarrassed, Adam. I assure you that I won't be shocked by whatever you tell me.' Matt looked the boy firmly in the eyes. 'Just spit it out and tell me what's wrong.'

'It's down here, you see,' Adam muttered, pointing to his groin. 'There's something…well, not right.'

'In what way?' Matt's tone was businesslike because he knew it was the fastest way to extract the information he needed. At this rate they would still be sitting here at midnight!

That reminded him of what he had planned for the evening but he managed to brush the thought aside. If he started thinking about Rachel and this dinner they were having, he would be in no better state than young Adam.

'Can you describe your symptoms for me, Adam?'

'I…um…I've had this sort of *discharge*,' Adam explained, his face turning even more fiery. 'And everything feels sort of *swollen*, you know.'

'I see. Right, I'll need to examine you so if you could just pop behind the screen and remove your trousers etcetera, I'll be with you in a moment.'

Matt gave the boy a couple of minutes to get ready then examined him. Adam's testicles were indeed swollen and he admitted that he experienced discomfort every time he passed urine. Add that to what the boy had told him about there being a discharge and Matt was soon able to make a diagnosis.

'It looks as though you have non-specific urethritis, Adam,' he told the teenager once they were sitting down again. 'The urethra has become inflamed and that's why you have these symptoms. My main concern now is to identify the micro-organism that has caused it, although most cases of NSU are due to a sexually transmitted disease like chlamydia. If that is the cause in this instance it means I shall have to contact all your sexual partners and check if they require treatment too.'

'Oh, no! I can't believe this is happening.' Adam put

his head in his hands and groaned. 'Will you have to tell my parents? They'll go mad if they find out!'

'No.' Matt shook his head. 'You're seventeen so there is no need to involve anyone apart from the girls you've slept with. It's imperative that they are checked out too because if it is chlamydia, it can have serious repercussions for them in the future. For you as well as it can cause infertility if it isn't treated.'

'I've only slept with one girl and that's the truth, Dr Thompson. It was my first time and I thought it was hers, too, but apparently not.'

Adam was obviously deeply upset by the idea that he had been misled. Matt gave Adam a moment to collect himself then carried on, wanting to get all the information he needed. He made a note of the girl's name and address then collected some samples to send to the lab for testing. He then wrote out a script for erythromycin and told Adam to come back to see him in a week's time when the lab results would be back. He would explain then that Adam would need to make follow-up visits for the next three months to make sure he hadn't suffered a relapse.

He made a note to check if Adam's girlfriend was a patient at the practice and buzzed in his next appointment, glancing at the clock as he did so. Just half an hour to go until surgery ended and he and Rachel could enjoy that dinner they had planned. Maybe it was only a working dinner but that didn't matter. Being with her was enough, probably more than he should allow himself given his parlous state of mind. However, he was only flesh and blood and he couldn't help wanting to spend time with her even if he wasn't sure if it was wise.

Rachel made a quick trip to the bathroom as soon as her last patient had left. If she'd had any idea that she would be going out that night she would have worn something more glamorous than the sober grey suit she had put on that morning. There wasn't much she could do about it now, so she washed her face, applied a fresh coat of lipstick and fluffed up her hair, wishing as she did every day that it would lie smoothly around her face instead of insisting on curling so riotously. Still, it was thick and glossy and that was something in its favour even if it refused to be tamed.

She went back to her room and was just attempting to struggle into her coat when Matt appeared. He looked so big and handsome as he came striding into the room that her heart gave a girlish leap of delight. She could just imagine him striding across the deck of a pirate ship, or riding hell for leather across an open plain. He was real hero material from the top of his dark hair to the tips of his well-shod feet, she decided dreamily.

'Need a hand with that?'

He took the coat from her and slid it up her arms before she could blink, and she shivered when she felt his hands smoothing the collar into place. Even though there were several layers of clothing between his hands and her flesh, she could feel her skin tingling, tiny flurries of heat that scorched along her veins and made it difficult to think. It was only when he removed his hands that she was able to pull herself together and she sighed softly. She needed to keep her emotions under far tighter control if she wasn't to make a fool of herself tonight.

'Thanks. I just need to get my bag then I'm ready to leave,' she told him, determined not to get sidetracked again. She bent over to open the bottom drawer of the desk, quite forgetting about her injured knee, and gasped when it suddenly gave way beneath her.

'Careful!' Matt grabbed hold of her arm and steadied her. He shook his head. 'What did I say before about you asking for help, Rachel? Leave it. I'll get it.' Bending down, he retrieved the bag, grimacing when he discovered how heavy it was. 'What on earth do you keep in this thing? It weighs a ton.'

'Oh, just the usual things,' she replied, making a mental note to be more careful in future. She was trying to remain on even keel and that wouldn't be possible if at every turn Matt ended up touching her. Her heart lurched as she recalled the strength of his grasp as he had set her safely back on her feet and she hurried on. 'The problem is that I never seem to get round to clearing out the clutter and just keep adding to it.'

'You women and your handbags,' Matt declared, rolling his eyes as she limped around the desk.

'Look who's talking,' she retorted, glancing pointedly at his case. 'You don't exactly travel light yourself, do you?'

'Ah, but the difference is that all I keep in here are essentials—pills and potions, etcetera.' He tucked her hand into the crook of his arm as naturally as though it had been part of their daily routine for ever and laughed, mercifully covering the tiny gasp that escaped her when she found herself pressed against the solid length of his body.

'And that's it? You're willing to swear on oath that you don't keep anything else in there?' she retorted, doing her best to keep her emotions firmly leashed.

'Of course,' he declared loftily, pausing in the doorway to switch off the lights. 'Everything this case contains is work-related.'

They headed along the corridor at a snail's pace, Matt adjusting his speed to accommodate the fact that she couldn't hurry. Whilst Rachel appreciated his thoughtfulness it didn't help one little bit. Each slow, deliberate stride he took brought his hip and thigh into even closer contact with hers and it was the sweetest kind of torment imaginable. Even though she was wearing heavy winter clothing, she could feel the power and strength of his body as clearly as though they had both been naked.

Heat rushed through at the picture that instantly sprang to her mind and she bit her lip. The situation was going from bad to worse and she had no idea what to do about it. All she did know was that she mustn't let Matt suspect how she felt or it could ruin everything. She would rather have him as a friend and a colleague than not have him in her life at all.

They went to the same restaurant they had been to the previous night. Matt had suggested going somewhere different for a change but Rachel had claimed that she wasn't dressed for anywhere too upmarket. To his mind she looked fine, more than fine, wonderful, in fact, although he forbore to say so. This was a working dinner, he reminded himself as the waiter showed them to their table. It wasn't a date.

The thought of what a real date might have entailed shimmered in front of his eyes like a mirage. *If* they had been out on a date, he'd have been able to tell Rachel how he felt, admit that he was attracted to her, maybe even confess his fears about getting hurt. And after dinner was over they might even have decided to continue the evening. It wasn't as though they didn't know one another, so it wouldn't have felt as though he was rushing her if he'd invited her back to his house. They could have sat by the fire in the sitting room and drunk coffee, and then he would have kissed her, slowly, deeply, passionately.

His body tingled as he imagined how sweet her lips would taste, like honeyed nectar. He would kiss her once then kiss her again and keep on kissing her until it was no longer enough for either of them. Even though Rachel had never chosen to have a long-term relationship, he knew that she would be a passionate and responsive lover, a tender and giving lover too. It was her nature to be generous and there would be no holding back. She would give herself to him with all the generosity of the person she was and he would bury himself in her softness, her sweetness, and allow it to heal him. He would become whole again in her arms, fearless and unafraid of the future. The thought was almost too tempting to resist.

'I'm going to have the same as I had last night.'

Rachel closed her menu and placed it on the table.

Matt's head whirled as he struggled to separate the mirage from what was actually happening. 'Good idea. I think I will too.'

He placed his menu on top of hers, forcing out the images that crowded his head. Rachel deserved to be loved and cherished, nothing less, and he wasn't sure yet if he could do that. 'So have you had any more thoughts about this new advisory service?' he asked to distract himself from that strangely unsettling thought.

'Just one. I was wondering if we should offer contraceptive advice as well.' Rachel paused as though she hadn't made up her mind about the benefits of such a service and Matt nodded encouragingly. He wanted to fill his head with as many new ideas as possible in the hope they would shut out everything else.

'It would make a lot of sense. Dalverston has never had a proper family planning clinic and, in my opinion, it's a huge oversight. Admittedly, the number of unplanned pregnancies in the town is relatively low compared to some other places, but they still happen. Kids need to understand that they have to behave responsibly, and not just to avoid getting pregnant either.'

'STDs, you mean?' Rachel queried.

'Yes. I had a young man in tonight who's a prime example of the value of such a service. It looks very much as though he's caught some sort of sexually transmitted disease—probably chlamydia—and it was the first time he had slept with a girl too. Youngsters like him need to understand that they can't afford to take any chances whether it's their first time or their hundredth.'

'I agree, although I suppose that must sound rather hypocritical.'

'Hypocritical?' He frowned. 'What do you mean?'

'That I'm hardly a shining example of how to behave sensibly seeing as I was a teenage mum myself,' she explained wryly.

'That's just plain silly, Rachel. All right, so you didn't plan on having Ross, but everyone is allowed to make one mistake in their lives.'

'Thank you. And I have to confess that I wouldn't change things even if I could. Having Ross was the best thing that ever happened to me. I know I worked twice as hard as I would have done if I hadn't had to support him.'

'There you go, then. You've nothing to feel bad about. In fact, I can't think of a better role model for the kids than you.'

Matt heard the husky note in his voice and picked up his glass of water, hoping that Rachel wouldn't thank him for the compliment. If she did he might be tempted to hand out a few more and that would be the wrong thing to do. He had to remember that he wasn't in a position to court her.

The incongruity of the old-fashioned term should have made him laugh, yet it was the best way to describe how he felt. He wanted to *court* her, to woo her and charm her into liking him. He tried to remember if he had felt the same way when he had met Claire but it was too long ago to recall his feelings. His love for Claire had been both rich and fulfilling, but it had changed over the years they'd been married. Their passion had mellowed, the urgency they had felt in the beginning turning into a closeness that had sustained them both. But all of a sudden he knew that if he fell in love with Rachel it wouldn't be the same. It couldn't be. He couldn't imagine the passion he felt for her growing weaker with time.

Matt's breath caught as he was forced to acknowledge the truth. Loving Rachel would be a very different experience from loving Claire. Admitting it seemed like the ultimate betrayal.

CHAPTER SEVEN

RACHEL sensed a certain undercurrent bubbling away while they ate. It wasn't anything Matt said, but a feeling she had that something was troubling him. To all intents and purposes he behaved exactly the same as normal but she was too sensitive when it came to him to miss even the smallest signs. The thought unsettled her so that when he suggested having coffee after their meal, she refused. It seemed wiser to bring the evening to an end rather than prolong it.

They left the restaurant a short time later and walked over to where they had parked the car. There was a thick layer of frost on the windscreen and once Matt had settled her in the passenger seat, he got out a can of de-icer and set to work. Rachel huddled deeper into her coat, although it wasn't the chill of the night that was making her feel so cold but the worry of it all. Had Matt sensed something amiss from her own behaviour, perhaps?

'Let's get this heater going.' Matt got into the car, bringing with him a blast of icy air. He frowned when he saw her shiver. 'You're frozen solid! I should have turned on the engine instead of leaving you sitting here.'

He sounded genuinely upset and she couldn't bear to hear him berate himself when she was the one at fault. She had to get over this ridiculous crush and set everything back on a normal footing.

'I'll live,' she said lightly, making a determined effort to sound upbeat. 'I'll have you know that I'm a lot tougher than I look!'

'Oh, I don't doubt it.' He grinned at her. 'I bet you tear up telephone directories with your bare hands for fun, don't you?'

'You'd better believe it!' Rachel flexed her fingers and laughed, feeling easier now that their usual harmony had been restored. Maybe she had been reading too much into the situation, she thought, glancing at Matt as he drove them out of the car park. He'd probably been concentrating on the pros and cons of this new venture, making sure that it would be worth all the extra work involved. She had rather sprung it on him and maybe she should have given him more time to weigh it all up.

'Look, Matt, if you have any reservations about this proposal of mine, please, say so. I know how stretched we are and offering a new service like this is bound to stretch us even more.' She shrugged. 'I don't want to cause problems for everyone, believe me.'

'You aren't. As we agreed earlier it could end up saving us a lot of time. Add in the very real benefits to both the mums and their babies and it has to be a good idea. No, I can honestly say that I don't have any reservations at all. It's an excellent idea.'

'Oh, right. Good. I'm glad you feel like that.'

There was no doubt in her mind that he meant what he said and Rachel let the subject drop. They passed through the town centre and headed towards the outskirts of the town. Matt drew up at the side of the road when they reached the lane where she lived and turned to her.

'I know you'll think I'm fussing, Rachel, but are you sure you can manage tonight with that knee? I'd hate to think of you taking a tumble down those stairs of yours.'

'I won't,' Rachel replied, swivelling sideways so she could look at him. Her breath caught when she saw the concern in his eyes but she refused to allow herself to get carried away. Matt was just being his usual kind and thoughtful self. She held up her hand as though swearing an oath. 'I promise on my honour that I shall be extra careful what I do. Does that set your mind at rest?'

'A bit, but I'd feel better if you would stay at my house tonight.' He hurried on, obviously keen to forestall any objections she might make. 'And before you say anything, you won't be putting me out. Just the opposite, in fact. You'll be doing me a favour.'

'A favour?' she repeated numbly, struggling to get her head round the idea.

'Mmm. I won't get a wink of sleep if I'm worrying about you falling down those wretched stairs.' He smiled at her, a smile of such tenderness that her heart immediately melted. Could he have looked at her that way if he didn't genuinely care? she wondered giddily. The thought was so mind-blowing that it was hard to concentrate when he continued.

'You can have the bedroom in the annexe. It's en suite so there's no stairs to negotiate if you need to use the loo during the night. There's even a little fold-down seat in the shower which should make life easier for you, shouldn't it?'

'I…er…I suppose so,' Rachel murmured, hoping to gain herself a little time. She groaned because even if she'd had a couple of hours to decide, it wouldn't have made the decision any easier. It wasn't the safety factor she was worried about, or at least not where it concerned her knee. It was the thought of spending the night under Matt's roof that was giving her hot and cold chills. That was far more dangerous.

'It's the ideal place for you to stay while your knee heals. You'll be able to potter about and not do yourself any more damage.' He leant over and squeezed her hand. 'Say you'll stay, Rachel, even if it's only for tonight. Please. Just for me.'

'There's clean sheets on the bed and fresh towels in the bathroom. Heather often invited one of her friends to stay over so the place is always ready for guests.'

Matt stepped aside so that Rachel could see into the small but functional bathroom. Everywhere gleamed brightly, the black and white tiles sparkling in the light, and she nodded, battening down the urge to laugh. Matt was acting like a hotelier, pointing out the room's good points, and she was acting like a guest. How ridiculous was that?

She went back into the bedroom, taking stock of the quilted throw on the king-sized bed, the comfy chair positioned next to the dressing table. It was an attractive room and she knew she would be comfortable sleeping there, but was she mad to have agreed? Surely she was making a difficult situation worse by sleeping in Matt's home even if she wasn't actually sleeping with *him*.

Heat rushed up her cheeks and she busied herself with removing her coat to hide her embarrassment. Matt must have seen her struggling because he immediately stepped forward to help. He slid the coat off her shoulders and it was all she could do to hide her shiver when she felt his hand brush against the side of her neck. Even though it was only the briefest of contacts she felt it register in every cell of her body like a surge of electricity. She heard Matt draw in a ragged breath and glanced round in surprise, wondering if he had felt it too, but he was already moving away.

'How about a cup of tea?' he suggested, hanging her coat in the wardrobe.

'That would be lovely. Thank you.'

Rachel waited until he had left then sank down on the bed. She must stop wondering if Matt felt the same way as she did or this night would turn into a disaster. Unbuttoning her jacket, she laid it on the quilt then smoothed down the front of her blouse. It was warm in the house and what with that plus her own inner thermostat going haywire, it felt as though she was burning up. Somehow, she had to remain calm no matter what happened.

Once again her temperature spiked as a whole raft of possibilities flooded her mind. They ranged from the innocuous—Matt giving her a goodnight peck on the cheek—to the preposterous—a night of unbridled passion—and she moaned. What a time for her imagination to run riot!

'Tea's ready,' Matt shouted, and she struggled to her feet. Tea and some undemanding conversation were just what she needed to calm her nerves.

She made her way along the hall and found Matt coming out of the kitchen, carrying a tray. He smiled as he nodded towards the sitting room.

'We may as well drink it in here. It's more comfortable.'

He led the way, placing the tray on a table before going over to the window to draw the curtains. He'd already lit the fire and the logs were starting to spit as they caught light. Rachel sat down in one of the squashy armchairs, sighing with pleasure as she looked around the room.

'This is such a lovely room, Matt. It always feels so welcoming.'

'I've always loved it,' he agreed, passing her one of the cups before sitting down on the sofa. 'I suppose that's the main reason why I haven't redecorated it for years. I like it just the way it is, although I'm going to have to buy a new sofa at some point. There's more sag than bounce in these cushions, I'm afraid.'

Rachel laughed at his wry expression. 'It looks fine to me, but there again my own sofa isn't exactly in its first flush of youth.'

'Obviously a woman after my own heart. You like to get full value out of your furniture too.'

He returned her smile, mercifully missing the start she gave. Of course she wasn't after his heart, she told herself sternly. That was ridiculous. She took a sip of her tea then looked up when the phone suddenly rang. Matt frowned as he got up to answer it.

'I wonder who that can be at this time of the night.'

Rachel watched as he crossed the room and picked up the receiver. He had his back to her and she found herself studying the strong, straight line of his spine. Everything about him was solid and dependable, she thought, both inside and out. He possessed the rare gift of making people feel that no matter what mishap befell them, he would help them sort it out. It was one of his major strengths as a GP and it was also one of the things that appealed to her most. Matt was someone she could turn to in a crisis and he would never let her down. She had never thought that about any man before.

'No, please don't apologise. I quite understand why you're worried, Mrs Morris. Leave it with me. I should be there in about ten minutes' time.'

Rachel frowned when she heard what he had said. 'What's happened?'

'That was Mrs Morris from Prescott Lane on the phone. One of her boys is running a temperature and he also has a strange rash on his legs.'

'Has she phoned the on-call service?' Rachel asked.

'Yes, over an hour ago, apparently, but nobody's turned up yet and that's why she phoned me.' Matt's tone was grim. 'There's been two cases of meningitis in the area recently so I appreciate why she's so worried. We can't afford to take any chances that this might be another one.'

'Certainly not,' Rachel agreed. 'Are you going over there now?'

'Yes. I know the on-call service should cover it but that isn't the point. The boy needs to be seen sooner rather than later.' He headed to the door then paused and glanced back. 'I don't know how long I'll be so don't wait up for me, Rachel. I'll see you in the morning.'

'Of course. Be careful, though, Matt. The roads are very icy tonight. You don't want to have an accident.'

'Don't worry, I shall be extremely careful. We can't afford to have two of us hobbling around the surgery, can we?'

He smiled at her and just for a second his face was unguarded. Rachel's breath caught but before she could react, he swung round and a moment later she heard the front door slam. She struggled to her feet and made it to the window in time to watch him drive away. Resting her forehead against the glass, she tried to recall the expression on his face. Had she imagined it, seen what she had wanted to see? She wasn't sure, but for a moment there'd seemed to be such hunger in his eyes as he had looked at her, such need, that just thinking about it made her shiver.

She sighed as she stared out at the darkness. Even if Matt did feel something for her there was no reason to believe that he would do anything about it.

'The good news is that I'm ninety-nine percent certain that Robbie doesn't have meningitis.'

Matt sympathised when he heard the boy's parents gasp in relief. As a parent himself, he understood how worried they must have been. He smiled at them, trying not to think about all the other worrying issues he had to contend with at the moment.

'Whilst Robbie undoubtedly has a fever and a rash, there's nothing else that points towards it being meningitis. There's no neck stiffness, no sign of photophobia—that's an aversion to light—no headache or sickness.'

He pressed a glass tumbler against the blotches on the boy's legs, blanking out all thoughts of what had happened before he'd left the house. The desire he'd felt for Rachel had almost overwhelmed him. If he hadn't made such a rapid exit he would have had the devil of a job to contain it. The thought was enough to make his heart race.

'As you can see, the rash disappears when you press the glass against it. That doesn't happen with the meningitis rash.'

'So you think it's some sort of a virus?' Robbie's father queried.

'It could be.' Matt turned to the boy, his gut instinct telling him to probe a bit more deeply. 'Is there anything else that you haven't mentioned, Robbie? Something that's happened which you haven't told your mum and dad about?'

Robbie bit his lip, looking so sheepish that Matt knew he was right. He sat down on the edge of the bed and said firmly, 'Nobody is going to tell you off if you've done something silly, son. We just want to find out what's making you feel so ill.'

'It was the rat,' Robbie muttered, glancing warily at his parents.

'A pet rat?' Matt said, shaking his head. Mrs Morris opened her mouth to speak. He didn't want any interruptions now that Robbie had got this far.

'No, just a rat down by the river. Me and my friends were playing there the other day and we found this rats' nest, you see. We weren't going to hurt them,' Robbie said quickly. 'We just wanted to have a look at them. We got a stick and poked around a bit, but then one of them bit me on the ankle. Just here. See.'

'That looks nasty,' Matt said as the boy rolled down his sock and showed him his ankle. The area surrounding the bite was badly inflamed, pointing towards it being infected. 'It would definitely explain why the lymph nodes in your groin are swollen. The infection has spread throughout your body. No wonder you've been feeling so poorly.'

'But rats carry the plague, don't they, Doctor?' Mrs Morris put in fearfully. 'I saw a programme on the television a few months ago and they said that the plague started because the country was overrun with rats!'

'Usually it's the fleas off the rats that bite people and pass on the plague,' Matt explained patiently. 'Thankfully, we don't have that problem in this country any more, although there are other diseases that rats can carry. That's why anyone who's bitten by a rat should always seek medical attention as soon as possible.' He glanced at the boy. 'Robbie is probably suffering from rat-bite fever and the good news is that we can clear it up with antibiotics. However, no more poking about in rats' nests, young man. Steer well clear in future.'

'I will.'

Robbie lay down, looking very sorry for himself. Matt wrote out a script for penicillin once he'd made sure the boy wasn't allergic to it. He handed it to the parents along with a couple of sachets of the medicine which he happened to have in his case. At least Robbie wouldn't need to wait until the morning when the prescription was filled before he started on the medication.

'Thank you, Dr Thompson,' Mrs Morris said gratefully. 'And thank you for coming out as well. We're really grateful, aren't we, love?'

'We are indeed,' her husband agreed.

'I'm only sorry that you had to wait so long,' Matt told them as they saw him out. 'I don't know what went wrong tonight but I'll get onto our on-call service and make sure it doesn't happen again.'

'Should I phone them and let them know we don't need a doctor to call now?' Mr Morris queried.

Matt shook his head. 'There's no need. I'll do it.'

He went out to his car and put through a call to the on-call service. He explained that there was no longer any need for a doctor to visit the family then asked why there had been such a delay sending someone out. He sighed when he was briskly informed that it was due to a combination of the number of calls they had received and staff shortages. He hated to think that their patients might not be getting the service they deserved.

He drove home, making good time until he reached the outskirts of the town where a heavy layer of frost on the tarmac made him slow down. As he had told Rachel earlier, the practice couldn't afford to have two of them injured. Thinking about Rachel immediately set loose a whole host of emotions. The temptation to go and see her when he got in was very strong, but he had to resist it. He simply couldn't trust himself to be around her at the moment and not do something silly, although maybe it would be all right if he just made sure that she had everything she needed. It would take only a moment and he could retire to his bed, duty done.

Matt grimaced as he drew up outside the front door. He knew that he was merely looking for an excuse to see her, but admitting it wasn't enough to deter him. He went straight to the annexe, pausing outside the door while he mustered his composure. The last thing he wanted was to make Rachel feel that he was coming onto her.

CHAPTER EIGHT

RACHEL was about to switch off the bedside lamp when she heard Matt's car turning into the drive. She hesitated, undecided what to do. Although he had told her not to wait up, she was tempted to go and see how he had got on. She sighed when she heard the front door open. Interested though she may be in their patients' welfare, it wasn't the real reason she wanted to see him, was it?

She reached for the switch but before she could turn off the lamp, there was a knock on the door. Rachel froze. Although a moment ago she had been longing to see him, the thought of seeing him now was suddenly giving her hot and cold chills. How could she hope to carry on a conversation when she was in this frame of mind?

'Rachel, are you awake?' His voice carried softly through the door and she knew that she had to answer. Matt must have seen that her light was on as he drove up and it would look very strange if she didn't reply.

'Yes, I'm awake,' she croaked, groaning when she

realised how strained her voice sounded. Matt would soon realise there was something wrong if she carried on like this. 'Come in,' she called firmly.

'I spotted your light was still on,' he explained as he came into the room. 'I thought I'd better check that you have everything you need.'

'Yes, thank you.' Rachel returned his smile, hoping he couldn't tell how on edge she felt. This was a whole new territory for her because she'd never entertained him in her bedroom before.

Nerves assailed her once more but fortunately he didn't appear to notice her discomfort. Walking over to the window, he drew the curtains tightly together. 'We may as well keep out any draughts. It's bitterly cold out tonight. I wouldn't be surprised if the temperature drops below freezing point.'

'It's been heading that way for the past few days,' she agreed, although the state of the weather was the least of her problems. All night long she had kept returning to that moment before Matt had left but she still hadn't decided if she'd been right to think that he had wanted her and the uncertainty of not knowing was the worse thing of all. If she knew how he felt then she might know what to do about it.

The thought made her heart lurch and she hurried on. 'So how did you get on? Was it another case of meningitis?'

'No, I'm glad to say.' He came over to the bed. 'It turns out that young Robbie managed to get himself bitten by a rat and has rat bite fever. A course of antibiotics will soon sort it out.'

'Well, that's good news. I'm sure his parents must be relieved.'

'Oh, they are. I'm only sorry they had to wait so long for a doctor to turn up and set their minds at rest.'

'Did you phone the on-call service to find out why there'd been a delay?'

'I did. Sheer number of calls, apparently, plus they have a couple of their staff off sick.'

'That wretched bug, no doubt,' she said ruefully, and he nodded.

'I expect so, although it's not really good enough, is it? Patients shouldn't have to wait so long for help to arrive. I was always uneasy about employing an on-call service before we signed up to it and this proves I was right to have my doubts.'

'But we've never had a problem before,' she protested.

'Maybe not, but that's no excuse. Our patients deserve a reliable service every single day of the year and it's up to me to make sure they receive it.'

'That's ridiculous, Matt! It's not your fault that they happen to be short-staffed when it's a particularly busy night.' Rachel could tell that he wasn't convinced and leant forward, determined to make him see sense. 'You can't blame yourself for what happened tonight.'

'No, but I intend to keep a closer eye on what's happening from now on.' He shrugged. 'It's only by the grace of God that it wasn't another case of meningitis we were dealing with.'

He turned away but she caught hold of his hand. 'Just because there was a glitch tonight, it doesn't mean it will happen again,' she countered, trying to ignore the tingles that were spreading up her arm. Matt's hand felt so big and warm that she was loath to release it even though she knew that she should. 'They're a reliable firm and you have to trust them to get on with the job.'

'Yes, ma'am!' Matt said smartly. He eased his hand out from hers, making a great production of flexing his fingers, and Rachel laughed.

'If you're trying to make me feel bad about crushing your hand, forget it. There's no way that I hurt you. I mean, look at the size of your hand compared to mine.'

Rachel laid her hand, palm up, on the quilt, feeling her heart jolt when Matt laid his on top of it. His hand was so much larger than hers that it completely engulfed it. She could feel the roughness of his palm against the smoothness of hers, the strength of his fingers, and shuddered. It had been a long time since a man had touched her like this, a long time since she had wanted this kind of contact either.

Her eyes rose to his face and her breath caught when she saw the expression it held. There was an awareness there that she understood only too well, but it was tinged with something else, something that made her blood heat. All of a sudden she knew that she hadn't imagined what had happened before. Matt had wanted her then and he wanted her now, wanted her in every way a man could want a woman. Finally seeing the proof of that broke down the barriers she had erected around herself to guard against making any mistakes.

She reached up towards him but he was already bending down to her so that they met halfway. Rachel felt heat envelop her when their mouths met and she gasped, heard him gasp as well. The kiss could have lasted no longer than a second but she was trembling when they drew apart and could see that Matt was trembling too. Maybe they hadn't planned on this happening but it was what they both desperately needed.

Matt looked at her for a long moment, his eyes grazing over her face before they came to rest on her mouth. 'If you want me to stop, you only have to say so,' he said, his voice grating in the quiet of the room.

Rachel took a quick little breath but her own voice sounded equally ragged when it emerged. 'I don't want you to stop, though. Really I don't.'

He was reaching for her before she had finished speaking but she didn't care. When he sat down on the bed and drew her into his arms, she went willingly, letting the soft curves of her body nestle against the hard contours of his. He held her close against him while he trailed fiery little kisses over her eyes, her nose, the line of her jaw, so that she was dizzy with need by the time he claimed her mouth again.

Rachel clung to him as she kissed him back, making no attempt to hide the hunger she felt. She wanted this so much, wanted Matt to kiss her, hold her, make love to her. When his hands went to the buttons on the borrowed pyjamas she wore, she helped him, working them free until the top fell open. She heard him take a shuddering breath as his hands went to the edges of the fabric. She could tell that he was struggling for control as he parted the jacket, and shivered. That Matt should want her this much was more than she had dared hope for.

'You're beautiful, Rachel, so very, very beautiful.'

His tone was reverent as he studied her lush curves. When he reached out and gently cupped her breasts in the palms of his hands, she closed her eyes and gave herself up to the sensations that were flooding through her. She had made love before but not once had she felt this way, filled with passion, overwhelmed by need. Making love with Matt was very different to anything she had experienced before.

He stroked and caressed her breasts until she could barely contain the desire that was building inside her. When he bent and placed his mouth over her nipple, she cried out. He drew back, his eyes intent as he searched her face and what he saw there obviously reassured him because he bent and kissed her other breast, drawing the rigid nipple into his mouth and suckling her.

Rachel gasped as a rush of desire flowed through her. Burying her fingers in his hair, she held his head against her, whimpering softly as he continued to lavish attention on her breasts before letting his mouth glide down her body. He kissed her waist, encircling her ribs with nibbling little kisses that made her twist and writhe with unbearable pleasure. Then when his tongue found her navel and dipped in and out, she groaned. Nothing had prepared her for how Matt made her feel.

His mouth retraced its route, stopping frequently to scatter more kisses over her body until Rachel could barely think. When he drew back and stood up, she could only murmur in protest, but he shook his head.

'I'm not going anywhere, Rachel. Not unless you tell me to.'

'I don't want you to go,' she said huskily.

'Good.' He dropped another deliciously sexy kiss on her mouth then stripped off her pyjama pants and his own clothes as well. Rachel just had a moment to marvel at the power and beauty of his aroused body before he lay down beside her and took her in his arms, holding her so close that she could feel his erection pressing against her.

'You can still say no, Rachel,' he whispered, his breath warm and sweet on her cheek. 'If this isn't what you want, we can stop right now.'

'It is what I want, though.' She looked deep into his eyes so there would be no mistake. 'I already told you that, Matt, and I meant it.'

'It's what I want as well.'

His voice throbbed with need and she shuddered when she heard the hunger it held. Opening her arms, she welcomed him into her embrace, her body suffused with desire when he entered her in one swift, breath-taking thrust. They made love with a desperation that spoke volumes, then made love a second time with a pure unbridled joy that brought tears to both their eyes.

Rachel knew that she had never shared this kind of closeness with anyone before and never would. It was only with Matt that she felt secure enough to give herself so completely, to shed all the restraints and allow herself to feel each and every emotion. She trusted Matt and that made all the difference. For the first time in her life she felt safe, secure, wanted, although she shied away from the one word that would have made the ex-perience perfect. Until she knew how Matt truly felt, she couldn't claim that she felt loved.

* * *

Day came slowly, the darkness gradually fading as dawn crept in. Matt was already awake and had been awake for hours. He had been too keyed up to sleep and had spent the night listening to the sound of Rachel's breathing as she had lain beside him. Now, as he studied the delicate beauty of her profile, he was assailed by doubts. Had he made a mistake by sleeping with her?

Last night he had been caught up in the throes of a kind of madness, his body demanding the release that only making love to her could give him. Now he'd had time to think and panic was setting in. He may have sated his hunger but at what cost? He would never forgive himself if he hurt Rachel, yet he was aware of how easy it would be to do so. After all, what could he offer her? One night of passion wasn't enough, but he wasn't able to offer her anything more. Not yet.

He rolled onto his back, feeling the emotions welling up inside him. Guilt and joy, sadness and elation were all mixed up together so that it was hard to know how he really felt. Had he betrayed Claire's memory by making love to another woman?

Guilt swamped him even though his head rejected the idea, insisted that he had nothing to feel guilty about, that it was time he moved on and lived his life in the present instead of the past. However, it wasn't the only issue, was it? There was Heather—how would she feel if she found out? Would she be upset that he had slept with another woman, especially when that woman was Ross's mother? He knew that Heather liked Rachel but that wasn't the point. By sleeping with Rachel, he may have made the situation even more difficult for his daughter. The thought made him feel even worse.

'Don't.'

Matt jumped when Rachel suddenly spoke. Rolling onto his side, he felt the maelstrom of emotions inside him shift once more when he saw the sadness on her face. Obviously, she had guessed that he had doubts about what they had done and it grieved him to know that he was hurting her this way.

'I'm sorry.' He ran the tip of his finger down her cheek in gentle apology, feeling the tremor that started in the pit of his stomach when he discovered all over again how wonderfully soft her skin felt. He may have caressed every inch of her beautiful body just hours before, but touching her now, it felt like the very first time. His breath caught as he was forced to acknowledge the truth: he may have doubts about what they had done but he still wanted her. That hadn't changed.

'We didn't do anything wrong, Matt,' she said quietly, her eyes holding his. 'We're both free agents, so don't beat yourself up about last night. It's over and done with, and now we can forget all about it.'

Was that what she wanted? he wondered in gut-wrenching dismay. To forget what they had shared and how magical it had been? He searched her face but could find nothing there to make him think that she hadn't meant it. Rachel wanted to put the episode behind her and whilst he doubted if he could do that, if it was what she wanted then at the very least he had to try.

'If that's what you want, it's fine by me,' he said

flatly, loath to admit how much it hurt him to comply. Last night had been a turning point in his life even though he wasn't sure if it had been a turn for the better. However, evidently it hadn't been the same for her.

Pain lanced through him and he tossed back the quilt, afraid that his feelings would become only too apparent if he remained there. 'I'd better go and have a shower. Breakfast in ten minutes. OK?'

'Fine.'

She gave him a quick smile but Matt didn't linger. There was no reason to when she had made it clear that last night had been a one-off and there wasn't going to be a repeat. The thought accompanied him back to his room, stayed with him while he showered, like a black cloud hovering over his head. He knew it was going to take time before he shrugged off the feeling of rejection and cursed his own stupidity.

He wasn't a teenager, for heaven's sake! He was a grown man and he'd had relationships before he had married. Granted, he'd not had any since Claire had died, but it had been his choice to remain celibate, just as it had been his choice to sleep with Rachel. Now he had to do as she had requested and put it behind him. It shouldn't be that difficult. One night of passion wasn't going to completely alter the course of his life. Maybe it had seemed like a milestone because it had been the first time he had slept with anyone in years, but it wouldn't be the last time. Now he had taken that first step, it would be easier the next time.

He went into the kitchen and plugged in the kettle, closing his mind to the thought that he couldn't imagine wanting any woman the way he had wanted Rachel. That was nonsense, complete and utter nonsense. It wasn't as though he was in love with Rachel, was it?

CHAPTER NINE

A WEEK passed, the longest week of Rachel's life. Although Matt was unfailingly polite whenever they spoke, he never made any reference to what had happened that night. Whilst she didn't regret sleeping with him, she did regret the fact that it had caused him so much heartache. The memory of how distraught he had looked the following morning would haunt her for a long time to come.

In an effort to minimise the stress it had caused for both of them, she avoided being alone with him as much as possible. Fortunately, her knee had healed and apart from the odd twinge, it didn't cause her any major problems. She applied herself to her job with a diligence that allowed little time for anything else. At least while she was working it stopped her thinking about Matt.

There was a team meeting scheduled for the Monday afternoon. They tried to hold a meeting most weeks, although sometimes pressure of work made it impossible. However, Matt was adamant that he wanted the meeting to go ahead that day so as soon as she had finished her lunch, Rachel made her way to the staffroom. Ross was already there, sitting beside Gemma Craven, one of their practice nurses. Pam Whiteside, the other nurse, arrived a few seconds later accompanied by two members of the reception staff, Carol Walters and Beverley Humphreys.

'I've left Dianne manning the phone,' Carol explained, hurrying over to her. 'It's been bedlam this morning and if someone doesn't stay behind to answer it, we'll be running backwards and forwards. I'll fill her in later if that's all right?'

'Fine by me,' Rachel agreed, glancing round when Fraser Kennedy, their locum, came to join them.

'I can't stay long as I'm on call this afternoon. I thought I'd take Hannah with me if you don't need her,' he added, referring to their new trainee GP, Hannah Jeffries. 'She's not been out to any house calls yet and it will be good experience for her.'

'Good idea,' someone said behind them, and Rachel felt her heart lurch when she recognised Matt's deep voice.

She hurriedly took her seat, doing her best to calm down. The others would soon realise there was something wrong if she didn't get a grip of herself. The thought of everyone in the surgery finding out what had happened steadied her and by the time Matt opened the meeting, she felt more in control.

'I know everyone's got a busy afternoon ahead so I won't waste time,' he said, glancing around. His gaze skimmed over Rachel before it moved on and she wasn't sure if she felt vexed or pleased by his indifference. While she had been torturing herself with guilt, it appeared that Matt had put the episode behind him.

'We've discovered that the locum who worked here before Fraser didn't order various tests to be carried out,' Matt informed them bluntly. 'It means that a number of patients will need to be recalled.'

A shocked murmur ran around the room as the staff exchanged horrified looks. This kind of situation was unprecedented.

'You're not serious!' Rachel exclaimed, voicing everyone's dismay.

'I'm afraid I am.'

This time his gaze landed squarely on her and remained there. Rachel felt heat course through her veins when she saw the glimmer of some emotion in his eyes. Maybe Matt wasn't as indifferent to her as he was pretending? The thought caused such turmoil inside her that she had to force herself to concentrate as he continued.

'Ross and Gemma went through the files over the weekend and pulled out any that will need to be followed up. I had a look at them this morning and from what I've seen, it's imperative that we get people back in here as soon as we can.'

'What kind of tests are we talking about?' Rachel demanded, knowing that she couldn't afford to let herself be sidetracked. It had been difficult enough to carry on knowing that Matt regretted what they had done, but it would be impossible if she allowed herself to think that he had changed his mind.

'A whole range of things,' Ross answered. 'There's one patient who was diagnosed with fibroadenosis but she wasn't sent for a mammogram to rule out the possibility of it being breast cancer. Then there's another who has angina but no blood tests were ordered. We have no idea if his angina is linked to anaemia or possibly an over-production of thyroid hormones.'

'But that's unforgivable!' Fraser exploded. 'Those tests are purely routine, so why on earth didn't the fellow make sure they were done?'

'Probably because he couldn't be bothered completing the paperwork.' Matt's tone was harsh. 'I'm sure those of us who worked with him remember how he was always bragging that he could get through his lists faster than anyone else could do. Little wonder when he was doing only half the job.'

Dianne poked her head round the door just then to tell Ross there was a phone call for him in Reception and he excused himself. Fraser announced that he and Hannah would have to leave too and followed him out. Matt explained to the others that he would let everyone know how he intended to handle the recalls and the meeting broke up, but Rachel didn't leave with the others. She could tell how worried Matt was about this development and couldn't bear to leave him to deal with the problem by himself.

'How many people will we need to recall, do you know?' she asked.

'At the moment it stands at just over three dozen, although I'll go through the case notes again in case anyone's been missed out.'

'Do you really need to do that?' she protested. 'If Ross and Gemma have checked the files then I can't see that they'll have overlooked anyone.'

'Probably not, but at the end of the day I'm responsible for the patients who are registered with this practice so it's down to me to make sure that everyone who needs to be recalled is seen.'

Rachel sighed. 'I've said this before, Matt, but you can't be responsible for every single thing that happens here. It's too much for anyone, including you.'

'That may be so, but it doesn't alter the fact that ultimately I'm to blame if things go wrong.' He shrugged. 'Anyway, I prefer to do the job myself. That way I'm not disappointed if other people don't come up to my expectations.'

'I used to think like that, too, was always afraid of being let down. But sometimes you have to take a risk and trust people.' Rachel could hear the plea in her voice. They may have been discussing the running of the surgery but she was aware that their comments could apply to more than their work. If Matt would take a risk in his private life, she thought sadly, his life could be very different.

The realisation that she would probably never be a part of his life even if he did so was too hard to bear. Rachel excused herself and left, feeling a sense of loss welling up inside her. That night they had spent together had made her long for more, more nights and days too. The truth was that she wanted Matt in her life week in and week out, year after year, and the thought brought a rush of tears to her eyes because it was unlikely to happen. Matt may have enjoyed making love to her but he didn't want her to play a permanent role in his future. He couldn't do when he so obviously regretted what had gone on.

Rachel went back to her room, forcing down the tide of emotions that threatened to engulf her. She wouldn't cry, not now, not here. Here in the surgery she had a role to fulfil and she would do it to the best of her ability. She wasn't a woman with a bruised and battered heart but a doctor who had patients who relied on her.

It was something to cling to, what gave her life purpose even though it was no longer enough to fill it the way it had done in the past. Now that she knew how good it felt to love someone, she longed for more, but if it wasn't to be, she had to accept that. She certainly couldn't make Matt love her in return and wouldn't try. For love to mean anything it had to be true to itself—it couldn't be forced or coerced.

Matt understood that because he had loved his late wife. Maybe one day he would reach a point where he could move on, but it wouldn't be her, Rachel Mackenzie, he gave his heart to. It would be some other woman who reaped that reward.

Matt could feel that black cloud hovering over him again all afternoon long. It was partly the fact that it felt as though everything was falling apart around him, but mainly because Rachel had been so distant towards him recently. Even that afternoon, when he would have expected her to help him thrash out this problem, she had made an excuse and left. She was determined to put their night of passion behind her and he wished he could do the same. Oh, he had tried all right, but he knew to his cost how spectacularly unsuccessful he had been. He merely had to be near her and his body was instantly on the alert, as it had been that day!

Matt cursed under his breath as he checked that all the lights were off and locked up. He got into his car and headed for home, taking his time as the roads were extremely busy. With less than a week to go before Christmas, the shops were staying open late and that explained all the extra traffic. He reached the centre of town at last and joined the queue at the intersection to wait for the lights to change, inching his way forward until there was just one car in front of him.

The lights changed again and the car ahead of him moved forward. It was halfway across the junction when a van came hurtling out of one of the side roads, ignoring the fact that the traffic lights were against it. It rammed into the car and sent it spinning across the road where it came to rest wedged up against a lamppost. The van didn't stop but sped on, clipping the sides of several other vehicles that were waiting to enter the multi-storey car park as it hurtled off down the road.

Unsurprisingly, there was chaos after that. People were leaping out of their cars to see what damage had been done, bringing the traffic to a standstill. Matt ignored what was going on around him as he leapt out of his car and ran across the road to where the first car had ended up. There were two girls in it and he could tell at once that both were injured. A middle-aged man suddenly pushed past him and wrenched open the passenger side door, obviously intending to lift the nearest girl out, and Matt hurriedly intervened.

'Don't move her!' he ordered, elbowing the man

aside. Crouching down, he checked the girl's pulse and was relieved when he found it to be rather rapid but reassuringly strong. She had a nasty cut on the side of her head just above her left ear which he guessed had happened when the side window had shattered. She was obviously shocked and disorientated, but apart from that she didn't appear to be too badly injured. However, one thing he had learned over the years was never to take anything at face value. He turned to the other man.

'I'm a doctor and although I don't think she's too badly injured, I don't want her moved until I'm sure it's safe to do so. Can you stand here while I check the driver and stop anyone else from moving her?'

The man looked doubtful. He was obviously loath to follow Matt's instructions until a woman in the crowd suddenly piped up. 'You do what Dr Thompson tells you, Alf. He's the expert so don't you go moving her until he says so.'

Matt silently blessed her as he hurried round the car to check on the driver, a girl in her teens who looked scarcely old enough to hold a licence. The driver's door was crumpled in and it was impossible to open it, but with the help of a bystander, he managed to force open the hatchback and climbed into the car that way. There wasn't much room to manoeuvre as the driver's seat had broken in two and the top half was resting on the rear seat.

Matt inched himself forward as far as he could go and placed his fingers on the carotid artery in the girl's neck. His heart sank because he couldn't detect a pulse at first. He tried again and finally felt the tiniest flutter beneath his fingertips. She was alive but only just from the look of it.

'Matt?'

He looked round when he heard a familiar voice calling him and felt his heart lift when he saw Rachel peering through the open hatchback. 'Good timing! I could do with some help,' he said, trying not to let her know how pleased he was to see her. Rachel had made no bones about the fact that she wasn't looking for commitment and that night they had spent together had proved it beyond any doubt. She couldn't have dismissed what had happened so easily if it had meant anything to her.

He forced the thought to the back of his mind because it was neither the time nor the place to dwell on it. Leaning forward, he tried to assess the girl's injuries, but it was impossible to see very much. It appeared that her legs had been trapped when the car's bonnet had been crushed and he simply couldn't tell how serious her injuries were.

'Damn!' he cursed, carefully easing his way back out of the vehicle. It was an old car and it hadn't stood much of a chance when the van had hit it. There were chunks of metal protruding into the interior and they proved a major hazard when getting in and out. He finally made it unscathed and turned to Rachel, trying not to notice how pretty she looked in the glow from the streetlamps.

'She's alive but that's about all I can tell you. I can't assess how badly injured she is because I can't get to her. However, her pulse is very faint. If I had to hazard a guess, I'd say she's bleeding internally.'

'Maybe I can get a better look,' Rachel suggested. 'I'm smaller than you and I should be able to wriggle further into the car.'

'It's worth a try,' he agreed. 'But be careful. There's chunks of metal sticking out all over the place—you don't want to cut yourself.'

'I certainly don't.' Rachel shrugged off her coat and handed it to him. 'It will be easier without this and we can use it to cover her up with once I've examined her. It's freezing tonight and she needs to be kept warm.'

She climbed into the car and Matt found himself holding his breath as he watched her lean through the gap between the front seats. Part of the front axle had broken through the floor and there were a lot of sharp pieces of metal about.

'Careful!' he warned. 'Mind where you put your hands.'

Rachel nodded, preferring to save her breath for the difficult task of inching herself far enough forward to reach the lower half of the girl's body. Matt caught a tantalising glimpse of her shapely bottom before he averted his eyes. He made his way round to the passenger side to check on the other casualty. She seemed a little less shocked, he noted in relief, although he put out a restraining hand when she tried to unbuckle her seat belt.

'Just give me a moment to check you over before you try to move. We don't want you doing yourself any more damage, do we?'

'It was that van driver's fault, not Katie's,' the girl said shakily. 'He came racing through the lights on red…' She gulped as she cast a look at her friend, although with Rachel in the middle of the seats she couldn't see her clearly.

'I know. I was in the car behind you and I saw what happened,' Matt said soothingly, checking her pulse again. 'I'm a doctor, by the way. My name's Matthew Thompson and the lady in the middle is also a doctor. Her name is Rachel Mackenzie. We both work at Dalverston Surgery.'

'Oh, you're my mum's doctor! She's always singing your praises and saying how lovely you are!' the girl exclaimed, then blushed.

'Thank you kindly. It's always good to know that you don't scare your patients.' Matt smiled at her. 'So what's your name? I don't remember seeing you in the surgery.'

'Megan Bradley, and you haven't seen me 'cos I haven't been ill since we moved here.' She grimaced. 'Not up till now, anyway.'

'Well, if it's any consolation, Megan, I don't think you're badly injured from what I can tell,' he assured her. 'But you're the best person to know how you feel. Is there anywhere that hurts really badly?'

'Just my ribs. They sort of ache but I expect it's because of the seat belt.' Tears welled up in her eyes all of a sudden. 'Katie's been hurt far more than me, hasn't she?'

'I'm afraid so.' Matt ran a gentle hand down the girl's spine to check for any signs of misalignment in the vertebrae. From what he could tell, everything was fine and he nodded. 'Right, we're going to get you out of there but we're going to do it really slowly, understand?'

'Like they do in those TV series?' Megan asked him.

'Exactly like that,' he agreed, inwardly blessing the writers of the popular dramas. The general public's knowledge had increased tenfold thanks to a steady diet of medical soap operas and in his view that was a good thing.

'I've a collar in my bag and I'm going to put it around your neck to protect the top of your spine. It will feel a little uncomfortable but it's worth wearing it.'

'I don't mind,' Megan assured him. 'I'm hoping to train as a nurse when I leave school next year so it will be good practice for me to know how it feels.'

'Definitely!' Matt gave her a warm smile, thanking his lucky stars that she was obviously a practical girl and not given to hysterics. It made his job that much easier.

He stood up and hurried over to his car. He hadn't got round to unpacking all the extra equipment he had taken with him to that incident at the canal, which was fortunate. He sighed as he found a collar plus everything he needed to set up a drip for the young driver It felt like years had passed since that day. So much had happened since then that it felt as though he had packed in several years worth of living.

His gaze moved to Rachel as he headed back across the road and he felt an ache of such intensity start up inside him that he had to pause. He could lie to himself but what was the point? Since Claire had died he had been merely going through the motions of living. That night he and Rachel had spent together had proved that to him. It wasn't what Claire would have wanted, either. She would have been appalled, in fact. Claire would have hated to think of him wasting his life the way he had been doing. She would have wanted him to be happy.

Matt started walking again and it felt as though he was leaving the past behind him at last. He had no regrets, strangely enough, because that had been then and this was now, although what the future held was another matter. Nobody could foretell what lay in store for them and he was glad. He didn't want to look too far ahead in case he was disappointed. He just wanted to enjoy what he had now.

His gaze rested on Rachel as he drew closer and he felt warmth well up inside him because at this very moment he had Rachel here beside him.

CHAPTER TEN

IT WAS well over an hour before the emergency services finally managed to free the injured driver. It had been a very difficult and complicated task as the firemen had needed to remove the engine as well as the roof of the car. Matt had insisted on remaining in the car while the work had been carried out, monitoring the girl's condition and reassuring her as she had drifted in and out of consciousness.

Once Katie had been lifted out of the vehicle, the paramedics hurriedly transferred her to an ambulance. Rachel sighed as she watched it drive away with its siren blaring and its lights flashing. The girl had a fractured pelvis, which explained the massive blood loss she'd suffered, and there was bound to be internal injuries too. Although everyone had done all they possibly could, it was touch and go whether she would pull through.

'I think it's a case of crossing our fingers and hoping, don't you?'

Matt came back from giving a statement to the police. Rachel nodded when she heard what he said. It had been more or less what she had been thinking too. 'How do you rate her chances?'

'Not all that high, I'm afraid.' He shrugged, his handsome face looking very grim. 'If the fire brigade had been able to get her out sooner, she would have stood a much better chance.'

'They did their best,' Rachel replied, watching a couple of the crew from the local fire station gathering together the equipment they had used.

'They did, and it wasn't meant as a criticism. Nobody could have got her out of that car any faster. It was in such a bad state. However, it doesn't alter the fact that the delay is bound to have affected her chances of survival.'

His voice sounded flat but Rachel understood why. To see a young life possibly cut short this way was always distressing. Without pausing to think, she laid her hand on his arm. 'She still has a chance, Matt. The fact that you were here when the accident happened and were able to give her immediate assistance is bound to have worked in her favour.'

'Thank you. That makes me feel a lot better, although I can't take all the credit. You did more than your share, Rachel. I would never have been able to set up that drip without your help.' He smiled at her, his eyes filling with a warmth that immediately made her feel warm too. 'It was a real team effort.'

'I suppose so.' Rachel hurriedly removed her hand. She couldn't afford to start hoping that his smile might mean anything. She grimaced as she looked around at the scene of chaos that surrounded them. There were vehicles scattered all over the place and people standing in the road. Nobody was being allowed to leave until they had been questioned by the police whose main priority now was to find the van driver who had caused the accident. 'What a mess!'

'It'll take a while to sort it all out by the look of it,' Matt observed.

'It will.' Rachel sighed as she turned and looked at the multi-storey car park. 'Heaven only knows when I'll be able to get my car out of the car park. The exit is completely blocked by traffic and there's a huge tailback of cars along all the ramps. It's going to take ages to clear them away.'

'It is.' Matt frowned as he studied the build-up of traffic. 'Have you finished all your shopping?'

'More or less. To be honest, I don't really feel like doing any more tonight,' she admitted.

'Then why don't you leave your car where it is and let me drive you home?' He pointed across the road to where his car was still standing in the same spot he had abandoned it well over an hour before. 'I've given the police a statement and I'm free to leave. It seems pointless for you to hang around here when I can give you a lift, doesn't it?'

It did and Rachel was tempted, very tempted indeed. However, would it be wise to accept the offer after what had happened since that night they had slept together? She had done her best to stay out of Matt's way and allowing him to drive her home certainly wasn't the best way to maintain her distance.

'It's kind of you, Matt, but I'm not sure if it's safe to leave my car there overnight.'

He sighed heavily. 'I doubt if that's the real reason, is it? Look, Rachel, I know you're keen to forget what happened between us that night—you've made that perfectly plain. However, all I'm offering you is a lift home, nothing more.'

Rachel flushed, embarrassed by his bluntness. 'It just seemed better to give you some space,' she said quietly. 'I could tell you were upset about what we'd done the following morning and I didn't want to make the situation even more difficult for you.'

'I appreciate that, although I think you were just as keen to put it behind you,' he said flatly, and she frowned when she heard the echo of hurt in his voice.

'In a way, yes, I was, but not because I regretted what we'd done. I just don't want you getting hurt, Matt. That's all.'

'And here I was thinking that you didn't give a damn. How wrong could I be?' He smiled at her, his eyes filled with such tenderness that some of the ice that had filled her heart started to melt. Was it possible that they had been at cross-purposes?

The thought was way too enticing. Rachel bit her lip, afraid of what she might say if she allowed herself to speak. Matt brushed her cheek with his knuckles and she could feel the tremor that passed through him as his fingers glided over her skin.

'I think we need to talk, Rachel, don't you? Let me drive you home and see if we can sort this out.'

Rachel nodded, surprised to find that now she couldn't have forced out a single word. She followed him across the road to his car and settled herself in the passenger seat and still she didn't say anything. She had no idea how they were going to resolve this problem if she was still struck dumb when they reached his house, but it didn't seem to matter. The fact that Matt cared enough to want to clear up this misunderstanding far outweighed everything else.

It took them a bare ten minutes to reach Matt's house. He drew up outside the front door and turned to look at her. 'Are you all right here? We can go to yours if you'd feel more comfortable there. I should have checked with you before.'

'No, here is fine,' she replied, trying to control the tide of heat that threatened to engulf her. Was he remembering what had happened the last time she had been in his home? Recalling in exquisite, exhilarating detail their love-making and how wonderful it had been?

Her legs felt as though they had turned to jelly as she followed him into the house. It wasn't surprising either when her mind was busily unreeling a whole series of tantalising images, pictures of them lying together, their limbs entwined, their bodies fused in the most intimate fashion possible. Matt had been the most ardent and yet the gentlest of lovers and she knew that she would never experience the joy he had shown her that night with anyone else. She couldn't do. It was only Matt she wanted, only him she loved.

The realisation filled her with joy but it also scared her. It made her see just how very vulnerable she was.

Matt could hear his heart thumping as he led the way into the kitchen and switched on the lights. It was making such a racket that he would be amazed if Rachel couldn't hear it too. He glanced at her as he plugged in the kettle but her face gave away very little about her feelings. In fact, she looked ever so slightly stunned, as though she had suffered a shock and was desperately trying to deal with it.

He grimaced as he reached for the jar of coffee. They had just attended a major accident so was it any wonder if she felt shocked? What she needed at this moment was a cup of coffee and some time to get herself together before they talked about them.

His heart gave another noisy drum roll at the word 'them' and he gritted his teeth. There wasn't a *them*, at least not yet there wasn't. There was Rachel and there was him, and just because they'd had sex it didn't make them a couple, not even when it had been the most mind-blowing sex he had ever experienced!

Heat scorched through his veins and he hurriedly applied himself to making the coffee as he fought to get a grip on himself. Making love with Rachel had been a truly memorable experience, but he was only flesh and blood and he had needs like any other man, needs that he had suppressed for a very long time. It was hardly surprising their love-making had been such a huge success, bearing all that in mind.

It was the most logical explanation, even though in his heart Matt had great difficulty believing it was the real reason why making love with Rachel had been so wonderful. However, he couldn't afford to let himself get carried away when they needed to talk everything through.

He poured the coffee, placing the mugs on the

kitchen table because it would seem less intimate if they talked in here rather than in the sitting room. Soft lights and a crackling fire were all well and good, he thought as he went to fetch the milk out of the fridge, but he hadn't brought Rachel here to seduce her...Well, not consciously, although the idea was *very* tempting now that he thought about it.

His mind drifted off before he could stop it, soaking up the delights of firelight flickering on smooth alabaster skin, and he groaned under his breath. Now, that really was too much temptation for any man!

'Matt?'

Rachel's voice roused him and he realised that he had missed what she had said. 'Sorry. I was miles away,' he apologised as he placed the milk jug on the table and sat down. 'What did you say?'

'Worrying about that poor girl, I expect.' She sighed, completely misinterpreting the reason for his abstraction. 'I do hope she's all right.'

'So do I, although I wasn't actually thinking about her. I was thinking about us.' He added some milk to his coffee, wondering if he was mad to admit it, but he refused to lie. There had been enough misunderstandings recently without deliberately creating any more.

'Oh! I see,' she said shakily and he felt his heart swell with tenderness when he heard the breathless note in her voice. It was obvious that it was as important to Rachel as it was to him to sort out this mess.

The thought gave a welcome boost to his courage and he carried on. 'I know that night we spent together has changed things, Rachel. And you were right to say that I was upset the following morning because it's true. However, it doesn't mean that I regret sleeping with you.'

He paused, needing a moment to work out the best way to explain how he had felt. He wasn't used to opening his heart this way but he knew that he owed her the truth and nothing less. 'Making love with you was wonderful, *you* were wonderful. If I was upset afterwards it was because I couldn't help feeling that I had let Claire down in some way.'

'It must be hard for you, Matt. I know what a wonderful marriage you had. I can't imagine how difficult it must have been for you when you lost Claire. I…I've never loved anyone that much.'

There was something in her voice that brought his eyes to her face but she wasn't looking at him. She was staring down at her cup, making it impossible for him to see her expression clearly. Matt frowned. Had there been a hint of doubt in that claim she had made about never having really loved anyone? he wondered, then immediately dismissed the idea. There was no reason for her to lie to him, was there?

'It was difficult. The only way I could cope was by focussing on my job and taking care of Heather. However, Heather is all grown up now and she no longer needs me to look after her.' He smiled ruefully. 'I don't think she's needed me to do so for some time, but she knew I needed her. That's why she came back to Dalverston after she finished her nurse's training.'

'Heather loves you, Matt. She wouldn't have seen it as a hardship to come back here.'

'How did you know what I was thinking?' he exclaimed.

'Because I've often wondered the same thing myself about Ross. Did he decide to settle in Dalverston because of me?' She laughed softly. 'He would never admit it, of course!'

'Maybe not but his actions speak for themselves, don't they? Ross chose to live here because he loves you, Rachel, and he appreciates how hard you've worked to bring him up.' He reached across the table and squeezed her hand. 'You've been a wonderful mother to him.'

'Thank you for saying that. It means such a lot to me.'

Tears glistened in her eyes before she blinked them away. Matt released her hand and picked up his cup, giving her a moment to collect herself. They were here to talk about their relationship, not their respective roles as parents.

Once again his heart clamoured at the thought of them having a relationship and this time he didn't correct himself. He and Rachel did have a relationship. They'd had one for a number of years and it had been a highly successful one too. The fact that it had altered recently was the sticking point and they needed to decide what they were going to do about it.

Matt drank his coffee, wondering how to raise the subject in a way that wouldn't cause Rachel any embarrassment. Coming straight out and asking her how she felt about them having an affair seemed so crass but that was what it amounted to. He wasn't ready yet to offer her anything more, although at some point in the future…

He cut short that thought before it could run away with him. 'Look, Rachel,' he began.

'How do you feel about us trying again?'

They both spoke at once and both stopped. Matt took a deep breath as he felt his head reel. That Rachel should have suggested what he'd been going to say stunned him. He was still trying to work out how to reply when she continued.

'If what happened was a one-off, Matt, then fine. I understand. But if you feel that one night wasn't enough, I think you need to be totally upfront about that too.'

'How do you feel about it?' he said, his voice sounding hoarse.

She shrugged. 'I asked first.'

Oh, hell! This was difficult, more difficult than anything he had ever done before. Matt's blood pressure rose until it felt as though he was going to burst from the pressure building up inside him. And yet in his heart he knew there was only one answer, only one *truthful* answer, at least. He refused to be a coward and lie to her about something as important as this.

'One night wasn't enough for me, Rachel. It never could be enough when I felt things that night that I've never felt before.'

His eyes held hers fast and he saw her pupils dilate when she realised what he was saying, that not even with Claire had he felt the way he had felt when he had made love to her. For a moment all the old guilt came rushing back and swamped him and then, miraculously, his head cleared. All he could think about was Rachel and what she was offering him, something so precious that he would be a fool to turn it down.

Capturing her hands, he pulled her to her feet and drew her into his arms, holding her so close that he could feel the firm swell of her breasts pushing against his chest, feel the exact moment when her nipples hardened with desire. His own body quickened and he heard her suck in a sharp little breath when she realised he was aroused too and didn't give a damn. He was past pretending, way past the point of playing games.

'I don't know how long this will last, Rachel, and I don't care. I just know that I want you more than I've wanted anyone in a very long time.'

'I'm not asking you for a guarantee, Matt,' she whispered. 'Nobody can foretell how long a relationship will last.'

'No, they can't,' he agreed, refusing to think about how devastated he would be if he lost her. 'But what I can do is promise you on my honour that whatever happens we will deal with it like two sensible adults.'

'Can you really be sensible when you feel like this?' she murmured, moving her hips against his and making him groan.

'No, I can't. I don't even want to try. I just want to make mad, passionate love to you right here and right now. Is it enough to be going on with?'

'Yes. More than enough for me.'

Reaching up on tiptoe, she pressed her mouth to his, her lips parting to invite his to open too. Matt felt the rush of desire hit him like a sledgehammer as he pulled her hard against him, letting her feel in intimate detail exactly what she was doing to him. The coffee cups went flying as he lifted her onto the table but he didn't care. What did some broken china matter when his heart was being healed?

They made love right there in the kitchen and it was even better than the first time, amazingly enough. Matt knew that he scaled new heights that night and that he couldn't have done that with anyone but Rachel. As her body opened to him, he realised that he was on the brink of falling in love with her, but he also knew it was a step too far at this stage. Rachel hadn't asked for love or commitment, just that they be together. He had to be content with that. For now.

They climaxed together, crying out each other's name in unison, and even if it wasn't an omen for the future, it proved they had made the right decision at this moment. He could live with that, live in the present and enjoy what he had. He only hoped Rachel could do so too for a very long time.

Matt was still asleep when Rachel got up the following morning. It was very early and the central heating hadn't switched itself on yet. She shivered as she unhooked his robe from the behind the bedroom door and pulled it on. It was far too big for her but she rolled up the sleeves and tightened the belt around her waist. The real bonus apart from an immediate feeling of warmth was that it smelled of Matt and she sniffed appreciatively as she made her way down the stairs. Being enveloped in his scent might not be as good as being held in his arms but it was the next best thing.

A smile curled her mouth as she set to work to make them some breakfast. The bacon was crisping and the eggs were sizzling by the time Matt appeared looking wonderfully sexy as he padded into the kitchen wearing nothing more than a pair of boxer shorts. He grinned as he came over to her and pulled her into his arms.

'Aha, so you're the culprit.'

'I am?' Rachel smiled into his eyes, loving the way his hair fell in a disorderly wave onto his forehead. Matt was normally impeccably groomed and it was a rare and pleasant surprise to see him looking less than perfect for once.

She brushed the lock of hair back into its rightful place, revelling in the fact that she had the right to enjoy such intimacies. 'You'll have to enlighten me. What is it I'm supposed to have done?'

'Oh, there's no supposed about it, not when the evidence is clear to see.' His hands went to the belt on the robe. 'You, Dr Mackenzie, stole my dressing gown and for that you deserve to be suitably punished.'

'Oh, but I didn't *steal* it,' Rachel objected, keen to point out that she had merely borrowed it. However, it appeared that Matt wasn't interested in hearing her defence.

He peeled the robe off her and tossed it aside, his mouth claiming hers in a drugging kiss that made her forget every argument she had been about to make. When he pressed her back against the wall, she didn't protest but gave in willingly. It felt so good to have him kiss her, hold her and make her his. Their love-making would have reached its natural conclusion if the sudden shrilling of an angry smoke alarm hadn't interrupted them.

Matt chuckled as he let her go and switched off the gas. 'Looks as though the bacon has gone for a burton.'

'And the eggs.' Rachel shook her head as she poked at the blackened remains in the frying pan. 'You do realise that you've missed out on having breakfast in bed?'

'That's a shame, although I have to confess that I prefer the alternative.'

He leered comically at her and she laughed as she aimed a playful cuff at his ear. 'You are completely shameless, Matthew Thompson!'

'Good. It's music to my ears to hear you say that. I was in danger of turning into a real old fuddy-duddy and I rather like the idea of being seen as someone whose attitude to life is a bit more risqué.'

'Fuddy-duddy! No way could you be described as that. According to my friends, you're a real babe.'

'Is that a fact?' He grinned at her. 'Whilst I feel I should point out that I'm a tad long in the tooth to be called a babe, I certainly won't dispute it. However, what interests me most of all is if you agree with your friends. Do you?'

'Now, *that* would be telling!'

Rachel shot past him as she beat a hasty retreat. Matt was hard on her heels as she flew up the stairs but, then, she wasn't trying all that hard to outrun him. They made love in his bedroom then took a shower together and made love in there too and it was wonderful again. Rachel had never enjoyed this kind of closeness with anyone before and revelled in it. She could get used to living like this, she thought later as she got dressed, very used to waking up with Matt each morning and falling asleep beside him each night. However, she had to remember that this wasn't for ever but just for now.

She sighed as she finished buttoning up her blouse. She may have found her soulmate, but it took two people to build a lasting relationship. She had absolutely no experience of making a lifelong commitment, although she could learn. As for Matt, he had the experience because he had done it before, but she didn't know yet if he would want to do it all over again with her. All she could do was hope that he would.

CHAPTER ELEVEN

MATT was amazed by how happy he felt in the days that followed. Not even the problems they were currently experiencing at the surgery seemed to trouble him the way they once would have done. He knew it was all down to his relationship with Rachel.

It had added a new dimension to his life, one that had been missing for far too long, and he found himself praying that it would continue. Maybe they hadn't made a commitment but what they did have felt so right that he never wanted it to end. The idea that he was falling in love with her crossed his mind with increasing frequency but he didn't allow himself to dwell on it. He was afraid that he would spoil things if he wished for more than he had. Although Rachel hadn't moved in with him, she spent most nights at his house and their sex life continued to be amazing. He kept wondering if a time would arrive when they settled into a routine but it never happened. Each time they made love it felt as though it was the first time and it blew his mind.

Christmas came, the best Christmas he could remember in years. Ross joined them for lunch and although he didn't say anything, Matt had a feeling that Ross had guessed there was something going on between him and Rachel. He also got the impression that Ross was genuinely pleased for them and it was a relief to know that their relationship wasn't going to create problems in that area. When Heather phoned to wish him a happy Christmas, he was tempted to tell her about Rachel but something held him back. Maybe it would be safer not to tempt fate.

After Christmas it was time to finish sorting out the mess created by their former locum. They had managed to whittle down the number of recalls to just half a dozen by then. Alison Bradshaw, the woman who had been diagnosed with fibroadenosis, was his first appointment when he returned to work after the festive break. She'd been on holiday when they had tried to contact her and that had caused an added delay. Matt brought up her file on the computer and was reading through the decidedly scrappy notes the locum had made when Rachel tapped on his door.

'You look very industrious. Heavy list this morning?'

'About average for this time of the year.' Matt tipped back his chair and smiled at her, wondering if he would ever reach a point where he felt indifferent to her. It was just over an hour since they had got out of bed yet his heart was already kicking up a storm.

Rachel closed the door and came around the desk to drop a kiss on his lips. They had agreed to keep their relationship a secret from their colleagues. Neither of them relished the thought of being gossiped about so they were very discreet when they were at work. That

Rachel had broken their rules and kissed him made his heart race with delight.

'I thought you might need a top-up to help you through the morning.'

'Mmm, I do. I do.' Matt pulled her down onto his lap and kissed her soundly, smiling when she eagerly responded. He loved the fact that she never pretended but let him know exactly how she felt. He scattered a shower of butterfly-soft kisses over her face and neck then reluctantly drew back. 'That will have to keep me going until lunchtime, although I'll probably need another top-up by then.'

'Always happy to help out a colleague in need,' she replied saucily, laughing at him.

That remark would have prompted a reprisal if the buzzer on his desk hadn't sounded to warn him his first appointment was waiting in Reception. Matt groaned as he tipped her off his knee. 'Action stations. It's time to knuckle down to some work.'

'Aye, aye, Captain!'

Rachel saluted smartly then headed for the door, leaving him chuckling. She had that effect on him, made him feel more positive about life than he had felt in ages. She was everything he admired in a woman—warm, caring, sexy...

He made himself stop right there, knowing from experience how fast his thoughts could run away with him. He called in Alison Bradshaw and set about explaining why he wanted to send her for a mammogram. She was naturally worried so he phoned up the hospital and made an appointment for her to be seen the following week.

Thankfully, her symptoms had settled down and on checking her breasts, he found nothing to indicate there might be a problem. However, he would only truly relax when the results of the mammogram came back and proved that everything was clear.

He saw her out and worked his way through the rest of his list. His last patient had just left when Carol phoned with a query about someone else who was on the recall list. Matt told her that he would come to the office to sort it out and gathered up the case notes he'd used. He was just walking along the corridor when a girl came out of the treatment room and he paused when he realised it was Megan Bradley, the passenger in the car that had been involved in that accident in the town centre.

'Hello! What are you doing here?'

'Having my stitches out,' Megan explained, pushing back her hair so that he could see the thin red scar above her ear. 'I was dreading having it done in case it hurt, but the nurse was so gentle I hardly felt a thing.'

'Good,' Matt smiled at her. 'So you're fully recovered, are you?'

'Yes, thank you. I felt a bit shaky for a few days afterwards and my head hurt but all things considered I got off very lightly.'

'And what about your friend who was driving—Katie? I telephoned the hospital and know that she came through the operation to repair her pelvis. Is she making good progress?'

'Not too bad, but it will be a while before she's up and about again.' Mel sighed. 'The police still haven't found the van driver. They were able to trace who owned the van from the CCTV pictures but it had been reported as stolen a couple of days before the accident. I hate to think the driver is going to get away with it after all the damage he's caused.'

'I'm sure the police will track him down eventually,' Matt said soothingly. 'The main thing is that both you and Katie are going to be all right.'

'You're right, Dr Mackenzie. Of course you are.'

Mel gave him a beaming smile and left. Matt went to the office and sorted out Carol's query in a buoyant mood. It was good to know that both girls would recover from their ordeal. The upside of feeling so happy himself was that he wanted only good things to happen for everyone else. He certainly didn't want any disasters to spoil what he and Rachel had now or in the future.

He frowned as he went back to his room. Once again he was thinking long term and it wasn't wise to do that. All he could do was hope that their relationship meant as much to Rachel as it meant to him.

It was the most wonderful time of Rachel's entire life. She couldn't remember when she had felt so happy before. Being with Matt both in and out of work was like a dream come true.

Amazingly their professional relationship didn't suffer. Matt still treated her with the same respect and courtesy when they were in the surgery, even if the look in his eyes did raise matters onto a very different plane! Rachel knew without the shadow of a doubt that she had found the man she wanted to spend her life with.

However, until Matt admitted that he felt the same way, she mustn't get carried away.

The thought of what might happen in the future was the only blot on the horizon and she refused to let it ruin things. Thankfully she was so busy that she had very little time to dwell on it. Having to fit in the patients they needed to recall meant they were all pushed to the limit. Morning and evening lists were longer than ever.

Then there was a near crisis when their practice nurse, Gemma Craven, attended a call at one of the outlying farms and got lost in a snowstorm. Rachel was surprised when she saw how worried Ross was when Gemma went missing. It made her wonder if there was something going on between them. Quite frankly, she would be glad if there was because Ross deserved to be happy and Gemma was a lovely girl. She was tempted to ask him but in the end decided that she wouldn't interfere. She knew how it felt to want to protect a new and very precious relationship.

It was the beginning of February when Rachel discovered that something had happened that was bound to affect her relationship with Matt. She had been feeling off-colour for several days, nauseous and dizzy, and had put it down to that wretched bug that was still doing the rounds. However, when she was violently sick one morning as she got up, she was forced to consider some other options and was shocked by what she came up with. Was it possible that she was pregnant?

She hurried back to the bedroom and took her diary out of her bag. Although it was normal for a woman's menstrual cycle to alter as she approached the menopause, hers had been remarkably regular up till now. However on checking the date, she realised that her period was almost two weeks late. She tried to tell herself that there was no need to panic but she couldn't help adding everything up, the dizziness and nausea, the bout of sickness that morning and the missed period, and they all pointed towards the same conclusion: she could be pregnant.

Rachel's head was reeling as she went downstairs. She was forty-six years old and she couldn't have a baby at her age! It wasn't as though she and Matt had taken any chances either because they had always used contraception. However, as a doctor she knew only too well that no contraceptive was one hundred per cent guaranteed. Her heart sank as she sat down at the kitchen table and wondered how Matt would react if she told him of her suspicions. She couldn't imagine he would be pleased when he had made it clear that he wasn't looking for commitment. After all, a child was the ultimate commitment of all.

'Are you feeling all right, sweetheart? You look awfully pale this morning.'

Matt came and crouched down beside her, his face filled with such concern that Rachel was hard pressed not to bawl her eyes out. Becoming a father again at this stage in his life would be the last thing he'd choose.

'I think I may be coming down with that bug that's been doing the rounds,' she murmured, hating the fact that she had to lie to him, although she had no choice. She needed to find out if she really was pregnant before she said anything. She dredged up a watery smile. 'I feel really rotten, if I'm honest.'

'Then there's no way that you're going into work today,' he said firmly. He got up and poured her a cup of tea then helped her to her feet. 'It's back to bed for you. Doctor's orders!'

Rachel laughed but there was a hollow ring to it. She allowed him to help her back up the stairs and lay down obediently on the bed. He placed the cup of tea on the bedside table then bent and brushed her forehead with a gentle kiss.

'Stay there and try to sleep. I'll pop back at lunchtime to see if you're all right.' He took the phone out of its charger and placed it on the pillow beside her. 'Phone me if you feel any worse, though. Promise?'

'Promise,' Rachel whispered, wondering if it was possible to feel any worse than she did. Tears trickled from her eyes and she turned her face into the pillow so that he wouldn't see her crying as he left the room. She had never felt more desolate in her life, not even when she had found out that she was expecting Ross.

As soon as Matt had left for work she got dressed and drove into town to buy a pregnancy testing kit. She took it back to her own home and did the test there. Waiting for the results was agonising but finally she had confirmation that her suspicions were correct. She was pregnant and now she needed to decide what she was going to do.

At her age there were added risks to having a baby and she would need to undergo various tests if she went ahead with the pregnancy. Nobody would blame her if she decided not to go through with it, yet she shied away from the idea of having a termination. How she was going to tell Matt was something she still hadn't worked out. It would have been different if they had made a real commitment to each other but their relationship was founded on the here and now, and she certainly wouldn't *blackmail* him into staying with her because of their child.

Matt had a highly developed sense of duty and she knew that he would feel he had to support her if they were still together when she broke the news to him. She couldn't bear to think that he could end up resenting her one day. Tears stung her eyes but she really didn't have a choice. It would be better to end things now than run the risk of that happening.

Matt couldn't stop worrying about Rachel all morning long. Her illness seemed to have come on remarkably quickly even if it was that wretched bug. He waited until there was a gap between patients and phoned the house, feeling more concerned than ever when there was no reply. Surely she must have heard the phone ringing, he thought as he replaced the receiver. So why hadn't she answered it?

He tried telling himself that she was probably fast asleep but he could barely wait for lunchtime to arrive. There was another delay then because the results of various tests had come back and he needed to check them. The results of Alison Bradshaw's mammogram were amongst them and he was relieved to see that it was clear. He asked Carol to phone Alison to make sure

she'd received a copy then made his escape before
anything else could delay him.

He drove straight home, frowning when he discovered that Rachel's car had gone. Had she felt better and
decided to go home? He set off down the lane, letting
out a sigh of relief when he saw her car parked outside
the cottage. Although he had no idea why she had come
back to her own home, at least she was safe.

Rachel opened the door to his knock but instead of
inviting him in, she just stood and looked at him. Matt
wasn't sure what was going on but it was obvious that
there was something very wrong and his insides
churned in sudden apprehension. It took every scrap of
willpower he possessed to smile at her when it felt as
though his world was on the brink of falling apart.

'Hi! I see you decided to come home. Does that
mean you're feeling better?'

'Yes, thank you.' Her tone was clipped and the
churning in his guts intensified.

'Is there something wrong, Rachel?' he demanded,
his own voice sounding equally harsh.

'No. I just need some space, time on my own for a
change.'

There was no smile to soften the words, nothing but the
starkness of the statement, and something warm and
tender shrivelled up inside him. Was she tiring of him
already, he wondered sickly, wanting to end their relationship so soon? The thought almost brought him to his
knees.

'You should have said so this morning if that's how
you feel. There was no need to pretend you were ill.'

'As I said, I needed time on my own to think everything through.'

'And now you've had the time you needed, you've come to a decision?'

'Yes. I have.'

'I see.' He shrugged, hoping she couldn't tell how terrified he felt. 'I assume it has something to do with us, so why don't you tell me what you've decided?'

'I think we need to take a break from one another.'

It was what he had feared she'd been going to say and his heart seemed to shrivel up inside him. It was all he could do not to beg her to reconsider but pride dictated that he shouldn't embarrass them both. After all, he had known from the outset that they hadn't promised each other a lifetime of commitment.

'If that's how you feel then there's not a lot I can say, is there?' He shrugged, praying that she couldn't tell how devastated he felt. 'You could be right. Maybe we do need to cool things a bit. It's been very full on recently, hasn't it, Rachel?'

'It has. I…I think we need to take a step back, Matt, don't you?'

There was the tiniest quaver in her voice which gave him some measure of hope that she wasn't convinced about that, but there was nothing to sustain it when he shot a searching look at her face. She looked so distant that it was like looking at a stranger rather than the woman he had grown to love with all his heart.

It seemed too cruel that he had finally admitted how he felt when he was on the point of losing her. Matt knew that he couldn't keep up the pretence any longer and swung round. 'As usual you're spot on in your assessment of the situation, Rachel. I suggest we see how we feel in a couple of weeks' time.'

'I think it would be for the best, too,' she said calmly, and he inwardly cringed as another shaft of pain shot through him. It was hard to believe that she could show so little sign of emotion when he was in such agony.

'I'll take the rest of the day off, if you don't mind,' she continued. 'It will look very odd if I suddenly turn up for work when I'm supposed to be ill.'

'Fine. Do whatever you feel is right.'

Matt went back to his car and got it. Rachel had already closed the door by the time he slipped the key into the ignition and he didn't linger before he drove away. Maybe it was the shock of what had happened but he felt icily cold. He had simply never expected their relationship to end like this. There'd been no tears, no arguments, no recriminations, just a polite indifference that was so much worse. It simply proved how little he had meant to her if Rachel could let him go with so little sign of emotion.

His eyes blurred and he pulled up at the side of the road. Maybe Rachel didn't deem it worth crying about but he did. He had lost the woman he loved for a second time and no matter what happened in the future he would never allow himself to suffer this kind of agony again.

CHAPTER TWELVE

RACHEL sobbed her heart out after Matt had left. It was as though a dam had burst and all the tears she'd been holding back suddenly came gushing out. She felt completely drained afterwards but calmer, better able to think.

She had been right not to tell him just yet that she was pregnant, she realised. The calm and controlled way he had behaved just now had proved that. If he hadn't felt it was worth fighting to keep her then she didn't want him to think that the baby changed anything. She couldn't bear it if Matt felt he had to do the *right* thing. That would be the route to a lifetime of unhappiness for all of them.

The situation was going to be difficult enough as it was. Rachel couldn't imagine how hard it was going to be once the baby was born. Working together each and every day would be a strain for both of them in the circumstances. Although she loved working in Dalverston, it might be better if she found herself a job somewhere else.

The thought of having to start afresh was a daunting one but Rachel knew in her heart it was the right thing to do. What she was going to tell Ross was something she would need to think about, although it could wait for now. Her main concern was to find herself another job as quickly as possible.

She hunted out some back copies of the various medical journals she subscribed to and checked the positions vacant pages. There were a number of possibilities and she marked them all, although her pregnancy could prove a handicap when applying for another post. Most general practices were understaffed and they wouldn't be keen to take on someone who would be able to work for only a few months.

She sighed as she laid the magazines aside. She would deal with that hurdle when she came to it. If nothing else came up, she could always do locum work for a few months to tide her over. She had some savings but they wouldn't last very long if she had to live on them. It could take a while before she sold the cottage and she would have to rent somewhere else in the meantime, so she needed to earn enough to support herself.

Knowing Matt as well as she did, he would probably offer financial support for the baby, although she wasn't sure if she should accept it. The child was her responsibility and she intended to make that clear to him, although she was willing to allow him access if that was what he wanted.

Her heart caught painfully when it struck her that it might be the only time she saw him. The odd couple of hours here and there weren't very much to look forward to after how close they had been, but she knew she had made the right decision. She wouldn't put him under any kind of pressure, wouldn't run the risk of him ending up resenting her. She loved him too much to ruin the rest of his life.

Matt felt as though the rug had been pulled right out from under his feet when Rachel announced that she was looking for another job. In one tiny corner of his mind where hope still resided, he had convinced himself that somehow, some way, they would work through this glitch and come out all the stronger for it on the other side. However, he certainly couldn't see a way out of this. If Rachel left Dalverston that would be the end of them. For good.

'Naturally, I'll work the required period as laid out in my contract. It's two months less any holiday I'm owed.' She consulted her diary. 'That brings it down to six weeks by my reckoning.'

'I'll make a note of that,' he said gruffly, the pain bubbling up inside him so that he had to clamp his teeth together to stop it escaping. He wasn't sure what was worse, the fact that she was planning on leaving or that she could talk about it with so little emotion.

'Don't you want to check that I'm right?' Rachel asked him in surprise, and he shook his head.

'I'm sure you've worked it all out correctly. It's not something you'd make a mistake about, is it?' His tone was brusque but he'd be damned if he would apologise for it. Didn't she know how hard this was for him, didn't she even care?

'No, it isn't.'

There was the tiniest hint of a plea in her voice but

he wasn't going to make the mistake of thinking she was asking for his understanding. She had made up her mind what she intended to do and she didn't give a damn about the effect it would have on him.

He stood up abruptly. 'I take it that you'll be applying for another post?'

'Yes. I've already seen a couple of jobs that look suitable,' she agreed, digging in the knife that bit further. She certainly wasn't wasting any time, he thought savagely. Obviously, she was keen to put some distance between them as soon as she possibly could!

'I see,' he said, clamping down on the emotions that were churning around inside him. He would be damned if he'd let her know how angry and hurt he felt, especially when she didn't care. He shrugged, feigning an indifference he wished he felt. 'It goes without saying that I'll be happy to provide you with a reference. You've done an excellent job while you've been here, Rachel. Any practice will be lucky to have you as part of their team.'

'Thank you.'

Her voice caught on the words but Matt didn't wait to see what had caused it. His control was held by a thread and he was desperate not to embarrass himself in front of her. He went to the door, pausing briefly to glance back, but she wasn't looking at him. She was staring down at her diary, probably counting the days until she could shake off the dust of her old life in Dalverston and set off on a new adventure somewhere else.

Had it been their ill-fated affair that had pushed her

into making the move? he wondered bitterly, then hurriedly blanked out the answer. He didn't want to know if *he* was responsible for driving her away.

'Leaving?'

'Yes.' Rachel summoned a smile but it wasn't easy when she felt so devastated inside. 'I know it's probably come as a shock to you, darling…'

'Too damned right it has!' Ross slumped down onto a chair and stared at her in bewilderment. 'Why on earth do you want to leave? I thought you loved it here in Dalverston.'

'I do…I mean, I did, but recently I've had the feeling that I'm stuck in a bit of a rut.' She perched on the edge of the sofa, willing her son to accept her explanation without probing too deeply. The last thing she wanted was Ross discovering the truth at this stage, although he would have to know at some point.

'This hasn't anything to do with Matt, has it? You two haven't…well, fallen out?'

'What do you mean?' she asked in surprise, flushing when Ross gave her a speaking look.

'There's no point denying it, Mum. It was obvious that you two were an item at Christmas.'

'I…um…was it?'

'Yes, and before you ask, I was delighted for you both.' He leant forward. 'It's about time the pair of you thought about yourselves for a change. I really like Matt and to my mind you two are ideally suited. If something has happened, are you sure you can't work it out between you?'

'I'm afraid not. That's one of the reasons why I've decided I need to make some changes to my life, although it's not the only reason.' For a moment she was tempted to tell him about the baby but it would be wrong to tell Ross before she told Matt and then expect him to keep her secret. She hurried on, trying to put a positive spin on her plans.

'I'm not getting any younger, Ross, and if I don't make the move now then I'll never do it. I don't want to end up regretting it in a few years' time.'

'Is that the truth?' Ross demanded.

Rachel felt herself colour when she heard the scepticism in his voice even though it was true in a way. If she stayed in Dalverston she could cause untold problems for Matt and that was something she would regret bitterly for the rest of her life. 'Yes. Of course it's true!' she exclaimed with, hopefully, a convincing amount of indignation. 'Do you really think I would lie to you?'

'Sorry, of course you wouldn't.' Ross sighed. 'It's just that I can't bear to think that you're leaving because of some sort of silly misunderstanding that could very well be cleared up.'

'I'm not. I've thought long and hard about this decision and I know it's the right thing to do.' She quickly changed the subject, afraid that she would let something slip if Ross kept pushing her. 'Anyway, enough about me. How are you and Gemma getting on?'

'Great! I never thought I'd feel like this about anyone. I'm head over heels in love with her.'

'I'm so happy for you, Ross,' Rachel said sincerely.

'Are you? I was afraid you'd think it was too soon

after what happened with Heather…' He stopped abruptly, looking deeply concerned. 'I hope it wasn't that which caused you and Matt to split up? I've no idea how he feels about me and Gemma seeing each other because he's never said anything to me. But it can't be easy for him to accept that I've met someone else so soon. I do hope I haven't caused a rift between you two.'

'You haven't,' she said firmly. 'I can say with my hand on my heart that me breaking up with Matt had nothing whatsoever to do with you, darling.'

'Thanks heavens for that!' Ross laughed ruefully. 'I'd hate to think that I had caused you a whole load of grief at my age.'

'You have never caused me any problems at any age,' she told him truthfully. 'Having you was the best thing that ever happened to me, darling. Believe me, it's true.'

'And you are the best mother in the world.'

Ross stood up and hugged her. He seemed a lot happier after that, eager to hear about the plans she had made. Rachel told him what she could, carefully avoiding any outright lies. She would tell him about the baby once all the tests had been done and everything was clear. How he would take the news was open to question but she would deal with that when it arose.

Ross left a short time later, promising to do all he could to help make the move as stress-free as possible for her. Rachel locked up and went upstairs to bed, wishing with all her heart it was as simple as that. Leaving her home and her job would have been stress-ful enough but factor in all the rest—Matt and the baby—and the stress factor achieved whole new levels. However, she would cope because she had to. She would cope because it was the right thing to do. She wouldn't trap Matt into a situation he wouldn't welcome, although she couldn't help thinking wistfully how different things might have been if they had been truly committed to one another when she had found out she was pregnant. They could have had something to celebrate then.

Matt felt as though he was caught up in some terrible nightmare. Every day that passed brought the day when Rachel might leave ever closer and he had no idea how he was going to cope when it happened. What made it worse was that she was so distant with him, confining any contact they had to strictly work-related matters. After their recent closeness, he felt her withdrawal all the more keenly and couldn't understand it.

Why had she changed her mind about him so suddenly? One minute she had seemed as blissfully happy as he had been and the next she hadn't wanted anything to do with him. The more he thought about it the stranger it appeared and he knew that he wouldn't rest until he found out what had gone wrong. It was having the opportunity to ask her that was the problem. There was no time to discuss it at work—she made sure they were never together long enough to give him the opportunity. As for going to see her after work, he knew it would be a waste of time—she would probably refuse to speak to him. No, he needed to find a time and a place when she couldn't avoid him.

He finally got his chance one evening. Carol had organised a fortieth birthday 'do' after work—dinner and drinks at a local pub—for Dianne, the newest member of their reception team. Matt had no intention of going when it was first mentioned to him. Quite frankly, the last thing he felt like doing was celebrating, so he made an excuse. However, when he discovered on the day that Rachel was going, he changed his mind. It could be his one and only chance to talk to her. After all, she could hardly ignore him with everyone there watching them.

Carol was standing at the bar when he arrived that night. She smiled in delight when she saw him coming in. 'Oh, wonderful, you've decided to come after all.' She pointed towards the far side of the room. 'We've managed to grab ourselves a table over there. What do you want to drink? I'm just about to order.'

'Oh, just a bottle of beer for me, please.' He took out his wallet and handed her several twenty-pound notes. 'Here, use this.'

Carol whistled. 'That's very generous of you, Matt. I'm doubly glad you managed to get here now!'

Matt laughed dutifully then made his way across the room, replying automatically to the friendly greetings that met him. Rachel was sitting in the corner and he frowned when he saw how pale and drawn she looked. She smiled politely as he pulled out a chair, but he could see the alarm in her eyes and knew that he was the last person she'd expected to see. 'Hello, Matt. I didn't know you were coming.'

'I wasn't planning to, but I changed my mind at the last minute.' He leant forward, subjecting her to a searching look. 'Are you sure you should be here, though? You look worn out.'

His eyes held hers fast although he had no idea what she could see on his face at that moment. All of a sudden he didn't give a damn either. This might be his only chance to sort out this mess and he refused to waste it by pretending he didn't care.

He did care, he cared a lot, loved her too, and only wished he could tell her that. The fact that she was unlikely to welcome such an admission was incidental. It didn't stop him feeling how he did. He loved her more than life itself and if there was any way to make her understand that she was wrong to leave him then, by heaven, he'd find it.

'It…it's been rather hectic in work lately, hasn't it? I expect that's why I'm looking so tired.'

Rachel could feel her heart pounding as she looked away from Matt's probing gaze. She had only agreed to come because Carol had told her that Matt wouldn't be there, so it had been a shock to see him coming into the pub. She cast him a wary look from under her eyelashes and felt her breath catch when she discovered that he was still watching her. She had no idea what was going on but the expression on his face stunned her. Why was he looking at her as though he genuinely cared?

'Okey-dokey, folks, it's drinkie time! Here you go, Rachel. A nice big G&T to perk you up and put some colour in your cheeks.'

Carol came back with a loaded tray and plonked a glass down in front of her. She held up her hand when

Rachel opened her mouth to protest it wasn't what she had ordered. 'Forget it. There is no way that you're having orange juice tonight. We're here to celebrate Dianne's birthday and you need a proper drink to do that!'

Rachel summoned a smile when everyone cheered, but she could have done without this. She couldn't drink alcohol in her condition, although how she could avoid it without causing a fuss was another matter. Picking up the glass, she pretended to take a sip. 'Mmm, that's delicious.'

'Good. Get it down you, then. There's plenty more where that came from, courtesy of our beloved leader.'

Carol looked pointedly at Matt and Rachel realised that with typical generosity he must have paid for their drinks. Once everyone had a glass in front of them, Fraser stood up and proposed a toast.

'To Dianne and the next forty years. May they be filled with health, wealth and happiness.'

Everyone raised their glasses aloft. Rachel went to pick up her drink and gasped when the glass suddenly flew across the table. Gin and tonic went everywhere, causing pandemonium as they all leapt out of the way.

'Sorry, sorry! My fault,' Matt apologised, grabbing a handful of paper napkins and hurriedly mopping up the mess. 'I must have knocked the glass over when I went to pick up my bottle of beer.' He glanced at Rachel. 'I'll get you another one.'

He got up and went to the bar, returning a few minutes later with a fresh glass. Placing it carefully on a coaster, he smiled at her. 'Try that. It should be just right for you.'

Rachel cautiously raised the glass to her lips, feeling

shock run through her when she tasted the sharp, undiluted bitterness of pure tonic water. How had he guessed that she didn't want to drink any alcohol? she wondered giddily. Surely he didn't suspect that she was pregnant?

The thought made her insides churn with apprehension and she hastily excused herself as she headed to the ladies' lavatories. Although the bouts of morning sickness had tailed off, there were times throughout the day when she felt nauseous and this was one of them. She sluiced her face with cold water then sat on the little stool in front of the vanity bench and took several deep breaths, feeling better as her panic started to subside. There was nothing the least significant about Matt buying her that drink. He had simply heard Carol's comment about her asking for a non-alcoholic drink and with typical thoughtfulness he had taken account of that. There was certainly no reason to believe that he had guessed she was pregnant.

Rachel stood up, feeling calmer now that she had reasoned everything out. She opened the door to go back and join the others, and came to an abrupt halt when she saw Matt leaning against the wall. It was obvious that he was waiting for her and her stomach lurched once again as she found herself wondering what he wanted.

All of a sudden it was just too much for her to deal with. With a tiny moan, she fled back into the toilets and was violently sick. Crouching down on the floor of the stall, she closed her eyes in despair. Even if Matt hadn't worked out already that she was pregnant, it wouldn't take him long to do so!

CHAPTER THIRTEEN

MATT could feel the shock wave spreading up from his toes. It reached his knees, moved up to his hips, his chest and finally arrived at his brain. He closed his eyes, desperately trying to find another explanation for what had happened that night but he really couldn't think of one. Was it possible that Rachel was pregnant?

His eyes flew open again because he just knew it was true. It explained so much that had made no sense before. Rachel was expecting a baby, his baby, and that was why she had decided to leave Dalverston. It hadn't anything to do with her lack of feelings for him—well, hopefully, not—she had just got it into her head that it was the right thing to do. He could actually understand her reasoning now that he thought about it: they hadn't made a commitment; she had no idea how he really felt about her; she was far too proud to make it appear as though she was using the baby to *force* him into staying with her—as if that would have been necessary!

Matt pushed open the restroom door, his heart aching when he saw her crouched on the floor of the nearest stall. He knelt down beside her and drew her into his arms, knowing that he would never forgive himself for putting her through this ordeal. 'It's all right, sweetheart. Everything is going to be fine, I promise you that.'

'How can it be?' she whispered, raising teardrenched eyes to his.

'Because there's no problem in the world that we can't solve so long as we do it together.' He brushed the damp curls off her forehead. 'You, me and our baby.'

Her eyes widened in shock. 'How did you guess?'

'It wasn't that difficult.' He kissed her gently on the cheek. 'I am a doctor, don't forget—I've been trained to recognise the signs.'

'I'm so sorry, Matt. I never meant it to happen. I just didn't think that it would when we were always so careful.'

Her voice rose on a wail and he pulled her closer, rocking her to and fro while she sobbed out all the fear and heartache of the last few weeks. Matt couldn't bear to imagine what she must have been through and blamed himself for it too. If only he'd told her how much he loved her then none of this would have happened.

He waited until she was a little calmer then urged her to her feet. 'Let's get out of here. We need to talk, Rachel, and we can't do it in here, can we?'

'But what about the others?' she protested as he steered her along the passageway that led out to the car park. 'They'll think it's very odd if we just up and leave without saying anything.'

'What people think is the least of my worries,' he said firmly, unlocking the car and helping her inside. He dropped a kiss on her forehead then fastened her seat belt for her. 'Anyway, I doubt we'll be missed for very long. They'll be too busy celebrating.'

'Well, if you're sure it's all right…'

'It will be fine. Don't worry.' He tilted her face up to his and kissed her lips. 'We have more important things to think about.'

'I don't want you to feel that you have to do anything you don't want to do,' she began, and he sighed softly as he placed a gentle finger against her lips.

'I don't, so you can get that idea right out of your head.' He looked deep into her eyes. 'I love you, Rachel. I only wish I'd told you that sooner but I was too afraid to admit how I felt to myself or to you.'

'You love me?' she whispered, her eyes enormous as she stared back at him.

'Yes. Now, let's go home and see if we can sort this all out.'

Rachel nodded mutely. She appeared too stunned to say anything. Matt got into the car and drove them back to his house, hoping that he had managed to convince her he was telling the truth. He couldn't bear it if she thought he had only said he loved her because of the baby, when it wasn't true.

The thought nagged away at him as he ushered her into the sitting room. The fire had died down so he added a fresh log and soon had it blazing away. His breath caught as he turned and saw how beautiful Rachel looked with the firelight bringing out the chestnut glints in her hair. He loved her more than life itself and there was no way that he was prepared to lose her.

'Would you like something to drink?' he asked as his resolve hardened.

'A cup of tea would be nice,' she said quietly, not quite meeting his eyes. 'Although I'd like to brush my teeth first, if you don't mind.'

'Of course I don't mind. You know where everything is, so help yourself.'

'Thank you.' She started towards the door, stopped and turned back. 'About the baby, Matt—'

'Later. We'll talk about everything once you've tidied yourself up.' He closed the gap between them and dropped a gentle kiss on her cheek. 'Just remember that I love you, Rachel, and that nothing will ever change that.'

'I had no idea,' she whispered.

'How could you have known when I made such a good job of hiding my feelings?' He rubbed the pad of his thumb along her jaw and felt her tremble. His confidence soared because it proved she wasn't indifferent to him. 'I only wish I'd told you the truth before now, then we could have avoided all this upset.'

'I never gave you the chance to say how you felt about anything,' she said, her voice catching. 'It's not your fault, Matt, it's mine. All of it.'

'It's nobody's fault,' he said firmly. He kissed her again then headed to the kitchen and set about making the tea. Rachel hadn't said how she felt about him yet, but he refused to believe that she didn't care about him. The fact that she intended to have his baby proved that she did.

He smiled as he dropped tea bags into the pot. From now on life was going to be very different. There would be no more holding back, no more guilt, definitely no regrets. He would embrace the future and what lay in store for them all—him, Rachel and their son or daughter.

Rachel sighed she made her way back down the stairs a short time later. Matt's reaction to the news that she was pregnant had stunned her. She was very much aware that she had done him a grave injustice. She had simply assumed that he would be upset about the baby instead of letting him tell her how he felt himself. It just seemed to confirm how little she really knew about relationships.

It was an unsettling thought and it was hard to shrug it off as she went into the sitting room. Matt had poured their tea and placed the cups on the table in front of the fire. Rachel sat down on the sofa, feeling incredibly nervous as she picked up her cup and saucer. It wasn't just Matt's reaction to her being pregnant that had shocked her, of course. She'd been stunned when he had told her that he loved her. Although she desperately wanted to believe him, she couldn't help having doubts. What if he had only told her that because he'd felt it was the right thing to do in the circumstances?

The cup clattered back onto its saucer and she saw Matt look at her. Even though it was tempting just to accept what he said, she knew in her heart that she needed to be absolutely sure about his feelings for her. 'I don't want you to feel that you have to…well, pretend, Matt.'

'What do you mean?'

'You said that you loved me but are you sure that it's true? You're not just saying that because of the baby?'

'No, I'm not!' he exclaimed forcefully. 'I know it's taken me a long time to admit it but I love you, and it has nothing to do with the fact that you're having my baby.'

Rachel's heart overflowed with happiness when she heard the conviction in his voice. 'You can't imagine how wonderful it feels to hear you say that and know that you mean it.'

'Oh, I think I can.' He smiled at her with a wealth of tenderness in his eyes. 'I can imagine only too well how marvellous it must feel to know that you're loved.'

Rachel knew what he was asking her and all of a sudden it was the simplest thing in the world to give him the answer he wanted. 'You don't need to imagine it any longer because it's true. I love you, Matt. So very, very much.'

'Wow!' He laughed deeply. 'It feels even better than I thought it would, especially as I'd convinced myself that you didn't care a fig about me after you announced that you were leaving Dalverston.'

'I never wanted to leave,' she admitted. 'I just thought it was the right thing to do.'

'Because you didn't know how I'd feel about becoming a father again?'

'Yes. I…I thought you'd be horrified and I was afraid that you would end up hating me.'

'I could never hate you,' he said so sincerely that it brought tears to her eyes. He leant forward and she saw fleeting sadness cross his face. 'If I hadn't found out tonight by accident, would you have left without saying anything?'

'No! I always intended to tell you about the baby,

Matt. I just decided that it would be better if we weren't together at the time. That way you wouldn't feel as though you had to stay with me for the sake of our child. I didn't want you to feel trapped.'

He shook his head. 'I would never have felt like that, Rachel. I'm thrilled to bits that I'm going to be a dad again.'

'You really mean that, don't you?' She smiled at him, uncaring that tears were streaming down her cheeks.

'Of course I do.' He came and knelt in front of her, his face filled with wonderment as he placed his hand ever so gently on her stomach. 'The thought that there is a new life growing in there all because of our love for each other is just so wonderful. Thank you, Rachel. Thank you so much for giving me such a marvellous gift.'

'There's no guarantee the pregnancy will go to term,' she said quickly. Even though she didn't want anything to spoil this moment for them, she had to be honest about the risks involved. 'I'll need to have all kinds of tests done because of my age…'

'I realise that. But no matter what happens, darling, it won't change how I feel. It couldn't do. I love you and I want to be with you for ever. This baby is just a wonderful bonus.'

He kissed her softly on the lips, a kiss of great tenderness that quickly turned to one of passion. Rachel kissed him back, wanting him to know how much she loved him. They made love right there on the rug in front of the fire, their bodies warmed by the blaze as well as the heat of their desire. Rachel's heart overflowed with happiness as she gave herself up to Matt's tender ministrations and allowed all the misery of the past few weeks to melt away. She would never ever doubt him again. She knew now in her heart that he would always be true to her, that he loved her and wanted her for evermore. Maybe that was the key to a lasting relationship, she thought in surprise: trust. She had never trusted anyone before but she trusted Matt and nothing that happened from this moment on would destroy that trust.

It was a moment of revelation she would remember for the rest of her life, a life she would share with Matt and their child, hopefully. When they finally drew apart she told him that and saw the tears that shimmered in his eyes as he realised she was giving him another precious gift. He kissed her hungrily then drew her close, pulling a throw off the sofa and covering them with it so that they were cocooned in their happiness and she couldn't begin to explain how it made her feel, safe, secure, loved. She had the whole world right here, she thought dreamily, everything she wanted and needed. How lucky she was.

Matt felt a wave of relief wash away the nightmare that he had lived with for weeks. There wasn't a doubt in his mind that Rachel had meant it when she had said that she loved him and he couldn't describe how it made him feel. To know that this beautiful, caring woman wanted him for ever and ever was too much to take in. He kissed her hair, feeling the silky waves clinging to his lips. He had been given the rarest, most precious gift of all: he was loved.

'What are you thinking?'

He tipped his head to the side and smiled at her. 'That I'm the luckiest man alive to be loved by you.'

'And I'm the luckiest woman alive to be loved by *you*,' she replied softly, kissing the side of his jaw.

'Hmm, that feels so good,' he murmured, drawing her closer so that she could feel exactly how good it had been, and she giggled, a girlish, happy sound that filled him with delight.

'You are insatiable, Matthew Thompson!'

'Guilty as charged,' he replied, nibbling her bare shoulder. 'I'm not going to argue with you, so does that win me any extra brownie points?'

'No, it doesn't…well, maybe a few,' she relented as he drew her even closer. 'However, I think we need to finish our talk before we tot up how many points you've scored.'

'About us and the baby, you mean?' He lay back on the rug, drawing her into his arms so that her head was cushioned on his bare chest. 'That's easy. Obviously, we're going to get married and live happily ever after…'

'Whoa! Hang on a second.' She sat up and stared at him. 'Did you say married?'

'Of course.' He ran a finger down her cheek, let it flow on towards her collar bone, his intentions clear until she grabbed hold of his hand.

'There is no "of course" about it! Marriage is a huge commitment.'

'So is having a baby and we're doing that, aren't we?' He smiled up at her. 'Call me old-fashioned, Rachel, but I believe in marriage. I think it's the best basis for two people who want to build a life together. It also offers stability when there are children involved.'

'Hmph! You make it sound very romantic. What happened to love and lust, etcetera?'

'Oh, there will be lots of that!' He pulled her down beside him and gently rolled her onto her back then kissed her lips. 'I want to marry you because I love you, because I want to spend the rest of my life with you. I want to know that you're mine and that no matter what happens we'll always be together.'

He kissed her lingeringly, savouring the sweetness of her mouth. It was an effort to continue when he finally drew back. 'I also swear on my honour that once we are married I shall see it as my duty to keep lust alive and fully functioning. I definitely don't intend to take you for granted if that's what you're worried about.'

'It did cross my mind,' she said, grinning shamelessly up at him.

'Then don't let it cross it again.' He rose to his knees and took hold of her hand. 'So will you marry me, Rachel Mackenzie, and make me the happiest as well as the luckiest man in the world?'

'I'll need to think about it,' she replied, pretending to give the idea due thought. She squealed when he pulled her into his arms and kissed her soundly. 'All right, then, yes! Yes, I'll marry you, Matt, although what Heather and Ross are going to think about us getting married is anyone's guess.'

'They'll be thrilled to bits, especially when they find out about the baby,' he assured her with a confidence that stemmed from pure joy. Nothing would spoil their happiness. He wouldn't let it!

'Let's hope they are both up for a spot of babysitting,' Rachel murmured, pulling him towards her.

That marked the end of the conversation, not that

Matt was sorry. They had far better things to do and they did them too. As they lay together in his bed later that night, he felt as though he was floating on air. He had found the woman who was going to make his world complete again and they were having a child. Life couldn't get any better than this!

Two years later....

A soft breeze blew in off the ocean, cooling the heat of the day to a bearable level. Matt stood beside the platform that had been built above the shore and watched the waves lapping at the glistening white sand. It was his wedding day and he knew that it was going to be a very special occasion, one he and Rachel would remember for the rest of their lives with pleasure.

They had flown to Thailand at the beginning of the week and spent several days in Bangkok completing the formalities. Once that was done they and their guests had been driven to Hua Hin on the coast. Rachel had confessed that it had always been her dream to be married by the ocean and he had pulled out all the stops to make sure that she had the wedding she wanted. It was winter back home in England but here in this tropical paradise the sun shone each and every day. Another wonderful omen for their life together.

The music suddenly changed, the triumphant strains of the Wedding March heralding his bride's arrival. Matt turned to face her, feeling his heart overflow with love. She had been very secretive about her dress and had forbidden him to take even the tiniest peek at it, but it had been worth the wait. Rachel looked a vision in the simple silk gown she had chosen for the occasion with tiny, star-like white flowers in her hair.

His smiled at her then let his gaze move on to the people who had travelled all that way to celebrate them getting married. Heather was here with her husband, Archie, both of them looking so gloriously happy that Matt's own pleasure intensified. Ross was also here with Gemma at his side and it was obvious that they were very much in love too. Ben and Zoe were laughing as they held hands with their daughter, who was skipping along beside them. They too had the look that all couples in love shared, one of happiness and pride. How odd that a cancelled wedding had led to so many people finding true love.

'Dada!'

Matt's smiled widened when he recognised a familiar little voice. He stepped forward and lifted the little girl out of her mother's arms. Sophie Jane Thompson was the image of her mother from her shiny chestnut curls to her huge brown eyes and he adored her.

'Hello, princess. Have you been a good girl for Mummy?'

Sophie nodded her head, setting the tiny flowers that had been woven through her hair bobbing. She was wearing a white dress too, with frilly white socks and white satin shoes. Matt put her down on the ground and took a firm hold of her hand as he smiled at Rachel.

'You look beautiful,' he said softly, loving her with his eyes.

'Thank you,' she replied, smiling up at him as she

slipped her hand into his. 'Not changed your mind, have you? You still want to go ahead with this?'

'Oh, most definitely.'

He dropped a kiss on her lips then led her towards the arch of flowers that marked the entrance to the podium that had been erected for the ceremony. There was a muslin canopy overhead to shade them from the sun and more flowers arranged in huge vividly coloured displays, but Matt was barely aware of his surroundings as he made his vows to love and cherish Rachel until the day he died.

This was what mattered most, he thought. These promises they made. He meant every word and knew that Rachel meant them too, and happiness filled him to the brim. They were going to have the most wonderful life together.

GREEK DOCTOR
CLAIMS HIS BRIDE

BY

MARGARET BARKER

MILLS & BOON

First published in Great Britain 2009
Paperback edition 2010
Harlequin Mills & Boon Limited,
Eton House, 18-24 Paradise Road, Richmond, Surrey TW9 1SR

© Margaret Barker 2009

ISBN: 978 0 263 86986 6

Harlequin Mills & Boon policy is to use papers that are natural, renewable and recyclable products and made from wood grown in sustainable forests. The logging and manufacturing process conform to the legal environmental regulations of the country of origin.

Printed and bound in Spain
by Litografia Rosés, S.A., Barcelona

Margaret Barker has enjoyed a variety of interesting careers. A State Registered Nurse and qualified teacher, she holds a degree in French and Linguistics, and is a Licentiate of the Royal Academy of Music. As a full-time writer, Margaret says, 'Writing is my most interesting career, because it fits perfectly into family life. Sadly, my husband died of cancer in 2006, but I still live in our idyllic sixteenth-century house near the East Anglian coast. Our grown-up children have flown the nest, but they often fly back again, bringing their own young families with them for wonderful weekend and holiday reunions.'

CHAPTER ONE

TANYA hurled the mop with the spider still clinging to it straight out of the window. It was a trick she'd learned from her grandmother when she had been very small and absolutely petrified of the giant spiders that had scurried along the floor of her bedroom.

"Just pick up a mop, dangle it over the spider and it will cling on, thinking it's found a friend," Grandmother Katerina had told her all those years ago, and it was still a good solution.

"Ouch!"

The sound of a deep masculine voice muttering a few choice Greek expletives rose up from the courtyard below her window. Tanya leaned out so that she could see the swarthy man beneath her and for a brief moment she thought she might be dreaming. It couldn't be…no, the low evening sunshine was playing tricks with her eyes…Manolis Stangos was in London, not here on the island…wasn't he?

"Tanya?"

"Manolis?"

"For a moment I thought you were Grandmother Katerina moving back into her old house."

He was speaking rapidly in Greek as if to a stranger, none of the smooth, silky tones he'd used when they had been together all those years ago. Tanya ran a hand over her long auburn hair. She was sure her afternoon cleaning session had done nothing to help her jet-lagged appearance. A cobweb was still clinging to her hand but thankfully the large scary spider was now scuttling away across the courtyard.

"Thanks very much! I know it's a long time since you saw me but I can't have aged all that much. Anyway…" Tanya swallowed hard as she rubbed a dusty hand over her moist eyes "…Grandmother—Katerina—died a few months ago…"

"I'm sorry. It's just that you were the last person I expected to see here."

His voice was softer now. Tanya took a deep breath as she tried to remain calm. This unexpected encounter was playing havoc with her emotions.

"Considering it's now my house, I feel I've every right to be here."

"I'm getting a crick in my neck looking up at you. Aren't you going to come down and check if you've fractured my skull with that mop, Dr Tanya?"

He smiled, and she could see the flash of his strong white teeth in his dark, rugged face.

"News filtered through to me in London that you'd qualified. I always knew you would in spite of…in spite of everything that might have stopped you."

She looked down at Manolis and found herself relaxing.

"I'll come down and check you out, although you could surely do that yourself, Dr Manolis," she said as she turned away from the window, taking her time to negotiate the narrow wooden staircase.

By the time she'd reached the tiny, low-beamed kitchen, Manolis had come in through the open door. Nobody ever closed their doors on this idyllic island of Ceres where she'd been born. Doors were closed when you went out. That was to make sure a stray goat or donkey didn't wander in and help itself to the food in the larder, but the key to the house was always left in the lock on the outside so that friends and neighbours would be able to get in if they needed to.

Meeting up with Manolis again after six long years had almost taken her breath away. She'd forgotten how handsome he was. Eight years older than her, he must be…what? Quick mathematical moment…thirty-six, because she was twenty-eight.

She remembered them celebrating her twenty-second birthday together. She'd just told him she was pregnant. She remembered how shocked he'd looked, how confused she'd felt.

"OK, are you going to check whether you've cracked my skull?"

"Sit down, Manolis. You're too tall for me to check it when you're towering above me, and you make me nervous."

"Nervous?" Manolis laughed. "When were you ever nervous of me?"

He pulled a chair out from under the check-clothed table and sank down, spreading his long legs out in front of him. She remembered that as a child when the impossibly tall Manolis had come into her grandmother's tiny kitchen he'd seemed to fill the whole room. She'd tried so hard to get his attention in those far-off days but he'd barely seemed to notice her.

"Keep still, will you?"

Her fingers were actually trembling as she smoothed back the thick black hair that framed his dark, rugged face. How many times had she run her fingers through his hair? And yet her reaction had always been the same. That sexy frisson she got from simply touching him. It travelled all the way down through her body and before she knew it her legs were turning into jelly, and as for her insides—well, that was almost impossible to cope with at such close quarters.

She sat down quickly on a chair. Her eyes were almost level with his.

"I can't see anything wrong with your forehead. Not a mark on it. You're just making a fuss about nothing."

If she continued using her bantering tone she could cover up the fact that she was so deeply moved she wanted to give in to her impossible desire. She wanted to laugh and cry at the same time. She wished she could turn the clock back to the time when they'd been so deliriously happy, so madly in love.

Manolis stirred on the small hard chair, unable to believe that he was so close to Tanya again. He had to clench his hands to stop himself reaching out and pulling her into his arms. Desire was rising up inside him, that familiar stirring in his loins that wouldn't cease until they'd made love again. But that would never happen. He'd known when she'd turned down his proposal of marriage for the second time that he would never try again. She was lost to him for ever and they couldn't go back.

"I think you'll live," Tanya said as she resisted the temptation to place her lips on his forehead in the pretence that she was kissing it better.

For a moment she wondered how he would react if she gave in to temptation. She could try…but he had a hard look on his face now. The moment had passed.

"I've got to go," he said evenly.

"Does your mother still live on the end of the street? Are you visiting her?"

He hesitated. "She still lives there. But actually I bought the house next to yours when I came back to Ceres a couple of years ago."

"Next door? In Villa Agapi?" She drew in her breath. Agapi was the Greek word for love. She had just come to live in Villa Irini, which meant peace. Love and peace next door to each other.

"Manolis, are you here on holiday?"

"I work here on the island again. I wanted to return and it was better for…"

He broke off as the sound of a child's voice came from the street.

"Papa, Papa? Where are you?"

Manolis hurried through the courtyard and stood by the open door that led to the street.

"Papa!" The little girl flung herself at him. He lifted

her high into the air. She was laughing and screaming with delight as he lowered her into his arms.

Tanya remained absolutely still as she watched the joyous reunion of a little girl with her father. Her hands were clenching the side of the table to steady herself as she listened to the rapid non-stop Greek words that flowed from the child as she told her father she'd had the most exciting day. It emerged that she'd brought her papa a picture she'd painted at school but she'd put it down on a stone at the side of the path as she'd bent to take her shoes off because she hated wearing shoes when it was hot and the wind had blown it away and she wanted to paint another one now as soon as they got home because…

The story came out in one long breath. As she listened to the chatter, Tanya felt tears prickling behind her eyelids. This child, this beautiful little girl, couldn't be much younger than the child she'd lost. Their child. She and Manolis should have had a child like this one but…

"Chrysanthe, *agapi mou*," Manolis said, setting his excited daughter down on the cobbles of the courtyard. "Come inside and meet an old friend of mine. Tanya, this is Chrysanthe."

The little girl hurried across the small courtyard and through the open door of the kitchen, smiling, friendly, totally trusting.

Tanya tried to swallow the lump in her throat. This wasn't what she'd thought would happen today. It was all too poignant. Her confused emotions were draining her strength away. She reached out a hand towards the child.

Chrysanthe smiled as she placed her hand in Tanya's.

A pretty little dimple had appeared in the adorable child's cheek. Who did she get that from? Must have been from her mother. The unknown woman who'd obviously taken Tanya's place so soon after they'd split up. How could he have met up with someone and conceived a child so quickly?

"Do you live here, Tanya?" Such a lovely lilt to the lisping childish tone.

Tanya cleared her throat. "Yes. I've just moved in today."

"I like your hair." The little girl took her hand out of Tanya's and reached up to stroke her auburn hair. She looked up at her father. "Daddy, why couldn't my hair have been this colour?"

Oh, no, please don't say things like that!

Tanya heard Manolis's swift intake of breath.

"It's very…unusual," he said quickly. "You can't… er…choose which colour your hair will be when you're born. Sometimes the colour comes from your daddy and sometimes from your mummy."

"My mummy's got blonde hair but she says it's out of a bottle. Could I get some of this colour out of a bottle, Tanya?"

"You probably could, but I prefer your hair the colour it is."

"Like Daddy's?"

Tanya swallowed hard. "Yes, like Daddy's." Her eyes met Manolis's and she turned away to avoid the poignancy of this discussion.

"Did you have a good journey, Tanya?" Manolis said quickly, breaking the uncomfortable silence.

"I'm always relieved when I get here because it seems to take for ever."

"Where did you come from?" Chrysanthe asked.

"Australia."

"Australia? My daddy used to live there, didn't you, Daddy?" The little girl had started to speak English now. "He told me all about it. It's a long way from here, isn't it? It's got lots of croccy... What are they called, Daddy?"

"Crocodiles."

Tanya noticed his voice was husky. He was reaching down and hoisting his daughter onto his shoulder.

"Your English is very good, Chrysanthe."

"My mummy's English. Are you English or Greek, Tanya?" The little girl looked down at Tanya from Manolis's shoulders.

"I'm both—like you. English mummy, Greek daddy. But I was born here on Ceres."

"I was born in England but I like living here best. Daddy used to bring me out to stay with Grandma Anna and all my cousins. I love being in my grandma's house. It's such fun playing with my cousins. Look, I can touch the ceiling! Daddy, I can touch the ceiling!"

"Tanya, I'll take Chrysanthe away and we'll leave you in peace. I'm sure you've got lots to do still."

Peace! How did he ever think she could be at peace when there were so many questions to be answered? She'd come back here to escape her stressful life in Australia but had never imagined she would have to face the turmoil of the past. Yes, she'd come to find peace but that wouldn't happen now, not while she was living next door to Manolis.

Manolis cleared his throat. "I know you've had a long journey, Tanya, but would you consider coming out for supper with me this evening?"

She'd never heard him sound so nervous. As if he was expecting her to squash the idea as impossible. Well, she had turned him down just before they'd split, only to bitterly regret it when it had been too late to change things.

"That would be after I've settled Chrysanthe with Mother. She stays with her when I'm on call. My mother has a huge bedroom—with plenty of room for her grandchildren—and they all love to stay there. We're a very close family, as you know, and…"

His voice trailed away. He was looking down at her, his eyes betraying how much he wanted to see her again that evening.

"Yes, I'd like that. There are so many questions I want to ask."

"Me too. So, I'll call in about eight. We could go to Giorgio's."

"How is he?"

"His health isn't too good but he sits in the corner and watches the rest of his family do all the work." He turned away, one hand still holding onto the child on his shoulders. "Bend your head, my darling, as we go through the door."

"Goodbye Chrysanthe. Come again to see me." She meant it wholeheartedly.

"Ooh yes, I will. Daddy, I'm still taller than you. When I'm grown up I might really be taller than you. When you're an old man I'll put you on my shoulder and…"

The voices became indistinguishable as father and daughter made their way down the street. Chrysanthe was a beautiful little girl, but Tanya had never imagined that Manolis could have moved on so quickly after they had split up.

He'd moved on. She mustn't dwell on it. She would remember only the happy times. She found herself wishing that little Chrysanthe was her child but stopped herself as soon as the thought occurred. No regrets. She had to move on with her life and not spend time wishing for the impossible.

Upstairs again, she ran hot water into the half-size hip bath in her tiny bathroom. As a child she'd loved to be bathed by her Grandmother Katerina when she'd been staying with her. She'd never dreamed that her grandmother would leave this house to her. Katerina must have realised how much Tanya loved it.

Tanya stripped off and stepped into the warm water. Mmm, it was bliss to lie back with the bath foam she'd bought in the airport shop in Sydney only yesterday. It hadn't occurred to her that today she would be preparing to go out for supper with Manolis. Once more she had to remind herself that nothing had changed between them. And now that Manolis was a married man, the gap between them must remain wide.

She closed her eyes and smoothed some more foam over her skin as she leaned her head against the back of her bath…

Tanya woke with a start and her arms flapped around in the cold water as she heard someone calling her from downstairs. Above the bath she could see moonlight shining through the tiny little window.

Manolis stood downstairs with his hand resting on the wooden banister. "Tanya, are you OK up there?"

"Yes, yes, I'm fine." She hauled herself out of the bath, spilling water onto the tiles. "I must have fallen asleep."

Manolis heard the splashing water and had a sudden mental image of Tanya's slim, lithe figure emerging from the tiny bath where Grandmother Katerina had often bathed him when he had been a small child and his mother had been too busy to cope as she'd fed the latest baby. He was sorely tempted to ask if he could join her upstairs but he knew what the answer would be. Still, a man could dream, couldn't he?

He put on his sternest voice so that Tanya would have no idea how much she'd already affected him. "That's a dangerous thing to do—fall asleep in the bath. You should never do that!"

Tanya was already climbing the narrow wooden steps up to her bedroom, clutching the towel around her. If it slipped and Manolis looked up through the rungs of the wooden stairs that connected the kitchen with the top floor… She glanced down as she stepped off the stairs into her bedroom but couldn't see him below her.

"I know it's dangerous but the bath's so small my knees were up to my chin so it's unlikely I could have slipped under the water," she called breathlessly, as she searched for something to put on. Not the smelly travel clothes…how about these trousers? She pulled them out of her case along with new, lacy black knickers. They were to make her feel good, nothing to do with the fact that she was going out with the sexiest man on the island—in the world.

It took her barely five minutes to emerge from her room fully clothed in three-quarter cut-off denims, white T-shirt and flip-flops. She'd spent a lot of time swimming and running at the beach near the hospital just outside Sydney and rarely used make-up for a casual night out. She would blend in with the tourists in Giorgio's taverna. And she knew for a fact that Manolis preferred a natural-looking face—not that it was any concern of hers!

He turned as she came down the stairs and in spite of his resolutions he whistled. "Mmm, you scrub up well, Tanya!" he said in English.

She laughed. "You haven't lost the Australian accent you picked up, Doctor. Are you trying to make me feel at home?"

"Something like that." He moved to the bottom of the stairs, placing his hands, which seemed to have a mind of their own, on her shoulders. For a brief moment he hesitated before pulling her gently against him and kissing her on both cheeks.

"Welcome home," he said in the sexiest, most unplatonic tone. He hadn't meant to inject all that warmth and innuendo into his words but spending five minutes waiting for Tanya, knowing that she was first naked, then semi-naked then…well, it had played havoc with his intentions.

She tried to move backwards to escape his arms but she was pinned against the end of the banister.

She took a deep breath as she prepared to ask the big question. "Manolis, is your wife with you here on the island?"

"We're divorced. My ex-wife is in London," he said evenly.

She pushed her hands against his chest, making it quite clear that she wanted to escape this potentially dangerous embrace. There were too many questions that needed answers before she could begin to relax with him. But the fact that he was a free man made the situation a little easier…no, it didn't! Her emotions were already in turmoil.

"Let's go," she said quietly. "I'm looking forward to being back in Giorgio's."

She stepped out into the narrow cobbled street, terribly aware of Manolis's huge frame close behind her. She wasn't small by any means—her legs were long but she was quite short—so she'd always felt that Manolis towered above her. Glancing up at him as they walked together over the uneven cobbles, she missed her footing. He put out a hand to prevent her falling as she stumbled.

"Careful!" He took hold of her hand. The touch of his fingers unnerved her completely. "This part of the street is so dark," Manolis said as he waved his other hand upwards towards the light at the bend in the street. "There! That's better."

White light flooded down over them. "I know every stone along this street. You'll soon get used to it. How long do you intend to stay, Tanya?"

She gave a nervous attempt at a laugh. "Good question. The shortest answer is I don't know. It all depends…"

"On what?"

"On how I feel after I've had some time here."

There was a comfortable silence before Manolis spoke again. "The only thing is, if you didn't have any plans to return to Australia in a hurry, I was going to put a proposition to you."

She took her hand out of his. No! He wouldn't propose to her again, would he? The clock could never be turned back.

As if reading her mind, Manolis said, "That was perhaps an unfortunate phrase to use. This is a professional proposition. You see, I'm medical director of the hospital here and we need another doctor because it's the beginning of the tourist season."

He paused and took a deep breath before continuing. "There is a hospital board of governors who have the final say when a doctor is appointed but I'm the one who assesses the medical credentials of a candidate."

She was still listening, even appearing slightly interested. Well, he could but ask. "Would you like me to put your name forward?"

Tanya remained silent as she reviewed all the implications. Manolis walked on beside her, making absolutely sure that he didn't touch her. He wanted to tell her that he would never propose marriage to her again. Two proposals, two rejections from the love of his life was more than any man could suffer. But they did need a good doctor at the island hospital and he did want to have her near him as much as possible while she was here. He had no plans beyond that.

CHAPTER TWO

THE emotional warmth given out by the revellers, tourists and islanders in Giorgio's Taverna welcomed and wrapped around Tanya as if she'd never been away. As a small girl she'd been carried in here many times by her parents, elder brother, uncles, cousins and had often fallen asleep on somebody's lap, the music lulling her to sleep as the evening progressed. She would wake up in her own bed either at home with her parents or at Grandmother Katerina's, wondering how she'd been transported there.

Her brother Costas, who like his friend Manolis was eight years older than she, would sometimes tell her the fairies had carried her home in a special coach that ran over the cobbles without a sound. She'd liked to think that was true and whenever she found herself falling asleep at the table she'd made an effort to stay awake so that she could enjoy the journey home. But, however she'd tried, sleep had always got the better of her.

Manolis was trying to guide her to a table, one hand gently in the small of her back, but many people wanted to talk to them as they passed by.

"Dr Manolis, come over here! There's room on my table."

"Thank you… I'll see you later on…" Manolis was smiling as he repeated his friendly phrase and moved on between the tables.

"I'm heading for that table in the corner," he whispered as he stooped down towards her.

Tanya was aware of the many glances in their direction. One middle-aged lady put out a hand to detain her.

"It can't be!" she said in Greek. "You're Katerina's granddaughter, aren't you? You're the absolute image of her when she was young and beautiful like you. Apart from the colour of your hair. You got that from your lovely mother, didn't you? I remember when she arrived here from England. Very soon she was going out with your father, our young Dr Sotiris. Ah, he was such a handsome man." She giggled. "All the girls fancied him. Including me!"

The giggle turned into joyful laughter.

Tanya smiled, wanting to give the lady her full attention even though Manolis was making his impatience to move on very obvious

"How is your father? Still living in Australia?"

Tanya swallowed hard. "He died of cancer five years ago."

"Oh, I'm sorry. How's your mother?"

"She's married again to an old friend. She's happy."

She felt Manolis's hand putting pressure on her to escape if she could.

"Lovely to see you again!" Tanya moved away,

still smiling as she and Manolis finally reached the corner table.

Giorgio's son had seen them making their way through the crowded taverna and was already standing over the table they coveted, fending off potential occupants.

"*Efharisto*. Thank you, Michaelis," Tanya said, as she sank down on to the seat that was being held out for her.

"Good to see you back, Tanya. Have you come to work with Dr Manolis in the hospital?"

She hesitated. "I'm not sure what I'm going to do. First I need some holiday and then…who knows?"

Manolis smiled. "I'm trying to get her interested in applying for the newly vacant position."

Michaelis shrugged his shoulders. "What is there to think about? Tanya, you would be ideal as an island doctor. We have a beautiful hospital now. Not like the old days when your father had to cope with a small surgery and not enough medical help. Come into the kitchen to decide what you want to eat. Mama has got everything laid out on top of the ovens. The chicken in mataxa brandy is very good!"

"Did your mother make it?" Tanya asked.

"Of course!"

"Then I'd love to have some."

"Me too!" Manolis said. "And bring us a small selection of meze to start with, *parakalor*."

The sound of Giorgio playing on his accordion drifted over the happy voices. In spite of the general clamour, as she looked across the table at Manolis she felt as if they were the only two people in the room. It was almost as if they were back in their favourite Greek restaurant on the outskirts of Sydney.

A bottle of wine was placed on their table. "On the house," Michaelis said. "It's from my father to welcome Tanya back to where she belongs."

Tanya looked across and mouthed her thanks to Giorgio. He raised a hand from his accordion.

"What a welcome!" Manolis said as he poured the wine. "Does it make you want to live here permanently?"

"As I told you, I have no plans at the moment," Tanya said. Her words came out more sharply than she'd intended.

Manolis reined in his enthusiasm. Tanya had always had a mind of her own. "I didn't intend to upset you," he said evenly.

"I'm not upset. I just need time to think. I came here for a holiday and I don't want to have to make any decisions while I'm still jet-lagged."

"Of course you don't. It was just an idea. Take all the time you need regarding the vacancy at the hospital. The post has already been advertised and we've had a couple of applications. The current doctor is returning to England to take up a post in London. He's not going until the end of the month but we're expecting an influx of tourists very soon."

Michaelis poured wine into Tanya's glass. Manolis put a hand over his. "I'm on call tonight, Michaelis, so would you bring me a bottle of still water?"

Michaelis called the order to a young waiter who threaded his way through the tables and poured a glass of water for Manolis.

Manolis was anxious to return to their discussion about the vacant position but he waited until they were alone before continuing.

"We particularly need someone who knows the islanders and someone like you who was born here is absolutely ideal. In the past we've had outsiders who didn't really understand what working on Ceres involved. So, at the last meeting of the hospital board it was decided that if we could find an islander with good medical qualifications, that would be the candidate we would take. As I say, you would, of course, be ideal but it has to be your decision. I know you have a mind of your own."

He gave her a wry smile as he said this. For a few moments neither of them spoke. Tanya knew what he was referring to. She remembered that fateful day when she'd turned down his second proposal. How different her life would have been if she'd said yes.

She looked across the table. He lifted his glass towards her. "Here's to your stay here on the island, whatever you decide."

She raised her glass and took a sip. "I would have to be approved by the hospital board as well as you, wouldn't I?"

"Of course. We now do more operations than we used to. We're licensed to perform emergency operations when it would be counterproductive to try to get the patient over to Rhodes. And we do some elective surgery as well. So I'm still able to make use of the surgical skills and qualifications I needed in my previous London job as head of surgery. Our hospital grew from a very small surgery not so many years ago, as you will remember, so our rules here have to be more fluid than on Rhodes or on the Greek mainland."

He could feel his hopes rising as he saw the expression of increasing interest on her face. "But knowing the excellent grades you got in your finals and the fact that you're an islander born and bred, I know—"

"You know an awful lot about me." She looked across the table, her gaze unwavering. "Did you check my exam grades?"

He leaned back against his chair. "I contacted Costas around the time I knew you should have finished your finals. I wanted to make sure that…you were OK after…after everything that had happened. I knew you wouldn't have dropped out of medical school altogether but you might have needed to take some time off."

"I didn't take much time off."

"I think it would have been a good idea. Your health had suffered."

"Yes, yes." She looked around her. Nobody could hear what they were saying because of the noise. "You were probably right when you advised me to take a year off."

She swallowed hard as she remembered how confused she'd been after the miscarriage. She'd realised too late that her hormones and emotions had been all over the place. Still feeling that a baby was on the way and yet having to come to terms with the fact that she was no longer pregnant.

"I chose to continue and, of course, I didn't drop out of medical school. It had always been my dream to qualify as a doctor. All my life. Especially when I was very young and you and Costas were making fun of me or ignoring me completely. I thought to myself, One day I'll show you big boys and my dad I'm not just a silly little girl who enjoys playing with her dolls."

Manolis stared at her. He'd never heard her say anything like that before.

"I didn't know you felt like that." He paused and took a deep breath. "Were we awful to you, Costas and I, when you were growing up?"

Tanya attempted to shrug it off, wishing she hadn't been quite so vehement about something that had bugged her for years.

"Oh, you were OK," she said, lightly. "You were behaving like boys do when girls are around. Trying to be macho. Sometimes you even noticed me."

"We were only teasing you, Tanya," he said gently. "When you came out to Australia to begin your medical training I could see you were a force to be reckoned with. Ambitious, clever, full of potential. Wow, I wouldn't have dared to tease you then."

She smiled to try and lighten the mood she'd created. "Oh, you were wonderful with me—really supportive. I never felt patronised by the fact that you were a qualified doctor and I was only a student. It was just something I wanted to do for myself at that point in time. I suppose I was ambitious. I was one of the generation of girls who wanted everything. I didn't want to miss out on anything."

She lowered her voice. "When I found out I was pregnant I still wanted to continue with my studies. As I told you at the time, my mother had agreed to help me.

You probably remember she was actually delighted at the prospect of her first grandchild."

Her voice cracked as she reached her final heart-rending words.

He leaned across the table and took hold of her hand. She remained very still but she could feel the prickly tears at the back of her eyes waiting to be released.

"I couldn't understand why you wouldn't take time off," he said gently. "Why you wouldn't let me take care of you, why you turned me down when—"

"I think my hormones were jumping around too much. I wasn't sure if you were proposing because… well, because you thought it was the dutiful thing to do."

"Was that why you turned me down for the second time?"

"Manolis, let's defer this discussion, shall we?" she whispered. "I can see people looking at us."

"Of course."

She knew now she'd been mistaken to turn down his proposal. In the agonising weeks after they'd split up she'd realised how stupid she'd been. She'd destroyed the most essential part of her life. The love of the person she'd admired as a child and desired when she'd become an adult. And by the time she'd come to her senses it had been too late.

She swallowed hard, very aware of the big hand holding hers.

One of the young waiters put more meze on the table. Taramosalata this time to add to the kalimara and the Greek salad, all of which remained largely untouched.

Manolis held out a plate towards her. "Try some of these Ceres shrimps. You used to like them when your parents invited me for supper, I remember."

She removed her hand from his and took some of the tiny pink shrimps. "Delicious as always." She chewed slowly. "Some things never change."

"And some things do. You, for instance," he said gently.

She leaned back against her chair. "How have I changed?"

"Well...you always were stubborn but—"

"Stubborn? I suppose you mean when I didn't agree with something you wanted?"

He smiled. "Possibly."

She nodded. "I have to admit that some of the ideas I had when I was younger have changed. I don't think I would be quite so...well...stubborn, as you put it, now."

He wondered if he was in with a chance now with this older, wiser woman. No, of course not! If they were ever to become close again and he was to raise the question of marriage she would dash his hopes again. What did she mean when she'd questioned if his proposal had been merely dutiful? When the time was more convenient he'd quiz her further.

"So, you got all your information about me from Costas?"

"Mostly. We rather lost touch when he went to South America to work in that rural area. He hasn't answered any of my letters for ages!"

"He's chosen to live in a remote hospital near the Amazon. Sometimes he doesn't get his mail for weeks, months or at all. Often he can't get his letters sent out of the area. He's very dedicated to his work and doesn't have much spare time to worry about the outside world. My mother worries continually about him, of course, but she's adamant that he'll tire of this difficult life when he's had enough deprivation."

"He had a relationship in Australia that went wrong, I believe," Manolis said, quietly.

"Yes." She sighed. "These things happen."

Their eyes met and Tanya saw the moistness in Manolis's gaze before he looked down at his plate and began crumbling a piece of bread.

"You haven't drunk your wine."

Tanya took a small sip. "The jet-lag is getting to me. I'd better not drink it. It might make me sleepy and I want to stay awake. I feel that we…well, we're getting to know each other again."

"I was completely surprised when you turned up here today. I'd had no news of you for ages."

The people on the next table had now gone. He waited before he dared to broach the subject of their disastrous break-up again. He'd been so unhappy, so completely devastated and depressed that he couldn't imagine how Tanya had suffered when her physical health had been at an all-time low and she'd had to cope with the emotional confusion as well.

"I was so proud that you coped by yourself after I left Australia. It couldn't have been easy after…"

"After I'd lost the baby?" she said quietly.

"Yes. Costas said you went straight back to medical school."

"I was still in a state of shock, I think. As I said, I now know I should have taken some time off but I was very confused. Keeping busy kept me sane—or so I thought. You must have done something similar when you went off to England and almost immediately married."

She tried but failed miserably to disguise the bitterness in her tone of voice.

"Tanya! I…"

The young waiter was placing the main course plates in front of them, having removed the scarcely touched meze dishes.

"Tanya, it wasn't like that!" he continued when they were alone again. "You'd made it clear that you didn't want me. My old tutor in London had already contacted me about a newly created post as head of surgery which he said would be perfect for me. I was holding off discussing it with you because I wouldn't have gone over to London without you. When you virtually sent me away I decided to go for it. There was nothing to keep me in Australia any more. Victoria and I were old friends and we just happened to meet up again."

"How convenient!" She couldn't hold back the jealous anguish she'd experienced when she'd heard that he'd gone straight into the arms of another woman.

She took a deep breath. "And then married and had a baby very shortly after."

"On the rebound, I suppose," he said quickly, regretting how much she must have been hurt when she'd found he had a child. "But in mitigation…I'm not trying to sound as if I'm in the dock being tried for something…"

She watched him, anguished about what he'd done but still unable to crush her feelings for him.

"Go on, Manolis, tell me why you're hoping to be forgiven for jumping from one bed to another in double-quick time."

His eyes flashed. "You'd turned me down, told me to go away, said I was making things worse for you by staying, didn't you?"

"Yes, I did," she said quietly.

"So, Victoria being an old friend helped to salve my wounds. Somehow the comfort she gave me turned to sex. She fell pregnant. We married in haste and repented at leisure, as the old saying goes. It didn't take us long to realise that we would drive each other mad if we stayed together. We split up when Chrysanthe was six months old. Victoria was busy with her career and agreed with me that Chrysanthe would be brought up well on Ceres with the extended family here. My mother was overjoyed to add another granddaughter to her brood, and I came over as often as I could. I was on a long-term contract at the time so I had to wait before I could give in my notice. When a vacancy came up here on Ceres I applied and was accepted."

"They must have been delighted to have you here."

He nodded. "Yes. After a while I was offered the newly created post of Medical Director. We've had to expand in recent years because of the long tourist season from April to November. Better boats, more tourist facilities…"

His voice trailed away. He hoped he'd helped to justify what had happened since he'd walked away from her. She'd asked him to go, but maybe, just maybe she hadn't meant it.

He gave a deep sigh. There he went again, giving himself hope that he could turn the clock back to the time when they'd been so idyllically happy together.

"Dr Manolis." The young waiter was standing beside his chair. "There's a lady in the kitchen who wants to speak to you. She's climbed all the way up the *kali strata* to find you. Her granddaughter is having a baby in her house and there's some problem that I…"

The young man paused in embarrassment. Manolis was standing now, his hand on the young waiter's shoulders.

"I'll come and see her. In the kitchen, you say?"

Tanya was also on her feet. She'd heard what had been said and her medical training was taking over. She was holding her jet-lag in check as she followed Manolis up the three worn old stone steps that led from the main restaurant part of the taverna into the ancient kitchen with the moussandra platform in the high ceiling where Giorgio and his wife had first slept when the taverna had been their home before the six children had arrived.

The agitated elderly lady was sitting on a chair sipping a brandy that Giorgio had poured for her.

It took only a couple of minutes to elicit the medical information they needed. Manolis ascertained that there was someone with the woman who was in labour before telling the grandmother to stay where she was. Someone from the hospital would come to collect her later. Yes, he knew the house where she lived.

As they hurried down the *kali strata*, Manolis was on his mobile phone, speaking to the hospital maternity section, giving them instructions, telling them to send a midwife, a stretcher with a couple of porters, and have an ambulance standing by at the bottom of the *kali strata* in case an immediate transfer to hospital was required, as well as the medication and instruments he would require if that happened.

Tanya was trying desperately to keep up with him but the ancient cobblestones beneath her feet were treacherous and slippery and the moon was covered in clouds again. Manolis, sensing her difficulty, took hold of her hand.

"Nearly there," Tanya said in a breathless, thankful voice. "I know the house where this family lives. My father used to say the houses in this area are in the worst place to get to for an emergency. Neither up nor down."

"Exactly! And yet nobody around here has a phone," he said in exasperation as he reached for the old brass door knocker.

The door was opened almost immediately.

"Doctor! Thank goodness you are here. My daughter…"

Manolis and Tanya stepped straight into the living room where the patient was lying on a bed. A low moaning sound came from her as Manolis gently placed his hand on her abdomen.

"It's OK, Helene. I'm just going to see how your baby's doing."

Tanya had immediately recognised Helene as an old friend from her schooldays. Helene smiled through the pain as she recognised Tanya, holding out her hands towards her.

One of the hospital porters arrived shortly afterwards, carrying the Entonax machine that Manolis had ordered. He explained briefly that the maternity unit was very busy and they weren't able to send a midwife yet but that one would arrive as soon as she was free.

Manolis nodded. "That's OK. Tanya will assist me."

While he was examining the patient Tanya fixed up the machine and placed the mask over Helene's face.

"Breathe deeply into this mask, Helene," Tanya said in Greek. "That's going to help the pain. No, don't push at the moment, Manolis will tell you when. I know it's hard for you. You're being very brave."

Helene clung to Tanya's hand as if her life depended on it.

Manolis began whispering to Tanya in English. He was totally calm and in control of the situation but she recognised the urgency in his voice.

"The baby is in breech position. I'm going to have to deliver it as soon as possible because it's showing signs of distress and the heartbeat is getting fainter. Take care of Helene and don't let her push yet. I've tried to turn... No, it's too late, I'll have to deliver the baby now. Ask Helene to push now so I can get the baby's buttocks through... Yes, that's fine... No hold it for a moment— I'll need to do an episiotomy. Pass me that sterile pack." He took out a scalpel and some local anaesthetic injection and performed the procedure.

It seemed like an age as Tanya, almost holding her breath, kept her cool with the patient.

"Manolis has everything under control, Helene."

Please, God, she thought. Don't let her lose this baby. She knew the anguish of losing her own baby and wouldn't wish that on anybody. Helene had carried this baby to full term and she couldn't imagine anything worse than losing it at this late stage.

"The baby's buttocks are through, Tanya," Manolis said. "You can ask Helene to push. One last push should… There, brilliant!"

As he lifted the slippery baby up it gave a faint mewling cry, rather like a kitten that had been disturbed from its warm, cosy sleep.

"Let me see, let me see my baby!" Helene held out her arms.

"In a moment, Helene," Tanya said, gently. "Manolis will—"

"Tanya, will you cut the cord while I put a couple of stitches in?" Manolis said quietly.

Tanya quickly scrubbed up. Taking the surgical scissors from the sterile pack, she cut the cord and wrapped the protesting infant in a clean dressing towel.

"You've got a little boy, Helene," she said gently as she put the baby in her arms. Tears sprang to her eyes as she saw the wonderful first meeting of mother and son. She dabbed her eyes with a tissue and held back the tears. She had to stay professional and think only of her patient. But she sensed that Manolis was looking at her. He was standing beside her now and had put a hand on her shoulder.

She looked up into his eyes and saw they were moist and knew he was thinking of their baby. She swallowed hard. How could she have hardened her heart and told him to leave her? Why had he not understood in the first place what a miscarriage did to a woman? Would they ever recover from what might have been? Would it ever be possible to repair the damage they'd done to each other?

The future was impossible to predict. She would take one day at a time, but she knew without a shadow of a doubt that she wanted to stay here on Ceres for a long time, whatever happened. This was where she belonged.

She looked around the room, which had become rather crowded during the time that she and Manolis had been taking care of their patient. Standing near the door that led straight out on to the *kali strata* was a midwife, two porters and a young man who now identified himself as Lefteris, the baby's father. The midwife had held him back when he'd arrived a few moments ago.

"Baby's father is here, Manolis," Tanya said. "Is it OK if…?"

Too late! The young father had already sprung forward to embrace Helene and his son.

"We'll need to do some tests on your baby, Lefteris," Manolis said gently after a short while. "He had a rough passage into the world and we need to check him over." He smiled. "Although from the way he's crying, there doesn't seem to be anything wrong with him."

The midwife came forward and said that someone from the postnatal team would do the tests as soon as they got baby and mother settled into the hospital. The ambulance was waiting at the bottom of the *kali strata* for them now.

* * *

As they emerged from the crowded room into the cooler night air Tanya took a deep breath.

"It's such a relief that we got here in time," Manolis said, taking her hand in what seemed to have become a natural instinct again. "It could have been otherwise."

His hand tightened on hers as he became animated about a subject close to his heart. "It's so strange here on the island. On the one hand we've got the latest technology at the hospital and on the other we've got people who haven't even got a phone living in a difficult place to reach, yet within minutes of help."

He broke off in frustration at the situation. "Sorry, Tanya. I don't want to offload my problems on you." He let go of her hand and turned her to face him.

In the moonlight she could see his eyes shining with happiness as he looked down at her. "We could be such a good team you and I—I'm talking professionally, you understand," he added quickly. "It felt so right working together just now. We seemed to sense that."

"Yes, I felt the rapport between us was…natural," she said quietly.

He lowered his head and kissed her gently on the mouth.

Oh, those lips, those sexy, wonderful lips. She'd never thought she would ever feel them on hers again. She'd cried with frustration when she'd realised how much she wanted him and he was never coming back. But here he was.

He raised his head and murmured against her lips.

"So, do you want me to put your name forward as a candidate, Dr Tanya?"

Shivers were running down her spine. "Let's talk about it later," she murmured as she looked into his eyes.

She was making it patently obvious that she wanted him to kiss her again…

CHAPTER THREE

FROM somewhere in the distance Tanya could hear a cock crowing. She was hotter than usual. Where was she? She stirred in the strange bed and opened her eyes. Wooden rafters above her…where was the window?

The mists of her mind suddenly cleared. She was at Grandmother Katerina's, snug in the big bedroom at the top of the house. For several seconds she went back in time. She couldn't remember the end of the evening. She'd been in Giorgio's and… It was almost as if she'd been transported back here in the mythical fairy coach. There was a feeling of happiness tinged with sadness in the air.

And then she remembered. That kiss…that wonderful kiss! She'd murmured something to Manolis, held her face ready for another kiss, practically thrown herself at him. What did a woman have to do to make it obvious she would be putty in his hands? Oh, no! How humiliating to be rejected like that. Like what? She couldn't remember the details. Only the feeling that she'd expected Manolis to take her in his arms and…

She squirmed with embarrassment as she remembered how he'd made it clear that the kiss had been a one-off, the sort of thing that happened between old friends when they met again after a long time. Oh, he hadn't said that, in so many words. As far as she could remember, he hadn't said anything apart from suggesting they should get back.

At that point, the jet-lag she'd been holding off while she'd assisted at the birth of Helene's baby came back with a vengeance and she'd found herself agreeing with him. He'd held her hand but only in a courteous way so that she wouldn't slip on the treacherous cobblestones. As they'd reached Chorio, the upper town, they'd passed the door of Giorgio's Taverna where the door was closed but the revelry was continuing as always well into the night, and she'd found herself hoping Manolis would suggest they go in and join in the fun.

But they had kept on walking until he'd delivered her to her door and said goodnight. Not even a peck on the cheek! She told herself it was best they hadn't got emotionally involved. Too much too soon. Yes, Manolis had been very wise and she'd been stupid to think they could turn back the clock. There was too much between them to jump straight into any kind of relationship other than professional.

She began to doubt now whether she'd been too negative in her reaction to the idea of working at the Ceres hospital. She hoped that Manolis would put her name forward as soon as possible because, having worked with him last night and having had time to reflect on the proposition, she realised it would be ideal.

Her thoughts swung back to that idyllic period in her life when she and Manolis had lived together in

Australia. The key stages of their relationship came flooding back to her. Their initial friendship when they'd first met again in the hospital, she a medical student, he a well-respected doctor. He'd asked her to have a coffee with him so she could tell him what she'd been doing since he'd last seen her on Ceres when she'd still been a schoolgirl of sixteen and he'd just qualified as a doctor at the grand old age of twenty-four.

She'd looked around her as they'd entered the staff common room she remembered. Seen the envious glances of the female staff as she was escorted in by this fabulously handsome, tall, athletic, long-limbed, highly desirable doctor. She and Manolis had seemed to be on the same wavelength right from the start of their new adult relationship. That evening he'd taken her out to a Greek restaurant near the hospital, wined and dined her, and she'd fallen hopelessly in love.

Four weeks later, at his suggestion, she left her hospital accommodation and moved into his apartment. It was pure heaven! Somehow she managed to keep her mind on her medical studies and clinical work during the day but, oh, the nights! In that amazingly luxurious bed that always looked as if a herd of elephants had trampled over it in the morning!

She never really worked out why the contraceptive pill she was taking at the time failed. Whatever had caused it, she was totally unprepared when she realised her period was late. She remembered the shock as the result of her pregnancy test came out positive.

She experienced the awful conflicting emotions of wanting a baby with Manolis, yet wanting to plough on unencumbered to reach her goal of becoming a doctor as soon as possible. And then she realised that she could have both of these dreams. Many women had careers and children as well. She went to talk it over with her mother, who was truly delighted at the prospect of becoming a young grandmother.

She remembered the characteristic way her mother ran her hands through her still beautiful, shiny, long, auburn hair and pulled a wry face. "Not very good timing, Tanya, with your medical exams to get through, but don't you dare tell me you're not going to have my first grandchild! I'll take care of him or her while you're studying and working in the hospital. There won't be a problem…"

She saw the tears of happiness in her mother's eyes as she hugged her. When they separated her mother dabbed at her eyes with a tissue. "You go for it, my darling, and I'll be with you every step of the way."

"What will Daddy say?" Tanya asked tentatively.

"Oh, don't you worry about your father. I can handle him. He's a pussy cat really, although he may find it a bit irregular. Now, you run along and get back to that wonderful man of yours and tell him…well, break it gently. Men can be a bit strange at times like this but he'll come round to the idea if you give him time. I've known Manolis since he was a child and he's a good man. He'll stand by you. After all, it's not as if you got pregnant by yourself. It takes two to tango…"

When Manolis arrived back that evening she waited until after supper, having cooked one of his favourites, a chicken casserole. Then she told him the news. Oh, the shock on his face! She told him to sit down because he looked like he might faint. Then she joined him on the sofa. She told him she was definitely going to go through with it.

He said, "Of course you are!" Then he paused as if he was weighing his words. "And, of course, we must get married."

It was his tone of voice that had made her think he was simply doing the dutiful thing. He was still in a state of shock. She remembered her mother's words. *He's a good man. He'll stand by you.* Did she really want someone who was simply being dutiful?

"I don't think we should rush things," she told him.

"Are you saying you don't want to marry me?"

She took a deep breath before saying, "It's not as straightforward as that. I'm going to have a baby. Let's do one thing at a time. For the moment I want to make my preparations for being a good mother and also I need to get on with my studies."

But nothing prepared her for the agony of her miscarriage at fourteen weeks. It was all such a blur now. The sudden bleeding, Manolis driving her to hospital, being told she'd lost the baby, rushed into Theatre for a D and C.

She stifled the sob that rose at the back of her throat and looked out at the bright sunshine beyond the bedroom window, breathing deeply to calm herself again.

She had a sudden vision of Manolis standing by her hospital bed, telling her that he wanted to take care of her until she was well again. He was again asking her to marry him, to be his wife so that he could look after her. His voice had been so tender and kind. But she remembered the feeling of panic. Her hormones had been in control of her body, not she. She couldn't make decisions at a time like this when she was grieving for the baby that had died inside her. Couldn't commit to anything so life-changing as marriage.

So she'd looked up at Manolis and said she couldn't marry him. That it was best they separate until she didn't feel so confused. They'd only been together for a few months and everything had happened so quickly.

She turned her head to look around Grandma Katerina's bedroom, her bedroom now, and decided that was enough reminiscing for today. Time to get back to the present and continue with her new life.

No time for nostalgic reflection now! It was high time she got herself moving and sorted out her clothes. Just in case Manolis phoned to say she should go down to the hospital for an interview.

In the house next door Manolis stared up at the ceiling. He couldn't believe he'd passed up the opportunity of a night with Tanya. How often had he dreamed that she'd come back to him, that they were together again?

She had obviously been aroused by his kiss last night. Or had she just been pretending so as not to hurt his feelings? He could never be sure with Tanya. He'd lived with her for a few months, loved her, conceived a child with her and mourned with her when their unborn child had died in the womb. But he still couldn't understand her!

He remembered the night she'd told him she was pregnant. The shock of it had almost taken his breath away. He'd felt so guilty at giving her an added burden to the load of getting through her studies and exams. He had been so worried it would all be too much for her that it had only been in the next few weeks that he'd had time to begin anticipating how wonderful it would be to have a child with Tanya. She'd seemed so happy, and so capable of handling the situation that he'd begun to relax with her again.

She'd made it quite clear this was what she wanted, a child and a medical career. He'd realised that life was going to be wonderful when they were a family and not just a couple.

Then had come the awful evening when she'd started to bleed. She had been fourteen weeks, he remembered. He'd driven her to hospital, made sure she was admitted immediately but there had been nothing anyone could do to save their baby.

He swallowed hard as the awful sadness of their loss hit him again. His grief had been almost impossible to bear. But he'd forced himself to stay strong for Tanya. He wanted to protect her, to take care of her while she'd been weak and vulnerable. That was when he'd made the mistake—he realised it now—of again asking to marry her. He'd told her that he wanted to look after her, to make sure as a doctor that she had the best treatment until she was strong again. He'd told her not to rush herself with her answer. He would wait until she was stronger.

But she'd looked at him as if he was a stranger. Her eyes had been blank, he remembered. This wasn't the girl he knew and loved. He'd worked in obstetrics and witnessed how hormonal a woman could be when she'd lost a child. But it would pass—surely Tania would realise that her current situation was temporary.

He looked up at the ceiling as he tried to bring his emotions back under control. He hadn't been prepared for her rejection of him. She'd asked him to leave her.

He remembered going out through the ward door. Her mother had been coming towards him down the corridor. She'd put out her hand and taken hold of his. "It's best you leave Tanya alone for a while, Manolis. She's very confused. We're going to take her home for a while until she's strong again."

After she'd sent him away, rejecting the love he wanted to give her for the rest of his life, he'd felt he would never understand her. Not in a million years!

But last night, as he'd kissed her, he'd felt the desire rising in him as she'd snuggled against him and he'd felt that it might be possible to take this embrace to its obvious conclusion. But the old fears of rejection had nagged him. No, he'd been deluding himself, elated by the successful conclusion of a working partnership when they'd safely delivered Helene's baby together.

Oh, yes, she might have gone to bed with him. But he wanted more than a no-strings relationship with Tanya. But he could tell she valued her freedom. He could understand that now. She'd worked hard to become a qualified and now experienced doctor. She didn't need marriage.

Not like he did. As a young man he'd had two ambitions—one, to become a doctor and, two, to raise a family with the woman of his dreams. He'd had several no-strings relationships before he'd gone to Australia to take up a post in the hospital where Costas had been working. Meeting up with Costas's sister Tanya again when he'd been twenty-eight and she was a promising medical student of twenty-two had been like a bolt of lightning.

He'd been amazed when he had seen her for the first time for six years. The last time he'd seen her had been just before her father had taken the family out to Australia. He'd just spent his first year as a qualified doctor in the London hospital where he'd trained and had come over to Ceres for a short break. Tanya had been with Costas one time when they'd all walked down from Chorio to the harbour for drinks together as night fell.

He'd noticed she was growing into a very attractive young lady. But she had just been his friend's sister and far too young for him. But when he'd met her again six years later in Sydney he'd realised she was mind-blowing, with her fabulous, flowing, long auburn hair! Beautiful, attractive, intelligent, everything he'd ever dreamed of.

He remembered looking into her eyes, realising that she admired him too. Four weeks later he'd asked her to move into his apartment with him. They'd been idyl-lically happy until she'd told him she was pregnant. He'd been so worried about her, but he'd come to terms with it and relaxed, finally beginning to look forward to being a father. Then she had miscarried and their lives had changed completely. He had been totally rejected by the woman he adored at a time when he'd wanted to give her all his love and take care of her for ever.

The only way out of the impossible situation had been to start a new life and try to forget her.

"Papa!"

The sound of his daughter's voice brought him back to the present. She was downstairs, having come from his mother's house to see if he could take her to school. He always took her to school if he wasn't already working at the hospital. The school wasn't far away and the path was perfectly safe, but he liked to go with her.

"Chrysanthe, I'm coming, my love!"

The pile of clothes Tanya had brought from her suitcase to the bedroom could wait until she'd had some breakfast. She'd hardly eaten any supper at Giorgio's. She set off to walk round to the baker's to get some bread. As she stepped into the street, she caught a glimpse of Manolis turning the corner and the sound of his daughter's chatter. If she hurried she could catch him up before he reached the main street. No, she needed to cool down. She wasn't sure how she was going to face him today.

She lingered a while to make sure he was well on the way to Chrysanthe's school. She wasn't ready to face him just yet. Not until she'd made a cafetière of strong coffee and had some breakfast. He would probably phone later from the hospital and ask her down to discuss the job. At least, that was what she was hoping.

But he didn't! She spent the entire morning doing more cleaning, organising the kitchen, organising the bedroom, hanging up clothes, neatly placing her pants and bras in one drawer, her T-shirts in another, her swimwear in another...

"He should have phoned by now!"

She realised she'd spoken out loud. Maybe that was what happened to people who lived by themselves. She needed to get out more! The sun was shining outside. To hell with him! She wasn't waiting around any longer. She knew she really wanted this job now and so if he wasn't going to contact her she would go to the hospital and ask for it herself. Her father had been one of the founders of the new hospital, for heaven's sake! She would go in there with her head held high and ask to see the chairman of the board, whoever he might be these days.

Choosing the right clothes when you wanted to impress had always been a problem, because she preferred a casual look. Somewhere in the middle? Her cream linen suit? With a pale pink silk shirt underneath in case the heat got to her? Yes, that looked fine.

She sat down at her grandmother's dressing table. Looking in the mirror, she smiled at herself to remove the worry lines that had appeared on her forehead. At twenty-eight she needed to take care not to get real wrinkles settling there. The light tan she'd had since she'd gone to live in Australia needed very little makeup. A little foundation cream and a dash of lipstick was all she'd use. There!

Several strokes of the hairbrush smoothed out the long auburn hair and made it shine. She was glad she'd taken the time to wash it that morning. She could, of course, coil it up so that she looked more professional. Yes, that would definitely impress the chairman of the board, the old boy she was going to see. He was bound to be old, wasn't he? These types always were.

She piled her hair up on top and stuck it in place with several pins and grips. Over the years she'd practised this so often that it wasn't difficult for her. She immediately felt more efficient, intelligent, a better doctor, somebody that the chairman would take seriously.

"In short, Dr Tanya," she told her reflection, "you are the perfect candidate we've been looking for. The job is yours."

She smiled. "Thank you, sir. I accept."

Outside, the midday sun was stronger than she'd realised and the smart court shoes were hardly conducive to the cobblestones. Still, by the time she'd gone through the upper town and tried to persuade a taxi to collect her it would be quicker and easier to simply make her way on foot down the *kali strata*.

Halfway down, the door to Helene's house was wide open. Helene's grandmother was standing on the step and called out to her.

They chatted together. Tanya explained that she was on her way to the hospital and wouldn't come in for a drink. Yes, she would try to see Helene at the hospital and was glad that all was well with her. With praise ringing in her ears about the way that she and Manolis had delivered the baby, she continued on her way.

It was marginally cooler as she walked through the narrow streets of Yialos, the town by the harbour. The hospital, referred to by everybody as the New Hospital, was set back from the harbour near the church. It had started off as the doctors' surgery, she remembered, and had then been extended a great deal to qualify as a real hospital. It had certainly grown since she was last here.

She walked in through the front doors that led from the area where a couple of ambulances were parked. The reception area was very smart and, luxury of luxuries, it was air-conditioned! She really hadn't expected anything quite so grand here on Ceres. She began to feel slightly overwhelmed. And definitely overdressed. And the fact that she'd assumed she could just walk in and demand to see the chairman of the board was perhaps a little…

"Can I help you?" an English voice asked.

She moved forward to confront the white-uniformed receptionist who, unsmilingly, didn't seem as if she wanted to help at all.

"Actually, I was hoping to see…I'd like to make an appointment to see the chairman of the hospital board."

The young woman frowned. "Could you give me some details, Miss…?"

She cleared her throat and straightened her back. "I'm Dr Tanya Angelapoulos."

"Tanya!"

She turned at the sound of Manolis's voice—his most welcome voice! For a moment she felt like the young girl who'd craved his attention. No, she was all grown up now and didn't need his help—did she?

He came towards her, looking so handsome in his theatre greens, a mask still dangling round his throat, that she was sure her heart missed a beat.

"I've been in Theatre all morning. I was going to call you when I got a moment to spare about the job. I haven't been able to contact any of the board. Wheels run slowly out here and now everything closes down for lunch. Why are you here?"

"I just happened to be down in the town, shopping, and I thought I'd drop in to…er get the feel of the place, see if I might like to work here," she improvised.

He looked taken aback, she thought, and wished fervently that she hadn't arrived unannounced. He didn't seem at all pleased to see her.

"Look, come along to my office. I'll fill you in on what's involved with the job." He turned to looked at the receptionist, who was desperately trying to find out what was going on. "It's OK, Melissa, I'll look after Dr Tanya."

He put a hand on her back as he guided her out of Reception. He hadn't even noticed she was smiling.

Tanya could feel the gentle, soothing touch of Manolis's hand in the small of her back as they walked along the corridor. He was pushing open a door that led into a spacious room. He was obviously very important here. She'd noticed the sign on the door that read "HOSPITAL DIRECTOR." He was the one who'd got her interested in this job. Surely he could bypass the usual rules and sign her in?

As if reading her mind, he said, "If you've come about the job, I have to tell you we'll have to go by the book—at least in principle."

He waved an arm toward the seat at the other side of his desk. "There are only three men on the board, mainly chosen for their influence on the island. Two are retired doctors and worked with your father—so that's a definite plus. The other used to be mayor and can be a bit difficult."

"Manolis, I want to be appointed to this job on my own merit, not because the doctors on the board worked with my father."

"Of course you do, and you will be. You have brilliant qualifications, hospital experience and background. I'll get on the phone as soon as everybody wakes up from lunch and siesta which, as you know, is obligatory on Ceres."

"I'd forgotten about the routine here on Ceres. I've been away for twelve years and the routines you follow here…"

She looked up into his dark brown eyes and saw them twinkle with amusement. "It's not so much routine as necessity, Tanya. After a long morning in Theatre I need a break. Some lunch—why don't you join me?"

He managed to make it sound like he'd only just thought of it, although he'd been wondering how he could drag it into the conversation without eliciting a negative response. Playing hard to get was more difficult than he'd thought it would be this morning. Trying to hold down his feelings for this woman was almost impossible.

She hesitated, just long enough to make him think she was considering her answer.

"Yes, I'd like that," she said, giving him a cool little smile, not too much, not too little. Hopefully, just cool enough to make him forget how she'd looked up into his eyes last night, practically begging him to kiss her again.

"OK. I'm going to have a quick shower. Help

yourself to a magazine from the patients' waiting area over there. I'll be with you in a couple of minutes."

He was actually three minutes because she was timing him. She'd got a magazine open on her lap but the sound of the shower coming from his bathroom next door was tantalising her. She couldn't help thinking about that wonderful muscular body that had been hers all those years ago. Hers to snuggle next to in the night after they'd made wild, passionate love.

She remembered the way he would move languidly round to hold her in his arms again. And even though she'd thought she was exhausted she'd felt herself reviving, the whole of her body alive to his touch. She breathed deeply as she felt that even here. As she waited for him to finish his shower, she was becoming aroused. The thought that she could just walk across, open that door and—

"Hope you're not getting bored out here."

He stood at the other side of the room now, a white towelling robe covering his magnificent body, one hand furiously rubbing his thick dark hair with a towel.

"No...you were very quick, really." She stood up, hoping she didn't sound too eager to agree with him.

He strode across the room.

How could he stand next to her dressed like that? She only had to reach out and take hold of that belt, give it a tweak and...hey, presto, they would be on the carpet in no time at all!

"Are you OK, Tanya?"

"I'm fine. Hungry, I think. Been a long morning."

She turned and deliberately moved into the patients'

area to replace the magazine. She heard him close his bathroom door again. When he returned he was wearing hip-hugging jeans and a T-shirt. Now she really did feel overdressed!

They walked out through the deserted reception area. Everybody, it seemed, was on their lunch and siesta break.

"No doubt somebody is still in the hospital to take care of the patients and deal with any emergencies," she said as they moved down the busy street outside.

"Oh, we're all in touch by phone. And there are nurses in the wards, taking care of the patients. At the back of the hospital the accident and emergency unit is functioning as normal. But as much as possible we like to keep the work down in the afternoon."

They'd reached the harbour. Manolis slowed the pace as people milled around everywhere, tourists stopped in small groups chatting before deciding where to have lunch.

"Everything gets back to normal from five o' clock, doesn't it?" Tanya said. "I'd forgotten what life was like on Ceres."

"Yes, shops are closing now but they'll reopen when people begin to emerge for the evening. You'll soon be back in the swing of Ceres again."

He looked down at her and unable to contain himself any longer he reached for her hand. She looked up at him questioningly. For an instant she thought she'd glimpsed the old Manolis, the man she now suspected might have been totally committed to her. But she'd killed that commitment, hadn't she?

It would obviously be emotionally safer if she didn't

try to resurrect what they'd had between them. Just get on with her life here on Ceres. Or should she tell him how, only weeks after she'd lost their baby she'd felt strong again and had come to her senses? Should she tell him that she'd regretted asking him to leave and missed him with an ache in her heart that was almost physical and wouldn't go away?

He'd dropped her hand again. She followed him to the table he'd selected outside Pachos Taverna. She remembered coming here with her family for evening drinks.

"Is Pachos still here, Manolis?"

"He retired a few years ago. His son has now taken over and he does delicious snacks at lunchtime. It's near enough to the hospital for me to pop out in the middle of the day if I'm not working. Would you like a glass of wine—or an ouzo perhaps?"

"A glass of retsina," she said, boldly. "Then I shall really feel I'm back on Ceres."

"I've got to work again this evening so I'd better stick to water."

A waiter came to take their order. They ordered Greek salad and Ceres shrimps.

"Nice and light, so that I can go out again for supper," she said, hoping that didn't sound like she was angling for an invitation.

He hesitated. He'd been holding back long enough. "I'm working late tonight, otherwise I could have joined you." He hesitated, sure that she seemed disappointed. "I'm due for a day off at the end of the week. Would you like to come out in the boat with me?"

"You've got a boat?"

"Don't sound so surprised! I'm not as impoverished as I was when I was a junior doctor. It's my pride and joy, as you'll find if you come with me. How about Saturday? Are you free?"

She hesitated just long enough. Was she free? What a question!

"I think so."

"Well you can let me know. I'll be going anyway—and probably Chrysanthe. She loves the sea. We can—"

"Manolis!" A tall, distinguished-looking man was standing by their table. "So this is the mysterious young lady you've been keeping to yourself."

"Demetrius!" Manolis was standing, holding out his hand to shake the older man's. "I was going to phone you this morning but I've been tied up in Theatre. Dr Demetrius Capodistrias, let me introduce you to Dr Tanya Angelopoulos."

"Not Sotiris's daughter? Yes, of course you are. With that wonderful hair, you're the image of your mother."

Tanya felt a firm grasp as she extended her arm towards Demetrius.

"Do join us, Demetrius." Manolis was pulling up a chair. "Let me get you a drink."

"Thank you. What did you want to speak to me about, Manolis?"

"I was hoping you could convene a meeting of the hospital board fairly soon. Tanya is interested in applying for the post that's soon to be vacant."

"That's why I'm here. News travels fast on Ceres and when I heard that Sotiris's daughter had helped to deliver Helene's baby last night I knew I had to suggest she apply for the post. We need someone like you, born and bred on the island with a medical background." He smiled at her. "And rumour has it that your own qualifications are excellent."

"Actually, Manolis said there would be a vacancy for a doctor in the hospital soon so I've already given it some thought. I'd like to be considered if—"

"Splendid! I'll get in touch with the rest of the board this afternoon. Could you be free for an interview about six, Dr Angelapoulos?"

"Yes, of course."

"And you, Manolis. We'll need you there in your capacity as medical director."

"Yes, I'll be there."

Demetrius raised his glass towards Tanya. "I used to be a junior doctor when your father was in charge here. He was a great man to work with. We were all saddened, everybody who'd known your father, when we heard that he'd died."

"Yes." She swallowed hard. It still hurt.

"And your mother?"

"She's fine. Did you know she'd married again?"

"No, I hadn't heard that."

"An old friend of my father's. I'm glad my mother is content again."

Manolis's mobile was ringing. She could tell it was an emergency by the way he was speaking.

He stood up. "Sorry, I'll have to get back to the hospital. There's been a crash on the waterfront. One of the cars has gone into the sea and the passengers are being brought in."

"I'll come with you, Manolis."

Manolis hesitated. "I suppose it's OK for Tanya to help out before she's been appointed to the staff, isn't it, Demetrius?"

"In an emergency, we're relieved to get all the help we can. We have to be totally independent here on our small island. Our emergency rules have to be flexible." Demetrius turned to Tanya. "Thank you. I'll see you at six, Dr Angelopoulos."

She was glad to be busy in the hospital during the afternoon, with no time to worry about the interview in the evening. The first thing she did was to change out of the smart, inappropriate suit and put on a white short-sleeved coat.

The small accident and emergency unit was crowded with relatives and friends of the drivers and passengers of the two cars that had collided on the narrow waterfront road. The driver of the car that had gone into the water and the woman who'd been sitting in the passenger seat were being treated already by a couple of nurses.

Manolis immediately took over the treatment of the driver while Tanya tried to revive the unconscious woman whose lungs were waterlogged. Tanya turned her on her side and gently but firmly tried to remove the water from her lungs with an aspirator. Seconds went by before a loud gurgling sound indicated that the lungs were disgorging water. She started to cough and water now came up from her stomach.

She opened her eyes. "Where am I?"

"It's OK. You're in hospital." Relief flooded through

her as she raised her patient to a sitting position and held a bowl under her mouth.

Meanwhile, she could see that Manolis had also been successful with his patient. The driver was already talking quietly, fretting about his wife, hoping everybody was going to survive. And how was the car?

Manolis gave his patient a wry smile. "Several metres under the sea, but everybody's alive, which is the main thing."

The two nurses took over from Manolis and Tanya, who were now required to deal with a patient whose leg was causing him a lot of pain. It wasn't difficult to diagnose that there was at least one fractured bone.

"We'd better have an X-ray of that leg. I'll do that because I know we haven't got a radiographer in the hospital this afternoon. Will you organise the plaster unit over there, Tanya?"

He put a hand on her arm. "Welcome to the real world of an island hospital! This is going to seem very different to the hospitals you've worked in."

"I know the score, Manolis. I used to watch my dad, remember. It was even more impromptu in his day."

By the time Manolis had X-rayed the distorted leg, he'd decided he would have to operate.

"It's worse than I thought," he told Tanya quietly. "I'll need to put in a steel plate and some screws in the tibia, which is shattered in several places. How much experience have you had in orthopaedic surgery?"

"I've assisted in Orthopaedic Theatre several times and passed my orthopaedics practical and theoretical examinations—with distinction," she added, just to set his mind at rest. "It won't be a problem."

"Excellent. The sooner we can get this leg in the right position again, the better will be the outcome for the patient. Check when the patient had his last food. I'll see you in Theatre when you've scrubbed up. The anaesthetist I've contacted should be with us shortly."

Minutes later she was standing across the other side of the operating table waiting for Manolis's instructions. The patient was anaesthetised and the anaesthetist was satisfied with his breathing. Tanya glanced at the monitor. Blood pressure was normal.

Above his mask Manolis's eyes registered calm. She'd never worked in Theatre with him before but she felt they were already a good team.

"Scalpel…"

CHAPTER FOUR

TANYA could feel the intense pressure under which the quickly assembled team was working. In this sort of emergency situation, where most of the team had expected to be off duty, the concentration required by them was paramount.

She watched as Manolis was cutting through the skin and outer layer of tissue to expose the tibia. As she'd seen on the X-ray, it was badly shattered. The front of the bone would require plating and other less damaged sections could be aligned with screws. In any case, whatever Manolis did, everything would depend on the healing process. If the bone didn't heal, amputation would be the only option.

As if reading her mind, Manolis began to explain to the team what he was doing and why. Whenever he was operating he tried to remember to pass on his skills to the team. He firmly believed that continual teaching was necessary in the operating Theatre. That was how he had learned. Textbooks were helpful but the real skills were learned by assisting and listening in the operating Theatre.

"We've got a young, otherwise healthy man here," Manolis concluded as he indicated to Tanya the steel plate he was going to insert. "There's no obvious reason why the bone shouldn't heal but always, in orthopaedic surgery, we cannot take anything for granted. Infection is always a possibility."

There was a murmur of assent from everyone. Manolis glanced across the table at Tanya. Beneath his mask she could tell he was smiling at her. The smile had reached his eyes. He was calm, totally in control, doing the job he was born to do—like she was.

For a brief instant she remembered the interview. She mustn't be too complacent about it. She wanted this job more than ever now she was actually working in the hospital. But now she had to concentrate on the work in hand. They had to save this young man's leg from amputation...

Three hours later, she pulled down her mask and breathed a sigh of relief. She was standing in the scrub room with Manolis, who was peeling off his gloves. A nurse and porter had just taken the patient to the orthopaedic ward. He was conscious now and Tanya had already removed his airway as his breathing was normal again.

"I'm quietly confident he's going to be OK," Manolis said, as he dropped the gloves in the nearest bin.

Tanya reached forward and released the Velcro fastening at the back of Manolis's gown. It was an automatic gesture which she'd done many times for whoever she'd been working with in Theatre.

Manolis swung round as he tossed the gown towards the large bin near the door. "It's a long time since you helped me to undress," he said, his voice much too husky and suggestive. He regretted the remark as soon as he'd made it. He waited for Tanya to retire into her shell again.

To his delight she smiled up at him. Her rich auburn glossy hair had tumbled down onto her shoulders as she'd removed the theatre cap that had been holding it in place. He remembered how it used to fan out on the pillow in the morning, all rumpled after a particularly fantastic night of sheer passion, love and...

"Purely second nature to me to assist the chief surgeon," she said, pleasantly but without a hint of sexual innuendo.

Good thing she couldn't read his thoughts! He reined in his feelings and physical arousal with great difficulty. They were standing so close now. Surely she could feel the emotional tension between them.

"I've got to go and see Helene in the postnatal unit," she said in the same tone. "I promised her grandmother I would."

He cleared his throat to remove all possibility that he would sound husky and provocative. "Don't be late for the interview."

"Of course not."

As she turned away she wondered how much longer she should put up the pretence that she wasn't interested in renewing their old relationship. They'd been standing so close just now. It had been all she could do not to take hold of his hand just to feel contact with him again. He'd had such a tense expression of control on his face.

As she walked out through the door she knew he was watching her. She could feel his eyes on her every movement. The door swung back again behind her and she walked away quickly before she had time to reveal her true feelings.

It wasn't going to be easy working with Manolis but she was determined to get this job. The old ambition was back. She still wanted to show him what she was made of!

She walked purposefully along the corridor towards the postnatal unit.

Helene was sitting in an armchair by her bed, feeding her tiny baby boy.

"Tanya! Grandmother said you were going to come in."

Helene patted her baby gently on the back as he finished feeding. A welcome burp came from the tiny mouth and she handed him to Tanya. "They checked him over but I'd like you to give your professional opinion."

Tanya ran her experienced eyes over the little body while she was changing his nappy to check that everything was in working order. As she removed his nappy a fountain of urine spurted into the air. They both laughed as Tanya narrowly missed being showered.

"He seems extremely healthy to me," Tanya said as she fixed a clean nappy and placed him back in his cot. "Have you got a name for him yet?"

"Lefteris, after his father."

They chatted together in Greek, both trying to fill in what had happened to them since they'd been together at school. Tanya was deliberately vague about her life in Australia, and managed not to mention that she'd had an affair with Manolis.

Helene began to tell Tanya about how difficult it now was that she and Lefteris were living with her grandmother. "It's kind of her to take us in but we're very cramped—it will be even more so now that our baby is here. You see, my parents don't approve of him. We're not married and unmarried lovers don't live together on Ceres, as everybody knows. When I found out I was pregnant my parents were furious. It was OK for me to live at home, even at the ripe old age of twenty-eight, but scandalous to get pregnant. We had a big row and Lefteris and I moved in with Grandmother."

"Do you know why your parents don't approve of Lefteris?"

"They think he's a drifter, never had a proper job. He's worked on the boats for a low wage for years and now he earns very little as a casual builder and labourer. My parents have forbidden me to marry him. They say he'll leave me when he wants to move on again."

"Perhaps they'll change their minds now that your baby is here."

"I doubt it! We could go ahead and have a quiet wedding without spending too much money but I don't want to disobey my father."

Tanya put her hand over her friend's. "I'm afraid I've got to go now. I'm due for an interview with the hospital board at six o' clock and I need to change out of this white coat into something more presentable."

"Are you going to be working here permanently?"

"I hope so."

"So do I. You'll come and see me again, won't you? They're going to keep me in for a few days in view of the difficult living conditions at my grandmother's."

"I'll come and see you again as soon as I can."

The hospital board was assembled in a large office near the reception area. Manolis went into the room first and introduced Tanya to the three men, before taking his place behind one of the desks. As he'd explained to her, there were two doctors—Demetrius, who she'd already met, and another retired doctor. Alexander Logothetis, the ex-mayor who still had a great deal of influence on various committees, the island council, the school board and the hospital, was the third man.

Manolis had told her that Alexander Logothetis might be a tough nut to crack.

"We'll have to play down the influence your father had when he was doctor in charge of all medical services on the island." Manolis had told her just before they'd entered the room.

"Alexander is not much younger than your father and I believe they didn't always see eye to eye when Alexander was trying to climb the ladder of success in the property world here. There were several disputes between them before the new hospital project got off the ground."

She had looked up at him with confidence she didn't entirely feel. "Don't worry about me, Manolis. I intend to get this job on my own merits."

"I'm sure you will," he said, quickly.

The interview lasted almost an hour. By the end of it Tanya was feeling very tired. It had been a long day and she could feel the tension in the room getting to her. As Manolis had predicted, Alexander Logothetis was the most difficult member of the board to convince.

He'd asked questions about her qualifications, experience, health and stamina, hinting that it was a tough job for a young woman, with long hours and a flexible attitude required to every situation.

She'd answered all his questions at length and hoped she'd convinced him she would be totally committed to her work. The medical questions put to her by Manolis and the other two doctors were easier to handle. She had a wide range of medical and surgical experience and rarely had a problem with the questions that examiners put to her.

At last the board members started shuffling their papers around and Manolis stood up to signify the end of the interview.

"Thank you, Dr Angelopoulos," he said in a formal voice. "If you would like to go along to the waiting room, I'll call you back when the board has reached its decision."

He escorted her to the door and opened it. She stepped out into the corridor and he closed it without even looking at her. Oh, dear, was that a bad sign? Had she fluffed it? She walked along to the small waiting room. There was a drinking-water dispenser. She felt in need of something stronger to calm her nerves. How long would they be in there?

She sipped her water slowly.

In the interview room Alexander Logothetis was making his views abundantly clear. He pointed out that there were two candidates who'd been interviewed by the agency in London who hadn't yet travelled out to Ceres. They seemed keen to settle on the island.

"They're both straight out of medical school, without the experience of Dr Angelopoulos," Manolis pointed out succinctly. "Tanya's qualifications are at a higher level than theirs."

He'd already given a glowing account of her medical qualifications and experience, which had been of great interest to the two doctors but seemed to bore the ex-mayor. "Also, they haven't yet experienced life on this island. How do we know they will be able to improvise and adapt to difficult conditions as Tanya, having been born and bred here, knows extremely well?"

"Only yesterday Tanya helped Manolis to deliver a breech baby in a small house halfway up the *kali strata*," Demetrius put in. "That's when her ability to improvise was fully shown."

"I have heard about that incident," Alexander said icily. "And also it's come to my ears that this young lady doctor was actually assisting in an operation here this afternoon. Has anybody looked into the irregular insurance situation? You, as Medical Director of this hospital, Manolis, should have known better than to allow such a thing to—"

"When it's a question of a patient's welfare I will be the judge of whether to worry about insurance," Manolis countered vehemently. "In actual fact, I have already made provision with our insurers and ensured that a clause has been inserted in our policy for each emergency case to be taken on its own merits. Don't forget, Alexander, that you are the only non-member of the medical profession in this room. I will defend my right to improvise in situations of life and death without worrying about unimportant issues."

This time it was Alexander who remained silent. Manolis could see that he was seething with anger. He had to convince him that Tanya was the best candidate they were every likely to get on the island.

"Tanya went to see Helene and her baby here in hospital just now," Manolis continued evenly. "Helene and Tanya were friends at school. From what Tanya has told me, the baby is in excellent health and Helene is extremely grateful that Tanya helped to deliver her baby. As for the operation we performed this afternoon, without her help it would have been—"

"OK, Manolis," Alexander interrupted impatiently. "Let's take a vote on it. You've made it quite clear how you will vote. I shall vote that it would be better for us to see the two candidates who—"

"And meanwhile have Manolis run the hospital without the full complement of staff!" Demetrius interjected furiously. "And have to pay the expenses of the two young, inexperienced men who may prove just as unsuitable as the present outgoing doctor."

Demetrius banged his fist on the table. "He's resigned apparently because of what he calls the difficult working conditions on the island. Alexander, doesn't this prove the case for appointing someone who was born and bred here and totally understands these so-called difficult working conditions?"

Manolis knew this was the moment he had to play his

trump card. "My secretary was making an important phone call when I had to leave her to attend this interview. She'd been notified earlier today that there was a possibility that the two other candidates may withdraw their applications. If we could hold off taking the vote a little longer until she's had time to—"

"It's time to take a formal vote, Manolis," Alexander said dismissively. "We shall know where we stand when everyone has voted."

A formal vote was taken. The outcome was a foregone conclusion. Manolis and the two retired doctors voted in favour of Tanya. Alexander Logothetis voted to postpone the appointment until all candidates had been seen.

There was a knock on the door. Manolis leapt to his feet. His secretary was standing on the threshhold with a piece of paper in her hand. "I've written out the details of the phone call, Dr Manolis."

"Thank you!" He glanced down and scanned the page before turning round, trying hard not to sound too triumphant. "Basically, gentlemen, it appears that both candidates have taken the jobs they'd previously applied for in London."

He paused for dramatic effect to give them time to let the news sink in. "Alexander, would you like me to re-advertise the post?" Another pause, still trying not to sound smug. "We could spend yet more hospital money on finding some other non-islander who is toying with the idea of working on a beautiful Greek island where they can spend their off duty sunning themselves on the beach…"

"OK, you've made your point, Manolis," Alexander conceded. "Under the circumstances I suppose—"

"The vote is carried in favour of Dr Tanya Angelothetis," Manolis declared, trying hard not to show how delighted he was, both on a professional and a personal level.

The sun was setting over the water down in the harbour as Manolis raised his glass of sparkling water towards Tanya. They'd both been busy after the interview, finalising plans for the work that Tanya would be expected to do.

Tanya sipped at her glass of wine, feeling excited about the outcome of the interview but apprehensive about the work she would be expected to do. She couldn't afford to let Manolis down when he'd been so supportive. She watched him now as he phoned his mother to find out if Chrysanthe was all right.

Even across the table, with the noise of the early evening chatter and laughter from the other tables outside the taverna, Tanya could hear the excited childish voice coming through on Manolis's mobile.

"Chrysanthe wants to speak to the pretty lady," he said, handing her the phone.

"When can I come to your house again, Tanya?"

She swallowed the lump in her throat. "You're welcome any time that Daddy says you can come. I've been very busy since I arrived but I'd love to see you again soon."

"*Daxi*. OK, Tanya! *Avrio?* Tomorrow?"

She looked across the table enquiringly at Manolis.

He nodded. "Tomorrow's fine. I shan't expect you to work tomorrow after all the extra work you've done already. So…"

She waited for him to continue. He reached across the table and took hold of her hand. It seemed the most natural gesture to make but the touch of his fingers grasping hers was affecting her emotions deeply. Why was he looking at her in that whimsical manner?

"So if you happen to be at home after school, maybe Chrysanthe could drop in?"

Tanya smiled her assent as she continued chatting to Chrysanthe. "Did you hear that, Chysanthe? Daddy says it's OK if you come to see me after school."

The squeals of delight made her feel happier than she had in a long time. She looked across the table at Manolis, her heart too full for words as she handed back the mobile. It was almost as if the baby that they'd so wanted had materialised in this lovely child.

No, she mustn't fantasise! She must stay in the real world. This child wasn't hers—but this was what it would have been like if fate had allowed them to keep their baby, to move on and become parents.

Instead, Manolis had started another baby with someone else, just months after the trauma of losing their own, which was something she'd not been able to understand. How could he have resolved his emotional turmoil so quickly? It had taken her years—and it was still unresolved. She could never really trust him again—could she?

Oh, it was all so confusing…just like it had been when the miscarriage had happened. She should have got her emotions sorted out by now, shouldn't she? How long did it take to get over an ex-lover?

Deep down she knew she could never get over Manolis. He was the only man she'd ever really loved. Yes, she'd had other relationships. But nothing to compare with the intensity of emotion she'd felt for Manolis. He'd been her life, her love, her reason for living, the centre of her universe. She stifled a moan of anguish at what she'd demolished by asking Manolis to leave her by herself all those years ago.

She'd wanted to sort out her emotions, to grieve for their baby by herself without any pressure about the future being put on her.

Some of the anguish she'd felt at that time was coming through to her again. She sighed as she realised she was going to have to work through this and decide if she dared give rein to her true feelings or…

"You're looking very solemn all of a sudden, Tanya." He frowned. "Are you having second thoughts?"

"About what?" she said sharply. It was almost as if he'd been able to see into her mind!

"About having Chrysanthe round to your house tomorrow? I'll try to get back early from the hospital to help you because I don't want to overload you with my family responsibilities."

"Oh, don't worry. It won't be a problem. Do get back early if you can. Obviously, it would be more fun the two of us looking after Chrysanthe. I'm sure she would enjoy having her dad and…me…at the same time…"

She leaned back against her chair, her eyes locking with his.

"You're a good father," she said quietly.

He hesitated. "I try to be." His husky voice trailed away.

They continued to look at each other, both instinctively knowing that the other was thinking about that other child which should have been theirs.

Manolis reached across the table and took her hand in his. "Are you thinking about…?" He couldn't finish his sentence.

She nodded. "Are you?"

He nodded, not trusting himself to speak.

Tanya leaned forward. "We need to talk about…what happened…when we split up."

Manolis squeezed her hand. "I think we should…if only to clear things up between us. Sort out where we go from here now that we're going to be working together."

"Exactly! So…"

He stood up. "I've got to get back to the hospital this evening. I'm doing a general practice surgery in a few minutes."

"I gathered you were going to be on duty when you ordered sparkling water."

He nodded. "But if you're going to stay down here by the harbour, I could meet you in a couple of hours for some supper."

"No, I've got to get back." Her words came out in a rush.

For a moment she'd panicked at the thought of the discussion about the past. She'd suddenly got cold feet. Was she really ready to face it head on with all the problems that needed to be resolved?

He was standing beside her now, looking down with an enigmatic expression, waiting for her to elaborate about why she had to get back, no doubt. She couldn't think of one reason why she couldn't enjoy a couple of hours here by the harbour so she remained silent. The thought of her empty house suddenly filled her with dread. But she really needed time to work out what it was she wanted.

To have him tell her he wanted to take care of her for the rest of her life? That she need never worry again if only she would play the little woman and let him do her worrying for her…as he had told her before? Well, not in so many words but that was how she'd worked out what he'd meant in her confused mind during and after her miscarriage.

Manolis looked down at her, his eyes troubled. He sensed she was going through some kind of emotional turmoil but he felt powerless to help. He'd been unable to reach out to her when they had both been trying to come to terms with the awful trauma of losing their baby. He hadn't understood what it was she'd wanted then and six years on he still didn't know! She must be the most complicated woman in the world!

"OK, I'll see you tomorrow, then, and we'll talk—yes?" He turned and strode off into the crowded harbour-side, back towards the hospital.

His hard, determined tone was ringing in her ears as she watched him until the crowd swallowed him up. The holidaymakers were still laughing and carefree but she felt a wedge of ice lodging on her heart. Once again she'd somehow managed to send Manolis away just when their troubled relationship was beginning to thaw out.

She made her way through the crowds towards the bottom of the *kali strata*, the steep cobbled climb that was the connection between Chorio, the older town at the top, and Yialos at the bottom. So many times she'd climbed this as a child, holding firmly to a grown-up's hand. She'd always belonged to somebody older and wiser than she.

But tonight she felt like a little lost girl with no hand to hold—and nobody waiting for her at home.

Reaching the top, she turned along her street and made her way over the cobbles to her house. From the end of the street she could hear the sound of laughter and chatter coming from the open door and windows of Anna's house. Manolis's mother was never alone. Always surrounded by her family, her children leaving their children in her care for a while or overnight.

She hadn't had time to go and visit Anna yet. She would make time tomorrow because she'd always loved her. As a child she'd always been welcomed into her house and treated like part of the family.

"Tanya!"

Chrysanthe's voice was, oh, so welcome at this moment of solitude as she was about to go into her empty house. She turned back into the street. The little girl was running over the cobbles, a beaming smile on her face, laughing for the sheer joy of living.

"Grandmother Anna wants to see you."

She had just time to glimpse the still good-looking older version of the Anna she remembered from her childhood before Chrysanthe grabbed her by the hand and began to tug her down the street.

"Grandma! I've found her."

Anna began walking up the street, her arms out-spread. "Tanya! You haven't been to see me!"

"I've been busy, Anna."

The older lady hugged her. "I know, my child. Manolis told me about your job interview. How did it go?"

Tanya smiled. "Well, Alexander Logothetis was a bit difficult but—"

"Oh, that old goat! I hope you took no notice of him."

"I was polite but Manolis managed to convince him I was the right person for the job."

"I knew you'd get it! You clever girl. Passing all those medical exams. Manolis is so proud of you and so happy you are back here on Ceres."

Anna lowered her voice, even though Chrysanthe had already darted off into the house to rejoin her cousins. "I never did understand why you and Manolis split up in Australia. What was the problem? You were made for each other, you two! He came back home for a little while after you'd broken up. Devastated. Inconsolable! But he wouldn't tell me what had happened. Me! His own mother! So…?"

Tanya could feel tears threatening to roll down her cheeks. "These things happen," she managed to say in a choking voice.

Anna, as if sensing she'd gone too far, put an arm round her waist.

"Come inside. You need a drink, my girl. Now, let me introduce you to some of my grandchildren. This little one is Rafaelo. He's Diana's first child. She's working in the pharmacy this evening. This is her baby son, Demetrius, and I was just going to feed him."

Anna picked up the feeding bottle from the bottle warmer.

"Let me do that Anna," Tanya said quickly. "You must be very busy with all these children around you."

Anna beamed. "My children are my life! What else would I do but look after my family? Here! Sit in this feeding chair. I've fed all of them on this chair—even Manolis. He was a handsome baby. I'll be in the kitchen, cooking, if you need me. You'll stay to supper, won't you? Keftedes tonight."

Anna smiled as she settled herself in the chair with baby Demetrius sucking contentedly on his bottle.

"Keftedes! How could I resist your home-made meat balls?"

She was totally absorbed into family life. Almost three hours had elapsed since they had all assembled around the large wooden kitchen table to eat supper. Baby Demetrius, who also needed some solid food, had sat on Tanya's lap while she'd spooned the semi-solid mixture of mashed potatoes and carrots into his mouth.

After supper Tanya had helped wash the children and put them down in their beds or cots. Chrysanthe had fallen asleep almost immediately.

"Will she sleep here tonight, Anna?" Tanya asked as she walked down the winding wooden staircase.

"I think it's better she does. Sometimes Manolis lifts her out of her bed and carries her back to her own bedroom, but tonight I'll suggest he leaves her."

"I must get back," Tanya said quickly.

"No hurry, child. Manolis will be home soon and you can— Well, talk of the devil!"

Tanya's heart skipped a beat as he appeared in the open doorway.

His face lit up.

"How was the surgery tonight?"

"Nothing too disturbing. I had to admit a patient with abdominal pains but I've checked him out thoroughly and the night staff are going to monitor his progress and call the doctor on duty if necessary. Which, fortunately, isn't me!"

"Well, I'll say goodnight."

"No, you won't!" He reached forward and put his hands on her shoulders, looking down meaningfully into her eyes.

"Chrysanthe is asleep," Anna said quickly. "I don't want you to disturb her. Leave her here till the morning, Manolis."

"In that case, Tanya, would you like to come back to my place for a nightcap?"

She looked up into those brown, melting, seductive eyes and all her resolutions disappeared.

How could she resist?

CHAPTER FIVE

MANOLIS closed the door behind them and for a brief instant he leaned against it, breathing heavily. He hadn't expected Tanya to agree to come back home with him. He hadn't expected her to now be looking up at him expectantly. If he took her in his arms now, would she vanish back into the dream he'd held onto for the past six years? He had to take that risk because he couldn't believe this was happening. But at the same time he had to consider her feelings. He knew how vulnerable she was. If he came on too strong, she would move away…

Oh, to hell with it! He was fed up with treading on eggshells around her! He reached forward and more roughly than he'd meant to he pulled her into his arms. To his excitement and utter amazement he heard her give a gentle moan. She was actually going to stay there in his arms while he…while he what? Dared he…dared he…?

He bent his head and pressed his lips against hers. She was so wonderfully pliant. He'd never thought she would ever mould herself against him as she was doing now…

Tanya moved to feel the maximum intimacy she could achieve without total abandonment. She had no idea why she'd thrown caution to the wind and she didn't care any more. She wanted so much to regain that wonderful relationship they'd had all those years ago. If only for a short time she would allow herself to pretend that they were both six years younger. She hadn't lost their baby, they hadn't had that awful row, she hadn't lost him, as she'd thought, for ever.

He was here with her now, his arms enfolding her, his body hard, muscles taut against her, needing her. Oh, she was so sure of how he needed her right at this moment! His manhood pressed hard and rigid against her own desperate body as his hands caressed her tenderly.

"Tanya?" he whispered as he held himself away from her for a brief moment.

She looked up into his eyes and saw that wonderful expression of total commitment that she'd once cherished so much, and had then destroyed.

She was aware that he was carrying her up the narrow wooden stairs. Once he bumped his head on the low ceiling of the ancient house. They both laughed and the tension relaxed. They'd been taking each other too seriously. Their previous relationship had been full of laughter, lightness, enjoyment.

She knew she could relax now. There was nothing serious about this romantic moment. They would make love…oh, yes, they would make love. Nothing mattered except this exquisite moment in time.

He put her down gently on the wide bed in the centre of the room. She was briefly aware of the moon shining through the window. A profusion of twinkling stars added to the mystery of the dark velvet sky. And then she saw it. A shooting star seemed to be coming to land in the bedroom before it disappeared without trace. She held her breath as she made the only wish possible.

"Tanya?"

He was leaning over her, his eyes full of concern. "Are you still with me? For a moment I thought I'd lost you."

"No, you hadn't lost me," she whispered. "There was a falling star and I was making a wish."

"What did you wish?"

"I couldn't possibly tell you or it might not come true." She reached forward to unbutton his shirt.

"One day perhaps?" He was gently removing her bra with one hand, the other straying inside to tease her rigid nipples.

"Who knows what the future holds?" She sighed as she anticipated how it would feel when their vibrantly excited bodies merged together…

She had no idea where she was when she awoke. Through the strange window a dark cloud was half obscuring the moon. The stars had vanished. But she'd made a wish some time ago…hadn't she? Or was that years ago? Now she remembered! She'd just repeated the wish she'd made a long time ago in Australia after they'd made wonderful, mind-blowing love…just like they'd done before she'd gone to sleep.

Manolis gave a soft moan in his sleep.

"Manolis?" She touched him on his shoulder, still hot and damp from their love-making. "Are you awake?"

He opened his eyes and smiled as he stretched his long muscular limbs like a tiger waiting to pounce.

"I am now," he murmured huskily as he wrapped his arms around her, holding her so close that it was immediately obvious why he'd moaned in his sleep.

As he thrust himself inside her she echoed his moan of pleasure. Why had she ever doubted him? Why had she denied herself of a lifetime of love that was too precious to have been destroyed?

They slept again after their love-making, this time with their arms around each other as if making sure that nothing could ever change between them again.

The sun was creeping over the windowsill when she awoke again. She stretched herself gently so as not to awaken him and also to make sure she still had arms and legs of her own! She seemed to have spent the night absorbed by this hunky, magnificent body which had taken over and melted inside her.

She lay back against the pillows, staring up at the ceiling, and suddenly reality hit her...and hit her hard. Where should they go from here? She had to be completely sure of her feelings this time around, now that she was older and wiser and had suffered the agony of separation from Manolis. She also had to be sure of how he felt about her. Oh, it had been wonderful to spend the night with him. But passion aside, she had to think clearly about the future.

Manolis was waking up slowly. He felt wonderfully happy but the old worries were crowding in on him again. Their love-making had been out of this world, just as he'd always remembered it had been. But now he had to tread carefully so as not to frighten this fragile girl away. He knew that in some way he'd been too demanding when they'd been in Australia. He'd possibly tried to take over her whole life. She was like a delicate butterfly who needed to be handled with care or she would fly away from him.

She'd been totally abandoned during the night, just like when they'd been together before their split. But now that it was the morning, would she have put up her guard again, decided she needed her independence and didn't want to commit herself to anything with him? He thought about it for all of two seconds.

One little kiss wouldn't frighten her, would it? He would test it out very gently.

Before the thought had barely formed in his mind he'd drawn her gently into his arms, his lips seeking hers. Oh, yes, they were still as soft and moist as he remembered during their love-making. Her lips parted as he kissed her.

He checked the temptation to make love again. Later, he promised himself as he raised himself on one elbow, looking down at her lovely face.

"We decided yesterday we needed to talk," he said gently. "About what happened to us the last time we were together. I think we both need answers."

She took a deep breath. It was now or never. "Yes, we do. Er…you first."

He swallowed hard. "Why did you send me away when I came to see you in hospital? I was so hurt by the way you treated me. You'd had a terrible ordeal, but I was also grieving for our baby. I couldn't understand why you were being so…" He broke off, unable to put into words the horror of his rejection.

"I'm sorry, I'm so sorry." She was trying to hold back the tears as the memory of their last few moments together came flooding back to her.

He gathered her into his arms. "And I'm sorry if I was too pushy with my ideas for our future. When I asked you to marry me it was only because I wanted to take care of you."

"I know, I know…and I think that was one of the things I was scared of…losing my independence. We'd only been together for a short time. I was still very naïve. You were my first real lover—older and much more experienced than me. I'd never been on the Pill before and I managed to get unintentionally pregnant within the first few weeks of our relationship."

She gave a nervous laugh. "Then when I got used to the idea of having a baby I managed to make a mess of that. I was so confused by the speed at which my life had changed since I'd met you. And then you asked me to marry you. I realise now that my hormones were all over the place, adding to the confusion I felt about whether I wanted to commit to marriage."

"You make it sound like a life sentence."

"Well, that was how I saw it at the time." She softened her tone. "It was something I wanted eventually in my life, but there were so many things I had to do before I made an important commitment like marriage. But I didn't want to lose you. I wanted everything to revert to the way it had been between us." She paused. "And I never dreamt that you would go off and marry somebody else so quickly!"

"Tanya, I was devastated when you asked me to leave you alone. In effect you made it clear you didn't want any contact until you were ready to make it. I waited, heartbroken, for the girl I knew to come back to me and—"

"You didn't wait long. Six weeks after you left I went back to the hospital medical school to hear that you were working in London."

"Six weeks! You didn't want to know about me for six weeks!"

"You've no idea how ill I felt during that time! Then shortly after I started studying again I heard you were in a relationship with an ex-girlfriend. At that point I decided I had to try to forget you."

"Which was what I'd decided to do when you sent me away and didn't try to contact me. I saw no reason to stay in Australia when you didn't want me so I applied for and got the job in London."

"And who should you meet as soon as you arrived but your ex-girlfriend!"

She moved out of his arms so she could watch his expression.

He lay back on his pillow, looking up at the ceiling. "Victoria was actually on the interview panel."

"I don't believe it! How convenient! No wonder you got the job. No, I'm sorry. I shouldn't have said that. I'm sure you got it on your own merits. So what happened after the interview? Did you take her out for dinner, wine and dine her, like you did with me?"

She could feel jealousy rising up inside her. "How could you? So soon after…"

"You'd rejected me, told me stay away, you were better off without me! I was on the rebound. Victoria and I were friends and went out for dinner a lot. One night we both had too much to drink. We got a cab back to her place…"

"Fell into bed?"

"Something like that. First I'd drowned my sorrows in drink, then tried to forget you in the oblivion of another woman's arms. Classical situation for the rejected male. It was only when I woke up the next morning the regrets crept in. Then we discovered she was pregnant and…"

Both of them were trying to ignore the shrilling of Manolis's phone. With a groan of frustration Manolis reached out towards the bedside table.

"I'd better answer it. It might be Chrysanthe."

"*Kali mera*, Papa!" squeaked a delighted voice at the other end. "Are you awake?"

For the second time, Manolis said, "I am now."

"Good. Because I'd like to come and have breakfast with you. Will that be OK?"

He ran a hand through his damp, rumpled hair as he tried to get his thoughts together. "You mean now?"

Chrysanthe was laughing now. "Well, of course now! What's the matter with you, Daddy? I'll have to have breakfast now or I'll be late for school. Grandma says she wants to give me breakfast with my cousins but I want to see you. I missed you last night because you didn't wake me up when you came home. Why didn't you wake me up?"

"I'm sorry, darling. We thought it best not to wake

you. Grandma said you were very tired. Yes, come now for breakfast. Give me five minutes to take a shower."

Tanya was already out of bed, shrugging into her clothes. She would have a much-needed shower later but for the moment she wanted to make sure that she didn't shock Chrysanthe.

Manolis put out a playful hand to halt her from buttoning her shirt.

"Manolis, I have to go!"

His spirits sank as he withdrew his hand and went into the bathroom, deliberately closing the door so that he couldn't see how wonderful she looked half-dressed in the early morning light.

Five minutes later she was out of the door into the street, almost bumping into Chrysanthe who was eagerly skipping along over the cobbles to her door.

"Hi, Tanya. You're out early."

"Yes, I just came round to borrow something I need for my breakfast. Lovely to see you. I'll see you later this afternoon. Don't forget you're coming to my house after school."

"Oh, I won't forget. I'm looking forward to it."

"So am I."

She really meant it, but not right now! Not now when her body needed a good soak in the bath to remove the lingering odour of sex. As she hurried away she felt guilty at having spent the night with Manolis. This dear little innocent child. She didn't want to do anything that would upset her.

She closed the door behind her and made her way through the little courtyard into her kitchen and up the stairs as quickly as she could. Not until she'd peeled off her clothes and climbed into the bath did she begin to relax. She poured in some of her expensive bubble bath.

What a night! What a wonderful night! And she was glad they'd had their talk. At last they were beginning to understand each other again. So much had happened to both of them. It was essential they brought it out into the open. There had been far too much misunderstanding for far too long. She lay back amid the suds and simply wallowed in that wonderful post-coital, rapturous feeling that always came over her when she and Manolis had made love.

After a long soak and an effort to return to normality she'd continued sorting out the house, doing more cleaning and trying to get the place organised enough for her to entertain a five-year-old when she arrived after school.

The sound of a childish singing voice and the clattering of skipping feet outside in the street made her glance at the clock. Good heavens, was that the time?

"I'm here, Tanya!"

Breathless and excited, the little whirlwind was holding up her arms for a hug. Tanya bent down and lifted her up into her arms. She was warm and smelt of pencils and paint.

"Have you had a good day at school?"

Was that the sort of question children liked?

"It was OK. I've brought you a picture of my mummy. We had to paint one and take them home for our mummies to see but as my mummy's in London I thought I'd give it to you. Oops, it's got a bit crumpled. It'll look better when I've straightened it out…there! What do you think?"

Tanya put Chrysanthe gently on the worn rug that covered that part of the kitchen. Taking a deep breath, she held up the picture to the light coming in through the small window.

"Let's take it out on to the terrace, shall we? It looks beautiful to me. You're good at painting, Chrysanthe."

"My teacher said it was a good effort." Chrysanthe screwed up her face as she looked down again at her work, now a bit crumpled and grubby. "It was difficult to make it look like Mummy, you know."

"Is she very beautiful?"

"Oh, yes! I'm going to spend two weeks of my school holiday with her during the summer. She lives near a big park in London—I've forgotten the name of it but it has a lake in it and we go and feed the ducks."

"That must be lovely! Would you like a drink, Chrysanthe? Orange juice perhaps or…?"

"Orange juice, please."

Tanya went back into the kitchen while Chrysanthe settled herself on a chair by the small wrought-iron table in the middle of the terrace.

"You must be looking forward to going to see your mummy in London," Tanya said as she placed two glasses of orange juice on the table.

Chrysanthe smiled happily. "Yes, I love going over there. But I'll miss Daddy, of course—and Grandma, and all my cousins. But Daddy takes me there and brings me back and I love being on the boat and the plane with him and—Daddy!"

Tanya had only just noticed that Manolis had come through the kitchen and was standing on the edge of the terrace.

He smiled at the two of them as Chrysanthe leapt down from the table, knocking over her glass.

"Oops, sorry!"

"It's OK. I'll get a cloth."

Tanya pushed past Manolis as he lifted his daughter into his arms.

"May I have an orange juice?"

"Of course. Or something stronger?"

She was selecting a cleaning cloth for the dripping table and rinsing it before screwing it out. Manolis watched and thought she'd never looked so desirable to him. His heart ached for her to tell him that she wanted to start all over again.

"Something stronger?" she repeated. "I assume you're off duty for the day."

He gave her a wry smile. "Never assume anything when you're working at the island hospital. I'd better have an orange juice, please. I've got to go back in half an hour."

She handed him a glass of orange juice and put a fresh glass on the terrace table for Chrysanthe.

Chrysanthe was sitting on the floor, looking at one of the picture books that Tanya's grandmother had kept for her in the bookshelves by the kitchen door. Having discovered this treasure trove, the little girl was now oblivious to what the grown-ups were talking about.

Tanya sat down beside Manolis and took a sip of her orange juice. "I have to say the working hours seem very flexible at the hospital."

Manolis laughed. "You could say that. We have to cover any and every eventuality on the island. So one minute we're working as GPs in the outpatient surgery and the next we're scrubbing up for Theatre." He paused. "Talking of which—Theatre, that is—I'm operating this evening on Alexander Logothetis."

Her eyes widened. "Not our less than friendly ex-mayor? He seemed OK yesterday when he had all guns blazing at me during my interview. Did my appointment upset him too much?"

"He's had a suspected problem in the lower abdomen that could suggest appendicitis. A couple of times when he's been in pain I've taken him into hospital and given him a thorough examination, kept him in hospital for forty-eight hours, did all the tests that needed to be done. But after a couple of days or so the pain disappeared and I let him go home, calling him back into hospital every couple of months to be re-examined. He came to me last night when I was doing the GP surgery."

"Was that the patient you said you'd admitted?"

He nodded. "I kept him in overnight but I found his condition had worsened by this afternoon. He's now running a high temperature. I'm going to operate this evening."

Once more he paused. "I need another doctor with surgical experience. My surgical junior doctor has been on duty for nearly twenty-four hours. He's willing to assist me but really I need somebody who's not been working all day. Will you assist me, Tanya?"

"Of course! Oh, but what about Chrysanthe?"

The little girl looked up from her book at the sound of her name. "What about me, Daddy?"

She raised herself from the floor and pulled herself up onto Manolis's lap, still carrying the book. "Can you read this story to me?"

"I'm afraid I can't, darling. I've got to go back to the hospital."

"Do you need me right now, Manolis, or do I have time to read the story to Chrysanthe?"

He glanced at his watch. "I'll need you at the hospital to scrub up in half an hour. I'm leaving now."

"All right. Would you like to come here onto my lap, Chrysanthe? Daddy and I have to work tonight. If I read to you for ten minutes now, I'll finish the story tomorrow. Will that be OK with you?"

"Well, if you have to work at the hospital it'll have to be OK. Yes, thank you, Tanya." She snuggled closer to her nicely scented new friend. "I know that doctors have to work hard whenever they're needed. Daddy's told me that lots of times when he's gone back to the hospital. I'll go to Grandma's in ten minutes so let's get started, shall we? It's this story here, Tanya. Bye, Daddy."

"This was one of my favourites when I was a little girl. My grandma used to read it to me."

"Did you have a grandma in this house?"

"Yes, it was her house when I was small."

"What was her name?"

Manolis smiled to himself as he let himself out and

began to sprint along the street. Ten minutes would pass too quickly for his little daughter, who had obviously formed a close bond already with Tanya. If only…! He daren't allow himself to think of what might have been if their own child had survived.

As he hurried down the *kali strata* he turned all his thoughts to the operation ahead of him. He hoped the anaesthetist he'd contacted had got himself back to the hospital. He hoped the results of all the tests he'd ordered would be back. He hoped the operation was going to be a success. It made no difference that this was a man who'd always been difficult with him. This was a patient who needed all the surgical expertise he could offer him.

Manolis stopped briefing Tanya as they scrubbed up side by side in the antetheatre. "I'm impressed you made it here in half an hour. Was it difficult to get away?"

"No, you've trained your daughter very well to accept the inevitable."

"She takes after her father," he observed dryly.

She decided to ignore that remark. "You were telling me about Alexander turning up at your clinic last night. What were his symptoms then?"

"High temperature, pain to the right of the groin around the appendix area. Just like on previous occasions. This time the pain was worse and the temperature was higher. I suggested we arrange to have him taken by our helicopter ambulance over to Rhodes to be under the care of a surgical consultant. He refused, saying that it would be just the same as last time. It would go away in a couple of days. So I admitted him here."

A nurse put her head round the door. "We're ready for you now, Doctor."

"I'm coming now. Tanya, final briefing."

"I've just checked the ultrasound and there appears to be an abnormality with the colon. I think we may find that the appendix is tucked behind the colon. Could be tricky to remove the appendix if it's stuck to the colon. That's why Alexander has been having recurrent pain and all these false alarms. I may have to take out some of the colon, depending on what we find when I open him up."

"Will you have to do a colostomy?"

"It may be necessary—I hope not. Alexander isn't the sort of man who would tolerate having to deal with a colostomy."

A nurse pushed open the swing doors that led into Theatre. Tanya could feel all eyes on them as they took up their positions on either side of the patient.

She'd never felt so nervous in a hospital before! She looked across the table at Manolis and saw the crinkly lines around his eyes. And suddenly she felt totally calm, completely at peace with her chosen vocation. Her patient was safe with her. Manolis's hands were as steady as a rock. So were hers.

She cleared her throat. The Theatre was silent. No sounds except those made by the anaesthetic machine.

Manolis looked at the anaesthetist. "Everything OK with the patient, Nikolas?"

He nodded. "Yes, Manolis. Breathing excellent.

Blood pressure slightly raised but not at a dangerous level. I'll let you know if a problem arises."

"Fine." Manolis turned back to look across the table again. "Then let's begin. Scalpel please…"

Three hours later they were finally able to relax. The patient was settled in a room with intensive care equipment right next to the night nurses' station.

Tanya leaned back against the cushion of the wicker armchair on her terrace and looked across at Manolis, who was relaxing in the other armchair by her table, drinking the strong coffee she'd just made.

"I'm glad you agreed to hold our debriefing session back here," he said.

"Well, I decided if we stayed any longer in the hospital somebody would find something for us to do. At least this way we get to relax in comfort."

When Manolis had suggested they discuss the operation at his house she'd been adamant that it should be at hers. The memory of last night's love-making wouldn't help her concentration while they still needed to check out the details and make a report on the operation they'd performed that evening.

"I think we could say the operation was a success." Manolis was checking some notes he'd made earlier and adding to them. "I've given the night staff a detailed report already. I just want to make everything clear for all of us."

"It was a relief that we didn't need to do a colostomy. You took a large section of colon, didn't you?"

"I had to in order to get at the appendix, which was

tucked behind it as I thought, and I didn't want to try to separate the organs in case there was some malignancy there. If there's a trace of cancer it could spread to other areas of the body. You did put those biopsies into the path lab for checking tonight, didn't you?"

She nodded. "Of course. The pathologist on call was none too pleased when I phoned him, but he's agreed to come in and get on with the tests."

"Good. The sooner we can rule out malignancy, the sooner Alexander will be happy. And he can be an impatient man, as we both know."

"And irascible, cantankerous, difficult…"

He laughed. "Can't think why we saved the old—"

"Manolis! How can you say such a thing?"

"Only joking! A patient is a patient and they all get the same excellent treatment whatever we think about them. Will you go in and see him first thing in the morning, Tanya?"

"How first thing? It's nearly midnight now."

"Oh, eight o' clock, if you can make it. I'll be in by half past. I need to take Chrysanthe to school. Her teacher wants to see me about something." He paused. "Now, that's the end of our working day so no more talking shop. And I've made sure that we don't get called out again tonight by designating one of the surgical team to stay on the premises and be on hand for any eventuality. And I've got absolute faith in our excellent night sister."

He picked up both coffee cups and went into the kitchen. "I'll go and get a bottle of wine from my fridge."

Manolis disappeared next door. She felt totally exhausted but when he reappeared she came to life again.

"Where do you keep your corkscrew?"

"I don't know. In the knife drawer by the sink, I suppose, although I doubt if Grandma drank wine at home."

She joined him in the kitchen and found him already searching where she'd suggested.

"I'll have to get the kitchen sorted out. Oh, look, here it is—in with the clean dusters. Funny place to put it."

She turned round triumphantly, holding it in her hands. "Da-dah!"

He'd been right behind her, leaning over her, in fact. They were so close again.

He reached for the corkscrew and put it down on the draining board while with his other hand he drew her even closer, lowering his head to kiss her, gently at first but when he felt her responding he became daring again. Memories of their previous night of passion were bringing him hope that their relationship might be moving on. It hadn't been just a one-off for old times' sake.

A sigh escaped her lips as he released her from his arms and looked down at her quizzically, trying to gauge her mood. Deftly, he began to unbutton her shirt, his fingers unsure of how quickly to move, however, as he willed her to feel some of the excitement that being close together always generated.

His tantalising fingers were on her breasts, gently coaxing her into a state of impossible arousal. She could feel herself melting as her desire rose. Her heart was winning the contest. She was going with the flow, entering that well-remembered paradise in which there was no yesterday, no tomorrow, just the present…

She could tell she was in her own bed as she came round from a deep sleep. Her limbs felt delightfully relaxed. In fact, her whole body had a fluid feeling, as if she'd been swimming in a warm tropical pool all night.

She turned her head. In the early morning light coming through the tiny window beside the bed she could see the outline of Manolis's features. Oh, he looked so wonderfully desirable even though she should be feeling satisfied after their passionate night of love-making. Even when they'd been six years younger they'd never had such a night together.

She couldn't turn her back on such love. She had to trust it could continue. But she didn't want to look too far into the future. Making plans might jeopardise their happiness.

She touched his face gently. He opened his eyes and smiled as he reached out to draw her into his arms, skin against skin, breasts against his hard chest, damp bodies entwining with each other, exciting each other, arousing the senses so that they turned into one body that moved slowly, rapturously, until both of them cried out together as they climbed to the highest peak of their paradise…

Some time later, Tanya made a determined effort to escape from Manolis's arms and climb out of bed. She felt his restraining fingers on her thigh as her feet reached the floor.

"Manolis, I've got to go. I promised the boss I'd see this difficult patient at eight o'clock and I'm going to need a long soak in the bath before I can face the world."

He gave her a wry smile, "How about I help you bathe? That would make it much quicker for you and you could come back to bed now for a few minutes while I outline the patient's treatment."

She laughed as she shrugged into her robe. "The best plan is for you to go home in case your daughter arrives early."

"Spoilsport!" He pretended to sulk as he climbed out of bed and searched among the clothes strewn across the floor.

She gave one last fond look at the handsome hunk on his hands and knees.

"Duty calls," she said, as she slipped out of the door. Minutes later she heard him pattering down the stairs on his bare feet. She held her breath, expecting he would call into her bathroom to say goodbye. Her lips moistened at the thought of his lips on hers but she could hear his footsteps continuing to the ground floor.

Their idyll was over—for the moment.

CHAPTER SIX

HURRYING down the *kali strata* she still found time to pause and admire the view at the first corner after the initial descent from the upper town. She'd always stood right here since she'd been a child, holding her father's hand tightly so as not to slip on the well-worn cobbles.

The view of the harbour with the people on the boats beginning to wake up was spectacular as always. One tiny boat was making its way out to sea already. From this height, it looked like the blue boat she'd played with in her bath when she had been small.

She mustn't linger. She had a patient to see. He wasn't in any danger—she'd just checked again with the night sister but apparently he was being impatient about seeing her again.

A difficult patient, Night Sister had said. "You're telling me!" she'd replied, as she'd switched off her mobile. For a brief moment, she allowed herself to lift her eyes up to the horizon where an early morning mist had settled over the sea, making it difficult to figure out where the sea finished and the sky started.

And over there across the water on the hills of

Turkey the morning glow of the newly risen sun had bathed the grass of the hills in a special light. Mmm, she loved this island. She was so glad she'd come home again, especially now that she'd made her peace with Manolis.

Moving swiftly down the steps, she realised it wasn't so much making peace with him as allowing herself to be honest. She hadn't really had time to get to know him during the weeks they'd been lovers in Australia. Yes, they'd had a wonderful heady, sexy relationship. But now, six years on, she was beginning to find out so much more about what this wonderful man was really about. She realised that she loved him so much still! She could never let him go again. They needed to rediscover each other and find out exactly what each of them had been through during the last six years.

She turned the corner at the bottom and made her way through the wide terrace of tables outside a taverna where people were drinking their first coffee of the day.

"*Kali mera*, Tanya."

"*Kali mera*, good morning." She smiled as she greeted friends she remembered from her childhood.

She wended her way through the narrow streets, past the church and in through the front door of the hospital. It was still quiet. Nobody had dashed up to tell her she was needed yet. She checked with the night staff gathered round the nurses' station. Night Sister was giving her report to the newly arrived fresh faced, clean uniformed day staff.

She broke off to tell Tanya that nothing had changed since they'd spoken on the phone a short time ago.

Alexander's condition had improved steadily throughout the night and he was asking to see her again now.

Tanya nodded. "Thanks, Sister. I'll go in and see
him now."

Alexander's door was wide open, as it had been all
night so that the night staff could keep a constant check.
A young nurse was washing Alexander's face and
hands, while her patient protested that he wasn't a baby.
He didn't need all this fuss.

"Go away, Nurse. I want to speak to Dr Tanya."

He flapped a wet hand at the terrified nurse and indicated she should remove the bowl of soapy water from
his bedside table.

"And close the door! Doesn't a man deserve a little
privacy in this place? Do you realise who I am? In
case it's escaped your notice, I'm Chairman of the
Board of Governors at this hospital and I used to be
the mayor of Ceres!"

He tried to raise himself up but flopped back against
the pillows.

"Tanya, do I need all these tubes and things sticking
in my hand?"

"That's your morphine line, Alexander. I told you last
night before I left. You can press that little knob at the
end of this tube if you are in pain and—"

"Oh, I've been doing that all night. I feel as high
as a kite!"

The elderly patient gave a little giggle and held out
a still damp hand towards Tanya, indicating that she
should hold it in hers.

"I'm deeply grateful to what you and Manolis did

last night. I hope I wasn't too difficult with you in the interview, my dear. My wife is always telling me I'm cantankerous. But it's just my way of dealing with my own nerves, you know. I'm actually quite shy so I like to make people feel frightened of me—yes, I do! It means they won't walk all over me."

He broke off, looking confused. "I don't know why I'm telling you all this."

"It's the morphine. It loosens the tongue—a bit like alcohol."

"Oh, alcohol! I don't suppose you could smuggle in a small glass of ouzo, could you? Not even for medicinal purposes? No, I thought not."

"Give it a few days, Alexander. You've been through a big operation. We removed half your colon, your appendix, a couple of abscesses and—"

"You'll let me know when that pathologist man has done his tests, won't you, Tanya? I hope he gives me a clean bill of health. I don't want to die just yet. I enjoy life too much. Always have!"

"Now, I need to examine the wound."

"Never! Wait until Manolis comes. Lady doctors have their place but I don't want you fishing around under my sheets."

He gave another uncharacteristic giggle. Tanya let go of his hand and checked the oxygen flow from the cylinder by his bed. "You won't need this much longer," she said, indicating the tube with the oxygen flowing into his nostrils.

"Thank goodness. Stop fiddling about, woman, and sit down on the bedside where I can look at you. Yes, you're beautiful like your mother and stubborn like your father. We got on so well, Sotiris and me, especially when I was mayor. Everybody thought we were deadly enemies but it was all an act, you know. We used to sink a few drinks after we'd been together in a public meeting, both taking different sides just for the hell of it. Well here the boy comes…at last! Close the door behind you, Manolis! I've just sent out for a bottle of ouzo so we can celebrate."

Manolis shot a glance at Tanya and she gave him a wry smile and a tiny nod of amusement.

"Alexander's been overdoing it on the morphine, Manolis. He—"

"Just listen to the woman! Get her out of here, my boy, before I drag her into my bed and show her who's boss around here." He started muttering incoherently. "Never could resist a pretty woman."

Manolis put his hand on Tanya's arm and spoke quietly. "I'll take over, Tanya, if you'd like to start on the patient round, please. I think this is our most difficult patient so I'll deal with the wound."

"I heard that, young man! I'm not senile yet. Get this oxygen tube out of my nose and be quick about it or…" He continued ranting to himself.

Manolis moved over to open the door for Tanya. She looked up into his eyes. For a few seconds neither of them spoke.

"Come and have a coffee in my office when you've finished your rounds, Doctor."

"I will, Manolis," she promised quietly.

"You make a lovely couple," came the now calm

voice from the bed. "You'd better snap that beauty up before anybody else gets her. It was the same with her mother. I fancied her rotten but Sotiris got in there first. Mark my words, Manolis…"

Tanya closed the door on her patient's musings and headed for the obstetrics unit to check on Helene.

"Great to see you, Tanya!" Her friend was sitting in an armchair by her bed, cradling her newborn son. "I've just finished feeding so we can have a chat. I'll put Lefteris back in his cot."

"Let me do that, Helene. I need to check him out."

"Why?"

"Oh, just routine," Tanya said, as she placed the small baby on his cot and began her checks. "I'm on my rounds at the moment and I'll have to write a report on everybody I'm able to see so that the nurses know how to continue with their treatment today, what medication needs changing…that sort of thing."

"Well, can you put me down to go home? I'm getting bored in here and I'd love to be back at my grandmother's house with baby Lefteris's daddy."

"Well, as far as baby Lefteris is concerned, there are no problems. He's in excellent health. And as far as I can see from your chart, you've made an excellent recovery from your unscheduled home birth. You look great!"

Tanya settled the little boy in his cot and sat down on the edge of the bed. "I can't stay long. I've got to get round most of the patients and then spend the rest of the morning in Outpatients. Just wanted to see how you were doing."

"I really do want to go home!"

Tanya smiled. "Of course you do! It's only natural to want to be at home rather than be stuck in here. I'll recommend you're discharged today and if Manolis agrees…"

"Oh, thank you, Tanya! You know, I'm glad you're working with Manolis. When you were delivering my baby I could tell there was a spark between you two. It would be absolutely perfect if—"

"We're just a good team, that's all."

"Huh! Pull the other one!"

Tanya stood up. "I'll arrange for one of the nurses to go home with you later today to check that you settle in OK and have everything you need. Then a nurse will come in every morning for the next week to help you get used to being a mother. I think you'll be excellent."

"Can't wait to get started!"

Tanya smiled as she stood up. "I'll call in and see you later this morning when I've made the arrangements."

"So you're sure Manolis will accept your recommendation that I go home?"

"Of course! I mean, we seem to see eye to eye on most of our professional responsibilities," she added hastily.

Helene grinned. "Sounds perfect to me. See you later, then."

Tanya continued on her rounds. She had two more patients to see in Obstetrics. The nurses had reported that one of these patients wasn't enjoying breastfeeding and found it difficult.

"My baby just doesn't suck, like she's supposed to," the young mother said. "She either falls asleep or starts screaming. The nurse had to give her a bottle last night to keep her quiet so we could all get some sleep."

"According to your chart, the nurse gave baby Rosa a bottle because she was worried she wasn't getting enough nourishment."

"Same thing!"

"Do you want to keep on with breastfeeding, Lana?" Tanya said gently.

The young mother pulled a face. "Not particularly. My mother told me I should breastfeed like all mothers on Ceres do. But to be honest I'd prefer to put her on the bottle so my husband can help with the feeding in the night. I need my sleep—I get really tired if I don't sleep enough."

"Well, let's give it another couple of days, shall we? You're staying with us till the end of the week because you had a hard time at the birth."

"It was awful, Doctor! I'm not going through that ever again. I thought I was going to die—and I actually wanted to when there was all this pain. Ugh!"

Tanya took hold of the young mother's hand. She'd skimmed through the notes and realised that her patient's blood pressure had been way too high and she'd been suffering from pre-eclampsia, a dangerous condition that, if untreated, could sometimes cause the death of the mother, the baby or both.

"You know Lana, for you to suffer as you did during your first labour must have been very frightening. It will take a while for you to regain your strength and feel as if you want to care for your baby."

"Actually, Doctor, I feel it was my baby's fault I've

suffered so much. And it's hard to feel love for her when she was the cause of everything. She just cries all the time and I want to rest."

"You've had a very difficult time, Lana. Your beautiful little Rosa didn't ask to be born, did she? It's not her fault you had a bad time. You wanted her so much when you were strong. I'll get the nurses to see that you can rest more so that your strength returns. I'll ask them to give Rosa the occasional bottle but we'll also give you more help when you're trying to feed her."

"Thanks. I'd like that."

"You're so lucky to have such a healthy, beautiful baby. You might find you enjoy feeding her when you're feeling more rested and start getting to know Rosa. I'll come back and see you at the end of my morning."

By the end of her morning she was beginning to wish she hadn't promised to give so many patients a second visit. Fortunately, there were fewer outpatients than usual and those who came in weren't in a serious condition.

Amongst the patients she treated were a couple of tourists with mild sunstroke who only needed reassuring that if they stayed out of the sun till the end of their holiday, and applied the cream she gave them they would survive.

A small boy who'd fallen down in the school playground required a couple of stitches in his head and Tanya gave him a glass of milk and a biscuit because he said he hadn't had time for breakfast.

Another bigger boy required her to set his arm in a cast, having fallen from a tree and fractured his ulna.

The four friends who'd come with him wanted to sign his cast immediately and then the patient wanted Tanya to sign it and the two nurses who'd helped her.

She hurried round the patients requiring second visits. As she came out of the orthopaedic unit where she'd given a second visit to reassure the young man who'd been admitted during the night with a fractured jaw that he was first on the list in Theatre that afternoon, she saw Manolis heading towards her down the corridor.

"We never did get that coffee," he said, looking down at her as they both paused.

"Later," she said.

"Much later. I've just scheduled Thomas for two o' clock. Has he been starved?"

"He's complaining he's had no food since yesterday evening. Difficult to tell what he says with that fractured jaw but—"

"He shouldn't even be trying to speak."

"That's what I told him. I gave him a notepad and a pencil so he can write instead of speaking."

"Good!" He paused. "I need an assistant in Theatre this afternoon."

"I thought you might."

"Let's take a break."

"Not now. Manolis, I need to—"

"Whatever it is, delegate it. We need a break together before we spend the afternoon and possibly the evening in Theatre."

She gave him a whimsical smile. "So I'm included in your schedule today, am I?"

"If I had my way…" He paused and took a deep

breath while he stopped himself before he spoke his innermost thoughts. He mustn't say it—yet. He wanted to be absolutely certain of her feelings for him. He mustn't say that he wished she would be part of his whole life. He mustn't frighten her away again.

"Yes?"

"If I had my way, we wouldn't have so many emergency operations." He moved closer. "It would make life so much easier. But, then, we wouldn't have chosen to be doctors if we wanted an easy life."

He cleared his throat to get rid of the huskiness that had developed suddenly. Putting on his professional voice, he told her they would have a break together so that they could discuss the patient they were going to operate on that afternoon.

There was no one in the staff canteen when they arrived. A young waitress appeared from the kitchen and took their order. Manolis led the way to one of the small tables by the window, overlooking the harbour. He held the back of a chair until Tanya sat down on it. They looked at each other across the table.

Tanya had so many questions she wanted to ask Manolis about the six-year period in their lives when she'd tried to forget him. But now wasn't the time. Later, she hoped, there would be a real opportunity when they were alone and really off duty.

They discussed their patient, Thomas, while sipping their strong black Greek coffee as they waited for food to arrive.

"Apparently he was in that new nightclub on the

edge of the harbour road. He was coming down from the roof terrace when he missed his footing and fell head first onto the ground floor. He took the full force of his weight on his chin which, from the X-rays, looks as if it's shattered. I'll need to put a titanium plate in to keep the shards of bone from disseminating into the surrounding tissues, I think. But I'll decide exactly what needs to be done when I operate."

"Will you have to cut through the tissue at the front of the chin?"

"I'm going to try to approach it from the lower palate. As I say, it will become more obvious when I've got the patient under sedation."

He reached across the table and took her hand. She felt her body quiver imperceptibly at his touch. Even in the middle of a professional discussion her body could awaken with desire by the least physical contact.

"Thanks for agreeing to assist me. We work well together, don't we?"

She smiled, still very much aware of his fingers now stroking her hand. "It's my job to assist you when I'm needed."

The waitress had arrived with their food and was waiting to place it on the table. Manolis leaned back in his chair and simply looked across the table at the wonderful woman from his past who'd materialised in this unexpected way. He'd never thought he would get a second chance. He mustn't blow it this time.

Tanya looked at the Greek salad and kalimara they'd ordered. She watched as Manolis dressed it with oil and vinegar, before serving some onto her plate together with a few of the battered and deep-fried baby squid.

She smiled. "You remembered just how I like it."

"It was a long time ago but I seemed to remember automatically. It was that restaurant by the sea in Darling harbour, wasn't it?"

She laughed. "No, it was when we used to go to that Greek taverna by Bondi beach. Spend the whole day swimming. We always had Greek salad and kalimara because it was light enough for us to go in the water during the afternoon—after we'd had a short siesta under the trees."

"Yes, I remember now."

His eyes had taken on a distant look as his memory became nostalgic for those wonderful heady days of sun, sea, surf and sex with the most wonderful woman in the world. It could be like that again if…

"And now we're having the same meal because it's light enough to eat before a long afternoon in Theatre," Tanya said. "I'm enjoying the work here but I'm looking forward to the weekend to spend our off duty with you and Chrysanthe."

Manolis put down his fork and looked across the table. "There's been a change of plan, I'm afraid. We're expecting a large tourist vessel to be anchored off Ceres for the weekend. The tour company has informed us that the passengers are going to spend the whole weekend on the island." He hesitated. "I had to make the decision to cancel all weekend off duty."

She pulled a wry grin. "Oh, well, I suppose it was a wise decision. I'm disappointed but—"

"That's the problem with being in charge. I have to make wise but unpopular decisions. We'll get away one weekend soon. But now that the tourist season is in full swing, our off duty times will be a little unpredictable."

"I understand."

She did, she really did. But she longed to have more time with him. To sort out where they were both going together. A whole weekend together would have helped to cement this new uncertain relationship they were trying to sort out between work assignments.

She pushed her plate to one side and took the bold step of reaching across the table to take his hand in hers. "We'll just have to make the most of the time we can spend together."

He smiled across at her. "Always the pragmatic one. That's one of the things I like about you."

She smiled back. "Come on. We'd better get moving."

He glanced up at the clock. "Yes. The anaesthetist will be here in a few minutes and I want to fill him in on the patient's condition. He's got a history of high blood pressure…"

The operation was long and difficult but with the expertise of the surgical team it was a success. Manolis put two small titanium plates in the chin, which would ensure that the tiny fragments of bone were contained within their boundaries. The fractured jawbone required screws to hold it in place and he'd had to extract four molars, which were badly smashed and posed a danger at the back of the mouth.

Then he'd put four little hooks into the patient's gums so that he could fix elastic bands around them to limit mobility of the mouth. Thomas was put on a high-protein-fluids-only diet for the next six weeks until the bone healed.

As she settled their patient in his bed after several hours, Tanya breathed a sigh of relief.

"Am I OK, Doctor?" Thomas murmured.

"You're going to be fine. But don't try to talk yet. There's a nurse sitting here beside you and she'll be there all night. So, anything you want, just scribble it on your notepad. I'll be in tomorrow morning to see you."

Her patient's grateful eyes told her all she needed to know. He was a tough young man and would pull through very well.

"Your girlfriend's just arrived and I've told her she can stay the night here so you've got a nurse and a girlfriend to take care of you. The morphine will help you to sleep."

Manolis held her hand as they walked up the *kali strata*.

"Let's stop here for a moment," Tanya said, feeling slightly breathless. "I always like to admire the view and catch my breath. It seems ages since I was here this morning. Such a difference now that Ceres harbour is bathed in moonlight. The twinkling lights on the boats and the tavernas—and the club where Thomas fell down the stairs last night. Poor Thomas! He's a good patient."

He turned and drew her into his arms. "And you're a very good doctor, Tanya."

She looked up into his eyes, seeing his tender expression that seemed so poignant in the moonlight.

"I always longed for the day when you would say that, Manolis."

His expression turned to one of surprise. "Did you?"

"That was one of the reasons I worked so hard to become a doctor. So that you would take me seriously."

"I've always taken you seriously."

"Yes, you have, since I grew up. But you did used to tease me as a child, didn't you?"

"Boys always believe girls are there to be teased. Your brother was just the same, wasn't he?"

"Exactly. But, yes, you're right. I shouldn't have taken it to heart as I did. But that's the way most young girls react."

"But you must admit I took you seriously when we met again and I realised you were grown up."

She smiled. "Yes, you certainly took me seriously then."

"I'd noticed you when you were a teenager but at that time the age gap was too much. But when I saw you that first time in Australia, I was absolutely blown away!"

He bent his head and kissed her lips as they parted to welcome him. For several idyllic seconds they remained locked in an exquisite embrace before the sound of footsteps threatened to disturb them.

"Let's go home," Tanya murmured as she tried to gather her strength for the final climb.

"Your place or mine?" he whispered.

Tanya was the first to waken. They'd both slept after making exquisitely wild passionate love on the soft feather mattress of her bed. It was a hot night and

Manolis had thrown the sheet on to the floor where it lay entangled with their hastily discarded clothes. As she looked around her bedroom, with the early morning light filtering through the window, she felt glad that she'd suggested they sleep at her place last night. She loved waking up in her own bed with Manolis by her side.

She turned to look at him and her heart filled with love—real love this time, she realised. Had she experienced real love all those years ago when she had still been rather naïve about her emotions? Maybe. But not like she felt now.

He stirred beside her and opened his eyes, reaching for her, pulling her into his arms.

"Why are you looking so serious?

"I was just thinking how inexperienced I was when I moved in with you in Australia."

His eyes, so tender, locked with hers. "I didn't notice," he said huskily.

"Oh, I'm not talking about when we made love. That was just…just…"

"Wonderful? Out of this world?"

"Yes, it was, but emotionally I wasn't ready for the big commitment I was expected to make."

He leaned up on one elbow and stared down at her. "I hadn't realised that."

She swallowed hard. "When you asked me to marry you…I wasn't ready. It was such a big step. I wanted to be with you but…" Her voice trailed away.

"I'm sorry you felt…hassled?"

"Manolis, I didn't feel hassled. I just found that I had too many decisions to make all at once. My life had changed so completely in the space of a few weeks. When I told you I was pregnant and you proposed, I wondered if you were simply doing the dutiful thing and—"

"Of course I wasn't doing the dutiful thing! I wanted you to marry me so that we could bring up our child together!"

"And then again in the hospital after the miscarriage, I was in such a weakened state I couldn't think straight. I simply wanted time to sort out all my feelings." She took a deep breath. "If I could turn the clock back I think I would have done things differently. I wouldn't have asked you to leave like that. I just wanted you to go away for a while so I could sort out my confused feelings. I didn't think I might never see you again—"

He held her closer in his embrace. She was trying to hold back the tears. Between sobs she began again. "I remember the awful day, just a few weeks after I'd miscarried, when reality hit me and I realised how I'd mismanaged everything and you'd gone away for ever."

"I really thought that was what you wanted. Your mother had advised me not to contact you. I thought the best thing for everyone was if I started a new life and tried to forget you."

He was still holding her close as if to reassure himself that she wasn't going to vanish. This precious person, the only woman he'd ever really loved, was actually here with him and he had to tread carefully not to destroy his dreams.

"I was devastated when you sent me away," he said hoarsely as the memories came flooding back. "I don't even remember what I said to your mother when she advised me not to contact you. She asked me if I was OK, I remember, but the rest is a blur. I went straight back to the apartment and drank a beer, then another. Anything to dull the actual physical pain I was feeling. I'd lost my partner, my child, my whole life had changed in a matter of weeks and—"

"Darling, I'm sorry, I'm so sorry!" She stirred in his arms and raised her eyes to his. "If I'd been thinking normally I wouldn't have been so…so stupid as to break up what we had between us. What happened to you after that? What did you do the next day?"

"I wasn't fit for work. I wouldn't have let myself loose on the patients. I phoned in sick for a couple of days. Then I got a phone call from my old tutor in London—the one I told you about. He asked me if I'd thought about the post in London. I told him my circumstances; told him I was in a terrible emotional state. He advised me to resign and come straight over to London, told me I would feel better once I got away."

"So you went."

"There was nothing to hold me in Australia. I remember going through the interview, answering questions automatically, not even caring whether I got the job or not. I simply wanted the pain of losing you—and our child—to go away. And when I got the job, and started working, the pain started to ease. It wasn't so much physical then as a mental nagging at me that something wasn't right."

"But you had your new…girlfriend to comfort you."

"Yes, I suppose I had. But I couldn't help mentally comparing what I'd had with you, Tanya. I threw myself into my new job and it helped to be doing something I was trained to do, something that would help other people."

"Work always helps. I threw myself into my studies, worked hard at the practical work on the wards, tried not to think about what I'd lost, and little by little I returned to some sort of normality. Yes, the pain eased…" She swallowed hard as her voice began to falter.

"We've both suffered," she said softly as she started again. "Let's just take one day at a time. It's wonderful to be together again and…" Dared she say it? "And have a second chance at…at happiness together."

His lips sought hers. He'd wanted to kiss her as she struggled with her words, her emotions still confused, he could see. This time he wouldn't rush things. Wouldn't ask her to make decisions. His precious darling had to be treated gently, with great tenderness.

His kiss deepened as he felt himself become aroused once more. Tanya was responding, her beautiful body opening up to him. His breathing quickened.

Tanya cried out as they became one. Her body felt as if it was on fire with the sensual flames flickering through her. She climaxed over and over again until she lay spent with exhaustion, fulfilment and happiness in his arms…

CHAPTER SEVEN

ON THAT wonderful night when Manolis had taken her home after their lengthy session in Theatre, Tanya hadn't dreamed that it would be more than two weeks before the long-awaited day out on Manolis's boat. As she hurriedly packed a small bag with towel and spare bikini—she was already wearing her favourite white one under her jeans—her thoughts drifted back to that exquisite night they'd spent together.

It had certainly been a turning point in their relationship. She remembered how he'd carried her up the narrow stairs to her bedroom. They'd laughed at the romantic gesture that had always made them giggle when they'd been living together in his tiny apartment in Sydney.

The people who owned the apartment had been Greek and had built a small mezzanine floor with a moussandra—a raised platform—for the bed. Manolis had so often insisted on carrying her up the small staircase when it had been obvious to both of them that they were going to fall on to the bed and make love.

He'd carried her upstairs so gently when he'd come to terms with the fact that she was expecting their baby.

For a few days after she'd first told him she could tell he was shocked but it hadn't taken long before he'd said he was looking forward to being a father. He'd insisted on cooking supper for them that evening, she remembered, making her sit with her feet up on the sofa.

Afterwards he'd scooped her up in his arms and carried her carefully up the stairs.

"Our first child," he'd said as he'd laid her gently on the bed, treating her as if she were made of Dresden china. "I shall carry you upstairs from now on."

She'd laughed, telling him when she got as big as a house she wouldn't hold him to it. But that hadn't happen anyway because she hadn't got very far on the motherhood road...

She zipped up her bag and told herself she wasn't going to continue that train of thought. Their present relationship was sailing along beautifully now. She wouldn't allow herself to dwell on the past or the future. Only the present was what she cared about when she was with Manolis. They'd both established that fact when they'd made love a couple of weeks ago. It was as if they'd never had that six-year split. Their bodies were so tuned to each other's that...

She drew in her breath and shivered with remembered sensual passion. It had been the most wonderful night of her life—until the next night and the next night...

"Are you up there, Tanya?" came the recognisable voice of Chrysanthe.

Tanya's door was always open and Chrysanthe often wandered in when she knew that Tanya was home.

"Yes, come on up, *agapi mou*. I'm nearly ready."

"Daddy says we've got to go soon. He was using his cross voice so I think he means now."

The little girl arrived panting at the top of the stairs that led straight into Tanya's bedroom. She held out her arms for a hug. Tanya lifted her up and hugged her, revelling in the clean smell of soap and shampoo. She sat her down on the edge of the bed.

"Let me look at you, Chrysanthe. I love the new shorts!"

"Daddy bought them ages ago because I was sad we couldn't go out in the boat. He said it was because you both had to work every day because the tourists kept on breaking their bones or cutting their skin or getting sick."

"That's very true. But we've got a whole day off today."

"Why do the tourists make such a lot of work for you and Daddy? In the winter when it's just the people who live on the island you won't have to work so hard, will you? You and Daddy will be able to look after me properly, won't you?"

"What's that about looking after you properly?" came a whimsical deep voice from down below. "If you girls don't get a move on, I'll have to go without you."

Manolis took the stairs two at a time and stood at the top, half in and half out of her bedroom. It was as if his heart missed a beat when he saw the two people most precious to him. Together, just like mother and daughter. Only they weren't. They should have been if… Don't go there!

"What was that I heard you say, Chrysanthe? You don't think we look after you properly when the tourists are here? Are you trying to say you feel neglected?"

He was using a jocular tone but his daughter's words had reinforced the worry he had about the way his precious child was being brought up.

"What does neglect mean?"

Manolis looked across at Tanya as if he wanted her to help him out.

"Well it's a bit difficult," she began cautiously. "Would you like to spend more time with Daddy?"

"Yes, and you as well, Tanya. You're like my mummy now, aren't you?"

Tanya's eyes locked with Manolis's, both of them now pleading for help in a delicate situation.

It was Tanya who spoke first to ease the tension. "Well, I help to look after you, Chrysanthe, but you've already got a mummy in England, haven't you?"

"Yes, but you could be my mummy here on the island, couldn't you? I'd like that."

Manolis could feel his heartstrings pulling. He noticed that Tanya's eyes were moist. She was holding back her tears. He wanted to draw her into his arms, tell her he loved her, ask her to become the second mother to his daughter, make some more babies of their own…

Thoughts rushed through his head about all the things he wanted to do but didn't dare suggest. He had to take it more slowly this time round. He'd rushed her the last time when he'd asked her to marry him after only a few weeks together. They needed time to simply enjoy being together again.

"I enjoy looking after you and being with you, Chrysanthe," Tanya said carefully, deliberately avoiding Manolis's eyes.

"I think we should set off now," Manolis said briskly. "The harbour's getting busier by the minute and I've always found it hard to extricate my boat when the place is full of tourists."

Tanya rolled her eyes at Chrysanthe as she scooped her up into her arms. "Now he tells us!"

Chrysanthe dissolved into a fit of giggles. "I'll drive the boat, Daddy! I know how to do it. Uncle Lakis showed me. You just put your hand on the steering-wheel and—"

"OK, child genius," Manolis said, taking her from Tanya's arms and beginning the descent of the stairs. "I'll let you have a go with the boat when we're safely at the tiny island where we're going to have lunch."

"Can we have a barbecue?"

"Of course! But only if you help me catch a nice big fish."

It was, they all agreed, one of the biggest fish that had ever been caught on Ceres. Well, at least on the small rocky island where they'd moored the boat. It had taken Manolis and Chrysanthe only half an hour before it had taken their bait and got hauled in. Chrysanthe and Tanya had then spent a long time swimming and playing in the water while Manolis had gutted the fish and put it on the barbecue he'd rigged up at the edge of the sea.

"When's the food ready, Daddy?" Chrysanthe had called several times, only to be told it wouldn't be long but he needed a swim before he served it. They were finally all able to swim together, amid a lot of laughter and splashing about. As they came out of the water, the three of them holding hands with Chrysanthe in the middle, Manolis glanced across at Tanya, his heart full of love for the family that seemed to have emerged so suddenly.

She swallowed hard as she looked at him. Was this what parenting was about, would be about if only she could commit to Manolis again? But did he still want her? He needed her…yes…but…

"Smell that wonderful fish!" Manolis called, clambering back up the rocks to rescue the precious fish from the grill of the barbecue where an inquisitive goat was wondering if it dared brave the fire.

Manolis told the girls to sit down so that he could serve them and they crouched by the fire, accepting delicious offerings of fish, Greek salad and crusty bread, washed down with wine or fresh lime juice in Chrysanthe's case.

Tanya stretched out on her sandy towel and chewed on the delicious piece of fish that Manolis had just handed to her on the end of his fork. She'd taken it with her fingers and popped it into her mouth.

"Mmm, delicious! What is it?"

"It's some kind of *psari*, rather like tuna—I don't know it's name in English." They were talking in Greek, as they often did.

"It's *psari*, fish," Chrysanthe said.

Manolis smiled. "We know it's fish, darling, but we were wondering exactly what kind."

Chrysanthe shrugged. "I'll look it up in my picture book of fish when we get back. I often have to translate words when we're having our English lesson at school because my teacher says I'm bi-biling…something."

"Bilingual," Tanya supplied.

"What does it mean?"

"It means you can speak two languages."

"Can't everybody?"

"They often can if they've got one English parent and one Greek parent. That's why I'm bilingual."

"Just like me!" Chrysanthe snuggled closer, oblivious to the fact that she was putting her sticky fingers on Tanya's towel.

"Have you had enough fish, you two?"

"Absolutely! That was wonderful!"

"Would madam care for dessert?"

Tanya picked up a flat pebble and pretended to study the menu. "I'll have the crème caramel."

"I'm afraid it's off. Would madam settle for an orange?"

"If it's freshly picked from the tree."

Manolis reached up and pretended to take an orange from the branch overhanging their shady spot.

Chrysanthe had gone past giggling and was laughing loudly now. "Daddy, you and Tanya are so funny," she spluttered. "I like it when you don't have to work. You're much more fun. I'd like to live on this island, wouldn't you?"

"Oh, you'd get bored eventually," Manolis said as he rummaged through the hamper in search of the oranges.

Tanya stretched out on her towel, Chrysanthe having

suddenly decided to run down to the edge of the sea in search of some more shells.

She looked up at the blue cloudless sky and then glanced across at the smart new motorboat bobbing on the water nearby. It had been such fun as they'd left the harbour far behind and Manolis had been able to speed along over the waves. Chrysanthe had shouted with delight when they'd reached their little island. It was little more than a few rocks surrounded by sand but Chrysanthe had announced that it was their own special island from now on.

"We're completely alone on this island, aren't we?" she breathed as she took the orange that Manolis was handing to her. "It's like playing at Robinson Crusoe. I agree with Chrysanthe. I'd like to live here and eat nothing but fish and oranges."

He leaned across her and kissed her gently on the mouth. She responded, but not as much as she would have done if they'd been alone. Glancing across at the small figure by the water, she saw that Chrysanthe was fully occupied in gathering shells, which they would soon have to inspect. She allowed herself the luxury of parting her lips and savouring the moment. Her body was stirring with desire. She pulled away as gently as she could so as not to destroy the delicious ambience they'd created.

"Mmm, it's so peaceful."

"Utter bliss," Manolis said, his fingers lightly moving down her arm. "I'm having difficulty controlling myself."

"Me too!"

"Are you free this evening?"

"I'll have to check my diary first."

"Cancel everything," he murmured, drawing her closer.

"I might just do that," she murmured, before dragging herself away and holding out her hand to be pulled up. "It's time we gave some quality time to our little darling."

The word "our" wasn't lost on Manolis as he drew Tanya to her feet. "Is that how you think of her?"

She hesitated. "I'm afraid it is now," she said, slowly.

"Don't be afraid, Tanya. Enjoy this feeling of family that we now have. We're all so close and—"

"Daddy, Tanya, come and see this little fish in the water. It's nibbling my toes, come and see it."

They inspected the fish, before going further out into the bay to swim. Tanya was relieved to find that Chrysanthe swam like a fish. There was no need to worry about her, although she and Manolis swam one on each side of her.

When they came out of the sea Chrysanthe stretched out on the sand under the trees in their picnic spot at the edge of the shore where the sand turned to rocks. "I'm quite sleepy," she murmured as she curled into a ball, closed her eyes and drifted off to sleep like a baby.

Manolis took hold of Tanya's hand. "I'm quite sleepy too," he murmured as he gently took her to one side of the sleeping child and moved across to a shady spot where they could still keep an eye on Chrysanthe.

"You're so wicked," Tanya said as he drew her down on to the sand beside him.

"I know." His fingers toyed with the strap of her bikini top.

"No," she whispered, her hand covering his. "Not in front of your daughter."

He gave her a wry grin. "Prude!"

"I'm not! And you know it. It's just that if she were to wake up she'd be so shocked. Oh, I don't know. It's all part of learning about being a parent."

She stopped, knowing she'd said more than she meant to. "And I'm not even a parent so…I know my place in this family. I'm just a friend."

"My darling, you're more than a friend and you know it. You mean…such a lot to me. Now that you've come back into my life it's so natural that you're part of the family. That's how Chrysanthe thinks of you anyway."

"But I'm not part of the family!"

He drew her closer and kissed her gently as he felt her shoulders shaking. She was crying now. He didn't know how to handle this. He hadn't known how to handle her when she'd lost their baby. She'd cried and he'd felt so useless—just as he felt now. The last time she'd cried in his arms he'd begged her to marry him so he could take care of her. But she'd pushed him away, told him she wanted to be alone.

So this time he remained silent. Held her until the sobs subsided, kissed her gently on the lips and then released her from his embrace.

She was calm now as she turned to him. "I'm sorry. I just felt a bit strange, that's all. It sort of brought back memories I want to forget. I'm happy with the way we are now, aren't you, Manolis?"

"I'm glad you came back into my life," he said carefully.

He was holding himself in check now. One word too many and the whole bubble of his happiness would burst.

"We've been through such a lot together and now…I just don't know how to handle the parent thing." She looked into his eyes so earnestly locked with hers. "How do you think Victoria will feel when she finds out Chrysanthe regards me as a mother figure here?"

"Victoria was never very maternal. She was anxious to get on with her career and insisted on employing a nanny right from day one. I used to bring Chrysanthe out to Ceres as often as I could because she was so happy here. She adores my mother and her cousins. When she was about three she asked if we could come and live here with Grandma. That was when I handed in my notice in London and bought the house on the island. Victoria's reaction was one of relief. Oh, don't get me wrong. She loves Chrysanthe but she doesn't give out that natural warmth that she needs—like you do. You're doing magnificently, especially as you're not a parent. I mean…"

"I know what you mean. I should have been a parent. We should have been parents together…"

"Darling!" He held her close again as her sobs renewed.

She rubbed her eyes with the back of her hand. "Hey, I'd better snap out of this. I don't know what came over me. Haven't cried so much since…well, a long time ago, you know."

"I know." His tone was very gentle, so scared to break up the newfound bond that was developing between them. "Look, we've both been there, done that and survived." He cleared his throat. "So, how about we have a party tonight to celebrate?"

"A party?"

He reached forward again at the alarmed expression on her face. "Not a party party. Just the two of us at my place. A bottle of champagne—oh, yes, we can now get champagne on Ceres. Thing have changed since you lived here."

"Well, I certainly was never allowed to drink the imported champagne at any of the family weddings."

"You were too young." He ran his fingers through her hair. "But you started to grow up and I remember looking at you when you were sixteen or seventeen and thinking if you were only a few years older, you would be perfect for me."

"Did you really?" She snuggled against him.

"Of course I did! So did all my friends. You were absolutely gorgeous—but completely unaware how attractive you were."

"I wish I'd known I was attractive. I was so caught up in the idea of proving myself clever enough to be a doctor like my dad, my brother and you that I never wore make-up or short skirts or anything like that. Relationships with the opposite sex were all pushed to one side."

A thoughtful expression flitted across his face. "That might account for a lot of things."

"Like what?"

She lay back in his arms, looking up through the leaves above her head. A large heron was flying above her. It skimmed above her head, swooping down towards the sea before expertly lifting a small fish into its jaws and flying away over the calm blue waters.

"Like why it took all my powers of persuasion to get

you to move in with me in Sydney. You'd grown up to be a beautiful young woman by then but you still seemed completely unaware of the fact that you were enormously fanciable."

She grinned mischievously. "Oh, I was totally aware. I was just fed up with playing the little-woman bit. I'd realised that at long last friends and family took me seriously. At last I'd got the power to be independent. And I wasn't going to surrender all that so easily."

He swallowed hard. "So when you surrendered to me, as you put it, it was a kind of testing time, was it?"

"It was a wonderful time in my life…while it lasted."

"And now…back to the present. Will you come to my party tonight?" he said. "I promise, we won't talk about the future."

She smiled. "You know me so well."

He gave her a wry grin. "I'm beginning to."

"Then I'd love to come to your party."

She glanced across at Chrysanthe who was sitting up now, looking around her, slightly bewildered.

"Tanya! Daddy! Let's go swimming again, shall we?"

Tanya went in through the open door and sat down in Manolis's small kitchen.

"I'm here!" she called as her eyes became accustomed to the twinkling candles on the kitchen table and took in the champagne holder full of ice, waiting for the bottle, which was obviously chilling in the fridge.

"Come on up! I'm in the bedroom."

"Is that wise?"

"Probaby not, but come up anway."

He was standing at the top of the staircase. He was wearing one of the faded sarongs they'd bought from an Indonesian trader when they'd been in Australia. He looked like an Olympic athlete, every muscle of his well-honed body hard and ready for action. She stood up. In a couple of seconds he reached the ground floor and drew her into his arms.

He nuzzled her hair. "I've been waiting all day for this moment."

"Me too!"

"So you didn't enjoy our day on our island?"

"It was wonderful!" She raised her head for his kiss. "But like a tired non-parent, I'm ready for some adult fun."

"Adult fun! Well you've come to the right place." He bent down and blew out the candles. "Just in case we don't get down here for an hour or so."

He reached into the fridge, took out the bottle of champagne and dumped it into the champagne cooler. Holding this in one hand, he scooped her up into his arms with the other and made for the stairs.

This time when they made love it was exquisitely tender, each body dovetailing into the other as if they'd never been apart. He held her so close, so much part of him, so loved, that she thought she had never known such happiness.

And when she reached the pinnacle of her climax she cried out at the impossible wonder of being once more with the man she'd loved first in her life and maybe would go on to love…for…for a long time.

As she lay back against the pillows and looked into his eyes she knew she'd really come home this time. She would give up everything for him, she was ready now. She'd gone through the independent bit. It was possible to be a wife, a mother even and still have it all with a man like Manolis. If she could only convey this to him now. He'd asked her before and been turned down. Would he ever ask her again?

He stroked her cheek, his eyes locking with hers. "Why so serious now?"

"Am I serious?"

"If I didn't know you so well I'd say there was something important on your mind. You're going to make an announcement."

She hesitated. He wouldn't like it if she proposed to him. He really wouldn't. He was this macho Greek man, steeped in centuries of male dominance. The last thing she should do was make the first move—even if she wanted to. After the way she'd treated him in Australia she was probably the last woman on earth he'd ever propose to. Anyway, why was she so suddenly getting soft about marriage? She didn't need to be married, did she? Her love for Manolis was strong enough to survive anything now.

"No, I'm not going to make an announcement," she improvised. "Except to say I'm starving and about to call room service."

He kissed the tip of her nose before reaching for the champagne bottle on his bedside table.

"Room service coming right up."

As he was deftly pouring the fizzy liquid into her

glass and handing it to her, the thought occurred that it could be a good time to pop the question uppermost in his mind. But even as the thought came into his mind he dismissed it.

This woman would never surrender her independence. He could feel that she loved him again now but anything more was pure fantasy.

He would settle for the present, wonderful as it was, and leave the conventional ideas to other couples. Tanya still needed her freedom and he had to respect that.

CHAPTER EIGHT

"I'M GOING to see Mummy in England next week, Tanya—my English mummy—not you. Daddy told me this morning. But you'll still be here when I get back, won't you? You'll never leave me, will you?"

Tanya lifted the small excited girl into her arms and kissed her soft cheek. The beautiful, sensitive dark brown eyes— just like her father's—were pleading with her to stay for ever. How could she answer such a poignant request? Over the summer weeks she'd grown so close to Chrysanthe, to love this child as if she were her own. But how could she predict what the future held for Manolis and herself at this delicate stage in their relationship? She was going to do all she could to ensure that they continued to trust each other more and more but she still wasn't sure how Manolis felt about a permanent relationship now.

She swallowed hard. "Of course I'll be here when you get back from England." That was definitely true.

Chrysanthe looked around proudly as she saw her other small friends greeting their mothers at the school gate. A couple of her friends had already asked if the pretty doctor lady was her mother. She'd wanted to say yes, but she knew that would have been a naughty lie so she'd had to tell the truth. So she'd told them she had two mummies—one in England and one in Ceres.

Tanya was putting her down on the ground now. That was good. Lots of her friends had seen her being greeted by her wonderful Ceres mummy.

She grabbed hold of Tanya's hand and called goodbye to her nearest friend, who'd kept on all day in school about her new baby brother. She must find out about the possibility of a new baby brother or sister for herself. She wasn't quite sure how it worked. It was something to do with mummies and daddies getting together to plant a seed somewhere but her English mother had told her it probably wouldn't happen till her daddy got married again.

She squeezed Tanya's hand tightly. She'd have to work on that one. Grown-ups could be so difficult about things that seemed so simple. If Katia's mummy could get a baby brother for Katia, why couldn't one of her mummies get one for her?

"I told my friends you were my Ceres mummy." Chrysanthe looked up at Tanya as she skipped along beside her, anxious to see her reaction. You never knew with grown-ups. They had funny ideas about what was proper and what wasn't.

Tanya stopped walking for a moment and looked down at the adorable little girl. She loved her to bits but she could be so precocious at times. They'd reached the section of the *kali strata* where the steps became steeper before the final slog to the top. She looked away for a moment, trying to draw inspiration from the beautiful view of the harbour and the hills beyond, but nothing came into her head to resolve the situation.

"Did you, darling?" She knew this was no resolution but she had to say something when Chrysanthe was looking up at her so anxiously, obviously seeking approval.

"Well, they wanted to know if you were my mummy so I had to tell them you were my second mummy," Chrysanthe said quickly. "That wasn't a lie, was it?"

Tanya wasn't sure what to say now. She'd had a busy day in hospital and questioning from Chrysanthe was hard work right now. Especially when you weren't a parent! If only Manolis were here.

She'd left him in Theatre reconstructing a mangled leg. Their patient had somehow managed to get caught up in a two-car collision and been shunted by a car with dodgy brakes. Manolis had taken her to one side just before he'd started the operation and told her it was time she went off duty. He would get assistance from Yannis, their new doctor who'd trained in Athens but had recently returned to Ceres, where he'd been born. He'd applied for the temporary post during the tourist season that they'd recently advertised.

"I took him on for the season because he has excellent references. He comes from a good family here on Ceres. His wife died a couple of years ago and he's decided to make a break from their life together in Athens. Anyway, I'd like to give him a chance to show what he can do," he whispered. "If he's anything as good as you are..."

"Flattery will get you everywhere, Doctor," she told him. "I must admit that the thought of a long hot bath would—"

"Well, actually, I wondered if you could pick up Chrysanthe from school?"

"I knew there'd be a catch in it! Only joking! I'd love to. Haven't seen her for a couple of days."

"That's what she told me this morning. She asked if you could pick her up like a proper mummy."

Tanya had groaned. "She's obsessed with mummies at the moment."

"I think it's because she's off to London next week. And also she likes her friends to think you're her mummy."

She brought herself back to the current dilemma as Chrysanthe repeated the question that had to be answered now. "It wasn't a lie when I said you were my Ceres mummy, was it?"

"If that's how you think of me…then…"

"Oh, thank you, Tanya! I do love you!"

"And I love you too, Chrysanthe."

Tears were pricking her eyes as she held onto the hot, sticky hand that was tightly clinging to hers. She sniffed and wiped a tissue over her eyes with her other hand before they continued the final section of the steep steps.

"Now, what shall we do when we get back home?"

"Your home? We're going to your home, aren't we? I like your house. Can we do some baking like we did last time I came to see you? We could make some more of those little jam tarts."

"Yes, we could."

Tanya took a deep breath as she realised she must draw on her inner reserves of strength. She had to keep going at the end of this long, tiring day. She couldn't disappoint Chrysanthe.

By the time Chrysanthe had mixed the flour with butter and water, plunging her little fingers into the dough-like substance, they were both laughing. Tanya was reinvigorated and had completely forgotten she was tired as she joined in the excitement of producing the tarts, which they were planning to eat as soon as they were ready.

"Can I invite my cousins round to help us eat them?"

Tanya wiped a damp kitchen towel over Chrysanthe's sticky hands. "Of course. The more the merrier!"

Chrysanthe reached up her hands and put them round Tanya's neck so that she could pull down her face for a kiss on the cheek. "I'll go and see who's with Grandma today. Don't go away, will you, Tanya?"

"No, I won't go away…"

The following week, when it was time for Chrysanthe to go to London, Tanya felt sad that she wasn't going to see her little surrogate daughter for two whole weeks. She placed the chicken casserole she'd made on the kitchen table and looked across at Manolis, who'd come round for supper.

"I'm really going to miss her, you know."

She picked up the large soup ladle and put a generous helping on Manolis's plate.

"Mmm, this smells delicious. You always could make a good casserole." He put down his spoon and looked directly into her eyes. "Did I tell you I'm going to stay in London for three days when I take Chrysanthe to Victoria's house?"

She sat down and busied herself with the wax dripping onto the table from one of the candles she'd lit to make the little kitchen seem romantic.

"No, I don't believe you did," she said nonchalantly. "I rather thought you were coming straight back."

"Well, Victoria says it's time I got to know Toby, her boyfriend. She's moved into his big house near Hyde Park. Apparently, it was his idea that I should stay until Chrysanthe settles in."

"Sounds a very understanding sort of person."

She tried to swallow a small spoonful of chicken and look as if she was unaffected by the idea of Manolis spending three days in London with his ex-wife.

"He's a retired cardiac surgeon, I believe."

"Retired? So he's older than Victoria?"

"Oh, yes. He's got grown-up children and a couple of small grandchildren. His wife left him for a younger man, I believe. Victoria told me they started off having a platonic friendship and then one thing led to another. I don't think it's a passionate love affair but it seems to suit them both."

Manolis bent his head and applied himself to the casserole, hoping they could now drop the subject. He'd explained what was going to happen but Tanya seemed concerned.

Tanya swallowed her spoonful of chicken and tried to think of a different subject than the one now uppermost in her mind. Was she jealous or was it just that she couldn't bear the thought of being without Manolis for the best part of four days?

She cleared her throat. "How do you know all this… er…stuff about Victoria?"

"Oh, she often phones to ask about Chrysanthe…how she's getting on at school, that kind of thing… May I have some more of this fantastic casserole?"

"Help yourself."

"You've hardly eaten anything. Let me serve you."

"No, thanks. I'm OK. But you go ahead."

There was an awkward silence for a while as Manolis finished his food and Tanya toyed with hers.

After a while she spoke. "What time do you leave tomorrow?"

"The boat leaves at seven."

He reached across the table and took hold of her hand. "What is it, darling? You don't look your usual self tonight."

"I'm tired, that's all." She picked up her plate and took it over to the sink. "I think I'll have an early night—"

He rose slowly, languidly from his seat and came round the table, a seductive smile on his face as he stood looking down at her. "How about I join you?"

She looked up into his dark liquid eyes and thought he'd never looked more desirable.

He drew her into his arms and kissed her tenderly, first on the lips and then on her neck. She felt his hands undoing the top button of her blouse and her body began to quiver with the renewed passion that always rose when they were close together.

"Why not?" she whispered.

Their love-making was tinged with a certain sadness that night. As Tanya revelled in their intimate embrace afterwards, legs entwined together, she was feeling much more relaxed than she had done at the supper table.

"You said you would miss Chrysanthe," he whispered, his hands gently running through her hair. "Are you going to miss me?"

"You know I am!"

"I don't know unless you tell me. I never know what you're thinking about me. I never did understand what goes on in that pretty little head of yours."

He leaned on his elbow and looked down into her eyes. The moon was so bright that they hadn't put the light on, both having agreed wordlessly that it was more romantic to make love by moonlight.

"I shall miss you a lot," she said quietly. "Just like I did in Australia after you left me."

"I left because you told me to go."

"I know. I was confused. As I told you before, I thought your proposal was simply you being dutiful. I didn't realise you...had strong feelings for me. Yes, we'd always enjoyed making love together but a lifetime commitment was too big for me to contemplate. You know I'd do things differently now, don't you? I hope I've made that clear if you're in any doubt about it."

She looked up at him thinking he'd never looked more handsome, more desirable. His dark rumpled hair was partly obscuring his face but she'd memorised his seductive expression over and over again as they'd made love. She wanted to be able to conjure up his image in her mind during the time when he wasn't with her.

She knew, without a shadow of a doubt, that she wanted to move their relationship on a level. If he were to propose to her now…If only he would! Surely he could read her thoughts. Surely she was making it obvious that she wanted their relationship to be permanent this time round.

He watched the worried expression that was flitting across her face. Something was disturbing her. Was she still scared of commitment? She'd always been a strong, independent person who needed to be as free as a bird. If he were to voice his innermost desire to make her his wife, would she clam up and go all cold on him again? Better to enjoy the relationship they had now than risk losing her again. She'd said she would do things differently this time, but had she really thought about the consequences, the lifetime commitment?

A rasping sigh escaped his lips as he ran a hand through his hair, pulling it back from his eyes so that he could appreciate how beautiful, how infinitely desirable but how totally inaccessible she was.

"Why the big sigh?"

He took a deep breath. "I was thinking it was time…it was time I finished my packing."

"Packing! I'll set my alarm. You can't do it in the middle of the night!"

"Oh, but I can!" He was already out of bed, pulling on his trousers. "No, don't get up. You need your sleep. I'll see myself out. Goodnight, darling. Sleep well. I'll phone while I'm away."

He was leaning down, taking her in his arms for a final kiss. He really was leaving! She felt a moment of panic—not like when he left her before but something akin to that.

And then he was gone.

She buried her face in the pillow but she didn't cry. Her eyes were totally dry as she closed them and forced herself to remember that he was only going away for three nights. Three whole nights when he wouldn't come round from his house next door, take her in his arms, hold her through the night in his embrace…

The tears were beginning to make themselves felt behind her closed eyelids. She didn't want to cry. It was her own fault that their relationship had reached stalemate. She hadn't cried the first time round when she'd asked him to leave.

Yes, her hormones had been all over the place after her miscarriage. But at that stage in her life she hadn't realised that it would pass and she would arrive at the other side of the tragedy longing for the only man in the world who could help her put her life back together again.

She sat up in bed and reached for the box of tissues on the bedside table, rubbing her damp face vigorously. The moon had gone behind a cloud and her bedroom was dark now. She switched on the bedside lamp and leaned back against the pillows, staring up at the ceiling.

Supposing she were to bring up the subject of marriage with him? Couples sometimes just seemed to agree on marriage nowadays. It didn't seem to matter who brought up the idea. She'd met couples who'd just sort of drifted into marriage by common consent. But not with the background that Manolis had! Born here on Ceres, he was steeped in the importance of family. The man was the head of the family. When he was planning to take a wife and start his own family it was he who did the running, he who proposed to the woman of his choice.

He was macho through and through! As a boy he'd been made to feel how important he was. His mother, grandmother, sisters had all spoiled him, as was right and proper with the male of the species. With a family background like that he wouldn't dream of breaking the rules of life that had been set out long before his birth.

But she loved him more than life itself now. So it was up to her to make it clear—in a subtle way, of course—that she'd changed, that she was waiting for him to propose again and this time her answer would definitely be yes, yes, a thousand times yes!

When she got into hospital next day she went straight to see Patras, the patient who'd been involved in the car crash the previous day. She'd promised Manolis last night that she'd give him extra attention while he was away in London.

The doctor leaning over the patient's bed, inspecting the leg which Manolis had operated on, turned to look at her as she joined him.

"*Kali mera.* You must be Tanya. Manolis told me you would be here to help me while he's in London. I'm Yannis. I've recently come over from Athens and joined the team as a temporary doctor for the rest of the tourist season."

He smiled and held out his hand. She felt a firm grip

as she reciprocated the introduction, thinking all the while what a pleasant addition he was to the medical team. Tall and dark and definitely handsome, he would probably find the single members of the hospital staff fawning all over him! And some of the married ones too!

But not herself. She was so head over heels in love that she couldn't imagine how any woman could contemplate cheating on her man.

He was a consummate professional and a gentleman—she could see that by the deferential way he stepped back to allow her to examine their patient. He waited as she washed her hands at the sink close to the bed. When she turned round she saw something she hadn't noticed before—the aura of sadness that surrounded him in spite of his welcoming smile.

She remembered Manolis saying something about the new doctor having lost his wife a couple of years ago. How long did it take for someone to recover from the death of a loved one? Perhaps you never did.

He handed her the patient's notes. "I assisted Manolis yesterday in Theatre," he said quietly. "It was a difficult operation. These are the X-rays."

Yannis slotted them into the screen on the wall and switched on the light. She could see the shattered tallus had been pushed upwards and had impinged on the tibia, causing it to shatter into several fragments. She could see where Manolis had inserted screws and pins to hold the tibia in place so that it could, hopefully, knit together and form part of a viable leg when the healing process took over. Manolis had told her that Patras was basically a fit young man whose bones were very strong. It was only the intensity of the impact with part of the engine of the car he had been driving that had caused the bone to shatter.

Yannis removed the top part of the cast covering the leg so that Tanya could see the extent of the injury.

"How are you feeling, Patras?"

The young man grinned. "Better than I was. How long will I have to stay in, Doctor? Only I've got a hot date with a new girlfriend tonight and I'd rather like to get out. Couldn't you just give me some crutches and I'll be on my way?"

Tanya straightened up and looked down at her patient. "I'd love to be able to say it was that easy, Patras, but the fact is we're going to have to keep you in for a few days. At least until Dr Manolis gets back from London. This is a complicated break that's going to take—"

"When will Manolis be back?"

"In three days. He'll probably keep you in for a week at least, I'm afraid. So my advice is to phone your girl-friend and see if she wants to come in and see you. Have you got a mobile with you?"

Patras pulled a wry grin "It sank in the harbour along with my car. I got dragged out just in time. The driver of the other car—the one that was too far over on my side of the road and made me swerve—escaped without a mark on him."

"I'll bring you a landline and plug it into that socket by your bedside table," Tanya said. "We'll be taking you down to X-Ray soon. Manolis has requested new X-rays for his post operational records."

"Well, that's something to look forward to," the young man quipped. "I'm going to get so restless when I'm in here."

"I'll get you a television," Yannis said. "There's a football match you might you might like to watch this afternoon."

"Great! Thanks very much, Doctor."

CHAPTER NINE

SOMEHOW she got through the three nights and four days knowing that Manolis was living it up in London with his ex-wife. Well, that's what it seemed like to her! He'd phoned every day to give her an account of what was happening there but the phone calls were brief and to the point.

He seemed to be having a great time. Victoria's husband was a good host and entertained them well in the evenings. Mostly, he had "things to do, meetings with friends and colleagues during the day" so it was left to Victoria to take them around London seeing the sights and generally making sure that Chrysanthe was happy.

And it certainly sounded as if Victoria was making sure her ex-husband was happy. He always sounded exhilarated, relaxed. He never told her he was missing her. But why should he miss her? He'd spent six years without her. What was four days and three nights?

On the fourth day, the day he was coming back to Ceres, she lay in bed staring at the ceiling, trying to contain her excitement but failing miserably. She still had to work a whole day before he arrived. She had to be a good doctor to her patients. She mustn't think about Manolis, not at all! Until she went down to the harbour and met him off the boat at 8.30 that evening.

She showered, dressed, somehow got herself to eat a piece of yesterday's bread and drink a cup of coffee before hurrying to the hospital.

Yannis was already there, going round the patients. She'd decided he was an excellent, conscientious doctor, someone who would be a great asset to the permanent medical team. She must remember to recommend him to Manolis—and she must stop thinking about Manolis until this evening!

Patras was much happier today, having been allowed out of bed for a short while and given a pair of crutches. His wound, when she examined, it was beginning to heal and the X-rays were promising. She predicted to Yannis that they would be able to take the stitches out in a few days and put a permanent walking cast on. Well, permanent as in the next six weeks when hopefully the bone fragments would have knitted together.

"But we'll have to see what Manolis thinks," Yannis told their patient. He turned to look at Tanya. "What time does he get back today?"

"He'll be on the evening boat from Rhodes," she said calmly, though her pulses started racing every time someone reminded her of their evening reunion.

They settled their patient, answering his questions, making sure he was comfortable, before leaving his room together.

"So Manolis won't be coming in to the hospital?" Yannis asked as they walked down the corridor.

"I really couldn't say. I'm meeting the boat…well, I'll be down in the harbour anyway at 8.30 so… Was there something you wanted to see him about, Yannis?"

"Actually yes." He paused as if wondering whether to discuss it with his colleague. "I've been wondering if there would be a permanent post going in the near future. I'm enjoying my work here at the hospital and it's great to be back on Ceres again. I went to medical school in Athens and then after my wife and I married— she was a fellow student—we both worked in the hospital where we'd trained. Since she died I've felt there's nothing to keep me away from my family here on Ceres, parents, nephews and nieces, and, well, it's where I was brought up. I feel very much at home here."

She heard the crack in his voice when he spoke of his wife. She didn't want to pry and ask questions which might upset him.

"Leave it with me. I don't know what the staffing situation will be when the tourists stop coming in the winter but I'll speak to Manolis as soon as I can. From working with you while he was away I can tell we would be mad not to keep you on the team here."

She smiled at him. "You're a definite asset so I'll put in a good word for you."

He smiled back, relief showing on his handsome face. "Thanks." He hesitated. "Have you known Manolis long?"

"Since I was born—apparently. Manolis is eight years older than me. He was a friend of my brother so he remembers me from a very early age. I became aware of him much later, of course. But we…well, we didn't get together until we were both attached to the same hospital in Australia. I was still a medical student while he was a doctor, of course."

Her final sentence was delivered very quickly. "Sorry, I don't want to bore you with my life history."

"Not at all. I'm intrigued. I'm only a couple of years younger than Manolis but our paths didn't cross when I was a boy here. We lived on the other side of the island and communications weren't as good as they are today. So, when you met Manolis in Australia I presume… Look, I don't want to be impertinent but it's obvious there's a strong bond between you."

She sighed. "You could say that. We lived together for a while in Australia. We were very happy…and then it all went wrong. We've met up again six years later and…well, who knows what will happen the second time around?"

"Oh, but you've got to make it work! It's obvious the two of you are so much in love. I've never seen you together but I've heard Manolis speaking about you, unable to disguise the fact that he adores you. And every time you mention his name I just know you've got the kind of love that my wife and I shared."

His voice trailed away but then he took a deep breath and resumed in a hoarsely quiet tone of voice, "You've been given a second chance at a special relationship. You're so lucky. I'd give anything to be able to bring my wife back. Life's too short to…"

She swallowed hard as she saw the moistness in

Yannis's eyes. Her heart ached to see the sadness he was fighting against.

"I won't let our happiness together disappear a second time," she told him. "I was determined even before we had this conversation but you've made me doubly determined—if that's possible!"

"Go and meet the boat tonight. Don't let Manolis worry about the hospital. I'm on duty and I'll make sure that everything's in order. I had a very responsible post in Athens. Tell Manolis I'll only contact him if it's absolutely necessary. And make sure you have a good reunion."

She reached out and squeezed his hand. "Thank you, Yannis. And I'll make sure Manolis and I do everything we can to keep you on the hospital team."

She stood on the quayside, watching the evening ferry come in. All around the harbour lights twinkled in the waterside tavernas. The hillsides looked like dark velvet studded with diamonds. Above her the moon beamed down, lighting up the mysterious canvas of the night sky. The usually blue sea was black tinged with gold as the boat came ever nearer to her. Manolis's boat!

Would he be standing up on deck or would he be down in the saloon, chatting to friends, perhaps drinking a coffee, unaware that they were drawing into Ceres harbour? He must have done this journey so many times before that it was probably like taking the underground in London. Just another journey to get through, just another…

There he was! Standing on the deck, right at the front, his eyes scanning the quayside.

"Manolis!"

Her voice rang around the harbour, cutting through the noisy chatter, alarming or amusing the people nearest her. But she didn't care about their reaction. She was a young girl again, in love with the most wonderful, handsome, caring…

"Tanya!"

He'd seen her. He was waving madly. For a brief instant it occurred to her that they both had to maintain their decorum in hospital but out here they could behave as they wanted.

The boat was close to the harbourside now. One of the sailors threw a chain. A colleague caught it and began the arduous task of securing the large vessel as the captain cut the engines. The passengers were coming down the steps onto the boat deck. The people meeting the boat were surging forward. Now more people were calling out the names of the people they'd come to meet. She wasn't the only one excited. Manolis had disappeared somewhere in the stairwell.

Her heart turned over as she caught sight of him reaching the bottom of the stairs. She called his name again. He was smiling, waving to her now, hurrying down the landing board, making his way through the crush of people, the confusion of travellers and welcomers and…

She felt his arms wrap around her and she turned her face up to his, her eager lips seeking reassurance that he loved her.

"I've missed you so much," she whispered against his lips as he moved to release her from his embrace.

"I've missed you too."

She felt an enormous surge of happiness running through her. She'd perhaps engineered that he would tell her if he'd missed her but she wasn't going to dwell on that.

"Is everything OK at the hospital?"

"No problems at all," she said hastily, revelling in the feel of his large hand encasing hers. "Yannis, our highly efficient and well-qualified new doctor, is on duty and he's promised to contact you if necessary. But he's given his blessing for us to enjoy our evening together and not to worry."

"Sounds good to me."

An important-looking car was easing its way through the crush of people and vehicles.

"That's our car," she told Manolis as she glimpsed the peaked-capped chauffeur driving it. "I happened to meet Alexander, our ex-mayor..."

"Our ex-patient," Manolis said with a wry grin. "Don't tell me you persuaded him to send the mayoral car he's still allowed to use in his retirement!"

She laughed. "It was actually his suggestion—so how could I refuse?"

"Well, he's been so grateful since we operated on him and then looked after him so that he could resume his enjoyable life. That's what he said the last time he bought me a drink. I can't go into any taverna where he happens to be without him sending over a drink."

The chauffeur was opening the doors at the back of

the limousine. It was so incredibly over the top for a small island like Ceres that the two of them were having difficulty in concealing their laughter as they were ushered inside into the back seat.

"Where to, sir?" the chauffeur asked.

"To Chorio. We'll get out at Giorgio's and walk the rest of the way. I don't think you could get this large car down the street where we live."

As she leaned back against the fabulously comfortable leather seat she felt his arm sliding around her shoulders.

"What a homecoming!" he whispered as his lips sought hers.

"This is why celebrities have tinted windows in the back of their stretch limousines." Tanya giggled as they both came up for air. "So they can get up to whatever they like and nobody can see them."

"I don't think we've time to get up to what I would like because we're nearly there."

"Later," she whispered. "I've prepared a special welcome-home supper in my candlelit kitchen."

"I'm not hungry," he murmured huskily, holding her face in his hands as if he couldn't believe he was actually with her again. "Not yet. But I will be…later…"

They were hardly able to contain their passionate excitement as they removed each other's clothes in the candlelit kitchen. Manolis had remembered to secure the outside door to the street when they'd come in so that they wouldn't be disturbed. He'd turned off his mobile phone. Now reassured by Tanya that the hospital was running smoothly, he could relax. He'd secretly planned to take a couple of off-duty days which were due to him and mentioned the fact that he would confirm this when he returned from London if he was sure that the hospital team could function without him during this period.

He'd actually been in contact with Yannis by phone and email while he'd been away and was impressed with the support this new member of the team was giving him. If by any chance he wanted to stay on at the end of his temporary contract, he would ensure that he was appointed to a permanent post.

All these thoughts had gone through his mind as he'd come over on the boat just now. The world didn't revolve around him. He could now relax with the most wonderful woman in his life. The woman he wanted to make his wife...if only he could be sure she would say yes. If only he dared propose without upsetting the delicate balance of their relationship.

He gathered her up into his arms, taking care not to bang his head on the low beamed ancient ceiling as he carried her up the narrow stairs to the top of the house. The bedside lights were already on. He smiled to himself. So Tanya had thought through the possibility that they might have a romantic interlude before they had supper.

He laid her gently on the bed and gazed down at her beautiful naked body. Oh, how he'd missed her!

She looked up into his eyes as she felt his tantalising fingers delicately tracing the paths she knew they both loved the most. Deep down inside she could feel the familiar awakening of her sensual desires and her body melted into the passionate embrace as they joined together in perfect harmony…

Waking up was like a wonderful dream. He was here in her bed, not miles away in another country. He looked so desirable. Even though she'd felt totally satiated by their love-making a short time ago, when he languidly opened his eyes, his lips moving in a seductive smile, his arms reaching out to draw her closer, her body melted once more with delirious passion.

The dawn was breaking over the windowsill with a rosy glow when she awoke again to find Manolis leaning over her, resting himself on one elbow.

"I didn't want to wake you," he murmured before kissing her gently, first on the lips, then nuzzling the nape of her neck before leaning back against the pillows, his arms still around her.

She'd always loved the aftermath of their love-making. The feeling that she was utterly adored by her man. This wonderful hunk who she loved to distraction. Six years ago she hadn't looked any further than the next moment of their relationship but now she was aching to look into the future. A future where she would be part of Manolis for ever, where she would bear his children, happy in the knowledge that they belonged to each other for ever and ever.

They would grow old together with the memories of a full and happy life. And, of course, the children and grandchildren.

He traced the side of her cheek with his finger. "What are you thinking about?"

She swallowed hard. "I was thinking…"

Dared she broach the subject of marriage? No, it had to come from him. She mustn't force the issue.

She sat up quickly, extricating herself from his arms. "I was thinking about making something to eat. Shall we have supper or breakfast?"

She was reaching for her robe. He leaned across and drew her back into bed. "Don't worry about food. Come back to bed. Stay here, my princess, and I'll bring you something to drink. What would you like? Champagne? I brought a bottle from the airport and stashed it in your fridge before we came upstairs last night."

She snuggled against him, her resolve to be practical disappearing as her skin touched his.

"That's better." His arms wrapped around her so that she couldn't escape. "We ought to celebrate."

She held her breath for a moment. "What are we celebrating?"

"Our reunion, of course! I know I was only away for four days but it seemed like for ever."

"I thought you were having a great time."

"I was. Great to the extent that I could see Chrysanthe settling into the London life, getting used to sightseeing, shopping, visiting museums, and one time we even took her to the Theatre. So I was completely sure she wouldn't be homesick when I left her with Victoria."

"Well, she is her mother."

"Yes, but it wasn't always this easy when she was

very small and we were trying not to row in front of her, so that she wouldn't get upset. Anyway…"

He released her from his embrace, kissing the tip of her nose before springing out of bed and wrapping a towel around his waist.

"Don't go away while I'm downstairs."

She smiled. "I wouldn't dream of it."

She snuggled down into the warm place where his body had been, watching him through veiled lashes before he disappeared down the stairs. His firm, brown, muscular legs showing beneath the towel excited her more than she needed at this moment. She simply wanted to wind down, calm her feelings and enjoy the rest of their time together this morning.

In a few minutes she found herself drifting off to sleep so she just let herself go. It had been a fabulous but exhausting night…

The sound of an explosion awakened her.

"What the…?"

"Sorry, I didn't mean to wake you. I was simply opening the champagne."

She rubbed her eyes and looked at the delightful scene in front of her. Manolis, still wrapped around by a towel, was pouring champagne at her dressing table. She could smell hot croissants.

"It took me ages to put your oven on for the croissants. I remember standing by that same oven when I was a child, waiting for your grandmother to pull out the cake and cut a piece for Costas and me. It must be positively antique by now."

He turned and handed her a glass of champagne. "To the most beautiful girl in the world."

He entwined his arm with hers as they both took their first sip together.

"Another toast!" he said, his eyes firmly on hers. "To us…to…to the future, whatever life may hold."

"To us!"

It was all becoming so impossibly formal she began to fantasise that he was leading up to a proposal. In your dreams, said the still sane voice in her head. You had your chance, girl, and you blew it.

He unwrapped the towel, threw it in the direction of a chair and climbed back into bed, carrying the tray of croissants and apricot jam. The champagne was already firmly placed on the bedside table.

She took another sip of her champagne. "How long was I asleep?"

"Long enough for me to phone the hospital and establish that we're both taking two days off duty."

She stared at him. "But who did you speak to? It's only seven o'clock."

He smiled broadly. "When I switched on my mobile I found a text from Yannis asking me to phone him this morning. He said he was going to be on duty there all night. He told me that Alexander, our beloved chairman of the hospital board and ex-mayor and very difficult ex-patient, had called in to the hospital yesterday evening to ensure that you and I were going to have two days off duty before we resumed our work."

"Whatever is the man up to?"

Manolis laughed. "I think he's matchmaking, as you

would say in English. Perhaps he doesn't approve of our affair and wants us to…to make it…more formal."

She held her breath. He was leading up to it…he was…he really was. He was looking at her with a strange enigmatic expression that could only mean…

As Manolis studied her face he misinterpreted the expression of anxiety. She looked terrified! And that could only mean that she thought he was going to propose again. He hadn't given up hope but in the meantime they could continue as they were. Life was getting better by the minute.

"More champagne?" He picked up the bottle and leaned across the bed to top up her glass. A wicked thought passed through his mind that if he got her a bit tipsy she might be open to saying yes if he proposed. But would she regret it when she was sober and sensible again? Probably.

"So what's the plan if we're not going to work today, Manolis?"

"Would you like to go out to the little island where we took Chrysanthe?"

"I'd love it! We can take everything we need for a barbecue and a picnic."

"If we take some breakfast-type food, we could sleep overnight in the cabin."

He put down his glass and took her in his arms. "Would you like to sleep under the stars with the boat rocking gently on the waves as they lap the shore?"

"Sounds so…so romantic."

He began kissing her face, nuzzling her neck. She could feel his arousal as he drew her even closer.

"The boat will start rocking by itself when we settle ourselves in the cabin," he told her with a wry smile. "But there'll be nobody there to see it but a few sheep and maybe the odd goat…"

By midmorning they were all packed up and ready to set off. Tanya had made sure that Manolis phoned London to speak to Chrysanthe because he'd told her there would be no mobile signal on the island. Chrysanthe as usual was excited to speak to Manolis and also wanted to talk to Tanya.

"We'll call you as soon as we get back home tomorrow, Chrysanthe," Tanya told the little girl.

"Tomorrow! Are you going to sleep with the sheep?"

"Well, the sheep will be on the island but we'll be sleeping in the cabin on the boat."

"Oh, I wish I was with you! Will you take me with you some time when I get back to Ceres?"

"I'll ask Daddy."

"Tanya, will you meet me at the airport in Rhodes when I come back and take me back to Ceres on the ferry?"

"I'll see what Daddy's arranged, darling. He may have planned to meet you himself."

"Oh, I meant both of you to come and meet me. My London mummy is flying with me to Rhodes and then going straight back. You could meet her. I've told her all about you being my Ceres mummy."

"I'll let you know what Daddy's planned as soon as I can. Goodbye."

"Goodbye. I love you, Tanya."

"I love you too."

Manolis was standing by the door. "What was all that about?"

"Oh, I'll explain later. Decisions, decisions…!"

"Come on, let's leave it all behind. For one day only we're going to be completely alone."

"Bliss!'

CHAPTER TEN

THE sound of the sea lapping around the boat and the movement as the gentle waves took them by turn nearer then further away from the shore created an idyllic end to a perfect day. She revelled in the warmth of her sun-tanned skin contrasting with the coolness of her pillow as she lay relaxed and refreshed by her wonderful day on the island, waiting for Manolis to come back from securing the boat to its mooring.

Everything had gone right today. They'd even seen dolphins dancing in their remote bay as if to welcome them when they'd arrived. Manolis had caught a tuna, and had been well pleased. They'd feasted royally on their barbecued fish, sheltering under the trees to escape the rays of the hot mid afternoon sun. Then they'd had a decidedly sensual, sexy siesta curled up together, a couple of lovebirds in their shady nest, before rousing each other to go for another cooling swim.

The dolphins had disappeared by this time and the sun had slowly begun to make its descent over their little island. So they'd gathered up their belongings, which had been strewn all over the small pebbly beach and begun to prepare the boat for their evening and night aboard.

Tanya had spread the sheets out in the sun as soon as they'd arrived earlier in the day and the pillows, which had been stored in a locker, had needed a good airing. But by suppertime they both agreed there was nothing more to do except enjoy the feta cheese, salad, taramosolata and spinach pies they'd bought in Ceres town on their way to the boat. Washed down with a special bottle of wine from Crete, which Manolis produced from his small wine rack in the galley, they made themselves comfortable on deck to watch the sun making its descent into the sea.

Tanya gave a sigh of contentment as it seemed to plunge into the depths on the horizon, spreading a gold and red carpet of light over the surface of the sea, which extended as far as their boat.

"Happy?" Manolis asked her.

She smiled. "What do you think?"

"I don't think I needed to ask you. I can tell that…"

He drew her against his side and together they looked out over the darkening sea before he suggested she go inside the cabin and prepare for the night while he finished up the chores on deck and in the galley.

She'd listened to him moving about above her, jumping off the boat at one point, presumably to check the moorings. And now she could hear his footsteps coming down the ladder that led to the cabin.

She smiled as he came in and began stripping off his clothes. "Everything OK? The sea's calm now. The rocking of the boat won't be a problem tonight unless…"

He moved with one virile, seductive movement to climb in beside her on the bunk. She felt his hands beginning their impossibly arousing exploration of her eager body as his lips sought hers.

"Your skin feels so cool," he whispered. "Let's make the boat rock so that you can warm up…"

They lay back against the pillows after they'd made love. She could hear a sheep bleating on the shore, probably calling to its lamb. She'd seen the mother and baby that afternoon and noted the lamb was being particularly frisky. The mother would find it soon. Yes, she heard the lamb now, calling to its mother, and then she was sure she could hear the gentle sound of the baby sucking as it fed. Or maybe she was just imagining it, she thought idly.

It was so utterly peaceful here. Not a sound except the soft murmur of the lapping water. Nothing more except Manolis breathing beside her. If only this could go on for ever, just the two of them, nothing to impede their romance, no customs and conventions to say what they should or shouldn't do.

She turned to look at him, his profile illuminated in the moonlight that was streaming through the cabin window.

"I wish we could stay like this for ever," she told him, leaning over to brush her lips across his face.

"No reason why we shouldn't." He tried to keep his tone light and mischievous, entering into the spirit of make-believe. "We could set up an annexe of the hospital here. Request that the patients be shipped out here."

She laughed. "Will you arrange that?"

"Of course! We could live like Robinson Crusoe—apart from the hospital patients, who would require some attention occasionally."

"And Chrysanthe, of course."

He smiled down at her, propped up on his elbow now. "But she'll grow up and look after us soon."

"And the hospital," Tanya said, wishing life was always as easy as this fantasy game they were playing.

She raised her head and kissed him gently on the lips. "Goodnight, darling. It's been the most perfect day."

"Another one coming up tomorrow. And then back to the real world."

"Yes." She turned on her side. "We've got a good life out here, haven't we?"

"Couldn't be better now that we've found each other again," he murmured.

She lay quite still until she felt his breathing becoming steadily deeper as he fell asleep.

It couldn't be better, she told herself. Very soon he's got to broach the subject of a permanent relationship. It's all so nebulous at the moment. He talks about the future all the time and I'm always part of it.

For the moment she'd have to be satisfied with that. Sometimes she felt she was drowning in happiness. She mustn't spoil what they'd got.

The warm sun streaming through the cabin window woke her. She stretched out her hand to touch Manolis, but he wasn't there. She could hear him moving about on deck. Throwing back the sheet, she wrapped herself in a towel and went up the tiny wooden ladder.

The morning sun had already warmed the surface of the deck. She curled up against the cushions at the front of the boat and watched Manolis pouring out a cup of coffee from the ancient, blackened coffee jug.

"I thought you might surface if I made the coffee," he said, handing her one of the small coffee cups.

He squatted down beside her. "Sleep well?"

"You know I did," she murmured in mid-sip of the strong black coffee.

He put down his cup on the side of the boat. "When I wasn't disturbing you," he whispered, taking her face in his hands, tracing her beautiful skin with his fingers.

The coffee went cold as they made love. It was exquisite, Tanya thought as she lay back afterwards, the hot sun on her bare skin, listening to Manolis making more coffee in the galley. This life has to continue. Oh, not the make-believe Robinson Crusoe life they were emulating at the moment. A real relationship that would stand the test of time.

Her eyes were moist as she turned to watch the sheep trotting along the shoreline, its errant lamb following behind, looking docile today. Mother sheep was getting the message through that it shouldn't stay out late where there might be danger. When the sun set it should make sure it was safe with its mother.

Mother love was a wonderful thing. She found herself thinking about the baby she'd lost. Their baby. But they could have another baby…babies even! Manolis never talked about the baby they'd lost. Perhaps men didn't feel the pain of losing a baby as much as women did…or maybe they just put on a brave face and got on with life.

"Why are you looking so serious?" He was handing her a cup of fresh coffee.

"Do you ever think about the baby we lost?" she said quietly.

He swallowed hard. "Often. Especially when I'm with Chrysanthe. I think how wonderful it would be if our baby had lived. We wouldn't have split up, we would have been together all through those six years when we were both having a tough time." He looked up at the blue sky. "When Chrysanthe was a baby she helped me to forget some of the pain I'd felt at our loss. But it's always there, isn't it?"

He reached out and took her face in his hands. His voice had been so poignantly tender when he'd spoken. She hadn't realised he'd suffered their loss as much as she had.

"It must have been awful for you, just as it was for me," she whispered.

"It was…but life went on around me and I simply went with the flow for a while until the pain eased."

"I wish I could make it up to you."

"Oh, you can, you are now." He gathered her into his arms, revelling in the scent of her, which was so nostalgic of their previous affair. "Today we're going to live out our dream. No plans, no patients, no children—no worries, as we used to say out in Australia."

She laughed as he drew her to her feet so that they could both dive off the side of the boat together.

"Wow! The water's still cool." The dive had taken her breath away. As she came up for air now she found Manolis nearby, treading water.

"Cool but not cold. It's going to warm up as the day goes on." He hesitated. "I thought it would be a good idea to call in at the hospital on our way home tonight, just check that everything's OK."

"Why not? We've got to return some time."

"Meanwhile, how about scrambled eggs for breakfast?"

"Fantastic! My favourite breakfast."

He swam nearer. They trod water together while discussing the breakfast menu.

She was so glad that the macho image the Greek men liked to keep didn't exclude them from cooking when they were out in the open air. Kitchen utensils on land were regarded as OK for the fairer sex but anything to do with a barbecue or a boat was definitely their territory.

She swam back slowly and stretched out on deck, turning her face up to the sun. It was going to be another deliciously sexy, highly memorable day…

Yannis seemed surprised to see them when they turned up at the hospital that evening.

"I thought you were taking two days off duty, Manolis."

"This is only a social call. You haven't been working all the time, have you?"

"I've only just come back again. I slept all day. The team worked extremely well. I'm going to stay on till midnight and then I'll take the rest of the night off. By tomorrow my body clock will be normal again for day work." He hesitated. "There's an operation scheduled for tomorrow morning."

"What is it?"

Yannis began to explain. "It's Alexander's wife's hip replacement. He's kind of exerted pressure to jump the queue."

Manolis groaned. "I'll say he has. We prefer to send hip replacements over to Rhodes. In fact, I've put her on the list and she's got a date for next month."

"I know. I explained all that because I checked her notes and phoned him back. But he was adamant that she couldn't wait. And she also wouldn't have any other surgeon but Manolis. She remembers you as a little boy."

"Yes, yes. I'm sure she does but—"

"She's a great fan of yours—and Alexander was singing your praises over the phone to such an extent that—"

"Well, I'll have to do it! Always best to stay on the right side of the chairman of the board."

Tanya smiled indulgently. "Maybe that's why he's been so charming to us. Giving us the VIP treatment for the past two days."

"The wily old fox." Manolis frowned. "Well, I'll admit her to hospital tomorrow but I'm not operating on her till she's been fully prepared. I'll postpone surgery until the day after tomorrow. Any other problems, Yannis?"

"No, everything under control. Patras, the smashed tallus and tibia, keeps asking when he can see you."

"I'll go and see him now. No, it's OK, Tanya. You don't need to come. I'll only be a few minutes. Yannis, would you take Tanya for a decent cup of tea? I forgot the tea bags and I can see the English part of her is getting withdrawal symptoms."

The medics' staffroom was empty. Tanya put the kettle on and sat down in the comfiest chair by the window, waiting for it to boil.

"How was the honeymoon?" Yannis asked, with a wry grin.

"Wonderful!"

"And the proposal?"

She shook her head. "My English mother used to tell me an old English saying that you could lead a horse to water but you couldn't make it drink. I couldn't have made it clearer that I wanted us to stay together for ever."

The kettle was boiling. She half rose but Yannis got there first and was already pouring the boiling water over the tea leaves in the pot.

"Real tea leaves! What a treat!"

"That's how we make it in Athens."

"And here on Ceres—but not usually when we're on a boat." She sighed. "Yes, everything was perfect. So perfect that I wanted to propose to Manolis myself."

"Oh, you couldn't do that!" Yannis looked genuinely shocked. "Manolis would have been scandalised! And all his family too if the news had got out."

"But it's so old-fashioned!" She took a sip of tea to calm her frustration at the impossible situation.

"You must have realised by now that Ceres is old-fashioned. That's what makes it so charming. I always stick to the rules here. They've been bred into me and I certainly wouldn't have wanted my wife to propose to me."

"I know, I know. I was born here too, remember. I

remember my English mother crying with frustration at something my stubborn Ceres-born father wouldn't allow her to do."

"Well, are you sure you want to marry a Ceres-born macho, stubborn, bossy, authoritarian—?"

"Wonderful man," she finished off for him. "Yes, I do. I'm utterly convinced about that."

"Well, you'll just have to be patient, I'm afraid. It certainly looks like it. If only I could—"

The door swung open and Manolis walked in. Tanya put down her cup and made to cross the room to pick up the teapot.

"No tea for me, thanks." He looked from one to the other again. "I could swear you two were talking about me when I came in. You both went suddenly quiet."

"I was telling Yannis about the dolphins."

"No, you weren't." He gave her a wry smile.

She took a deep breath. "I was saying how conventional you men are on Ceres. Always sticking to the old-fashioned customs where it's not the done thing for a woman to propose marriage to a man."

"There would be a scandal if that happened in my family," he said lightly, his eyes scrutinising her expression. "How about your family, Yannis?"

"The same as yours. But, then, nobody's ever tried it, as far as I know."

"Of course not." Manolis hesitated, wondering if Tanya had been asking his advice. No, she must know the conventional rules on Ceres. They'd just been having a light chat together—or had they? Could she possibly be thinking about marriage? Never had he ever thought... No, he was jumping to conclusions—wasn't he?

"Come on," he said briskly. "Let's go home and have a long soak in the bath."

"The same bath?" Yannis pretended to look shocked.

"I wouldn't like to say," Manolis replied lightly. "Otherwise I might compromise Tanya's reputation."

Manolis placed his arm around her waist possessively and began to guide her to the door.

"Whatever happens, Yannis, we'll both be on duty tomorrow."

They were both down in the kitchen early the next morning, trying to get themselves into the mood for work.

"Come on, Manolis, it's not as if we don't like our work. You'll soon be back in the saddle again."

She was leaning over him to pour a cup of coffee from the fresh jug she'd just made. He took hold of the jug, placed it on the table and pulled her onto his lap.

"I was getting used to our idyllic life out there on the island," he whispered. "I'm glad I'm a doctor but the last two days have made me wish I'd been born a fisherman like my ancestors."

"That fish you caught wouldn't have fed a large family," she joked. "You'd have had to have a second string to your bow."

He laughed. "Quite right. OK, let's go and do some work, Doctor."

He kissed her on the lips before she could escape from his lap. They separated for their different tasks before meeting by the door to walk down to the hospital.

* * *

The pattern of their lives that evolved while Chrysanthe was in London soon became the norm. On the evening before she was due back, as Manolis lit the candles on the table in Tanya's kitchen she knew that they'd both enjoyed probably the most wonderful period of living together that they'd ever experienced.

Manolis blew out the match and looked across at her, his eyes tender and expressive.

"Are you thinking what I'm thinking, Tanya?"

"Probably. I love Chrysanthe to bits but we've had a great couple of weeks just the two of us, haven't we?"

He came round the table and drew her into his arms. "I'm looking forward to seeing my daughter again tomorrow, but this time when we've been completely alone in the evenings and that two days of fantasy on our little island without a care in the world. That was like our…"

He broke off. He'd been going to say "our honeymoon" but that would have meant he couldn't avoid bringing up the subject of marriage. And that could be enough to burst the bubble of their happiness.

She held her breath. "Like our what?"

"Like our first days together when we first moved into our flat. We were like a couple of kids."

"Well, let's face it. We were a couple of kids. I think we've both matured in the last six years, don't you?"

"Possibly," he said, a whimsical smile on his face.

He reached inside the fridge and took out the bottle of champagne he'd put in there when they'd first arrived back from the hospital.

Tanya placed the glasses on the table in front of him.

They clinked their glasses together, linking arms, as had now become something of a ritual.

"I had a phone call from Victoria today."

"Yes?" She was immediately alert, waiting to hear what his ex-wife wanted.

"Apparently, Chrysanthe would like you to meet her at Rhodes airport. She wants you to meet Victoria. Don't ask me why because I haven't a clue."

"It's the afternoon plane, isn't it?"

"Yes, you'll need to be there by about three."

"Oh, so you want me to go?"

"It's by special request. I thought I'd give you the day off and you can be the perfect Ceres mummy doing the transfer from Chrysanthe's English mummy."

"I think she might want you to be there."

"Impossible from a work point of view! It's you that Chrysanthe wants to meet her. You three girls can have a pleasant chat together. Victoria only has a few minutes before she takes the same plane back to London. Don't worry, she won't bite you. She's very civilised. Now, just relax and enjoy the rest of our evening."

He came round the table and drew her into his arms. She felt a frisson of excitement at the evening ahead…

Getting off the Rhodes ferry in the early afternoon, she walked along the harbourside to the taxi rank.

It was just as well that Manolis had given her the day off today because they hadn't had much sleep. It had been as if they'd both been clinging to the fantasy life they'd led and changing to become responsible adults with a child to consider was going to somehow intrude.

But they'd both agreed that the totally selfish life they'd enjoyed couldn't continue. They were both longing to have Chrysanthe back.

Tanya felt that their love for each other had grown stronger while the darling little girl had been away, but without children in their lives it would be a false sort of relationship. Sooner or later, Manolis would realise that. He had to! He had to propose sooner or later.

The taxi was drawing into the airport waiting area. She could feel her excitement mounting. It would be so good to have Chrysanthe back with them again.

CHAPTER ELEVEN

THE arrivals hall was in its usual state of turmoil. Tanya made her way through the crowds, her eyes scanning the nearest screen. Chrysanthe's plane had just landed. She moved as near as she could to the glass door where the people meeting those coming off the plane were waiting. She was lucky enough to find a seat in the corner where she could watch the door, which was now being opened.

Good sign. Hopefully she wouldn't have to wait long. She whiled away the time looking out through the glass windows, which gave a good view of the arriving coaches and taxis. A pleasant cooling stream of air was coming down from a vent just above her. Air-conditioning had been unheard of when she'd been small and had sat here with her parents, waiting to meet visiting relatives. The airport had been much smaller, much less organised and hopelessly chaotic in those days. As a child she'd wondered why on earth her parents had dragged her away from her island home to come to this noisy place to politely say hello to some unknown person. She'd had to be on her best behaviour, wear impossibly clean clothes, speak when she was spoken to and…

There she was! Her darling Chrysanthe was coming through the door, clasping the hand of a very elegant, tall slim woman whose eyes were searching around the spot where she was sitting. Her chic blonde hair was cut in a style that suited the high cheekbones and general air of elegance and sophistication.

She leapt to her feet, feeling all of a sudden hot and flustered compared to this vision who looked as if she'd spent the morning in a beauty shop but obviously couldn't have done. She must be one of these women who remained cool, calm and collected under difficult conditions.

"There she is," cried an easily recognisable little voice. "There's Tanya. Tanya, it's me, I'm home, I'm…"

And the tiny bundle of energy unleashed herself against Tanya's legs. Tanya picked her up, feeling tiny hands round her neck.

"Tanya, I've missed you so much! Has Daddy come?"

"No, he had to work at the hospital."

"Hi, I'm Victoria."

A firm, cool hand gripped hers.

"Good flight?"

"Not bad." She pulled a wry face. "I've had worse. Now, I've only got a few minutes before I've got to get along to Departures and go back to London on the same plane when they've managed to clean it out. There were so many kids on the plane it was in an awful state by the time we got here."

Chrysanthe had wriggled free and jumped down from Tanya's arms. "Mummy, Mummy, can I go to the crèche now? I'm going to meet that girl who was on the plane."

"Yes, just a moment, Chrysanthe. I'm talking to Tanya. Now, we must have a chat. I've arranged for Chrysanthe to go into the crèche for a short time. She's been in there before and is desperate to play with her new friend."

"It's over there, Mummy! I know the way. I'll just—"

"No, I'll take you then you must stay with the stewardess till Tanya or I come to pick you up."

"If you've only got a few minutes, Victoria, it's best if I pick up Chrysanthe."

"Good thinking! After all, you're her Ceres mummy, I hear." It was said in such a tone of approval that Tanya felt reassured that Chrysanthe's birth mother obviously didn't mind her stepping into her shoes when they were apart.

"So Chrysanthe explained that was how she describes me to her friends on Ceres."

"Oh, she talked of you all the time. I'll say goodbye now, darling. Tanya will collect you soon."

"OK. Bye, Mummy."

Chrysanthe disappeared into the crèche after a stewardess had taken details from Victoria and Tanya about who was collecting her and when.

"Well, that's a good innovation," Tanya said. "Wish they'd had that when I was a child. Hours I spent in this place, kicking my heels."

"We've just time for a cup of tea—or would you prefer coffee?" Victoria was heading over to the drinks dispenser. "It all comes out of the same container, I think, but… There you go."

They found a corner where there were two seats. "It's great to meet you at last. As I say, Chrysanthe is besotted with you. And also with the idea that you and Manolis are going to get married and give her a baby brother or sister just like the rest of her friends seem to be having."

Tanya tried a sip of her tea and put it straight into the nearest waste bin. "The tea hasn't changed!"

Victoria agreed as she also binned hers.

Tanya didn't mind the tea being awful. The bonding of the two women in Manolis's life was going much better than she'd dared to hope.

"I think it's a kind of one upmanship to have a baby brother or sister," she said carefully. "I'm not taking it too seriously."

"Oh, but you must! It's so obvious that you and Manolis were made for each other—just as it was obvious from the start that Manolis and I would never make a go of it. Talk about on the rebound! The poor man didn't know what to do with himself. He was utterly bereft. I felt so sorry for him. It was obvious he'd left his heart in Australia. He never stopped talking about you. I suppose I just wanted to comfort him at first and, well, you know how things develop when you've had too much to drink. Manolis was hell bent on drowning his sorrows. Somehow the comfort turned into sex…and then in no time at all I found I was pregnant."

Victoria fidgeted on the uncomfortable plastic chair.

"Of course, Manolis did what he thought was the honourable thing and asked me to marry him. You know, they're so old-fashioned over there on that quaint little island, aren't they? I would have been content to split up at that point and bring up the child myself—well, with the help of a nanny, of course, so I didn't have to take a career break—but, oh, no. Manolis said his child had to be legitimate. His family on Ceres would... Oh, you must have come across the sort of thing I'm talking about."

"Absolutely! That's the problem at the moment with our relationship. Manolis actually proposed marriage when we were in Australia and I turned him down—for various reasons which we don't need to go into. Anyway, we have a marvellous relationship now but... well, I'm waiting and waiting for the third proposal, which just isn't coming. And I daren't propose to him because it would be so frowned on."

"Well, of course it would. Oh, it's so easy to talk to you, Tanya." Victoria broke off as she looked at her diamond-encrusted watch. "Look, we must keep in touch. I'm sure you'll find a way of prompting Manolis. Oh, there's the announcement for my departure. I'd better go. Stick to your guns because, as I say, you two were made for each other. You could stick your neck out and just tell him it's for Chrysanthe's sake. She's desperate for a baby brother or sister."

They were both laughing together now as the woman who'd been sitting next to Victoria, leaning nearer so that she could take in the bizarre conversation, got up from her seat and walked away looking thoroughly shocked.

They stood up and air-kissed each other on both cheeks. "I feel as if I've known you for ages," Tanya said, feeling relieved that their short introduction to each other had gone so amicably.

"Well, in a way you have—through Chrysanthe. I wish we had more time to chat through this problem. When you've solved it—as I know you will—please invite me to the wedding. I'll just lurk in the shadows at the back of the church and I won't cause any problems. I won't hurl myself at the altar weeping and wailing…"

Tanya was giggling now. "I can't imagine you weeping and wailing about anything, Look, you'd better go or you'll miss your flight. I'll go and collect Chrysanthe."

She watched the slim figure disappearing through the crowds in the direction of the departure lounge. She turned as she went through the doors and waved, still smiling.

Tanya waved back. This certainly wasn't the meeting she'd dreaded. She'd made a true friend in a matter of minutes. That was a part of the relationship that would be easy. Chrysanthe having two mummies. It was the daddy who was the difficult one.

They enjoyed a smooth crossing on the ferry. So smooth that Chrysanthe fell asleep snuggled up to Tanya in the saloon. She had to be woken up a few minutes before they were due to dock.

The little girl smiled sleepily and was soon in conversational flow. A never-ending stream of thoughts and dreams had happened while she'd been asleep and she needed lots of answers from her Ceres mummy.

"Did my London mummy tell you that you and Daddy could easily get a baby brother or sister for me if you really tried?"

"I think she might have mentioned it but she was in such a hurry to catch her plane… Oh, look, we're nearly there. Daddy said he'd try to get out of the hospital in time to meet us. He's got such a busy day today."

"Mummy said all the daddy has to do is to plant a seed in the mummy. He's got this kind of injector thing. Does my daddy know how to do that?"

"I'll have to ask him. But not just now because, as I say, he will have had a busy day and he's probably tired."

Chrysanthe put her head on one side so that she could look up at Tanya and judge her mood. Grown-ups could be so weird. You could never tell what they were thinking. Best to change the subject because Tanya seemed really tense.

"Is Daddy cutting people up today? He really likes cutting up people, I think."

Tanya was relieved they'd been speaking Greek together since Chrysanthe woke up. The English tourist listening next to Chrysanthe didn't flinch at the little girl's words and smiled with complete incomprehension at the continual flow of Greek words from such a small child.

"I think he probably is. Can you pass me your jacket and I'll help you put it on."

"Is it difficult to put people back together again once you've cut them up? I mean, knowing which bit goes where?"

"Daddy's a very good surgeon so he knows exactly

what to do. You have to train a long time to be able to work like Daddy does."

"I'm going to be clever like Daddy and train for a long time. I think I'd like to cut people up. It's probably like doing jigsaw puzzles. Must be fun sorting out which bit goes where. You can do it, can't you, Tanya? Daddy was telling Grandma one day that you were the best doctor he'd had helping him in the operating theatre."

Tanya took hold of Chrysanthe's hand and led her firmly towards the top of the stairs that led to the boat deck.

"Grandma said your daddy used to cut people up and he was ever so good at getting babies for people. Didn't your daddy ever tell you where he got the babies from? Didn't you ever ask him?"

"Careful on the stairs, darling. Watch your step. Hold my hand tightly for this last little bit… There he is! There's Daddy."

Manolis had somehow managed to board the ferry as soon as it arrived. He could usually find the odd grateful patient who would bend the rules and let him aboard.

"Daddy!" Chrysanthe ran forward as Manolis bent down to greet her. He lifted her high in the air and swung her round. "Daddy! You're not tired, are you?"

"Of course not. Why should I be tired?"

"Well, Tanya wants to ask you… Oh, look, there's my new friend from the plane. Let me go and see her before she gets off the boat." Chrysanthe had wriggled her way out of Manolis's arms and was halfway down his legs, scrambling to the floor.

"No, hold onto my hand, Chrysanthe," Manolis said, as he reached for the escaping child.

Tanya screamed out. "Hold onto her, Manolis. They're letting the lorries off the car deck. They're—"

A deafening thud, the screech of brakes and then an awful silence around them. The worst thing had happened. Every parent's nightmare. Their child under the wheels of a vehicle.

"Chrysanthe, darling." Tears were streaming down Tanya's cheeks as she bent to reach the motionless child beneath the wheels of the large truck.

The driver was crying as he climbed out of his cab. "I slammed on my brakes as soon as I heard you call out. I never saw her. She came from nowhere. Is she OK? She's not…?"

Manolis was on his knees, crouched over his daughter. The wheels of the truck were resting against her head. She'd received a blow to the head but the wheel hadn't passed over her.

The driver was trembling with shock. "Get an ambulance! Quick. I couldn't help it. Nobody said the passengers were on this deck."

"It's OK," Manolis said quietly to his unconscious daughter.

Tanya was at his side.

At that point the captain arrived, saying frantically, "I've called an ambulance. I'm sorry, I'm sorry! There was a new sailor in charge of disembarkation today. He shouldn't have given the signal for the trucks to start their engines and move off early like that."

He was pleading with Manolis now. "Is there anything I can do, Doctor? She's not…?"

"I just need to get my daughter to the hospital…"

"Your daughter? Oh, Manolis I wouldn't have…"

They waited in silence until the ambulance arrived and the paramedics stabilised Chrysanthe's neck and head for the journey. The normally noisy, loquacious, lovable child lay pale and motionless while they tended to her and Manolis and Tanya looked helplessly on.

As Chrysanthe was carried to the ambulance, Manolis strode through the crowd with Tanya beside him in a state of total shock. She just knew she had to get Chrysanthe to the hospital before she allowed herself to cry. She had no idea how badly injured her daughter was. She wasn't her daughter—she knew that. But that was how she now thought of her.

They all went to the hospital in the back of the ambulance, Manolis checking out his little daughter with a paramedic en route. She was very still, eyes closed but she was breathing.

As the driver pulled in to the hospital forecourt and slammed on the brakes, Tanya opened the door and got out.

A porter with a trolley arrived and, with Chrysanthe lifted safely onto it, Manolis led them all hastily straight past Reception and along to the X-ray department.

"X-ray of skull please…now!"

In a very short time Manolis and Tanya were examining the X-ray images on the screen.

"There's no fracture of the skull," he said in a relieved tone. "No discernible subdural haematoma, which sometimes happens in a concussion like this. I'll get a CT scan to make sure. If blood has collected beneath the skull it won't be a problem for me to remove the haematoma provided I can do it quickly so— Ah, Yannis, don't you agree with me that—?"

"Absolutely, Manolis. But I think you should let me take over at this point if you don't mind me saying so. You're bound to be in a state of shock because this is your daughter. I'll take Chrysanthe for a CT scan and report back to you as soon as possible."

Tanya put her hand on his arm. "Manolis, my darling, just let Yannis take over for a little while. Sit here with me for a moment. I need you by my side, my love. You're shaking with the shock of it all."

"OK. Yes, you're probably right. I think I am in shock. But, Yannis, get back to me as soon as you can."

Gently, Yannis took the motionless child from her distraught father. "Chrysanthe will be fine with me. Take it easy, Manolis, and I'll keep you informed."

The lights in Chrysanthe's hospital room had been dimmed. The child was breathing steadily but was still unconscious. Tanya clung tightly to Manolis's hand as they sat together at the side of her bed. She was exhausted but knew she would never be able to sleep even if she'd taken up the offer of the bed in the corner of the room.

"Why don't you try and get some sleep, Manolis? You've been working all day."

He tried to smile but failed miserably. "I don't expect your day has been all that easy. How did you get on with Victoria?"

"Very well. She's easy to get on with."

"Really? What did you talk about?"

"Oh, this and that. Chrysanthe mainly."

He attempted a wry grin and succeeded. "And me?"

She smiled. "Possibly."

Yannis walked in. "All the tests show there's no hae-matoma. She has concussion, which we all know can be unpredictable. She could come round any minute or…or we may have to wait a while longer."

"Thank God! How about the swollen arm I pointed out to you? What did the X-rays show?"

"The ulna is cracked. I'm going to take her along to the plaster room and put a cast on now."

Manolis half rose. "Do you want me to do it?"

"No, I'd like to do it," he said, firmly taking the lead.

Tanya put her hand on his arm. "Better you rest while you can. Why don't you stretch out on the bed over there?"

"I might just do that while Yannis is putting the cast on Chrysanthe."

CHAPTER TWELVE

As THE morning sun tipped over the windowsill of the small room in Ceres Hospital, Manolis opened his eyes and took in the all too familiar scene. Tanya was still sitting by Chrysanthe's bed, holding her motionless hand, looking down at her with the gaze of a concerned mother and an experienced doctor.

Twice during the last three hours he'd got up from the bed in the corner of the room reserved for the patient's relatives and tried to persuade Tanya to take some rest. But she'd been adamant that she wanted to be there when Chrysanthe came round.

She'd looked at him with those intense, beautiful eyes where the sad expression told him that she knew as well as he did that it wasn't when she came around, but if. He'd stayed with her for a short time, hoping to give her some support. But she was one tough lady who'd done exactly what she felt was the right thing to do all her life. There was no changing her.

He watched for a few moments wondering what life would be like if she ever left him. They'd split up before and it had been hell. It mustn't happen again!

He threw back the light sheet that was covering him. He was still wearing the clothes he'd worn yesterday morning. At some point he'd try to have a shower—but not yet. Like Tanya, he didn't want to leave their precious daughter. He'd seen how Tanya had completely bonded with his child. Chrysanthe was only slightly younger than their child would have been.

In fact, looking at the scene of mother and child now, he doubted if Tanya could differentiate her feelings from what she would have felt if she'd actually given birth to Chrysanthe.

Tanya looked across the room at Manolis sitting on the narrow bed in his crumpled clothes, his dark hair flopping over his forehead, and her heart went out to him. Was his anguish worse than hers because he was the biological father of this precious child? She couldn't imagine anything worse than the agony she was going through.

A nurse came in through the half-open door. Tanya looked up expectantly.

"Do you have any more results of the tests?"

The nurse shook her head. "I came to see if you'd like some breakfast, Tanya."

"No, thank you."

The nurse looked across at Manolis. "Doctor?"

"No, thank you," he said in an absent tone of voice. He stood up and walked across to the bedside. "Maybe some coffee, strong please."

He sat down on the other side of Chrysanthe's bed and took hold of her limp, seemingly lifeless hand. His eyes scanned her face for any sign of life. Then he raised her arm, which was encased in a cast. He checked on the fingers.

"They're only slightly swollen," Tanya said. "I've been working on them every few minutes."

"Let me take over now. Why don't you go and have a shower?"

She gave him a faint smile. "Do I look grubby?"

"You look wonderful, darling. But if you feel anything like I do…"

"OK, I'll go off for a short time when I've had some coffee. Find some clean clothes to put on."

The nurse brought in a large coffee pot and two cups. Beside it she'd placed a plate with some small bread rolls.

"You must eat," she told them. "It could be a long time before…before your daughter regains consciousness. These rolls are freshly baked. I've just been out to the bakery in the harbour to get them."

The nurse hesitated by the door on her way out. She was much older than these two doctors. She'd become very fond of both of them since she'd come back to work now that her family were grown up.

"Please eat something to keep up your strength. Life must go on."

She closed the door quietly behind her.

Tanya picked up the plate and held it towards Manolis. "Sound advice. Take one of these."

Manolis dutifully finished his bread roll and took a gulp of the strong coffee.

Tanya forced something down. "This drip needs changing." She stood up. "Have we any more glucose saline in that fridge?"

"Yes, I checked a short time ago." He handed her a pack.

She scrubbed her hands and put on some sterile gloves before changing the nearly empty pack for a full one.

"Got to keep Chrysanthe hydrated."

Manolis nodded. "I'll send another blood sample to the path lab this morning for a full blood count and checks on how her body is coping."

"She'll need to be strong when she comes round and starts…" Tanya hesitated. "Starts talking again."

Her voice cracked as she came to the end of her sentence. She looked across the bed at Manolis. "It will be so wonderful to hear that little voice chattering again, won't it?"

He swallowed hard. "Yes. It will happen, you know, Tanya."

"I know, I know." She was choking back the tears now.

He stood up and came round the bed, drawing her to her feet so that he could take her in his arms. He pressed his lips against her tousled hair, murmuring gently.

"I'm so glad you're with me, darling. I love you so much."

He lowered his head and kissed her on the lips. It was a gentle kiss, devoid of all passion but infinitely soothing to her. But what was most reassuring to Tanya was his assertion that he loved her. She couldn't remember him saying that since they'd been together in Australia.

"I love you too, darling," she whispered.

He kissed her again, before smoothing away the tears from her face with his hand.

She gave him a long slow smile as she looked up into his swarthy but still handsome face.

"I'll go and take that shower. Won't be long. Don't go away."

"As if!" He was already holding his daughter's hand, checking her pulse. "You know, as long as she's breathing and her heart is beating…"

He broke off as Tanya turned at the door, listening to him clutching at straws.

"Look, we've both been with unconscious patients who've recovered and we've been with some who haven't," she said quietly. "We're doing all we can but medical science can only do so much." She took a deep breath. "I'm hopeful."

"So am I!"

She went down to the female staff shower room. It was empty. She'd checked the contents of her locker and found a brand-new packet of cotton knickers which she'd brought over from Australia. Not at all glamorous but perfectly serviceable. She'd picked up a clean white short-sleeved coat from the doctors' clean laundry pile outside the shower room.

The hot water tumbled down, washing over her sticky skin. Yesterday afternoon, waiting outside the airport, her clothes sticking to her skin, she'd promised herself that the first thing she would do when she reached home would be to have a bath. Hours later, it felt as if she'd died and gone to heaven.

She made a point of trying not to think about Chrysanthe. Manolis was with her. A large number of the hospital medical team were devoting their combined skills and energy to ensuring that this little girl wasn't going to die.

She stepped out of the shower wrapped in a hospital issue towel, ready to face whatever the day threw at her.

Somehow, they both got through the day without losing hope. But it was a tough one. As they resumed their places beside Chrysanthe's bed Manolis reached across the bed and took hold of her hand.

"She's going to make it!" he said firmly.

"Absolutely!"

Whenever her hopes dwindled during the day she'd taken hold of Manolis's hand and they'd both said their mantra together. Heaven knew, they'd done all they could during the day. And the rest of the medical team had been amazing. They'd pooled their ideas and theories, tried every test that could possibly give them a clue as to what was happening inside that little head. There was no evidence of a blood clot.

They sat either side of the bed for a while, both of them in deep contemplation. Manolis was first to break the silence.

"An unconscious state like this could last for weeks, months, years even before…before…"

"Before it's resolved," she put in quickly as she saw him floundering to find the right words without demolishing the hope they were hanging onto.

"Exactly!" He reached across the bed with his spare hand and squeezed Tanya's.

Neither of them must admit that their hope had grown thin during the day. Neither of them must give in to the temptation to face the medical facts of the situation. The longer this unconscious state lasted, the less likely they were to get their daughter back so that she could lead a normal life.

Tanya glanced once more at the clock across the room. Two a.m. This second night was proving harder than the first. She forced her heavy eyelids to stay open. They'd decided to take turns to have a two-hour sleep while the other watched. It was time for her to wake Manolis but he looked so peaceful. She'd give him another five minutes.

Her heart missed a beat as she thought she saw the faint fluttering of Chrysanthe's eyelashes. She leaned closer, not sure if it had really happened. Chrysanthe was completely still again. The small hand remained cold and motionless in her own. She'd imagined it.

Tomorrow she was going to play some of Chrysanthe's favourite CDs to see if there was any response to the music. She remembered a young patient in Australia who'd been roused from a coma after several weeks by the sound of his favourite music. But unfortunately his brain had been damaged by the length of his vegetative state.

That wasn't going to happen to Chrysanthe. Oh, no! She was going to…

That was a definite fluttering of the eyelids! She hadn't imagined it this time.

"Manolis, Manolis!"

He was immediately awake, throwing back the sheet, padding across the floor in his bare feet.

"She's opening her eyes. She's opening…"

A strange gurgling sound came from Chrysanthe's mouth as her lips began to move. They leaned over her, clinging to her hands.

"Chrysanthe," Manolis said gently. "Can you hear me, darling? Can you…?"

The eyelashes fluttered again and she opened her eyes. For a few seconds it appeared as if she couldn't focus her eyes on the faces hovering above her. And then she uttered another sound, a gentle animal sound like a small lamb calling for is mother.

"Mmm…mmm…Mummy. Mummy." Slowly she turned her head towards Tanya, then Manolis. "And Daddy…"

"Oh, thank God! She's OK." Tanya choked on her words as she leaned down to kiss the child's forehead.

"I was dreaming," Chrysanthe said slowly and very faintly. So faintly they both had to bend down as closely as they could to catch what she was saying. "I was dreaming. We were on the boat…. The sun was hot…"

She closed her eyes and became quiet again as if the effort of those first few words had exhausted her.

"We must be patient, not rush her progress," Tanya whispered.

Manolis nodded, his heart too full of emotion for him to speak.

Several hours later, Tanya had made her small patient comfortably propped up against her pillows. The few words she'd spoken had indicated that all her faculties were well and truly in place. Time, the great healer, would do the rest.

For the next seven days they all lived in the small hospital room. The medical team involved with Chrysanthe's care had insisted that they keep their patient in hospital until they all agreed that she was back to normal again.

Manolis and Tanya both agreed. They knew the odds on a case like this and didn't want to take any risks until Chrysanthe was out of danger. But exactly one week and two days since she'd been admitted to hospital the entire team agreed that the patient could go home.

It had helped that both parents were doctors and would pick up on any sign of deterioration in the patient's condition. Even so, Alexander had insisted that they have round-the-clock nursing care on hand at home. He didn't want the parents to tire themselves. And he'd also insisted his chauffeur drive them home. Only the best for the sleeping princess.

It was Alexander who'd first called her that when he'd visited her the first day she'd woken from her sleep as he'd put it.

"You were like Sleeping Beauty," he'd told her.

"Was I really?" Chrysanthe's eyes had become wider than they'd been since she'd fallen into her coma. "Am I a princess?"

"I think you are," Alexander said. "And so do your mummy and daddy."

And Manolis had whispered into Tanya's ear, "There's nothing wrong with our daughter's brain!"

"She'll soon be running rings around us again," Tanya said happily.

* * *

It seemed as if the whole of Ceres had heard about the doctor's sick child who'd woken from her coma. People were lining the streets down by the harbour. As the mayoral limousine drove slowly along the water's edge they were actually cheering.

"I'm not really a princess, am I, Daddy?"

"You are to us, my darling. And for the people of Ceres you're a princess for the day."

"Wow!"

Manolis closed the bedroom door behind him and walked quickly across to the bed.

"Don't you think we should leave the door ajar?" Tanya said, as she snuggled back against the pillows to admire Manolis's athletic muscles as he stripped off his robe.

"No reason why we should," he said firmly. "There's a trained night nurse in Chrysanthe's room ready to come and alert us to any change in her condition. But the way our little princess has been behaving today—even with the inconvenience of the cast on her arm—leads me to believe that she's completely OK."

He climbed into bed and drew her towards him.

"Completely OK? Is that your clinical diagnosis now, Doctor?"

"It is indeed. It's you who needs your head examined."

"Me? What clinical signs have drawn you to that ridiculous conclusion?"

"I've done a lot of thinking while we were going through the awful crisis of almost losing our precious child. I can't live without you, Tanya. Everybody who knows us—friends, colleagues, the world at large—acknowledges we are a great couple. Made for each other is the phrase often bandied about."

"Yes," she said, drawing out the word as slowly as she could.

"Chrysanthe regards you as her mummy now and—"

"Manolis, I think I know where this is going—"

"Please, hear me out before you start saying anything. I know what you're going to say but—"

"You do?" She was impatient with hope that he might, he just might be going to…

"Tanya. Six years ago I asked you to marry me and you turned me down—twice! But I'm going to ask you again anyway because it doesn't make sense to go on as we are doing. I agree with the general consensus of opinion that—"

"Ask me, Manolis," she said, breathlessly.

"What?"

"Ask me to marry you."

"Well, against all the odds I am going to ask you to marry me even if—"

"And I'm going to say yes."

"But no matter what you think or… What did you just say?"

"I'm thinking that if you were to get out of bed and go down on your bended knee I could give you my answer—the answer I've longed to give you for ages. So please put me out of my misery. The suspense is killing me."

He looked completely stunned as he climbed out of bed and went down on one knee. He felt as if he'd turned into a robot. He was simply obeying orders. This couldn't be the girl who'd turned him down twice admitting that maybe, just maybe it could be third time lucky.

He swallowed hard. "Tanya, will you marry me?"

"Of course I will. What took you so long?"

Waking up in Manolis's arms, the details of the previous evening when Manolis had proposed to her were sketchy to say the least. But the love-making that had ensued had been out of this world. That bit she did remember! She remembered him climbing back into bed after his proposal, covering her with kisses as she settled into his arms.

And waking up in his arms just now, stretching out as a new day began. A day when she would have to start planning the wedding of the year! Everybody on the island would want to be invited. And her mother and stepfather and all of Manolis's enormous family.

He was opening his eyes, drawing her closer to him.

"Manolis, darling, before we…before we… I need to talk to you about the wedding so… Mmm…well, perhaps later…"

Just over a month from Manolis proposing to her they were standing in the beautiful church on the hill overlooking the entrance to the harbour. Neither of them had seen any point in waiting to tie the long-awaited knot.

Tanya was intrigued by the knots of ribbon that were being made around the two of them by the priest and his assistants in front of the altar. It was at this point that she began to realise that she was actually going to be Manolis's wife after all these years of longing.

She felt little fingers touching the ivory silk of her fabulous long gown and J7bent to see Chrysanthe admiring the texture and feel of the hastily but beautifully made garment. Two of the best seamstresses on Ceres had worked flat out to have it finished in time for the wedding of the year.

She bent down to whisper to Chrysanthe, who was chief bridesmaid, looking pretty and demure in her ivory silk mid-calf-length dress. She'd wanted a long dress like Mummy Tanya but Manolis was so afraid she'd fall over in her exuberance at some point during the long day that he'd suggested she would look better in a shorter version. He'd X-rayed her arm yesterday and decided that after six weeks in a cast the ulna had healed perfectly. She'd parted happily with the cumbersome plaster regretting only the fact that she could no longer show off all the signatures from friends and family.

"Are you OK, Chrysanthe?" Tanya whispered.

Chrysanthe nodded. "Why are they tying you up with Daddy?"

"To show that I'll always be with him."

"And me?"

"Of course."

Chrysanthe squeezed Tanya's leg encased in the layers of silk. "How much longer do we have to stay here? I need to go to the loo. I ever so need a…"

Tanya could see Victoria watching from the back of the church. She nodded her head down towards their daughter. Victoria hurried forward and put out her hand to take hold of the chief bridesmaid. Tanya smiled and mouthed her thanks as mother and daughter walked off down the aisle.

This was the first contact she'd had with Victoria that day. She'd arrived at the last minute and had been keeping a low profile at the back of the church. Not exactly lurking, as she'd so poignantly put it when they'd talked about the possibility of a wedding, more trying to remain unobtrusive in her chic silver grey designer suit and impossibly high stilettos.

The service continued all around her with the priests chanting loudly and the guests becoming restless in the hot airless church. They'd deliberately chosen the wedding to be at the end of the holiday season so that the island wasn't too crowded and the weather was still good.

The weather today was hot, almost too hot, but she was so happy that she hardly noticed. Only the sight of the ladies in the congregation fanning themselves with their wedding programmes made her hope that the service wouldn't last much longer.

As soon as it ended, she and Manolis were surrounded by their guests before they'd had chance to leave the altar.

"Let's go outside," Manolis suggested to the nearest and dearest of his family, who were clinging to him, congratulating him, kissing him and generally holding him back from his bride, who was signalling to him they should leave.

They finally found a way of getting together before walking down the aisle and escaping into the fresh air, hands firmly clasped together, Chrysanthe holding onto Tanya's skirt so that she didn't fall over in the crush of people all trying to reach her Mummy and Daddy.

"Thanks, Victoria," Tanya said as she passed by the London mummy.

Victoria smiled. "Glad I could help. You look absolutely gorgeous. And so do you, my poppet." She bent to kiss her daughter. "What a good girl you've been."

Chrysanthe beamed and looked up at her Ceres mummy. "Are you and Daddy married yet?"

"We are," Tanya said as they posed for the cameras outside the porch.

"When will you start to make the new baby?"

"Let's talk about it later, Chrysanthe. Smile now for the camera."

She looked around at the enormous crowd. It had been a mammoth task to get all her relatives here. She had a particularly special smile for her brother Costas who'd miraculously phoned a couple of weeks before to say that he was going home to Australia from South Africa to introduce his new fiancée to his mother.

According to their mother—who was now coming forward to join the large family photograph to be taken on the grass to the side of the church under a large tree that would give them some shade—it hadn't occurred to Costas that the family might be worried about his whereabouts. So he'd simply got on with his work out there in the back of beyond.

Tanya's mother came closer to her now, kissing her cheek before moving to the appropriate place for the mother of the bride.

"I think Costas's fiancée is going to be a good influence on him," her mother whispered, before taking up her place.

Tanya smiled. "About time someone took my brother in hand."

"I heard that," Costas said, coming up to stand behind her. "Hey, Manolis. We've got a lot of catching up to do, my friend. How about I meet you tonight for a drink—after this show, of course."

"Sorry, Costas," Manolis said. "I've got an important date with the most wonderful woman in the world."

Costas looked around him. "So when's she arriving?"

"Quiet, Costas!" Tanya's mother said.

"And now just the bride and groom by themselves!" the fraught photographer boomed above the laughter and chattering.

Manolis took hold of her hand as the crowds moved back. "Happy?" he whispered.

"What do you think?"

"A kiss! The wedding kiss," the photographer called.

"This is the best bit," Manolis said as he drew her into his arms and kissed her. His kiss deepened and the crowd cheered.

Tanya pulled herself gently away. "Later," she whispered.

"Promise?"

Her eyes shone with the promise of the night to come, their first as a real married couple. "Can't wait…'

EPILOGUE

CHRYSANTHE climbed into bed, snuggling down between her mummy and daddy, taking care not to speak until they opened their eyes. Since her baby brother had arrived they'd been keen that she shouldn't talk and wake him up when they'd just got him to sleep. She glanced at the cradle at her mummy's side of the bed. He was a very small baby. She hoped he would start growing soon. He hadn't seemed to get any bigger since he was born three weeks ago.

Tanya lay very still, pretending she was still asleep. Baby Jack had needed two breastfeeds in the night and it seemed only a short time since she'd fed him.

Chrysanthe stared hard at her mummy. She was sure she wasn't really asleep. Perhaps if she just whispered to her, that would be OK.

"Are you awake, Mummy?"

"I am now."

"It's morning time. Look, the sun's shining outside. Daddy, can you see the sun?"

"Mmm?"

"The sun. It's shining. Must be time we all got up, don't you think?"

"Morning, darling." Manolis planted a kiss on his daughter's cheek before reaching across to his wife and kissing her on the lips. "How were the feeds last night? I think I might have slept through them."

"I think you did. But I forgive you because you had a long busy day at the hospital yesterday whereas—"

"Mummy and I did nothing all day yesterday but look after Jack. I loved it! Do I have to go to school today? I know it's Monday but—"

"Don't you want to go to school and tell all your friends how brilliant it is now that you've got a baby brother?" Tanya said.

"Yes, OK. But will you come and meet me and bring Jack in the pram?"

"Of course I will. Now, don't make a noise as you climb out of bed. Just go back to your own room for a couple of minutes and start putting on your clothes."

"OK. You'll come and help me, Mummy, won't you?"

"Yes, I'll be with you in two minutes. I just want to discuss something with Daddy."

Chrysanthe paused at her mummy's side of the bed and looked gravely at the eyes that were firmly closed again.

"You know, I told you it was easy making a baby, Mummy. You did really well. It seems to be the looking after the baby that tires you. But you've got me to help you, haven't you?"

Tanya opened her eyes and smiled at the child who now seemed as if she was her true firstborn. "Of course

I've got you to help me. I don't know what I'd do without you, darling."

She held out her arms and closed them around Chrysanthe. "Now, off you go and start getting ready for school, my love."

"What was it you wanted to discuss?" came a sleepy voice as the door closed behind their daughter.

Manolis drew her into his arms and she snuggled as close as she could get.

"I've forgotten. It will have to wait until this evening."

"Like everything else," he told her in his most seductive, provocative tone. "Unless…"

"Not now, Manolis!" She moved out of range and put her feet on the floor. "You won't be late tonight, will you? Because… I've forgotten what I was going to say again! It must be all these broken nights."

"They won't go on for ever. Can't wait to have you all to myself again." Manolis looked down at his sleeping son. "But I wouldn't be without this wonderful gift you gave me, darling. As Chrysanthe just said, you did well making our baby."

She laughed. "It was an absolute pleasure, I assure you."

"We could maybe make another one in the not too distant future," Manolis said gently.

She blew him a kiss. "It would be fun trying…"

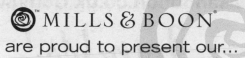

millsandboon.co.uk Community

Join Us!

The Community is the perfect place to meet and chat to kindred spirits who love books and reading as much as you do, but it's also the place to:

- **Get the inside scoop from authors about their latest books**
- **Learn how to write a romance book with advice from our editor**
- **Help us to continue publishing the best in women's fiction**
- **Share your thoughts on the books we publish**
- **Befriend other users**

Forums: Interact with each other as well as authors, editors and a whole host of other users worldwide.

Blogs: Every registered community member has their own blog to tell the world what they're up to and what's on their mind.

Book Challenge: We're aiming to read 5,000 books and have joined forces with The Reading Agency in our inaugural Book Challenge.

Profile Page: Showcase yourself and keep a record of your recent community activity.

Social Networking: We've added buttons at the end of every post to share via digg, Facebook, Google, Yahoo, technorati and de.licio.us.

www.millsandboon.co.uk

5

2 FREE BOOKS
AND A SURPRISE GIFT

We would like to take this opportunity to thank you for reading this Mills & Boon® book by offering you the chance to take TWO more specially selected books from the Medical™ series absolutely FREE! We're also making this offer to introduce you to the benefits of the Mills & Boon® Book Club™—

- **FREE home delivery**
- **FREE gifts and competitions**
- **FREE monthly Newsletter**
- **Exclusive Mills & Boon Book Club offers**
- **Books available before they're in the shops**

Accepting these FREE books and gift places you under no obligation to buy, you may cancel at any time, even after receiving your free books. Simply complete your details below and return the entire page to the address below. You don't even need a stamp!

YES Please send me 2 free Medical books and a surprise gift. I understand that unless you hear from me, I will receive 5 superb new stories every month including two 2-in-1 books priced at £4.99 each and a single book priced at £3.19, postage and packing free. I am under no obligation to purchase any books and may cancel my subscription at any time. The free books and gift will be mine to keep in any case.

Ms/Mrs/Miss/Mr _____ Initials _____

Surname _____

Address _____

_____

_____ Postcode _____

Send this whole page to: Mills & Boon Book Club, Free Book Offer, FREEPOST NAT 10298, Richmond, TW9 1BR